WAR RECORD

WAR RECORD

Mark Zaccaria

Dreams of a Stolen World

— Mark Zaccaria

www.WAR-Record.Com

TATE PUBLISHING
AND ENTERPRISES, LLC

Published by Tate Publishing & Enterprises, LLC
127 E. Trade Center Terrace | Mustang, Oklahoma 73064 USA
1.888.361.9473 | www.tatepublishing.com

Tate Publishing is committed to excellence in the publishing industry. The company reflects the philosophy established by the founders, based on Psalm 68:11,
"The Lord gave the word and great was the company of those who published it."

Published in the United States of America

ISBN: 978-1-61862-627-1
Fiction: Historical
12.03.02

Pvt. Leo V. Zaccaria, 1943

War Record

Dedication

This book could be dedicated to no one other than the indomitable spirit who lived the story and the spirit who has powered it into print both before and after his passing. It is dedicated to my father, Leo V. Zaccaria.

Prologue

It is early April, 1945, in Berga. That's a small German town in the Thuringia state, east of Düsseldorf and west of Leipzig by approximately equal measures. The weather is gray, and so is the mood. The residents of this unremarkable settlement on the Elster River have been constantly assaulted by ever worse news about the progress of the war their leader started for them nearly seven years before. Their response has been to turn inward and be more and more pessimistic. Those old enough to remember the dark days that followed the Great War of 1914-1919 have the uneasy feeling of history repeating itself.

Berga has another unsettling distinction though. It is the site of a prisoner of war encampment whose inmates are being forced to work as slave laborers. They are building a tunnel system intended to shield a proposed ammunition factory from the daily bombings that rain down from the gray and ominous skies. In two twelve-hour shifts, the skeletal remnants of once-vibrant young men are force-marched the mile or more from their cramped and soiled quarters to the tunnels in the rock cliffs that overlook the *Weiße Elster*. There, they drill the sedimentary slate faces of the tunnels for explosive charges set to shatter them so the ghost soldiers can come back to pack them away in jagged pieces.

These are the closing days of a war that has broken the spirit of every German. It is a war that has also consumed and digested hundreds of thousands of that nation's citizens. To be sure, a generation of young men has been decimated on the battlefield. Even more telling on the national spirit, though, the relentless air attacks on cities and manufacturing sites have left every civilian still alive in abject fear of each engine sound they hear above. From this broken pool of people, the few available to be guards at the *Berga an der Elster* camp are the old, the disillusioned, the frustrated, and the angry. By this cold, early April morning, it has long since become routine for all that anger and frustration to be taken out on the prisoners.

If you could observe the prison camp from above, you would see long, narrow wooden frame barracks laid out in ranks and files. There are two chimneys in each of the identical buildings, but none of them show smoke. There is no fuel for the small stoves at the bottom of each chimney. There is no food to warm on those stoves, even if they were fueled and fired. Inside the barracks, there are racks along each wall and protruding out to form bays. Little more than shelves, these racks are the prisoner's bunks. Most often, the men double up for warmth, and all too frequently, one of them awakens to find the other dead.

Prisoners are dying in Berga every day now. They die from exposure. They die from starvation. They die from exhaustion. They die from beatings administered to make them work or just simply to satisfy the guards' rage. Despite any of this, the main reason they die is that they give up. Sadly, many simply choose to die as a preferable alternative to the life that seems to lie before them. They stop fighting, and they lose the last thing they own: their lives.

The prisoners in the camp come from many different nations. There are captured adversaries from Poland, Russia, and elsewhere. There are former allies from Italy. And there are Americans.

In one of the two American barracks, shrouded in the pre-dawn gloom, you would see what appeared at first to be a pile of rags discarded next to a window. A closer inspection would reveal that a military great-coat seemed to have been dropped on its hem, sitting now roughly cone shaped to its buttoned collar. If you peered into the dark circle encompassed by that collar, you would be surprised to see an eye looking back at you.

The rag man by the window was positioned to quickly make his escape if the guards arrived with weapons blazing. His captivity had broken down any unit identity that might have been there at first. By now he was a man alone in a room full of his former comrades. His only thought was survival. He calculated his chances at all times. He connived to edge out his fellow prisoners by a few calories or, if possible, a few hundred calories whenever the opportunity presented itself. He made expert estimates of the minimum effort needed to make it look like he was working without spending any extra energy once he'd ensured he was safe from his captors' truncheons. He guarded his life with a singleness of purpose that was both angry and defiant, even as it was covert so that no attention would be attracted that might cut into his chances to survive.

During wakeful periods, the rag man was a beast who roamed a jungle, always ready to hide, or defend, or strike. Whatever was needed to keep him alive would be done. The beast he had become bore no resemblance to the young American who had answered the call to service. In fact, while he was awake, the beast within him prevented any thoughts of what had gone before. Consciousness was only about succeeding in his one mission: survival. There was no room for distractions that might make him miss an opportunity or a threat.

Now, though, in the pre-dawn, he hovered between the abyss of sleep and the alert wakefulness that he would require of himself soon. As he inhabited that no-man's-land of half sleep, the person the rag man had once been could raise his head figuratively, if briefly. He used the time to transport himself to a past that seemed so distant now. He wondered what twisted and tortured road had led him to this spot and its predicament. He

War Record

searched his own history to try to find a skill or some other asset there that could help him escape from the slowly closing vise in which he was being crushed. He went back over everything he had ever been, searching for a clue.

He dreamed about a world now taken from him, hoping it would be given back somehow in some measure at some time. As he dreamed, he also wondered whether or not he had time enough to regain that lost world.

The Making of a Man of His Times

Imagine the little boy growing up in two worlds at the same time. What sort of man would he become?

Inside his father's house, he might as well have been in Italy. Its language and customs, its artifacts and costumes, and its tastes and smells filled up the first-floor apartment. Only the front windows gave any hint that the building was located in some other country. Even so, they only showed the little piece of City Street that could be seen from their vantage point. To one who knew, the sight of a telltale Ford or of a milk wagon with its sign in English might have been a clue. When he first began to look out those windows, though, the little boy was not one who knew.

Still, he was one who would learn.

He learned things every day. He learned how to eat and how to walk. He learned how to act, which things would get him punished and which would get him praised. Most of all, he learned by exploring, and before long, he knew all the voids and spaces of the front room parlor. He had mapped the folds of the lace curtains from behind. He had seen the underside of the cushions of each of the chairs and could tell why one was softer than the next. Moving back through the house, he had puzzled over the arrangement of the little eight-sided tiles on the floor of the hallway that led to the kitchen. At length, he had understood the pattern of the black-and-white rough-edged circles they described.

He quickly learned the imperative of territory. This happened the moment he first tried to enter his older sisters' bedroom by himself. Because it was shut off to him after that, it exerted a mysterious attraction that was far more powerful than gravity.

The little boy learned because the people around him helped him to learn. They wanted him to know and to grow, so they gave him what he needed. They gave him love, of course. Perhaps as important, they gave him information and admitted him to all the production processes of family life. So he learned about laundry and about how to cook Neapolitan style. In summer, he watched his father turn the tiny patch of yard behind the house into a vegetable garden within a formal topiary of hedges and flowering shrubs. He felt an imposing and solemn responsibility when he was first allowed to trail his father down the cellar stairs to that inner sanctum of masculinity.

In the basement, he began to associate the musty smell of the dirt floor with the household work that was unique to his father. Did that not mean to all men? Down there, he saw tools hanging in order, removed one at a time for their special purposes, cleaned, and returned to the ready. He learned how the many-armed furnace sent hot air to the grates on all three floors. He helped by throwing two or three pieces of coal onto the banked fire after his father's shovelful had covered the red embers. He catalogued the hanging cheeses that his father had made and prepared his response for when he was asked which one should be chosen for Sunday dinner. He helped check both the wine and the beer that were resting after being bottled, and he paid attention to his father's inspections of it all so that he would learn what cues gave away the information that it was ready.

Yet there was always the sense of how much more there was to learn. As he grew, he absorbed everything that the house would yield. From the mundane to the mysterious, he took it all in, but he always understood that there was more outside.

Each work day, he saw his father leave the house. Each night, he would hear the tin growl of the electric buzzer that meant his father had come home. Soon, the boy himself was both tall enough and quick enough to return the salute by reaching for the second buzzer at the apartment entrance. This modern marvel would loosen the lock on the big outside door and let his father enter the building. Before long, he would also open the apartment door the two inches it would go until its chain caught. This, he knew, would let him verify the identity of a visitor without dropping all the castle's defenses.

What a formidable barrier that outside door was. It was too tall for its little windows to be of any use to anyone for looking out. It was too massive to be opened by a little boy, even if it were unlocked and unbound by the iron coil which forced it shut. It was too thick to let the sounds of the street come through as anything but a murmur. But it was a portal of magic and mystery because just on the other side was the second world in which the young man was to grow. Behind the great door, the little boy was safe in the arms of his family and the structure of life that they dictated and chose to live by. Outside it were places less and less bound by the rules of polite society.

The front windows offered a sterile peek at a piece of what was beyond. The front door made the promise of contact with everything on every street that existed anywhere on its other side.

When it did open, he was blinded by the light. He was deafened by the cacophony of street sounds. He smelled ozone from the electric trolley cars. He smelled the horses as the ice wagon was drawn by. Whenever the door was opened, the aromas of America began to creep in and around the hothouse flower of Italy that had been carefully cultivated inside the flat.

The front door was a much stronger attraction than the bedroom his sisters guarded so closely.

War Record

By the spring of 1930, he was allowed to open that new world gate himself and to venture out for even more exploration. What he found on the other side was East Boston.

Standing alone on the front stoop that first time, he squinted in the sunshine. He'd been out there before, of course, but always with an escort of adults. He had been hustled around the corner in a phalanx of his elders as the family went to visit relations who lived close by. This time, though, he measured the steepness of the three steps with the care that comes from responsibility. He gauged the sharpness of the ornamental spear points on the pickets of the iron gate. Could they be removed in an emergency and used as weapons? He looked carefully at the pitted gate latch. It had to be operated with a delicate touch or he would be stuck at the bottom of the stairs forever or, worse, unable to get back in.

Beyond the gate was a sidewalk, across the street a school yard. To the left and right, city blocks extended downhill to the waterfront or across town to Winthrop or Chelsea or Revere. What a flood of impressions crowded in on him during that first expedition, just two doors down. As he walked, he listened to the pleasing scrape of stiff leather soles on the gritty concrete. His eyes were drawn to the detritus of sawdust and horsehair from the iceman's wagon that floated on the trickle of wash water in the gutter. Then he saw the symmetry of the granite paving stones that cobbled the road. They looked newly set. They had sharp edges and mottled faces fresh from the shear. Best of all, he could read a pattern of half circles in their layout, just like the little floor tiles at home. The street had been made with the same pride and attention to its beauty.

As he smelled the crisp air and looked up at wispy clouds he craned his neck hard and thought of them as lying on a bright blue bed. For that moment, he was hanging from the street above and looking down on the sky. Lost in that little reverie, the boy was completely unaware of the invisible string he was on.

Mark Zaccaria

"Leo!" his mother called from the stoop, "you come back here right now!"

The string went taut and began to reel him back. He didn't resist. Without thinking about it, he was comforted by the protection of his parents. They were the foundations of his household and of his life. They were the bedrock upon which his family was built.

His family. It was an iron-bound association of people, starting with those closest to him and extending out to some he never saw. The family also extended far back into history, as was proven by all the stories told about those who had gone before. No one thought about it, but the assumption certainly was that the family would continue to extend endlessly into the future.

It gave form to everything that happened in his life because everything was judged in the context of how the family saw it. There were rules about how family acted and operated. Though unwritten, the rules were understood by everyone and obeyed in detail, without question. To later generations, such automatic compliance would be thought of as a lack of individual will. To Leo, there was nothing to think about. The rules of the family were like the rules of nature; they were just there. Could you make a ball fall up? Should a flower or a person grow young? To him, individual expression could begin only after a position had been established in the protective, enabling matrix of the family.

His mother and father were towering figures of authority and ability. They could do anything. His sisters were older than he, so they had both some authority over him and some responsibility for him. They might be delegated even more if his parents left him in their care. Or he might think a sister was overstepping her bounds and resist with a squawking petition to the parental judiciary. She might remember that and save it as a reason for payback when a future opportunity presented itself. Everyone knew, however, that when any real threat came up from outside the family, they would all take care of each other.

War Record

Leo was the oldest son. It gave him a prescribed position in the family organization. His place in the hierarchy was neither better nor worse than anyone else's; it was simply his. It defined him and always would. Although his little brother was just a baby, Leo knew that it would fall to him someday to instruct the youngster in all that he had learned. He would watch over his brother until it was all learned over again.

"Leo! Why didn't you tell me you were going down the block?"

"Aw, Mama. I said I was going out."

"Out is one thing," she said, looking him over for damage, "but you don't go down the block unless I know about it! You understand? You're only nine years old!"

"But, Mama, there are other kids down the block."

Back on the street, there were, indeed, other kids. Learning how to act with them was a whole new exploration all its own. You didn't owe other kids the way you owed family, but neither did they owe you. You couldn't ignore other kids because you wanted to be around them and have their approval as well as their comradeship. They wouldn't like you just because you wanted them to, though. You had to find some way to make them.

The second time out, the cobblestones did not distract him. He walked up the street this time and stood outside the iron gate three houses away. Inside the tiny enclosure, a boy sat on the bottom step. Leo's hair was straight and black, brushed back and held with hair dressing. This boy had short, curly hair that fell about his head like a cap.

Maybe his family came from Sicily, Leo thought, for his father always claimed that anyone different was a Sicilian.

From his seat, the new boy concentrated on a spot on the concrete at his feet. He watched this spot as he also tapped it rhythmically with a length of broomstick. The long dowel had split into a wedge with a short, round handle. To his mother, it had become junk. To him, it was the perfect tool, toy, and weapon.

Mark Zaccaria

Leo watched for a moment until the boy looked up, smiling. He stopped tapping and held the pointed end of the broomstick up, presenting it for inspection. His smile broadened as his eyes clearly stated that this stick was a prized possession. Leo understood but just looked down and shrugged. The boy read his response as envy and was even more pleased.

To Leo, the stick had no great value, so it didn't even cross his mind to take it for himself. Since there was no contest between them, the first step in a friendship had been made. Not one word had been spoken.

Each of the three-decker houses on his street had at least one apartment that was a little slice of Italy just like his own. But each was a slightly different slice. All the boys Leo's age had spoken Italian before they began to speak English, just as he had. Even so, the Italian language was spoken so differently from place to place in the old country that it would have been difficult for the adults to converse. Add to that that each family's contact with Italian had been cut off years before, when they first came to America, and that all the new words they had learned since then were from English or one of the other languages in the melting pot. The result was a schoolboy's argot based on English but heavily laced with names and action words from the dialects.

That's how the kids spoke to each other. American English was the melody with words from Italian or other languages thrown in for scherzo emphasis or to promote exclusivity in some minor key known only to that group.

"Hey, Wal-Yo. Ya wanna play?" It was the standard greeting.

"*Più Tarde, Cugino.* I can't right now."

"*Basta!* Whaddaya mean, no? *Andiamo, siamo pronto!*"

"Hey, it's my mama, *capishe?* We'll play later, okay?"

Adults just shook their heads, but in America, the work that supported the families was done in factories or warehouses. Since the men worked at their companies and were paid in cash, it was both impossible and unnecessary for them to bring their children along. Women used their sons for errands around the house but wouldn't permit them to completely take over any important tasks. Could they cook or clean like their sisters? Of course not! School was the only work the boys had, and when it was out, what were they to do? A new pastime evolved almost immediately: play.

In every predatory species, the young play as the start of their apprenticeship for combat. From play, they learn how to form packs and determine who's the boss. They learn how to identify prey or enemies posing a threat. They act on these understandings in ritual fashion, but it is all preparation for the day they will kill for real. Animal cubs wrestle and roll with their siblings, but the same one always finishes on top, especially when the pack starts hunting in earnest. They nip at each other's ears in mock victory, knowing that soon they will snarl and gnaw at the throat. This is as true of the wolf cubs in Yellowstone as it is of the lion cubs of the Serengeti.

In East Boston, the young did the same things, but the game they played was marbles.

To adults, a game of marbles was a benign pastime that had several things to recommend it. It kept the boys in one place for a while. There was little physical risk. Oh, the toes of shoes might get scuffed up but seldom did any clothing get torn. Best of all, it was a game that an adult could interrupt anytime they needed one of the boys. There was never any whining about whose turn was next or any foreign-sounding concerns about the *inning* or the *down*.

Did they really miss so much of what was right in front of them?

To the kids, the game contained all the elements of the relationships between nations. First and foremost, marbles was about possessions and the gaining or losing of them. This was an age where the mass production of nonessential articles was still a new

Mark Zaccaria

phenomenon. Access to such things as money was very rare for the kids, so an item like a marble was a prized belonging that could not easily be replaced. To risk its loss, even on a game of skill, was a big step for a child. Who knew when you would be able to find or make something worth trading for a marble? So if you lost your whole supply, it might be quite a while before you got back into the game. But the stakes were even higher than that.

Negotiations preceded every contest to determine which of the three or four marble games would be played and by what rules. Many a match was won or lost right there. The smaller boys learned that they had to accept the dictates of the bigger boys and then hope that their opponents would remain bound by the rules that they, themselves, had set in the event of a loss. When groups of players from different blocks met for the first time, the one with better scouting reports on the other had a tremendous advantage. Knowing what to expect let them know just how far to go in accepting the other's terms. Groups of friends contended hotly among themselves for practice. When a game was played with another group, however, they would quickly fall into a pattern of supporting each other as a team. Without a word, these teams would protect the identity of their champion until the opposition could be measured and it was time to go in for the kill.

The etiquette of marbles was as important as the game itself because it was a social function every bit as much as it was a sport. You never carried all your marbles with you. You never carried what you had in the same pocket. This gave you the option of playing poor boy while the rules were being set or of claiming to be cleaned out if you found yourself in too deep. Most of all your worth as a person was displayed to one and all by how nonchalantly you accepted a loss. This was especially important in the face of the braggart's dance you were forced to watch as the jubilant victor tried to record his win in the most epic terms.

War Record

Marbles was a game of rules, but just below its surface, there was always the threat of violence. If you lost and then fought, you'd better be sure that there had been a clear infraction. If it wasn't something that everybody saw and would swear to, you might win back your property, but your honor would be gone forever. Worse yet, you might be declared fair game for any who wanted to prove themselves over an unsympathetic victim.

The marbles themselves had different values and different roles in the game. Glassies were clear, machine-made marbles. Usually, they had bubbles and imperfections. They had the least value. Cat's eyes were glassies with a burst of color inside, though the color always seemed to be a cobalt blue. They had greater value, if only as a curiosity. Fake aggies were also made of glass, not agate like the real aggies. You could tell the fakes because over time, the opaque glass would show scratches and pock marks on its swirling, two-colored surface. Still, they looked like real aggies, so they were worth more than cat's eyes. Clay balls were handmade of glazed pottery. They varied widely in size, shape, and weight and so had to be treated with caution because it was hard to predict what they would do. In 1930, steelies were the latest advance in marble technology. They were the shiny, steel balls from a large ball bearing, and they could only be had by those who got lucky in the scrap yards. They were heavy for their size though, so they made the best shooters. Real aggies were talked about more than they were seen. Those who actually had one might show it off before a game as a sign of rank and importance. They would never really play with it though.

The object of all the games was to hit one marble with another. The target was called a pawn, a fish, or *una donna*, a woman. The marble used to hit the fish was flicked from inside a nearly clenched fist by popping it out with the thumb. This one was always called the shooter. The shooter's job was to send the pawn, either to put it into an awkward position or to knock it out entirely to capture it.

A shooter had to be big enough to hold and heavy enough to pack some wallop when it knocked a lady. There were no standard sizes for anything, but if a pawn was offered that was too small to be a worthy prize, the pre-game negotiations would take that much longer.

Leo picked all of this up and more. There were nuances to the arguing over rules as well as techniques both for shooting and for distracting an opponent when he was shooting. It all became reflex to him because the game itself was so important. It was important only because everyone thought it was important, but that was good enough. At the age of nine or ten, he was defined by marbles when he was outside of his home, and he used the game to claim the best position he could in his group of friends.

The school across from his house had a large exercise yard. There was an iron fence along the sidewalk, but that didn't stop anyone. The yard itself was paved with red brick in a herringbone pattern. At the two corners nearest the street, though, there had originally been trees planted. The trees were long gone, but the patches of exposed earth were more than large enough for marbles. They were also packed so densely by the endless line of schoolchildren marching over them that their hard, smooth surfaces made them the perfect places to play.

So perfect that there were always games in progress, both before and after school. When Leo and his friends first started, they couldn't compete at a level that would admit them to the schoolyard. They had to use the small patches of dirt from a sidewalk to a house, between the entryways. In the beginning, they wouldn't have had a chance against any of the regulars, so they practiced where they could. Before too long, though, they were ready.

The Sicilian kid from up the block was named Guido. That quickly became Gui. He trailed his buddy, Lee, and was followed

War Record

by three others as they crossed to the schoolyard to shoot some. It was late on a spring afternoon, and as the sun slid down, only the marble patch on the east end of the bricks still had good light. They both had games in progress, but Leo led his boys to the good one.

"Hey, Bambini!" he shouted while still walking up to the crouched combatants. "We got the winners." He couldn't really tell if there were two or three groups concentrating on the action. He didn't really care. When no one argued his call immediately, it assumed the force of law.

One kid looked up. He was the shooter, and he was irritated that the high art of his performance had been interrupted. He also knew he'd get his chance for revenge, so he went back to work.

Leo knew the kid who looked up. It was Joe the Barber's son. The barber's name was Giuseppe, of course, so it stood to reason that in America, he would be called Joe. He ran the only barbershop within a half a dozen blocks. This was an age when the men thought of a trimly clipped and well-groomed head of hair as a sign of good hygiene and, therefore, social position. So by common usage, he had become Joe the Barber. In fact, many of his clients spoke the name as if it were all one word. Leo had his hair cut there. All the boys did. So they all knew that this kid was Joe the Barber's son, even though they didn't know his name.

They were playing Ringer. The game was to knock the fish out of a circle so they became yours. Whoever won the most marbles won the game, but the circle they had drawn seemed smaller than normal.

Joe the Barber's son worked a group of three fish near the edge of the circle. He took a long time to shoot, seeming to think through every turn his shooter would make before firing it. When he did, however, he was rewarded with a double. His shooter hit a fish that was just in front of two others. The force of the collision made the first fish hit both of the others, sending them on diverging tangents across the line.

Mark Zaccaria

As he picked up his two prizes he looked them over and tried to make this little victory even sweeter by getting a response from his opponent. Both of his new girlfriends were just glassies. One was a purie, though; it had no bubbles or scratches, and it was a nice transparent blue. Not bad. He looked over at the loser to see if it would get any better. The other kid just shrugged and looked down.

Tough break, Leo thought. *That blue marble must have been new. It might have been a present. More likely, the kid inherited it from an older brother who had graduated to playing ball. Still, he had made the choice to put it into the game. Now he was taking its loss as he was supposed to. This kid's all right.*

The defeated team stepped back a little to lick their wounds and to make room for the new challengers. One or two of his friends tried to comfort the boy who had lost the purie, but he just shrugged. It was part of the game.

Angling for advantage in the next round was also part of the game, and Leo wasted no time getting started. He wanted to speed up the beginning of his match so that Joe the Barber's son and his bunch would be still feeling a letdown after their last victory when their next test began.

"Whaddaya mean playin' Ringer in a rain barrel?" he asked harshly.

Usually, the game was played in a large circle as much as ten feet across. Leo's comment about the small size of this circle called the winners' judgment and maybe their skill into question.

"This time let's make some room to play! Uno *campo grosso,* hey? Like the big boys."

"Hey, it's our patch; it's our call, *bambolini,*" the response came from one of the others. "You don't like it, go play at the racetrack."

"So that's it?" Leo asked, looking directly at the barber's son. "Hey, Little Joey, is this kid your rule maker? You gotta do what he says, Giusepini?" The taunt was a direct hit.

His anger was visible immediately.

War Record

"You see the circle," he said. A weak response, and he knew it. "We play Your-Side-My-Side and Shooters Out." He wanted each side's players to stay and to shoot from their own half of the circle. He also wanted the shooters to be removed from the field of play after each turn.

"Girls' rules," said Leo with disdain. "You want to play on a doughnut, okay. You can't handle dead wood. Okay, shooters out. But we play around, Cugino, and you guys throw in the extra. Or do you really want to play?"

The game started with an *X*-shaped formation of thirteen pawns in the center of the circle. The first team or player to capture seven was the winner. Leo wanted his opponents to supply the odd thirteenth pawn.

"Also," he continued, "last shooter plays out and losers play again. Okay?"

When a player knocked a fish out of the circle, he got another shot. When the seventh fish was caught and the game won, Leo wanted that player's turn to continue until he missed. It meant more chances to capture the ladies and was a show of confidence in the outcome.

"Or do you really want to play?" This was quickly becoming personal. Joe the Barber's son had no choice but to agree. He was also forced to accept small sides. Only two players from each group would contest the match. It was such a small circle, after all. The pregame carping over the rules ended when Leo agreed to let the winners shoot first. Ordinarily, the two teams would lag for the first shot. That was a test of skill. The player able to toss a shooter closest to a predetermined line won the advantage of the first shot.

The other guys have to get something, he thought.

So it was Lee and Gui facing off against little Joe and the jockey. That crack about the racetrack would not soon be forgotten. In a show of bravado of his own, little Joe put his new blue purie in the center of the circle to start the *X*. Then Lee and Gui

Mark Zaccaria

put their three fish each in place. Leo was careful to leave plenty of space between each pawn in the line, and Guido might have been called on placing his marbles out of turn, but he knew that the ones at the ends of the X would be the first to be lost. No one complained, and the shooting began.

The barber's son got down and carefully put the knuckles of his right hand on the hard dirt. He had to shoot from outside the circle, so he picked his biggest shooter and carefully fit it into his fist. He was surveying his options.

"Make it count," Leo intoned.

Again, the boy looked up with irritation that his ritual had been interrupted. That was the point, of course.

Back in his concentration, Little Joey was really working on this shot. He had to show the new guys who was boss, and he especially had to show his own guys the same thing. He looked at every little hump and dip in the packed dirt circle. Which way would each make his shooter turn? Which was the easiest pawn to knock? He was worried, and it made him take even longer.

Leo just looked at the jockey and then up at the lowering sun. Nothing had to be said.

Aware of the time all this was taking, he panicked a bit and let the shooter go with too much power and too little finesse. He shot it so hard that it skipped off of the hardpan rather than rolling. This changed its direction some and made it land just next to a pawn in the middle of the X. The pawn actually moved an inch or two and clicked into the next one out on its line. The shooter kept rolling, leaving the circle. It would have been halfway across the schoolyard but for one of Lee and Gui's supporters who blocked it with a foot and left it for its owner to collect.

"Nice shot," Guido observed as his teammate got down to business.

"I like that blue one," Leo said, knuckles down, as his fake aggie rolled on a line toward the center of the circle. It was the most difficult shot on the field, and that was the reason he chose it. Leo's shooter wasn't much bigger around than the purie, and it stopped dead when it made contact, transferring all of its energy and sending its target out of the circle with dispatch. One down, six to go.

Leo moved over to his opponents' side of the circle. This was as much to exercise his right to do so as it was to make them move. The barber's son was just getting back to the action after picking up his shooter. The purie was just disappearing into Leo's pocket.

"Let's clip this bird's wings," he said, taking aim at the end fish on one leg of the *X*. His second shot was as true as his first. Two down, five to go.

Leo didn't think excessively about his shots. He looked at the target and didn't think at all about his shooting hand. He couldn't have told you what he saw that made him know a shot was right, but he knew. After four were down and there were only three to go, he felt the flush of impending victory and started to enjoy it. He knew then that it was only a matter of time. When he knocked over the seventh lady, he just kept going. With nine down and four to go, he was just showing off.

"Hey, *pizan*," said Gui. "Don't I get a shot?"

"Next game," he replied, clearing the circle. "I hope I don't get a hole in my pocket!"

"Okay. Here are the rules for the next game." Leo was up now and facing the other team. "First, you're all playing or we'll know you're not wearing underpants. Second, we play in a real circle. Third, we lag for firsts. Fourth, shooters stay in and you shoot from where they stop. Last, no bellyaching! Any questions?" His shooting demonstration gave him serious authority, at least at that moment.

There were no questions.

"Jimmy-och," he finished. "Make a circle, will ya?"

The boys who had lost to the barber's son were still standing in the background, watching the show. They were joined now

Mark Zaccaria

by some others from the marble patch on the other side of the schoolyard. There was blood in the water, and the sharks were gathering to have some fun.

Little Joey was unhappy. His last shot had been a painful experience. He was worried, and he'd lost confidence. Still, he was smart enough not to say anything.

Leo was very happy. This was why anyone bothered with marbles. He was doing much more than just winning a game; he was vanquishing a foe. His excitement was visceral, and his smile was a natural response of baring the teeth. If he had been thinking like a good neighbor, he might not have rubbed it in so much, but he wasn't thinking at all. He was just responding.

Using a piece of string that he had wrapped on a stout little stick, Jimmy had drawn a perfect circle with a diameter of twice his height. Then he had used an artist's eye to draw two parallel lines tangent to the opposite ends of an imaginary diameter. One was the pitch line, and the other was the lag line. You stood on the first and tossed a shooter toward the second. The closest to the lag line won the first shot.

Gui was the best lagger in his group, so he stepped up. Following the performance his teammate had just turned in, he was eager to show what he could do. After all, he was ten and he was tough. He posed just a bit on the pitch line but had an iron eye all the way. He lofted his shooter so that it returned to Earth nearly vertically. It landed almost exactly in the groove Jimmy had cut and didn't roll a bit. It just settled into the little channel. Bull's-eye.

"Couldn't ya get any closer?" Leo scoffed approvingly.

Guido beamed. Joe the Barber's son felt ill. In the spectator's circle, there was a murmur as the lag was recounted and analyzed. Outside the spectator's circle, more sharks drifted in to see what was up. The jockey understood that he was about to lose some marbles.

War Record

Little Joey and his crew knew that Ringer was played on a big circle, but they had never practiced on one. Perhaps they had no place big enough. Perhaps it was too difficult and, by mutual consent, they didn't face the pain of it. Whatever the reason, they weren't up to what was ahead. Oh, they knocked over a few of the ladies, but it was all in a losing cause.

In any contest, when one of the rivals realizes that a loss is imminent, something chemical happens that can be sensed by the opposition. At that moment, the limbs get as heavy as lead and the reflexes slow to a crawl. Of course, this only energizes the other guy. In sports, when this happens, every move then attempted just shows one more proof of the failure that's in progress. In a fight, all you can do is cover up and hope your opponent doesn't really want to take your life.

So it was in the second game of Ringer that day. Lee and Gui led the way, but Jimmy and the others got their turns too. Prizes were collected by one and all. The losers' spirits were gleefully crushed with a disregard for feelings that can only be summoned up by the naive. The jockey and one other of his crew left before the game was even over. Leo caught the last two fish and Little Joey's shooter.

"That's mine!" the barber's son croaked through a thickening throat.

It wasn't really his anymore, and everyone knew it. Even so, Leo flipped it to him in a high arc. It fell at his feet.

"Here," said Leo triumphantly. "Now we can play again sometime." He also fished in his bulging pockets and found the blue purie. This he tossed to the kid who had first lost it.

The other boy was happy to have his prize back, but he looked dubious because of the way he'd recovered it.

"Keep your shirt on," Leo said. "You and I will play sometime, and maybe I'll win it back in a real game."

Joe the Barber's son had to walk through the ring of circling sharks to get to the gate. He only had one of his crew left with him, and they both had to endure the taunts and touches of the gallery.

"Hey, *chi chi*! You showed 'em!"

"Who taught you, your Mama?"

"Your game's kaput."

"*Va fa nabala,* short stuff!"

Depending on which side you took, either the triumph or the thrashing was absolutely complete. Moreover, the emotions that were generated by this simple ritual were towering. Leo and his bunch felt like giants striding across a pygmy landscape. For the losers, the embarrassment was total but very short-lived. By the time they got out of the schoolyard, it had already turned into anger. For most of them, it was anger at one or more of their teammates as they focused on a breach of strategy or a cold shooting streak. For one, the anger was aimed elsewhere.

Back at the patch, Guido was ecstatic. "I got enough fish now to play for a century!" He happily accepted the accolades that were pouring in on him.

Leo was smiling and enjoying the jostling of the exuberant crowd. He was thinking, however, about what he could trade for, using all these new marbles as a capital asset.

Since the concept of play was a new and foreign one to the adult community, the thought of getting toys for their children never occurred to them. In fact, Leo knew that his father would not allow such a superfluous item as a ball or a bat into the house. They had never spoken about it. Leo would never have asked. He knew his father too well. He didn't feel that that was in any way an injustice. It was just the way things were, a condition of his environment to be understood and accounted for when choosing his own course of action.

For the same reason, Leo knew that he could not tell his parents about the victory he had had that day. They would not have

War Record

given the accomplishment the credit it deserved because they thought of marbles only as a pastime. Telling his sisters was even more out of the question. Their values were far different from those of their kid brother, and they occasionally enjoyed being intolerant of him.

There were no further challenges that day, of course. Not only had the last match been a peak experience, but it was also getting close to dinnertime. The whole neighborhood followed virtually the same schedule, so the multitude began to disperse as if on cue.

Walking back across the street, Leo hefted the cache he had in his pockets, wondering just how good a pair of skates it would bring. He didn't head for the front door but rather went through the alley and hopped the fence into his father's garden. Slithering under the back porch, he crawled to the hiding place he used for illicit treasures. His vault was a coffee can covered with a tied rag. It was stuck behind some lengths of pipe that were stored under the porch. In it was a folded color picture from the Rotogravure Section of the Boston Traveler, a 1929 Lockheed Vega monoplane. There was also a single metal roller-skate wheel, with bearing, that was being saved for an unspecified future project. The can had a few extra marbles, just in case, and a special nail that had been extracted from a railroad cross tie. On its oversized head was engraved the number 98, indicating the year the tie had been installed. Leo was made solemn by the thought that it came from the nineteenth century.

While he loaded this little vault with all his newfound wealth, he was thinking that he would soon need more space. Where could he best hide all the sports equipment he imagined he would have? As usual, necessity would be the mother of invention.

Out from under the porch, he brushed himself off quickly and climbed the back stairs to the porch door. It led directly into the little bedroom he shared with his baby brother. After a quick check of the cleanliness of his shoes and pants, he walked out into the apartment's kitchen. It was warm and moist with the meal being prepared and crowded since the table had been pulled out and set for the family.

"Ah, Leo. Just in time," his mother said. "Go wash up your hands now, and then tell your father we're almost ready to eat."

She was moving with precision in a circle from the stove to the icebox to the table to the sink and back again. Without realizing it, she was ticking off items on a checklist and directing every detail of her half of the household so that dinner would go off without a hitch. Dinner was the magnum opus of her day. She concentrated on both the art and the science of it as a musician would on playing his theme song at a club where he had a permanent booking. She was just as good at her theme song as any headliner was at his.

"So, whad'ya do today, *feel-yo?*" his father asked.

The family was seated, working eagerly on chicken parts sautéed in tomato sauce. Pasta would follow, and then some meat.

"I went to school, Papa, and later shot marbles with my friends." Leo was careful not to use the term played marbles; he didn't want to offend his father.

"School, huh?" the old man asked. "So whad'ya learn?"

"Today, we had arithmetic, penmanship, and the history of the oceans," the child reported.

"The history of the oceans," his father repeated softly. He nodded and chuckled to himself over a topic so complicated and so useless. "You gonna be a professor someday," he concluded.

That Sunday afternoon, Leo was sent around the block to his aunt's house to deliver some fried pastries his mother had made.

"Tell Zia Concetta I didn't realize how many I was mixing up. She could have them later," he was instructed.

It was a move made in a game going on between the two women. This much Leo understood. How to interpret it, he couldn't say. He was happy he was only the messenger.

His aunt and uncle had a three-decker around the corner and down the hill. Like all building owners, they occupied the first-floor apartment. It was the best one, no different in layout from those above but with fewer stairs on which to carry everything coming in or out.

His aunt was a sturdy young woman with dark hair and darker eyes. Her hands and forearms were well developed from the physical labor of the housework she did. She was Leo's father's sister. Thanking him for running the sweets over to them, she pinched his cheek with an iron grip and exclaimed what a pretty boy he was. He thought he might have to get a tattoo to cover up the permanent mark she was surely leaving, but he didn't cry.

His uncle Paul was a workingman, powerful in the upper body but already beginning to stoop a little. He was a few years older than his wife. He was also the older brother of Leo's mother. While the boy rubbed his cheek casually, the two of them talked about the "base-a-ball" for a few minutes. Uncle Paul would have understood marbles. To him, Fenway Park was like the gladiatorial circus. When he went to a game or listened on the radio, he reacted like anyone would who was attending a blood sport. During the game, when Uncle Paul smiled, he showed his teeth.

As Leo was returning home, he passed a house with an alley on each side. Before he reached the second alley, Joe the Barber's son stepped out to confront him. Was it the look in his eye, or was it something Leo smelled or tasted in the air that told him this meant trouble? He just stood there, fists clenched, holding Leo's eye ten feet or so ahead. Behind him stood his little brother, obviously nervous but riveted to the situation.

Do they want to fight? Leo was incredulous. He could kick them both across the harbor. He might have thought to laugh at them, but just then, a piece of doubled-up clothesline rope was slipped over his head and tightened around his neck.

In a flash, Leo realized that it was real. In a second flash, though, there was anger or rage or some kind of animal power rising up in him.

How dare they do this? He was furious.

Mark Zaccaria

Grabbing the rope, he pulled like someone who meant it and twisted himself around one half a turn. His attacker was taller but was no expert with the garrote. Leo should have been at the mercy of the bigger boy, but instead, when he yanked, he moved the rope through the other's hands. This burned the attacker, and he let go. When Leo turned, he had the rope in his own hands, and he saw that Joe the Barber's older son was also a part of this. The rage just increased.

Leo used the rope as a whip and started beating the bigger boy, who ran toward his brothers. In three steps, Leo was whipping them all with the rope and running after them up the block. He didn't stop. He didn't even realize that when the three boys entered the front door of one of the houses that it smelled different from his own. They ran up the stairs, and he ran up after them, hearing their screams and cries for the first time echo in the tunnel of the stairwell.

At the first landing, the boys were beating on the apartment door, and Leo was beating on them. They were cornered until the door opened and a startled Joe the Barber stood over all of them. The brothers melted past their father, who looked in amazement at their ten-year-old assailant. Things like this just didn't happen in East Boston.

"What's goin' on?" Joe asked. He didn't really ask the boy before him. He just asked.

"This must be your rope," Leo said firmly. "Your sons put it around my neck to try to hurt me. You ask them!" He was breathing heavily. "That's wrong! Maybe you can make them understand." He continued, "If I see them again, they know what I'll do." With that, Leo dropped the rope at Joe the Barber's feet and started back down the stairs, his chest heaving as he recovered his wind.

Giuseppe Taurozzi was a tall man, a bit portly but with a low, booming voice that dominated a room. His black hair was thinning a bit, but his mustache was thick and large. He kept it well waxed and trained into a straight handlebar. His normal poise was gone at that moment though. His large hands just hung by his sides. He was amazed at what had just happened. Picking up the rope, he went back inside his apartment.

As Leo reached the sidewalk and turned toward home, he could hear the muffled sounds of the barber's big voice shaking the walls of the second-floor flat. Nobody saw any of the three boys for almost a week.

Mark Zaccaria

Day Begins at Berga

The door to the grim barracks at Berga was kicked open with a sharp report.

"*Achtung Hieraus, Schweinhunden!*" A tired guard shouted as he labored in. "*Hier Aus mit Die! Schnell! Schnell!*" he boomed.

Two other guards followed him into the quarters, blowing police whistles and banging on the racks with their batons. These two were halfhearted in their attempts to rouse the prisoners and get them moving. The noise they made didn't compare to the cacophony of whistles and percussion that had greeted Leo months before, when he was first captured. By then, the prisoners were halfhearted too. A slow motion dance ensued where scarecrow figures struggled to their feet before stooped and corpulent old jailers.

The day began. The dreams of home vanished from the clouded heads of all the Americans. Leo immediately went on the alert, sizing up the aged guards with a sideways glance through eyes that were slits. Once again, the jailers were unaware of the danger he posed as he sulked out into the yard for the morning count.

As he began the walk to the caves, Leo made the mental note to pick up where he left off when he was back again at the frontier between wakefulness and sleep.

War Record

The Schooling of a
Man of His Times .

In those days, marbles was a short-lived part of a boy's coming of age. As soon as his body started to sprout, he became interested in showing off his muscles as well as his mind.

There was value to that. It kept marbles a kids' game. It also kept kids from invading the ball fields, at least until they had learned a little about social hierarchy and until they could start to really play.

Marbles was a game. Playing ball was better; it was a sport. Whether it was baseball or track in the spring and summer, football in the fall, or basketball in the winter, team athletics were an unwritten requirement for the boys of Eastie. Like games, sports had all the rituals of etiquette and the strategies of playing the rules like a concert violinist plays his instrument. They also had the running and jumping and the being faster or stronger or just better that let young bodies do what they do best.

None of the players realized it, but they were living through their moment of peak physical health and peak athletic ability. Before very long at all, these teenagers would start smoking, or drinking and dancing late into the night, or working overtime in difficult environments. They would stop training to get on with adulthood. Then they would become so involved in careers and

War Record

families of their own that they would overlook the fact that no longer could they have trained if they'd wanted to. Before long, their only contributions to sport would be the advice they gave the players and the opinions they traded with their friends.

For now, though, these schoolboy athletes were the best that their neighborhoods had to offer and the best that any of their families could ever remember. They were better fed than any who had gone before, even in the best of times in the old country. They were better rested and raised since they had been spared the brute physical work of subsistence that had drained so many previous generations. They were better trained because they had formal coaching at school and informal coaching from every grown man they saw as the neighborhood lived vicariously through the exploits of its youth.

All this was reflected in their performance statistics. There might not have been good records of what previous champions had done. For sports new to Europeans, like baseball and football, there were no records at all. Still, all of the older men agreed that there had never been times or feats like the ones they were seeing then. Was it ever thus?

Leo and his classmates grew taller and stronger than their fathers. They were faster and better-drilled than the older men. They were measurably better, and they knew it. They were admired for their prowess all around the neighborhoods, and they knew that too.

So all of the boys strove to be the champion of something. They openly exulted at the thought of a run, or a hurtle, or an at-bat. They thought about their athletic performances before, during, and after actually making them. They used the thinking about one race to refine and improve their results in another. They secretly ranked themselves by position among their peers in every event they attempted. They reveled openly in the attention that came if they managed to win one. Points scored in sports were also points scored in the social order they all adhered to.

Even those who never won still broke down each event into components, telling themselves, and sometimes others, that no one was better at leaving the starting blocks or leaning into the finish than they were. It might have been moving to the left to cover second from shortstop. Maybe it was going out in the quarter-mile run. Whatever it was, each boy thought of himself as the champion of something.

As a result, they all carried themselves like the champions they were. When they walked down the street, they did it purposefully. They were going someplace. When they lifted a milk crate full of groceries for someone, they did it gracefully and seemingly without effort. Someone else might be watching. When they hopped a fence or bounded up a flight of stairs, it was an athletic event, and they treated it with the same respect and determination they would an actual match. Pride ran deep in the boys of East Boston, as it does in all boys everywhere.

The women and men of this largely immigrant community looked on all this as being completely proper. They each thought of themselves as the champion of something too.

On the street, when Leo heard the clattering staccato of a Model T engine approaching, he could look up and see a champion passing by. Invariably, the bonnet was not just black but glistening black. The wooden posts or panels of the truck were always varnished, and the driver sat proudly on his cushioned leather seat. Whether it was a delivery of meat or milk or newspapers, you could bet that the driver wore some uniform of his profession. It might be a butcher's apron, a dairyman's whites, or the paper hat of a printer's devil, but it was always accompanied by an erect posture and a necktie. It was unthinkable that a delivery truck not display a sign. The lettering was an art unto itself because the lion's share of all those signs proudly proclaimed the name of the man whose business it was.

The ground would vibrate as the even tom-tom beat of a Mack Bulldog's diesel engine announced the arrival of a real

War Record

truck. Its massive wooden spokes might be painted red with gold leaf details, its curved bonnet a French-styled sculpture in sheet metal painted dark green beneath the gold highlights. This was striking to the eye in a day when you could have a vehicle in any color you wanted, as long as you wanted black. With a load of coal or paving stones, this leviathan would labor up the hill only because of the Herculean efforts of its driver. As that man stepped down from his cab and adjusted his sooty gloves before continuing with his task, he was accepting the applause of every onlooker, whether there were any sounds or not.

When a welder from the shipyard chatted after dinner on Sunday with his brother-in-law, he spoke of his work in solemn terms because it was important. Realizing this, the in-law would listen intently to the briefing on striking an arc or flowing the weld into the grooved seam with a *C*-shaped motion. The listener would remember all this too. It might prove the breadth of his own understanding of the world to some other acquaintance later on. Then the welder would happily return the favor, hearing about the intricacies of road-building or baking or machining a gear. What they all heard were champions describing their most recent victories.

People in Leo's community defined themselves by their work and were happy about that. Most had come from far poorer circumstances, forced out of the places of their birth by poverty or politics. They had mastered life in a place so alien that it might have been another planet, and they were proud of that accomplishment. In the process, they had improved their living conditions remarkably. Many a one-time goat herder who was raised in a lean-to in the hills was now the owner of a three-decker house with central heat, running water, and inside toilets. Their forebears could not have imagined such a climb up the social ladder.

In the old country, they had lived by their wits. They had become champions despite the best efforts against them that were made by the social order or the political machines of their native towns or lands. They had to be champions in order to choose to succeed in a new world rather than remain subjugated in the old one. In the process, they had become self-sufficient in a way most Americans were not.

American literature, from Fenimore Cooper to Zane Grey, had taught the world that Americans were self-reliant in the wilderness. The ability to fell a tree and to singlehandedly use it to build house was thought to be indigenous in North America, especially by those who had never tried it. The immigrants who were forced out of Europe by the threats and degradation imposed on them by their own countrymen became self-sufficient philosophically.

Most of them were used to living in cities or towns where crafts and specialty services were readily available. They usually went to a baker when they wanted bread. As such, they preferred a crowded urban existence to the lonely hermitage of the legendary plainsmen. They were cynical, though, on the subject of government and on the motives of the aristocratic classes. Flag-waving American patriotism was thought to be naive by those who grew up under despotic systems that only gave way by force, and then only to other despotic systems. When they transplanted their families to America, they uprooted their opinions and ideas as well and brought them across the oceans along with some clothing and a few prized possessions.

This curious mix of social contact and radical politics combined to create a broad spectrum of special interest groups within the immigrant communities. New arrivals who had learned the hard way back home regarded the local police as American Cossacks or the city council as the Court of the Doge, whether or not it was true. But in the United States, they found themselves in a political environment where opposition comment was not only allowed but was exalted in song and story. Perhaps without realizing it, they all quickly learned that there is nothing like social acceptance to instantly blunt the sharp edge of anarchy.

War Record

Still, in all, they were champions. Certain standards had to be maintained. Antonio Zaccaria and his young wife, Maria, were well schooled in the vocabulary and patois of radical politics. Even so, Sunday dinner was a time to fill the house with friends, to drink some red wine, and to enjoy the fruits of a week's labor. Tony would nod his agreement to diatribes against the government, any government. He might even make an impassioned argument, himself, about the tribute exacted from an innocent population by a corrupt police force. Deep down, though, he knew that while American cops took some produce and a little money when it was offered from those they were sworn to protect and serve, they almost never broke bones or burned shops the way their European brothers had on occasion.

Mary was a beautiful young woman and liked having the position of attention and respect that went along with that. Sure, she dressed her young son in his best clothes and took him with her by streetcar all the way to Dedham to march outside the Norfolk County Courthouse in support of Sacco and Vanzetti. But not before she had carefully attended to her own looks and costume.

Anarchy was a philosophical avocation for some, but there were darker forces of greed and paranoia that had also been spawned in the old country. Those new citizens who followed this path when they came to America were far less flamboyant and far more interested in the tangible rewards they could gain than were their philosopher cousins. Everyone in Eastie knew of the existence of one or more "businesses" that displayed no proud signs proclaiming their ownership. Most avoided contact with those they knew to be associated with such enterprises, and that very isolation gave the rogue businessmen the silence and invisibility they needed in order to operate effectively. It was a real social ill that was tolerated even while so many imagined slights at the hands of the government were decried with a strident voice.

To Tony and Mary, radical politics was a hobby that put them in social touch with a number of other young, energetic immigrant thinkers. They already lived in a maelstrom of cultures and languages. Their hobby gave them a chance to entertain in it as well. It was more than just a bridge club or mah-jongg society though. There was elaborate talk of opposing forces and the occasional raid to knock hats off the policemen in the Columbus Day Parade. This gave them the excitement of feeling that they were underground without having to worry about going back to work on Monday.

In the thick Southern Italian accent of the Neapolitans, the classic insult "*Merda di cane*" was pronounced more like "*Mahra cone-ay.*" Their native language became like a secret code. When they referred to Americans as *mahra cones,* it sounded close, but they were participating in an exclusive little private joke.

Who were the Americans though? It was a question they never thought about. The answer was they were, themselves. Everyone they knew traced their family history back to some other country, virtually all of which were in Europe. Even the old Yankees had been English not too many generations ago. In school, their children learned about the long and successful campaign called King Philip's War waged by the Wampanoag Indians against the British Colonial Army. Still, no one ever actually saw any Native Americans around town, only Hollywood Indians on the silver screen.

As their family increased and their children grew up, parental instincts further quenched the fires of their political activity. They became concerned with the benefits the kids would receive in the America they were growing into. All of their political comrades were undergoing the same transformation. Some might have argued faintly that they were being co-opted by the system. In fact, they were benefiting from it and realizing more and more that it was reality and that all their indignant charges against the government were really just fantasy.

They were a part of an energized society that was growing strong producing things and infrastructure exactly because its entire population felt just the same way. It was the best tangible example of the American dream of real equality that there was, and it was an example the parents provided every day to their children.

The main work that their children had to do was to go to school. So it was natural that a generation of scholars should grow up. Without really thinking about it, the children were trying to prove and define themselves every day in the arena they were given. School was an occupation that was tantalizing to Leo and his classmates because of how relevant and interesting it was.

All around them, the city was bursting with energy. Skyscrapers were reaching upward to eighteen or twenty stories. A motor tunnel was being built that would let cars drive under the main channel of the harbor. New products and new improvements were announced daily in a blizzard of details so profuse that they made the head spin. All of this was fueled by inventions. The kids heard about new wonders of industry at least every week, new machines or processes they all remembered by name. Each was a promise of some faster or healthier or less expensive way to do something important. All of the inventions were based on science, however, and there the world of discovery and the world of school came together.

The immigrant parents of these children lived with the memory and the fear of poverty. As a result, they were incredibly conservative in matters of money. What that meant for the kids was that if they ever wanted to see any money themselves, they had to earn it themselves. The concept that a parent might give a child money for something was unheard of in East Boston.

This is why Leo had taken the marbles from his first big win and traded them for a pair of roller skates. They were the clip-on type and came without the key necessary to attach them to his shoes. That just meant trading for a skate key. Later, in return for the promise to repair them, Leo was able to secure the long-term loan of a pair of the more prized shoe skates. This freed up his clip-ons for use in acquiring a baseman's glove and a bat. All the while, he was ever on the lookout for chances to earn real cash.

He was quick to respectfully converse with his elders because they were all potential employers. When he made the acquaintance of an older lady in the next house, he found someone who needed the help of a willing young boy to run errands and bring packages up the three flights of stairs. Leo thought it odd that her religion forbade her to handle money or even to talk about commercial transactions on Saturdays, but he was happy to help her out of the jam it created.

Milk was delivered on Saturday, and it couldn't be left on the stoop to spoil. Before long, he knew to take her milk and her newspaper up to her flat, knock on the door, and wait. She admitted him silently on Saturdays and didn't even watch as he put the milk in the icebox, put the paper on the table, and collected the trash to be taken downstairs. She would then move to a side board in the kitchen where a napkin lay. Without looking herself, the lady would lift the napkin to reveal a penny. This was Leo's wage for the service he'd performed, and he took it gratefully. Going out, he nodded, almost bowed to her. He knew not to speak but felt that some formality was required.

With all this as the social environment, it should be no surprise that Leo and all of his peers were committed capitalists. Odd jobs and small business dealings were considered good by city kids without a second thought, just as farm kids automatically till a small vegetable plot. Big business was like the big leagues. Those who made it there were stars, and their box scores were discussed exhaustively. Care to know how many automobiles Henry Ford produced this month? That number always made the papers.

So if science was the key to invention, and invention was the key to new business opportunities, everybody wanted to know more about science. The girls, of course, were distracted greatly by the crushing weight of the social and biological imperatives of

War Record

impending motherhood. The boys, however, saw technology as the way to make good financially based on merit, without regard to social background, physical size, or luck. They understood the American Dream in a nutshell: It doesn't matter who you are; you can make it if you're smart and you work hard enough.

The children of Eastie came to school every day eager to participate in the process of learning. And the school system they came to? It was ready, willing, and able to do its part.

The inhabitants of Boston had sought to keep their social differences distinct from the beginnings of the settlement in 1630. Then the religious pilgrims wishing to establish a theocracy lived in different neighborhoods than the seafarers, trappers, and iron workers who were interested in exploiting natural resources while they enjoyed life to its fullest. By the 1930s, the city government belonged largely to the ethnic Irish who had first emigrated eighty years before. Police and fire companies were multi-generation family businesses. Italians found work in factories or on construction crews. Chinese had come to the area as laborers or as traders in the days when clipper ships connected Boston to Shanghai around the Horn. They stayed committed to their enclave neighborhood seemingly without regard to the economic benefits that might have been found in other sections. The old Yankees were descendants of the original British settlers. They were usually the brokers, attorneys, physicians, and businessmen. They were said to control all the real fortunes of the area, and in some cases, it was true.

Through all this, Teaching had become virtually the only acceptable profession for an educated woman. Since almost all of the educated women were Yankees in the Blue Stocking tradition, they were the group who bent to the task of satisfying the immigrant children's hunger for knowledge.

Mark Zaccaria

When he first met Mrs. Appleton, Leo thought of her as a curious but formidable guardian of the secret treasures of science. As a sixth-grade teacher, she handled the lecturing for all her student's academic subjects. She also carefully formulated a written opinion of all of them, which would be the main guide used to set a curriculum for each when they got to East Boston Junior High School the next year.

She was tall and very slender. Her white hair had long since submitted to being permanently swept back from her face and knotted savagely into a bun. Her eyes were blue, or rather had been at one time. Now they were more of a slate color and seemed always to have a bit of fluid in them. Yet they remained the windows to a sharp mind. Her dress never varied from the black straight skirts and white long-sleeved blouses that must have served her well for so long. The pale, flaccid folds of skin at her throat were always walled up in a high collar and locked in place with a cameo brooch. Her voice was strong, and it resonated with authority. When she spoke, all other activity in her classroom ended.

When she announced, "Now, children, we will begin *science*," the strength of the attention being paid to her was palpable.

Whatever restrictions she might have felt society placed on her outside the classroom, she felt completely free within it. She felt free to use her talents to mold the minds of her students. She felt free to use her own judgment regarding how best to do that. She felt free to approve of herself for the professional manner in which she concentrated on the students and thus did as good a job this year as last, even though the syllabus was exactly the same. Most of all, she felt free of gender, age, social station, and almost free of gravity when she used her intellect to get her students to use theirs. Beneath her impenetrable façade, she might also have been a free thinker.

War Record

Without doubt, she was a fine teacher, but most of her students would never really notice that because most of the rest of the faculty was similarly well equipped for the task.

"Please open your science texts to page ninety-six," she instructed. "Today, we will begin our discussion of magnetism." After a respectful rustling of desktops and school books, she delivered a tease line that would have been the envy of a carnival barker.

"Magnetism is a widely used and little understood force of the universe, without which no life, as we know it, could exist on our planet. With it, however, we have been able to create the mighty machines that power our electric lamps and drive our trolleys, ships, and soon our freight and passenger trains."

She told a tale of limitless economic application and continuous benefit for the citizens of the land. She then went on to subtly imply that when ages past thought of magnetism as an example of magic or sorcery, they might have had some grounds for their beliefs. She wondered openly whether or not people and automobiles would drift off into the regions of outer space if magnetism were to suddenly stop working, thus ending Earth's gravity. She hinted that magnetism was just the first of a number of physical forces she would explain and that each was more powerful than its predecessor.

The class was spellbound. Each new idea she introduced was skillfully woven to practical examples and benefits that each child understood and agreed with. Each time she established credibility for one idea, she used it as the pylon for an intellectual bridge to the next new thought she would disclose. Lines of force were displayed emanating from a permanent magnet using a plain piece of paper and a saltshaker filled with iron filings. Those same mysterious lines surrounded a rod of glass after it had been strenuously rubbed with lamb's wool. With the glass, though, there was a greater revelation. The crackle and spark of a static electric shock could be made to jump from the charged rod. Mrs. Appleton looked on with satisfaction as a link between magnetism and electricity was forged unbreakably in the minds of her students.

She brought all her subjects to life this way, but she didn't stop there. When Leo and one of his classmates asked for more information, Mrs. Appleton did not refer them to the abyss of the library's card catalogue. Rather, she took from her desk a copy of *Popular Science* magazine. She opened it for them to a story on the newest magneto that had been designed to withstand the stresses expected in the next generation of fighter planes now only on the drawing boards.

"Did you children know," she asked calmly, "that while maneuvering in combat, an airplane can be caused to double or even triple its weight?" Her sense of timing was well practiced. She gave that concept one beat to sink in, and then she continued. "That goes for the engine, its magneto, and the pilot as well." She had delivered the *coup de gras*. The questions bubbled up in their brains and spilled from their lips.

"Why does that happen?"

"How do you make it happen? How do you make it stop?"

"Why don't the wings fall off? Could the pilot die?"

"Does magnetism still work at that weight?"

She hushed them gently and took a moment to explain. That afternoon, the two budding physicists could be found swinging a bucket of water over their heads by a length of clothesline rope tied to its bale. They didn't spill a drop. Everything led to something important, and students in all the classes followed the trails eagerly.

That evening, at the dinner table, Leo was waiting for his father's question. When the meal had been eaten and the appropriate compliments made to the chef, the old man asked.

"So, Leo, whad'ya learn in school today?"

War Record

"Well, Papa," the son replied, "I learned to hold water in a bucket without a lid, even when it's turned upside down."

"Huh. Whaddaya mean, fil-yo? You talkin' crazy."

He had him. A demonstration was hastily organized in the garden.

"Hey, Lee-ooch," Papa admonished with a smile, "you no gonna break my tomatoes, huh? I break you backside."

"Don't worry, Pop. I'll be okay."

Leo was energized by the chance to show off what he'd just learned. He wanted his father to know that he was picking up important information in school. His mother was a little concerned that the boy not anger his father over anything. She and the girls thought of upside-down pails of water as a diversion only interesting to men, though, so they set about cleaning up.

When he watched the bucket swinging around its circular arc, Antonio Zaccaria knew intuitively what was going on. He understood just how the trick worked, and to his credit, he also understood that he would never have thought to do that himself if he lived for one hundred years.

"Humph," he said quietly. Nodding, he tacitly admitted that his son had done well. "Hey, professor, it still won't pay the rent," he observed, turning to go back inside.

Leo stayed at the bottom of the back stairs and swung his bucket of water a few more times, smiling in the dark.

In grade school and through junior high, Leo's academic career was not always such a romantic voyage of discovery. Despite the quality of the teaching, there were some subjects that just didn't captivate his interest. By and large, though, he and all his classmates were exposed to something of whatever was considered cultural by the society of that day.

He struggled through the instruction on music and the fine arts. In both cases, he was asked to listen to or look at things from another age and then remember about them. His music teacher benevolently noted that many of these works should have taken him back to his European roots. Sure, he could understand the words to the operatic pieces, but she never played enough of them in the right order for him to really get a whole story.

Leo's mother knew all about the operas. She loved to tell the story lines of them all. It proved that she had been a girl in Napoli, a big city where such items of refinement were available. When his older sister began to study voice, she brought home a phonograph and a number of recorded performances, including one by Caruso. This seemed to strangely vex the mother, though, and she never played the arias for herself. The fact was that most of the Italians in the neighborhood had been too young in the Old Country or had grown up in poor surroundings and had little firsthand knowledge of Verdi or Puccini. Once in a while, you might hear the strains of a dramatic tenor in the background on a warm summer evening. More often, though, it would be the scratchy growling reproduction of the voice of Fred Hoy, radio announcer for the Boston Red Sox.

The adults in the neighborhood recognized opera when they heard it and knew it to be an art form heavily influenced by Italian culture. The truth was that they were more likely to listen to Glen Miller or Tommy Dorsey than to Rossini or Leoncavallo. This fact was not lost on their children.

Leo's study of history was a much happier enterprise. In his mind's eye, he could gradually envision the whole continuum of human history, at least as it was recorded from the European perspective. At each of the major waypoints in this story, he could imagine the ships and weapons that were used, the main political pressures that made things happen, and the inventions and industrial advances that each civilization had made. These things interested him because he also understood all the same things about his own civilization and he was able to relate the two. The chariots of the Assyrians spelled the downfall of Pharaoh's armies

War Record

just as the Greek fire had doomed the Phoenicians. Roman highways were built throughout their empire. These allowed them to maintain rapid communications with all their outposts and to easily bring home all the spoils of their conquests. In a later time, the Royal Navy did the same things for the British Empire. It seemed clear that soon, radio would do it all again for the forty-eight states of the USA.

History seemed to teach a lesson that could be used in the present, so Leo tried to learn it.

Science was the real magnet that attracted him to school, though, and to get more of it than was offered in class he took to the library. There, he could read whatever interested him, from the latest magazines to the oldest texts. There was more to the library, though; it was a social center.

Leo's earliest memories of his parents' flat were of its enormous size. Yet, as he learned all its details and grew in size and outside interests himself, he felt confined. He wasn't alone. Despite the better standard of living, there were still too many people in most apartments for peace and tranquility to reign unless other places were found for them to get away from each other. Movie theaters and social clubs were fine for those who had a little money to spend. For most of the people in the neighborhood, though, public facilities were used extensively.

There were parks, of course, but also more elaborate city-run facilities. The Paris Street baths offered indoor athletics, mostly to young men. They were also the favorite place for both men and women to start their Saturday night with a shower and some gossip. Women of all ages would crowd into the ladies' side, helping the youngsters primp for parties and giving their mothers a chance to clean up away from the crowds at home. Community centers were established in vacant or unused buildings. These city-sponsored organizations provided a place for crafts training, entertaining lectures, and some social activities like luncheons or birthday celebrations.

Mark Zaccaria

In general, the neighborhood encouraged the use of these as acceptable places to be when not at home. So the library was a crossroads, and Leo used it like everyone else did. It afforded him a perch for people-watching and a great deal of fuel for the fires of his intelligence.

A nameplate of gold leaf on oak announced that the head librarian of the East Boston branch was Miss Emily Derby. She, too, had gotten her education at the end of the last century. She, too, loved her work because it freed her from the restrictions she felt elsewhere in society. Though her name was spelled like that of the famous hats, she always corrected people and insisted that it was pronounced, "Darby." Leo thought that odd. He once overheard her acknowledge that she was of *the* Derby family of Salem. He didn't know anything about that family, so he wasn't impressed.

As a spinster daughter of the renowned clan of seafaring traders, Miss Emily had brought her branch of the family tree to a dead end. Since women were not admitted to the business, the real wealth she might otherwise have been due had been diverted to her siblings. Certainly, she had a trust that kept her comfortable enough that she did not have to work for the city. The point was her situation at the library suited her just fine.

From her chair at the Eastie branch, she was able to sail the limitless seas of imagination. She kept up with politics around the country and around the world. She knew enough of the classics to know which ones she wanted to get back to at any time. Better yet, she knew which ones to recommend to all the different kinds of patrons who came in asking for suggestions. In fact, she served as a sort of private detective for a growing number of students, business people, and even academics who had known her and then come back to seek her help. With a simple request, you could set her on any case that held her interest, the more difficult or arcane the better. She was like a bloodhound as she prowled the stacks in search of clues to the answers sought by the library's patrons.

Mail came to her daily from professors at any of the colleges or universities in the metropolitan area. "Dear Miss Derby," they would write, "I have need to research the circumstances surrounding the editing and publication of the first edition of Darwin's *On the Origin of Species*. Would you be so kind as to suggest sources that might enrich my studies on this point?" Or, perhaps, "My dear Miss Derby, thank you so much for your recent advice on the import of the trials of Captain Alfred Dreyfus in the evolution of the Third Republic in France. Are you still in correspondence with the good captain? May I ask you to enquire of him on the following topic...?"

Any such request would launch Miss Emily on a fact-finding mission. Since she seemed never to forget a request or its outcome, she was increasingly able to quote sources and answers verbatim as time went on. This intrigued Leo and was seen as a challenge by many of the older students. They made a game out of trying to stump her. She had long since heard everything that the high school students were likely to come up with, although some of them, having moved on to undergraduate work, would return when they thought up a particularly difficult question for her. They were intellectual riddles really, and she relished the competition as a chance to prove her superior mettle. Secretly, she thought of herself as a soul mate of Edgar Allen Poe. One hundred years before, while editing the Baltimore Sun, he had publicly challenged anyone to offer any anagram, puzzle, or conundrum and had promised the solution in the next edition. Legend had it that he always delivered. When Miss Emily got a fatuous request from one of her sophomore patrons, she felt a responsibility to measure up to that standard.

Did any of her married cousins have this much fun keeping a home?

Mark Zaccaria

One Saturday afternoon, Leo was seated near the entrance to the periodical room engrossed in the latest *Popular Mechanics* magazine. Two young men came through the main entrance and directly to Miss Emily's desk. One was Johnny Russo. He'd graduated two years back and was then in college. His friend was not from the neighborhood. As the introductions were made, Leo could see what was coming and moved toward the foyer to listen in.

"Thank you, Miss Derby," the visitor was saying, "you are very kind to offer your assistance. My question is this: What was the name of the boat in which Shelley was sailing at the time of his unfortunate death by drowning?"

Leo barely knew who Shelley was. He had to admit that the question plumbed the depths of trivia. Still, his money was on Miss Emily.

She paused for a moment, not really in thought because she held her interrogator's eye the whole time. She, too, had a practiced sense of timing in these matters.

"Actually, Mr. Chapman," she began with a slight smile, "the boat had two names." Although she did not strut or make a physical display in any way, there was still no doubt that she was triumphant.

"The Italian boat builder," she continued, "a Signor Gommi, I believe, knew that he was dealing with one of the British expatriate poets. Sadly, he didn't seem to know which one. When he delivered the craft, its sail was emblazoned with the name, *Don Juan.*"

She pronounced the Spanish name with the English "J" sound rather than its native "W." That was, after all, how Lord Byron had rhymed it throughout his long poetic narrative.

"So as not to be confused," she continued, "Shelley later literally cut the name out of the sail and sewed an oval of red cloth in its place. Then, on the boat's transom, he painted the name he wanted, *Ariel.*"

The young Harvard man was not just vanquished; he was dumbfounded. Sensing his disbelief, Miss Emily set about leaving no question. "You recall Shelley's companion, Richards, do you not?" she asked. "He perished along with the poet, of course, but his wife kept a complete diary of their days in Italy. It was published, naturally. I have a copy here if you would like to look at it."

Chapman was a tall, gangly lad with fair skin and a large nose. When he smiled and blushed, though, he became charming since he had the grace to recognize his superior when he met her.

"That will not be necessary, ma'am," he said, offering his hand and making a slight bow. "*Ariel.* The wind sprite of mythology, of course. I thank you again for enlightening me so."

Their appointed task complete, the two classmates departed.

"What did I tell you, Chappie?" Johnny was heard to say as the young men passed back through the main entrance.

Once outside, Chappie's smile was broad. He reached for a cigarette as he nodded his approval of Miss Emily's command of the subject. Recounting the details of their interview with her, they stopped down the block for a roast sausage and a beer to fortify themselves for the street car ride back to Cambridge.

Back at the library, Miss Emily permitted herself a little smile after the boys were out the door. For Leo, that wasn't the tipoff as to what was going on within her. It was her eyes. As she looked after them, he clearly read a twinkle in her eyes that told him what she was feeling.

Like all of the women and most of the men of her day, Emily Derby was skilled at social camouflage. She hid easily behind those symbols of adulthood that were considered acceptable. Her dress, her hairstyle, her manner of speech, even her job had been carefully chosen to fit seamlessly into the social fabric of her time and place. With all this mastered, she disappeared within her social context every bit as well as a deer becomes invisible in the forest. Yet, unlike many of her peers, Miss Emily was conscious

Mark Zaccaria

of the fact that within this external matrix, she could use her intelligence, her creativity, and her animate spirit to satisfy herself without letting on to the outside world.

That's what she had just done, and that's what Leo picked up on as he watched her watching the doors her most recent victims had just used. Her pride was the same emotion that Leo felt as the victor at marbles. She had that same animal reaction that he had when he resolved a question of who would captain the ball team by delivering one punch to his rival's solar plexus. Her smile was very self-disciplined. She didn't show her teeth, but inside, the feeling was the same, and Leo knew it.

In that same moment, he was also aware of another dimension that Miss Emily displayed as a champion. He had seen any number of adults in the neighborhood referred to as great ball players, but in the past tense. Her game was one at which you were clearly able to improve with age. It was that fusion of predatory behavior and social conformity that made him realize for the first time that there was life after baseball.

Little discoveries like this are the waypoints of everyone's educations. The students of the Boston public school system enjoyed as rich an environment of learning as any others. In Leo's case, the library and his reading of the examples of the older students and of teachers like Mrs. Appleton and Miss Emily augmented his academic growth.

That is not to say that he had the most profitable or the most disciplined path through the educational labyrinth. At the library, he went wherever his desires took him. What piqued his interest captured his attention. What was thought to be dry or useless was ignored. Before long, he knew the delivery dates of *Popular Science* and *Life* magazines. After that, he was usually waiting for the postman to arrive at Miss Emily's desk. Within an hour, the new issue had been gutted. Stories of cars, airplanes, and locomotives were absorbed immediately. Stories on textiles or home furnishings were ignored. The long stream of "What's New" thumbnail descriptions of new products were relished at length, each becoming a part of a brief fantasy of possession. *What would I do if I had one of those?*

He certainly did not take the shortest route to pure enlightenment. Who does? He did keep his interest high on schoolwork in general, though, while bonding himself ever more tightly to science.

Early one Saturday morning during his sophomore year at East Boston High, Leo sheepishly approached the head librarian's desk.

"Pardon me, ma'am," he said quietly. "May I ask a question?"

She looked at him quizzically. Was this to be a riddle? She really didn't want students that young trying their hand at Stump the Librarian. She preferred that their intellectual skills be practiced more so that at least their questions would be thoughtful. She also didn't want a juvenile fad to evolve, which would take up so much of her time with what were sure to be such obvious questions.

"Certainly, Mr. Zaccaria," she replied, intentionally leaning on the tone of superiority in her voice. "What is it?"

Leo fumbled. It was becoming a good deal more difficult than he'd imagined. Still, there was no one around this early to see him squirm, so he forced out his request.

"I'm interested in a serious study of science, and I'd like your advice on which field would be the best one to concentrate on."

As he finished his statement, he finally met her eyes. It was just in time to see them soften.

"Of course," she said, quickly warming to the opportunity to be of help. "What is it about science that attracts you? Tell me what your interest is and I'll try to suggest a field. What do you think you want to do?"

He puzzled about this for a moment. Without asking, he took a seat in the bow-backed chair that was posted beside Miss Emily's desk. "I want to invent something," he finally said. "I know I'll have to learn about whatever kind of science I specialize in," he continued. "But I wonder which field will have the most discoveries to be made during my lifetime. I want to work on new things and be there when important discoveries are made." He looked back down for a moment and then finished. "Is that crazy?"

"It is most certainly *not* crazy, Mr. Zaccaria," she replied, bringing all of her formidable academic stature to his defense. "In fact," she asserted, "too many people have no reason whatsoever for going into their professional fields. By having a reason of any kind, you are already ahead of them in life's long race."

It was Miss Emily's turn to ponder the options. "Let me think for a moment about what you have said."

Most inventive thought processes actually take place fully in only a fraction of a second. So it is not odd that she had evaluated all the options, double-checked her assumptions, and formulated a detailed conclusion almost immediately. One has to admire the towering self-confidence she had, however, to believe that she had solved the problem of the boy's entire career in that one moment, without any question.

"Chemistry."

She said it simply but with finality. "Yes, that's it," she continued, "the study of the building blocks of the Earth and all it contains. It is a science that has thousands of years of history and that might really have just begun to be explored." She paused for a reaction.

Leo didn't really know what to say. Chemistry was one of the four or five fields he'd expected her to choose from. Still, her decision seemed to exclude several other possibilities, which suddenly seemed more attractive than they had been just the moment before.

War Record

"Why not astronomy, or physics, or radio?" he asked for no real reason.

"Young man," she lectured, "radio is not one of the exact sciences. Furthermore, you have asked me for my opinion and I have given it to you." She didn't want to frighten him off, so she softened her approach. "Let me explain," she said, trying to soothe him. "Have you heard of the Englishman William Perkin? Perhaps not. Just eighty years ago, he was an eighteen-year-old chemist. He invented a synthetic dye that was far superior to any of the natural dyes then in use either for ink or apparel. He might be personally responsible for the demise of indigo as a cash crop. My point is that now, as then, age is no barrier to excellence in chemistry.

"Second, are you aware yet that the basic chemical elements have only recently been understood in any scientific fashion and that perhaps only half of them have even been discovered? I will get you an article from *The Scientific American* magazine on the work of Professor Dimitri Mendeleev, the Russian chemist who first made sense of the organization of the elements according to their atomic structures. His first Periodic Table of the Elements was published about sixty years ago. Have you ever seen one?"

Here, Miss Emily paused to dig in the bookshelf immediately behind her desk. In a moment, she had retrieved a leather-bound text and opened it to the table.

"This text is in German," she said. "So do not bother trying to decipher it, but look here. This is Mendeleev's chart as it existed in nineteen twenty-nine. Notice the empty spaces? It is currently a hypothesis that each of these blanks represents an atomic structure that should exist but hasn't yet been discovered. And why? Perhaps some do not occur naturally on Earth. Who then will do the laboratory work to create them so that they might be used in other experiments and in industry? And what will you name the one that you discover, young man, Zaccarium?"

Leo was beginning to see her point. Derbyum was the name he actually thought of in response to her last question. *The building blocks of the Earth...and all it contains? New chemicals for use by industry?*

She could see him beginning to take her point. It was time for this argument's *coup de grace*. "You asked about radio a moment ago." She concluded, "It is my opinion that the only limit on the size or power of radio receivers, and possibly transmitters, is the materials now available with which to construct them. Who will discover the substances that will conduct electricity more efficiently or use less overall power to broadcast the same or greater distances? Think about it please. I will get you that article."

He walked slowly back to the periodical room. *The Scientific American* had replaced *Popular Mechanics*. He looked at the chart in the magazine's English text and read the groups and periods and atomic numbers without really knowing what it all was. How did hydrides differ from oxides? Maybe the article would explain. Finally, he concentrated on the blank locations in the table's matrix.

"New elements," he said softly, and then, "better radio."

He thought for a moment before starting to read.

"Chemistry," he said.

War Record

The Cycle of Life at Berga

A day in the life of one of the ghost soldiers of Berga involved fatigue more than anything else. They were all such poor physical specimens that almost any exertion at all was too much for muscles that had seen no protein to speak of for months. The dark walk from the barracks to the tunnels was slow and halting, but it left them all winded and needing a rest before they could pick up tools and make their way into the tunnels.

The walk home in the pre-dawn hours was made slightly more bearable by anticipation. When they returned to their meager quarters, there would be food of some sort. Usually, it was hot broth and a bit of bread. These days, the broth had been thinner and thinner as what little was available was stretched to cover all the POWs. The same applied to the bread. Each night, some number of small, round loaves were provided. Usually, it was black bread, and each night, the question was how many mouths each loaf would have to feed. On a good night, each roll was to be divided between five. On a bad night, it was ten or twelve. For most of the prisoners, it was all there was, though, so they looked forward to it as if it were Thanksgiving dinner.

And then there was sleep. There was no choice in the matter really. Despite the hunger, the stress, and the fear in each of them, fatigue always won. Whether they would come to later and worry away the rest of the dark hours or not, everyone fell into their bunks just minutes after whatever arrived for the daily meal. The room fell silent with exhausted figures seemingly draped at random on racks that were more plentiful as more of their users died.

Crouched under his US Army-issue greatcoat by the back window, the rag man was vigilant at first but soon gave way to sleep and then to dreams.

Mark Zaccaria

Radio Days

It is said that human language first developed as a means of better coordinating hunting in groups. Perhaps that was it. Certainly, the second use of this unique tool was to transmit news from group to group. More like gossip at first, ancient tribes were as hungry as modern tribes are for information on people elsewhere so they could compare themselves and decide who was better off.

A victory attributed to some other group raised envy in those who heard of it later. A defeat that befell someone else brought on a suppressed smile because it was them and not us. Sympathy would develop in those who had felt the same sting at some time past. Whichever way these stories went, they were eagerly sought after and quickly became the basis for all spectator entertainment.

Bazaars and markets grew up in the settlements of our early history. These were as much social entities as they were economic. People gathered to trade but also to look each other over and especially to hear each other's news. When strangers came to town, it was an event because new information from afar arrived with them. The universal interest in travelers and the envy of them stems from the belief that they possess some knowledge we do not. Envy quickly becomes anger and has often led to suspicion of strangers. That's a secondary response though. Our first impulse is to find out what the newcomer can tell us about the world outside our day-to-day reach.

For millennia, people's time sense regarding world and national events was calibrated by the interval required to get information back and forth. Many a military battle has been fought after the war had been ended but before news of that fact reached the armies in the field. Many an international negotiation proceeded like a chess game played through the mails as dispatches sailed back and forth across oceans in wooden ships or rode with messengers on horseback.

Through all this, the world went on about its business quite happily, accepting the pace at which events unfolded. Usually, when an advance in communications occurred, it was the exclusive domain of only a select few. The telegraph, and at first even the telephone, certainly followed this pattern. They were either too complex or too expensive for general use.

As usual, technology did not consider the social impact it would have when it shattered that pattern. Within just a handful of years, everyone in the United States had a radio. In terms of civilization, it was really just an instant of time before everyone in the nation could hear about something more or less at once. It was a lightning bolt of opportunity but one that struck almost without anyone taking notice.

In days gone by, the town square had been the meeting place for everyone in the community. There, while relaxing on a summer's evening, the townspeople could find out about all that was going on. This knowledge made them a part of the social group. They became members, actually, of a club whose privileges were open only to those sharing this firsthand knowledge of the town. People from other towns were encountered occasionally. They were immediately recognized as outsiders, though, and were suspected or feared because of it.

In the large cities that grew up in industrial America, it was the neighborhoods that took over this role. This was especially evident in the many immigrant populations whose local quarters were further differentiated by languages and cultures quite distinct from those nearby.

Then, in less than a decade, the whole country became aware of the feud between Jack Benny and Fred Allen. Sides were taken in local meeting places from coast to coast. Particularly delicious insults from the ongoing spat were recounted endlessly. People all over the continent were suddenly informed about the same debate, so they were engaged together in it.

To be sure, the mock combat between Benny and Allen was a contest only for entertainment's sake. It was just one of many things, though, that everyone quickly came to know about together. This made a vast number of people members of "Club America" in a very short time. It's arguable that the evolution of radio was the single most important factor of nation building in the history of the republic. Certainly, it glued the country together and provided a common culture that transcended regional differences. That alone is no small feat, but it was accomplished while everyone was unaware of what was going on.

While he was still a marbles shooter, Leo knew all about radio, even though he only rarely heard a broadcast. He read about the advances and designs of radio receivers in Popular Science. He heard the plotlines of all the programs favored by young people from the other kids at school. His uncle Paul even owned a set, but it was only turned on for the Braves or Red Sox games on Sunday afternoons.

Leo felt left out. Life was clearly passing his family by since they had no radio. He had to try to convince them to get a set. He knew in his head that his father wouldn't understand why he needed a radio and would refuse to spend the money. In his heart, though, he knew he needed that radio set, so he had to give it a try.

War Record

"Whaddaya mean, a radio?" his father asked irritably, eyes squinting as if they hurt. Maybe it was just disbelief. "What'sa big deal, hey? You wanna music? There's the record player." After his initial shock, he wanted to soften his response to his son. He tried to sound logical and soothing. "Hey, fil-yo, no radio, huh? I'm not mada money," he said, concluding the interview.

This didn't leave Leo with too many options. It was time to head back to the library.

Coming into the East Boston branch this time, he was a man on a mission. Miss Derby was his chief ally and the intelligence officer of the operation. She led him to several issues of *Popular Science* from the twenties, an illustrated how-to book from that decade, and a set of drawings published by the Howard Radio Company of Chicago. With those, he was able to map his strategy.

Once he understood the final task of his campaign, Leo was faced with serious logistical questions. The kinds of supplies he would need for this enterprise posed intriguing and completely new problems as compared to simply getting some sports equipment. To be sure, he was part of a sizable network of traders, each of whom had different specialized commodities to offer, but he'd never before tried to use it for items as exotic as a germanium crystal. Once his list was complete, though, and he knew what he had to do, his jaw was set and he looked only ahead.

His first stop was Alex Bang's boat yard. From the front door of Leo's house, the boatyard was only about a mile away. Even so, it was a part of another world. Down the Lexington Street hill he marched. From the square at the bottom, he turned right, along the waterfront, in the direction of the new suspension bridge across Chelsea Creek.

There were piers all along the half-mile stretch to the bridge. All were serviceable but none was too presentable. Each was home to one or a few hardscrabble businesses related to the water. Ship chandlers and outfitters supplied customers from the fishing fleet and the cargo steamers that called on the port. Boat brokers had an eye for every nickel's worth of value in anything that floated. They had to because along these wharves only the least valuable craft were offered for sale or salvage. There were divers and welders and riggers of one sort or another who worked occasionally and lived in their shacks on the piers in between jobs. One refrigerated warehouse took up an entire dock and its yard area. The smell of ammonia mixed with that of the day's catch. The warehouse sold ice to the fishermen, stored bananas and melons coming in from the steamers, and crated up everything from shoes to salted cod for shipment up and down the seaboard.

One hundred years before, all these docks had been a part of the shipbuilding empire organized by Donald MacKay. At these same piers, MacKay and his men had built the clipper ships. Then there had been a constant bustle of activity surrounding the launching of hulls and the building and outfitting of the boats. These narrow-beamed greyhounds of the sea were so long at the waterline and so sharp of prow that they fairly slid through the water. Their length made room for more masts, and their many masts made space for more sheets. With full sail aloft, a clipper could make way either before the gentlest breeze or pulled up to it in the tightest reach. These thoroughbreds kept sail-powered ocean commerce viable for a quarter century beyond the time when steam power might have first surpassed it.

By the time Leo was walking past, though, the activity was long since over. Even though there were parts of the skeletons of some of the clippers still in evidence here or there, the energy had been leached out of the whole area, and it was no longer a birthplace of ships. In fact, the salt, the wind, and the general lack of maintenance had conspired over the decades to suck the color out of these structures as well. As he walked by, the predominant shades were brown and gray. Even a lobsterman's buoys with their signature bands of bright paint were little more than marks of punctuation in a long sentence of weathered wood. In many ways, this was the perfect place for a junkyard.

War Record

Captain Bang would have indignantly insisted it was a salvage yard and that there was quite a difference between salvage and junk. He was a man in his mid-fifties who had lived by his wits for forty years on the coastal waters of New England. He'd fished. He'd towed. He'd manned the lighters or barges that fueled the oil-fired steamers. In the process, he had been touched by the great beauty of the sea but had also been cut to the quick by the fear of its unpredictable, unforgiving strength. As a young man, he had always been certain of his ability to cope with whatever happened afloat. His self-confidence was well placed since he always had. Once, in his late middle years, it had crossed his mind to wonder if he was still up to the rigors of life on the ocean. Directly after that, he had simply stayed ashore.

The old skipper was neither wistful nor nostalgic. He had done the right thing. He kept his yard and pier. He sat by the water's edge and looked across the inner harbor to the docks and granite storehouses of Boston proper, dominated by the spire of the custom house. He traded the bits and pieces of ships that came in and out more often by water than by land. He ran a tug up and down the harbor when need be but left the real boatman's work to his son. The lad was in his twenties, tall and strong and sure of himself. To the old man, this was as it should be.

Old Captain Bang was willing to trade with anyone whose word was good. He especially liked dealing with the boys from the Italian neighborhood up the hill. He had started early himself and still held the nineteenth-century notion that boys should be brought along young. The boys liked dealing with him because he had such treasures. Items of all types and descriptions were piled high in crates and stalls and just laid out all around the yard. They could explore and analyze each new bauble while slowly ferreting out the one they had come for. Brass and bright work were in one area. Shiv blocks and tackle sat in orderly piles in another. Winches and hoists marched in a line along one of the yard's boundaries. They were all that remained of old trawlers or

Mark Zaccaria

lobstermen whose wood had gone bad and whose hulls now rotted on the tidal flats somewhere up Little Mystic Channel. Leo loved looking closely at each item. He would turn them over in his hand, thinking about what each one was and where it had been. But there was no time for that on this visit.

It was a passable day, so Alex Bang sat on a bow-backed armchair he'd dragged outside his shack. That shack was actually the wheelhouse of an old steam tug that he'd hoisted into place near the path from his carriage yard down to his pier. It had a rounded front of tongue and grove wood slats that had been embalmed with brown paint for decades. Its helmsman's windows skirted this radius and gave occupants a 180-degree view that was no longer necessary but was still a nice symbol of where its owner had been. He wore a woolen pullover, stout flannel pants, a well-worn boatmen's cap, and a scraggle of white whiskers. Leo walked directly over to him.

"Good morning, Cap'n," he said. "Any weather comin' up?" The old salt chuckled at the question, but it still made him cast a critical eye to the heavens.

"Don't rightly know, boy," the captain replied in his flat Yankee accent. "Whatever does, though, I expect I can ride it out with no damage right here." He paused to silently go over the humor of what he had just said, shore bound as he was. "What brings you out today, son?"

"I need some gear for a radio I'm building," Leo said seriously. "I was hopin' you would have some of the parts and that we could arrange a swap."

The kid was all business, so the captain nodded gravely and avoided being too curious about what might be offered in return.

"Aa-yuh, I got some radio gear," he said, pronouncing this last word as if it had never been meant to have an *r*. "You see that shed yon-da, just seaward of the A-frame crane?"

Leo nodded.

"You look around in they-yuh and see what you can find."

War Record

Radio equipment was almost unheard of in those days aboard the kind of workboats and small trawlers that Alex Bang was likely to have had for salvage. Such stuff was also relatively new to the captain himself. Since he didn't really understand it or its value, it was the one type of gear that he never really kept ship shape. In fact, the little shed was a rat's nest of damaged parts and tangled wires. Corroded sheet metal frames were fitted with large tube sockets that were usually empty. The cabinets were mostly of varnished wood, but their metal knobs were designed to turn metal shafts through metal journals. All this metalwork had long since pitted in the salt air and, in most cases, a tool would be necessary to break them free.

Still, everything had to be looked over, and Leo was not one to give up early just because the task looked impossible. He knew he wasn't going to get anything unless he worked for it. That attitude was rewarded after a short while when he unearthed a pair of headphone speakers. They had US military markings from the 1919 Expeditionary Force. The small Bakelite disks, which pressed against the ears, were backed by a cylindrical form from which the wires protruded. The two earpieces were suspended from metal pins held by the arc of a twin wire metal frame that was covered in cracked and broken leather. The whole assembly was much heavier than one would think for its small size. Each speaker held a sizable permanent magnet, and the dense Bakelite earpieces had been designed to take a beating. As a result, they were in pretty good shape. The intertwined wires that hung from one side had woven cloth insulation that had seen better days, and they were cut off two feet from the phones, so it was hard to say what kind of connector they had once sported.

It might not sound like much, but to him, it was a find that energized his search through the remainder of the radio junk. He hung the headphones around his neck and got on with it.

All of the gear in Captain Bang's radio locker had once been marine equipment. That meant that it generally hadn't been intended to receive commercial broadcasts. In their day, the RDF sets could have been tuned to NBC or CBS, but by then, they were just giant maelstroms of broken tubes, frozen knobs, and wire-wound magnets. Leo couldn't recognize very much of what he was looking at as he sifted through the alien mess. At the bottom of one column of crazed aluminum and copper, there was a galvanized bucket that held some metal modules.

As he looked closely, Leo could see that the bucket was around half full of light oil, diesel fuel from the smell of it. Soaking in the oil were several mechanical devices. His eye went right to the one he wanted. Its black Bakelite knob had been above the oil level, but its interlocking circular metal fins had been submerged. This meant that he could handle it and that it still operated. It was a variable capacitor. He recognized it from his research, and he almost understood what it was for in design of a radio set. Every real marine locker has a rag in it someplace. He located one there and wrapped up the oily prize.

The triumph of his discoveries was quickly blunted by the recognition that he didn't have much to trade for them. It was time to go face the captain.

When he got back to the wheelhouse, the skipper was whittling and enjoying the sun. "Whatdja find, youngun?" he asked without looking up.

"I've got a couple things that might help, sir." The emphasis was much too strong on the word *might*. "Most of the gear in your radio locker is in pretty bad shape, you know."

"Aa-yuh," the captain agreed, looking up. "What's in the rag?"

"Well," Leo said, looking down. "I think it's a variable capacitor, but I'm not sure if it still works."

In the shed, he had tried the action and found that it was as smooth as silk. Careful inspection showed that none of the moving plates made contact with their stationary neighbors. Of course it would work, and since the old man knew about things, Leo decided to up the ante.

War Record

"Also, I'm not at all sure if it's the right size for the radio circuit I'm trying to make."

"Uh-huh," he acknowledged slowly, trying to sound sage without cracking a smile. "Those earphones look good on ya. D'ya think you can hear anything over 'em?"

Leo had to be truthful. "They're from the army, Cap'n. They were built tough, so I expect they still work." There was one ray of hope, though, and he held up the frayed end of the signal cord. "If I can figure out how to plug 'em in."

"Sure you can," the skipper said, dismissing the problem. "Now, if you're going to get those two, what am I going to get?" he asked.

It was the moment of truth, and the parts were so important to Leo that he couldn't hope to be convincing when he described anything else he had as being equal or greater in value.

"I was thinking about offering my roller skates," Leo said slowly. "They're shoe skates," he added quickly, hoping this would increase the appearance of their value. He was only thinking about this trade's value gap in his own terms, so he was genuinely shocked by what the captain said next.

"Sounds temptin', son, but I really don't do much roller skatin' these days, and I don't know what I'd do with 'em on a boat anyhow. Got anything else?"

Leo hadn't thought about a counter offer. His mind raced. "I see you're whittling, Cap'n," he said, grabbing for what was right there. "Could you use a first-class pen knife?"

"A pen knife," the captain said to himself. Then to Leo, he said, "It's a good one, you say?"

"Oh yes, sir," he replied and then let his sales pitch spill out in a stream of superlatives. "It's got a bone handle and two blades. It was made in Pennsylvania, and they really know about knives out there. I keep it real sharp, so it's all ready to go."

"Well then," Bang said encouragingly, "let's have a look at it."

Mark Zaccaria

He had been whittling with a blade that he had ground out of a broken bastard file. The handle was a piece of broomstick that had been jammed onto the file's tang.

"It might do better than this homemade job."

When he started out, Leo hadn't thought that the project would cost him his pocketknife. It didn't take any thought at all, though, for him to decide to put it up. He dug into his trousers and produced the little jack knife. Captain Bang took it from him and made a real show of inspecting it.

"Seems you do know how to sharpen a blade," he commented approvingly. "This is a mighty fine item," he continued, "and I don't want to take it unless I can give you equal value. Here's my suggestion. Since you're not sure about that variable *what's it*, why don't I just throw it in? Now those earphones are good quality, but I think I ought to put up somethin' mo-ah, just to make it fair. My son, Val, says you might be needin' one of these."

He pulled a small item from his pants pocket. It looked at first like a short stub of a pencil but grayish-white in color. Looking closely, a small metal band could be seen at each end. Leo's heart jumped into his throat. It was a germanium crystal, the only other hard thing to find before he could start to assemble his radio set.

"Val says that'd cost you five cents if you bought it in a store," the older man said with obvious amazement. "I confess I can't see its value, but if you can, I'll throw it in."

"Gee! Thanks, Cap'n!" Leo gasped with eyes wide. "It's a deal!"

He had completely forgotten about keeping up his poker face. In fact, he was so excited that it was an hour or two before he realized what a favor the old man had done for him. Alex Bang took the penknife and deposited it in his pocket, right next to the slightly larger one with the sharper blade that was already there. Leo thanked him energetically and hurried off in the direction of home. As he was leaving Bang's yard, he looked out across the glistening harbor. He was captured for a moment by the picture of a gray-hulled patrol boat slipping gently up the chan-

War Record

nel toward the other fighting ships docked at the Boston Naval Shipyard in Charlestown.

Back home, he stopped briefly under the back porch to collect another part he had stored there. It was the armature from a Ford Model A's generator. The casing and the shaft had been broken in a crash, and he had gotten the lump of copper wire from the auto save yard in return for some clean-up work one Saturday. This project was so important, though, that he felt authorized to use his father's workbench rather than sitting in the dirt.

Leo began by setting up his library book, open to the diagram he was trying to copy. Then he took a piece of scrap pine as a base for the whole assembly. He spent an hour unwinding copper wire from the generator coil. Next came a used baking powder container that his mother had thrown away. This was a cardboard cylinder, and it became the mandrel around which he wound the main radio coil. If he had not had the variable capacitor, he would have had to use the coil wires for tuning. Since his good fortune at the boatyard, though, he had a much more elegant solution.

Leaving plenty of running end, he wound the copper wire around and around the cardboard form. He was careful to see that none of the windings touched and that none were too far apart. When it was done, he coated it all with varnish, both as an insulator and to hold the fine wire in place. Next, the capacitor was mounted to the base. Then several nails were driven into the base as terminal blocks, their pattern closely mirroring that shown in the book. While the varnish cured, he took some more wire out to the porch.

The porch behind the first-floor apartment was duplicated on the second and third floors too. A wooden staircase zigzagged up along the corner opposite to the back door. This was a fire escape more than a service entrance. Since there was a floor above his family's porch, though, there were floor joists running overhead. Down the length of the porch between two of these, Leo strung a single antenna wire from nails driven into the wooden joists. The

Mark Zaccaria

wood insulated the antenna, and he was able to drop a tap off of it right next to his bedroom window.

Back to the workbench, he wrapped copper wire around the antenna nail and brought it to one end of the coil, which was then mounted on the base. One of the nails became a ground. Later, he would wire it to a water pipe. The crystal was held in place and wired to one of the two headphone nails. The other headphone nail went to ground. Wrapping the free ends of the signal wires from the headset, he used fiber electrical tape to hold them in place.

When everything was done, he carried the set to his room and connected the antenna and ground. He adjusted the headphones to his ears and then touched the free end of the crystal with a single piece of stripped wire that ran from the coil. This last part was called the cat's whisker.

At first, there was nothing in the earphones, but then he began adjusting his capacitor. There was a crackle of static. It was followed by a short, sharp sound. He was moving the tuner too fast. Coming back slowly, he found his reward. Bix Beiderbecke's horn cried in his ears, and a scratchy rhythm section danced behind it. He had jazz in his bedroom. What could be better?

For a day and a half, he spent all of his spare time finding his way around the commercial radio band. His capacitor had no dial or calibration, of course, so he used a modified version of the Braille method to find stations. With his eyes closed, he would turn the capacitor knob all the way to one stop and then advance it slowly until he heard the tin voices of the few stations with any real power. WBZ and WNAC broadcast from Boston. The first was part of the NBC Network and carried the familiar three-gong signature every quarter hour. Bob Emery soon became his favorite local personality. However, with recorded music and live remote broadcasts, Leo could expect to regularly hear such diverse celebrities as Tom Mix, Franklin Roosevelt, and Duke

War Record

Ellington. He felt like he had arrived. He was in touch with all the things that important people knew.

Before long, it was time to show off his radio to his father. He got ready to answer even the harshest criticism. He had all of his facts and figures ready. He waited until after dinner. Not only was the reception best then, but it was also the only moment of a normal day when he could get his father's attention for a frivolity. Leo began by trying to explain what he had while inviting the old man into his room.

"C'mon, Pop," he said. "I got a radio in here, and I want to show you. I built it myself."

"Whata you, talkin' crazy?" was the confused reply, but as a dutiful father, he went along to see what his son wanted.

What must it have looked like to him? All he saw was a piece of 2x10 floor joist cut almost square and laid flat. On it were some things that made no sense. The nails were not driven all the way in, and there was an empty paper tube with lots of wire on it but no connection to the wall. In fact, what had he heard of radio at all by then, and how much of it did he believe? His son quickly picked up the headset and turned one speaker around so that he could listen without donning the whole thing. Satisfied that there was something to hear, he broke into a smile.

"Here, Pop. Let me help you get these on," he said, reaching out to the top of his father's head with the alien bracket he held.

Antonio Zaccaria leaned back from the advancing headset almost imperceptibly. He didn't fear them; it went without saying that Leo would maintain respect for his father. He just didn't know what he was supposed to be doing with them.

When they were put in place, Leo said, "Listen."

The old man began to think, *Listen to what?* But then there it was. It wasn't very loud, so you had to concentrate. When you did, though, it was definitely one of the American popular orchestras playing some of that dance music all the kids listened to. As soon as he recognized what he was supposed recognize, he took the headset off, almost to avoid contamination.

"Hootchie kootchie music," he said. "Where's it come from?"

Leo beamed, thinking he had begun to get through to his father. "It comes from the air, Pop. It's broadcast from different stations all around the country. You want to hear something else?" The younger man took the phones and listened to one again as he adjusted the tuner to try for another station.

"Whaddaya mean, it comes from the air?" the older man asked, a little irritated that his son expected him to buy such an obviously groundless explanation. "It's no even plugged in a wall!" All of his experience with modern appliances told him that this was a trick.

"Really, Pop," Leo continued, "the big transmitters send out energy through the air, just like the dynamos send energy through the wires for the lights."

It was clear to Leo that his Father didn't believe a word of it, but he was still listening with complete attention, so the lad pushed on.

"The radio energy is called a signal, and it carries the patterns of what you hear by being stronger or weaker in the same way as the music."

The old man was completely lost now, and at a loss to know whether he should be angry with his son or to get him some medicine.

"The power to make the sounds you hear comes from the signal itself. Oh, sure, big table model radio sets use electricity from the wall, but that's just to make the sound powerful enough to come out of bigger speakers so everyone can hear it at once."

"*Basta*," his father said softly. "It's crazy. You talka crazy." He was shaking his head as he left the room.

He had heard every word of his son's explanation, and he understood the meaning of all of them and of the sentences in which they had been used. He just didn't believe it.

War Record

It wasn't long, though, before Antonio Zaccaria and virtually every other American was listening to radio, whether they understood the technology or not. In his case, his oldest daughter took singing lessons. These led to her being featured on a fifteen-minute program of Italian songs three times each week. This, in turn, meant that his wife had to hear the broadcasts. They had an American Bosch Magneto Corporation Model 60 console in their front room the next day. Before it, the family was held in a trance as they listened to Edith's soprano voice. By the end of the first show, they were all dedicated patrons of the program's sponsors.

"Sta sera il programa sta presentato per..."

It didn't really matter who. Whichever of the local shops or food specialty brands presented the broadcast had just locked four new customers into place.

Within the span of only a few years, there had been millions of individual stories like that one, all with the same outcome. They got a radio. By the mid-1930s, advances in industrial specialization and labor-saving machinery had given most of the population an hour or two to relax after dinner every day. At the same time, the mass introduction of radio had provided them with a national campfire they could all sit around to swap stories during that time.

"A fiery horse with the speed of light, a cloud of dust and a hearty 'Hi-yo, Silver!' The Lone Ranger rides again with his faithful Indian companion, Tonto, the daring and resourceful masked rider of the plains led the fight for law and order in the early western United States. Nowhere in the pages of history can one find a greater champion of justice. Return with us now to those thrilling days of yesteryear. From out of the past come the hoof beats of the great horse Silver. The Lone Ranger rides again!"

"Come on, Silver! Let's go, big fellow! Hi-yo, Silver, away!"

"At the end of yesterday's episode, Bud Titus stormed out of Sheriff Whalen's office…"

"Good evening, ladies and gentlemen. This is your News of the Airways, covering local, national, and international events of interest today.

"Washington: Speaking to a joint session of Congress, President Franklin D. Roosevelt strongly reiterated the government's commitment to friendly relations with all the countries of Europe and, in fact, the world. He was stern in advising Congress that the American people do not want to take sides in any argument that does not directly involve them.

"The President went on to stress that legitimate American interests should not be overlooked just because the Europeans are squabbling among themselves. 'Trade abroad means jobs at home,' Mr. Roosevelt said, concluding that sales of food, raw materials, and even munitions should be thought of as economic rather than political activities.

"Berlin: The government of Germany today announced the sudden death of its President, Herr Paul von Hindenburg. German Chancellor, Adolph Hitler, called upon all Germans to observe an official mourning period of three days.

"In June of this year, several prominent German political figures were murdered or died under mysterious circumstances. All were opponents of Herr Hitler, leading to speculation that he or his supporters were behind the violence. Now, with the death of President von Hindenburg, the chancellor becomes the undisputed leader of the German Third Reich.

"Closer to home now.

"Boston: Mayor James Michael Curley today dedicated the newly renovated park surrounding Jamaica Pond in the city's Jamaica Plain residential section. The public works project had

War Record

taken three months to complete, and it had provided employment for sixty-four laborers…"

"Who knows what evil lurks in the hearts of men?"

"The Shadow knows! Hahahahaha!"

"Your neighborhood Blue Coal dealer brings you the thrilling adventures of The Shadow, the hard and relentless fight of one man against the forces of evil. These dramatizations are designed to demonstrate forcefully to old and young alike that crime does not pay.

"Government forecasts indicate that homeowners may face another shortage of all types of fuel for home heating. You're fortunate if you heat with coal because you're able store fuel. Call your Blue Coal dealer tomorrow and place your order so he can schedule early delivery. Make sure you order the right size for your furnace. And, if you are not sure what it should be, ask your Blue Coal dealer. He'll be glad to inspect your heating plant and may be able to make recommendations too that will help you get more heat and burn less fuel. Tomorrow, first thing, call the nearest Blue Coal dealer. And ask him to schedule your supply of Blue Coal for early delivery.

"The Shadow, who aids the forces of law and order, is in reality Lamont Cranston…"

"Buck Rogers is back on the air! Buck and Wilma and all their fascinating friends and mysterious enemies in the superscientific twenty-fifth century.

"This program is brought to you by the makers of Ovaltine, the famous food drink that is a favorite with millions of Americans, young and old. Ovaltine is a favorite food drink for two reasons. First, because it's so downright good. You'll love its rich, satisfying flavor. Second, because Ovaltine is good for you. It brings you loads and loads of valuable vitamins, minerals, and other vital food elements that help build strong, healthy bodies, gives you the pep and energy to be wide awake and husky.

"So tell Mother you'd like to start drinking Ovaltine every single day.

"And now for Buck Rogers and his thrilling adventures five hundred years in the future..."

Radio quickly became the constant companion of every American home. The very fact that most had no idea how it worked gave the information gushing out of it even more credibility. If science had gone to such a length to create this marvelous means of communication, no one would dare use it for gossip or half-truths, would they? If they did, the scientists would know, wouldn't they?

Not long after the American Bosch console appeared in Leo's home, his mother began to serve three courses on the same plate at dinner. This was met with a raised eyebrow from his father. It was traditional to have each course separately, with everybody completing the first before the second was served.

"You needa have a balanced dinner plate," she said emphatically, "especially a green vegetable!" She then turned her attention to Leo. "And you and you brother gotta start drinking milk with the meal."

Of course you had to. That point was made repeatedly over the radio, and who was she to ignore such wise advice?

Before long, every listener had his or her favorite programs and personalities on the radio. This became far more than simple entertainment, however. Since it was assumed that everything said on the air was the truth, it was all accepted as the truth. Movie stars became examples of style, and the people went to films in part to keep up with the latest fashions. Movie stars

War Record

played different characters in every picture though. The fantasy was apparent.

Radio stars were far more persuasive because they tended to play the same characters over and over. Since more imagination was required of the listener, it was far more common for them to believe that the radio actors were playing themselves. Add to that the commentators and announcers who certainly were playing themselves. They were highly regarded by their listeners for their ideas, even though they were usually reading from a script. Multiply this by the large numbers of daily listening opportunities, as compared to the only occasional trip most made to the movies. The result was a tremendous impact on society made by a little electric box that attracted no fanfare for itself but only for its offerings.

In cities, towns, and rural backwaters all over America, people's actions were soon dictated by the social policy they received from the radio. In Baltimore as much as in Chicago or San Francisco, people in the neighborhoods would turn in the pettiest of thieves, in part because Bud Collier, playing Superman, led a constant fight for "Truth, justice, and the American way." In the hills and hollows of West Virginia, as in the ranches of Colorado's high plains, it came to be accepted that formal schooling was a goal that should be achieved if possible. Real life in either of these places might not seem to argue this position too well, but *Jack Armstrong, the All-American Boy*, demonstrated its importance weekly.

Once, just after his fifteenth birthday, Leo happened onto a case of street drama while walking home from an after-school job. On the sidewalk outside the iron gate to a three-decker, he saw a boy perhaps a bit older than he was pushing around a girl who was probably a little younger. Standing over her, the slender youth shouted menacingly. She seemed to be only able to cower and hope it would end.

Mark Zaccaria

"Give me that money, pipsqueak," he shouted, "or I'll bounce you off the gate some more!"

The girl was silent, hunching into a protective posture and only looking at the pavement.

Without an instant's hesitation, Leo picked up his step and put himself between the two.

"Hey, stupido," he said in a slow, menacing voice, "you keep your hands off the young lady, and you be real careful how you speak to her. *Capiche?*"

The two boy's eyes were locked. A test of wills began.

"Don't stick your nose in other people's business!" the older boy protested. "She's my sister. I say any money she gets is mine, and I'm takin' it. So just move along and you won't get hurt."

Leo dropped the books he was carrying in a strap. "What you do in your house is your family's business, sure, but what you do on the street is everybody's, and I say you don't treat a woman like that. I don't care who she is."

Letting go of his sister's sleeve, the boy turned to face Leo. "Why is it always me having to do these things?" he asked himself out loud, looking up theatrically.

He must have been thinking only about himself as well, because he drew back his right hand almost lazily to throw a punch at Leo. Somehow, he just assumed that his adversary would stand around, waiting for the blow.

Leo knew what was happening almost instantly. He actually sensed it, perhaps smelled it before he really saw it. In what must only have been a fraction of a second, he felt a rage build up in him, and his entire attention was on one thing: the boy. An immediate byproduct of the rage was strength. Before the bully had even completed his wind-up, he had been hit twice in the face. His first reaction was fear and surprise. His attention was completely on his foe now, but Leo's rage was overpowering, and the older boy could only adopt the pose his sister had used just moments before.

War Record

What was in progress at that point was purely animal in nature. Leo had his prey defeated immediately, but he continued to pummel the unfortunate lad. It wasn't just the humiliation of being slapped around. Leo was doing some real damage and was showing no signs of stopping. The older boy collapsed, and as quickly as it had begun, it was over. Leo stood over his victim, fists clenched, breath coming in giant gulps, triumphant. He made a quick abbreviated kick. He didn't intend to make contact, just to verify that his opponent would react and do so defensively. With that, he lowered his guard, spit on the pavement in front of the fallen boy, and turned to pick up his books and leave.

As he walked away, he felt ten feet tall. Was he Tarzan, turning to the bull elephant, Timba, after saving the day? Was he Tom Mix whistling for his trusty horse, Toni, ready to ride off into the sunset? Was he Sky King doing his preflight on the good ship *Songbird* before disappearing into the clouds? In fact, he was all of them and a few others. That he was physically able to prevail in hand-to-hand combat was a matter of biology. That he felt justified in doing so and completely innocent in his victory was a result of radio. He had conformed to the code of the West. His victim was a bad guy who deserved what he got. He had learned all that from the faceless mentor in the front room. The examples he had heard were legion, and each one reinforced the others. As he walked away from the beating he had just administered, his knuckles hurt, but nothing else did.

The girl had observed all this with a mix of emotions. She was pleased that her brother had been put in his place. She hoped he hadn't been hurt too badly. She worried at first that he would take his revenge out on her, but then she saw that his spirit had been drained.

At length, she just watched her departing champion. Her dark eyes shone. They were glistening almonds in a smooth, olive colored face. *He said I was a woman,* she thought.

Coming to, in Berga

These reveries on the young man he'd once been were comforting but also fleeting. As Leo rose up from the depths of sleep, the part of him that was repressed by day was allowed to briefly take control. He savored his moments of transport back to the world he'd once inhabited. In the end, though, he was still a prisoner in a forced labor camp. During his waking hours he was on guard, thinking only of survival.

As the vicious and vigilant Leo came to, he might have briefly sneered at his more emotional self for clinging to these memories. You couldn't eat them, after all. They wouldn't protect you from a beating or make you invisible if the camp's guards burst in with orders to dispose of you, along with all the other skeleton soldiers. After perhaps one thought of this type the animal Leo dispelled these misty thoughts and they evaporated as unremembered as any other dream.

With that he was fully awake. He cocked his head to make sure he still had a clear exit through the window after simply standing up. He didn't relish the thought of a three-foot fall if he had to use his window for escape, but he knew he'd do it in a heartbeat if something even less palatable suddenly came through the barracks door.

Next he shifted slightly and moved to touch the items he always kept with him. A pocket knife. It was his only tool. A pier spike he'd retrieved when he landed in Liverpool, keeping it with him throughout the bivouac without really knowing why. Maybe he'd use it to twist together the strands of barbed wire to cross a fence if he had no choice but to try an escape. A gold chain with a small gold crucifix. He'd traded tobacco with one of the prisoners to get them and soon he would trade the gold to the Jews across the camp for potatoes. He grinned thinking about the guy who bargained food for a smoke. Idiot.

Leo's clothing and equipment kit would look laughable to us today, and they'd smell even worse. To him, though, they were the thin thread from which he was hanging over the abyss. They were the only things he had to provide any kind of assurance that he would survive.

And survival was the only measure of success that he would consider during his wakeful hours.

Fully alert now, the emaciated rag man struggled to his feet. Every joint sang with pain. Every muscle fluttered on the verge of a cramp. But everything depended on his fitness, even such as it was after nearly five months of deprivation. He stood up without making a sound. The idea of courtesy to the others sleeping in the barracks would have been greeted by Leo with derision. He didn't care about them. He did care that any listening sentries miss the fact that he was awake. The more he moved, the more he could move. Even before the guards made their morning entrance he was easing through the door to find the latrine.

X

With the prisoners awakened and assembled, the pitiful formation shuffled more than marched from the barracks area off in the direction of the tunnels. No one spoke. It took too much energy. A few surveyed the fading light as they made their way to work.

Leo smiled thinly when he thought of being on the night shift. It was by far the better of the two schedules and he would have ignored any order to switch, if any of the guards had cared.

Mark Zaccaria

Their most calculating prisoner cared, though. He reckoned that there were bombing raids every night, and only sometimes during the day. When a raid came all work was shut down and all the electric lights in the tunnel doused to prevent targeting. That meant a period of rest. Since Leo also left one of the high-watt light bulbs burning, hiding it under his great coat to contain both the heat and light, a raid also meant warmth.

They walked along the banks of the Elster River, on roads long ago cut out of the same shale the men would be mining later. The tunnels were to be factories impervious to attack from above. For now, though, the prisoners who dug them thought they were walking into their own graves every night. It angered Leo to be forced to give up his precious energy this way. As usual when he started to see red his first reflex was to fight back.

In the tunnel he operated a pneumatic rock drill to start boring holes for the explosives. The act of lifting the increasingly heavy rig made him mad. The cramps he got in his lower back from keeping pressure on it to drive the bit into the brittle rock made him mad. So he leaned off center a little once the bit was well into the rock and it made the long drill curve slightly. That put excessive wear on the sides of the hexagonal shaft. Leo had worked these walls long enough to know not to bend the bit so much it bound up in the wall. That would be sure to get him a beating. By wearing it quickly, though, he hastened the moment when he'd have to bring the worn bit to Vulcan's Forge to be renewed. It was at the forge that he'd meet with other prisoners, especially the Jews who were so sure that having gold would save them.

Leo disagreed. He thought having potatoes would save him. Time would tell which of them was right.

For now, though, the nearly beaten prisoner was not beaten all the way. A part of him was still fighting. He might not have been fighting for his country, at least not the way the recruiting posters liked to portray it. He certainly wasn't fighting for his unit.

War Record

It was harder and harder for him to remember his days with the Bucket of Blood Division. He was fighting for more than just his life, though, despite what he thought during his waking hours.

He was fighting to get back to that moment between sleep and wakefulness where he could once again inhabit the world that had been stolen from him, even for just a moment.

He thought about the dreams of his lost world as the rock dust began to envelop him and he disappeared into the noisy cloud.

Mark Zaccaria

Coming of Age in America

America in the 1930s was truly a melting pot. The analogy to the swirl of ethnic cultures marbleizing the population is as easy as it is accurate. There were also philosophical and sociological forces coming to maturity at that time that made America a mélange of advances and opportunities, all of which created an exciting place to enter adulthood.

Every human has always been thrilled by the newness they discover at all points in the process of growing up socially, sexually, and, nowadays, economically. In the United States, in the decade before World War II, there was the extra sense that many advantages were available to young adults for the very first time in history. Of course, not everyone participated in this feeling of forward motion, but many did, and the fashions of the day were based on the premise that everything was new and good and available to one and all.

For nearly the first time, there was an accessible record of style and fashion that was open to virtually everybody in society: the movies. No longer was a knowledge and understanding of the basics of etiquette the sole province of the upper class. Everyone with a dime to spend on the silver screen once a month was presented with example after example of how the four hundred acted both at work and play. When it came time for ordinary folk to behave in public themselves, they did so in the new ways they

War Record

had learned. How a young man or young woman held their head or their hand baggage as they entered a diner or a subway car was closely patterned after the way in which Carole Lombard and Fredric March did so in the film *Nothing Sacred*.

Nor were the "rich" left out of the learning process. They, too, went to the movies, and perhaps more often. This gave them a singular window through which to see and learn about the Hoi Polloi. Certainly, the images they saw were stereotypes in such pictures as 1935's *Alice Adams*, 1936's *The Petrified Forest*, or 1937's *Thrill of a Lifetime*. Everyone else saw them too though and tried to emulate them. So life imitated art, causing art to become lifelike.

This familiarity between the social strata was unprecedented since the dawn of the Renaissance. Furthermore, in a country that taught its citizens about democracy, it created an environment where people could pass quite freely between social groups, even if they actually did so only on occasion and just for a moment.

In a time and place when you could get a Trilby and a beer for twenty cents at a booth in a neighborhood restaurant, people saved up for a once-a-year visit to the Brown Derby or the Latin Quarter. The Trilby, a hamburger patty served on white bread with raw onions, was the real world. On that annual adventure into the social stratosphere, however, any barber or welder or housewife or teacher would transform themselves into expert counterfeits of the stars to enjoy a fantasy world. They would gladly pay $1.50 each for cocktails that night and would consume them in a fashion at least as ritualized as the tea ceremony in Japan. As for the steaks? Don't ask. The man would summon a cigarette girl and pay for a 10-cent pack with a dollar bill, tipping her the remainder. The woman would beg, borrow, or steal the dress she could find that was most likely to draw her a look as she walked to the powder room, which she happily did at least two or three times during the evening. They would dance to the music of the Dorseys, Benny Goodman, Count Basie, Ruby Newman,

Glenn Miller, or the like, and always in person. At the end of the evening, they would leave in a taxicab rather than by streetcar.

Well, before the popularity of resort vacations for the masses, the occasional night out was a holiday worth paying for. Since they recounted the events of that night over and over again, the investment might actually be thought of as small when amortized over all those opportunities to relive the excitement. Most important of all, the average Jane and Joe were able to make the fantasy of the movies real and to be a part of it themselves. That initiated them as members of Club America, and it also validated the mores and the social structure portrayed on the silver screen.

All this rapidly made for a remarkably cohesive society. Everyone had the same values. Everyone shared the same goals. Everyone wore the same fashions.

When youngsters in the thirties got ready to go out to a Friday night dance at the Community House, the YMCA, or the JCC, their wardrobe was usually pretty well set. Nobody had a large range of outfits to choose from. This was an era that was just beginning to have enough extra resources to make leisure wear a reality. Most houses and apartments still didn't feature built-in closets, not because they couldn't be made but because they were considered unnecessary. Young people shared the same fashion ideals as their parents, and this was very convenient because frequently they had to borrow one or more items of formal clothing from them.

What the adolescent partygoer could choose, though, was his or her persona for the evening. In this area, everyone had a limitless assortment to select from.

While studying his features in the bathroom mirror and practicing key facial expressions, a young man went over his alternatives for a character.

War Record

"Tonight, I could be Clark Gable in *It Happened One Night*," he might announce to his reflection. "Cool and not too pushy, even if I'm being given the bum's rush by some dame. I don't feel overpowering enough to be Douglas Fairbanks in *The Private Life of Don Juan*," he might continue solemnly. "Or lucky enough," if he ended with a nod to reality. "There's always Charles Boyer in *Caravan*. Smooth and courteous with no fight in me at all. That drives the women wild," he would offer with complete confidence that he was correct. At length, some decision had to be taken. As he prepared to leave the sanctuary of the toilet, a final mental coin toss would be made. "Definitely Gable. I just have to remember to grin right."

Meanwhile, in a nearby apartment, a young lady he would meet at the dance was doing her own social calculus before the proscenium of an identical mirror.

"My features are too plain, but I could still be Katharine Hepburn, perhaps in *Spitfire*," she would say while watching herself analytically. It was an option that carried some risk. "If I really am that brazen, will they throw me out of the dance?" Perhaps something less controversial was in order. "I could be Maureen O'Sullivan in *Tarzan and His Mate*," she might continue critically. The social status implied by the title was appealing, but did she really want to put up with a strong, silent type lacking in the social graces? It took some thought. "No," she said at length. "I'll be Myrna Loy in *The Thin Man*. If I can find a reasonable copy of William Powell, at least he'll be dapper." The die was cast.

And when they got to the dance? The mating displays were certain to be legion and as heavily stylized and rigidly conformist as is any such behavior anywhere else in the wild. Birds parade to show off their plumage. Elk in the rut try to look as formidable as possible to frighten off competitors. Young city dwellers in the thirties demonstrated their command of fashionable manners.

They had all learned them at the movies, and they could each instantly judge how well anyone else had picked up the same things. To compete in this game, one had to be able to dance at least one of the popular steps. It was necessary to be able to chat engagingly about automobiles or even yachts. This was easy since there was little chance that anyone actually had either of those conveyances. Without doubt, the most important displays to be mastered were those surrounding smoking and the cocktail.

People were brought up to assume that since life was short, anything that could provide a moment's pleasure was to be grabbed without a second thought. Smoking cigarettes was a relatively new social pastime, and the thought that women might smoke them in public was still shocking in many quarters. It was just the sort of *avant garde* craze that was made to be overstated by the movies. As for cocktails, the end of the era of prohibition was still fresh in the collective memory. America, which had been a nation of alcoholics in its early years, was then racing head-long to assert its regained choice in the matter social drinking. Even though the Community House dances usually began with alcohol-free punch, the revelers still used the dainty glasses to practice their style as if they contained the real thing.

Gable sauntered confidently through the front door of the Community House. His strides were a little long, and his shoulders moved forward and back with the rhythm of the motion. His left hand was thrust into the slash pocket of his double-breasted suit coat, the thumb extended to keep his arm at just the right crook. With his right hand, he pulled slightly at the brim of his hat, nodding to the matron who guarded the door to the dance floor.

"Thanks, ma'am." He grinned. "But I think I'll wear it tonight."

It was a social breach to keep the hat on indoors, but it was also a requirement if he was to remain in character.

Walking into the dimly lit room, he stopped for a moment, framed by the light streaming through the arched doorway. From that pose, he surveyed the crowd. There was one other lad wearing a snap-brim hat. In his case, though, both the front and rear brims were turned down.

Leslie Howard, he thought. *No contest.*

Taking in the rest of the room, he noticed what seemed to be an excess of Jimmy Cagneys. Gable had been a good choice. When he spotted several of his friends standing in a group, he moved coolly toward them, completing his entrance.

Gable's performance had not gone unnoticed. Standing with her friends, Myrna Loy watched his moves with approval. He certainly had the grin down perfectly, and that hat, right on the dance floor, showed a delicious dash of the rebel. Unconsciously, she smoothed her hair back in each direction from its center part, checking the spit curls by touch. Myrna made a mental note to see whether or not this Gable could dance. If so, she might have to abandon *The Thin Man* for *Cain and Mabel.*

As with all mating rituals, these were developed for the benefit of the females. The young women had been drawn instinctively to the values so emphatically expressed as important in pictures. It was so clear to them all. If a woman could get a man of the proper type, who knew all the hep routines and could provide for her in the lavish fashion of the silver screen, she would have everything that was important. Better yet, any other woman would be able to see that at a glance.

The young men, as always, were blinded by their sex drives and so used enormous energy to make themselves conform to the rituals. In almost all of them, though, there was a nagging recognition of the reality of the situation. The movies demanded that each of them be rich, smart, cocky but not too cocky, motivated by the highest ideals of patriotism, willing to fight for the right (hopefully with a lethal left), and capable of romantic love which, with the right woman, would be as strong as iron bands. Add to this that they should be impervious to alcohol, able to fly a plane, brave enough to take on enemy agents, and be the close friend of a scientist or at least a policeman. It was impossible, of course.

Mark Zaccaria

Most young men would start out with jobs that were relatively menial until they reached their thirties. The demands of apprenticeship for a craft and the economic depression effectively upped the age at which a man of the city got married to thirty-two or thirty-three years old in most cases.

In the years between his late teens and his wedding, an ordinary man would socialize as much or more with his group of male friends than he would with any one woman. As the male group gained importance, at least to its members, it was thought of as macho for a young man to be unattached. In fact, when he became attached to a woman, a man instantly dropped out of his group and was in uncharted social territory unless he could financially manage a marriage.

Knowing all this, the women were extremely careful in granting their favors. Sexual intimacy was a goal of all concerned, as it has always been, and it occurred as regularly as it has throughout the millennia. Its value was much different, though, than in the more permissive or informed ages that preceded and followed the 1930s. Pregnancy was the great regulator of sexual activity, and it was usually a young lady's job to be careful that if the worst occurred, she could live with the consequences.

When Myrna Loy stepped in front of Gable at the punch bowl, she seemed a little surprised. She hadn't seen him there and made an apology. Gable was gracious, however. He tipped his hat by touching the brim.

"Never you mind, my dear." He grinned. "Here. Let me help you with that."

Ever the gentleman, he ladled her up some punch. She accepted the offering with a smile and a knowing eye. They played a short scene. Then they talked a bit about school and family. When the band struck up a waltz, she was delighted to find that not only could he dance but that he took command of the team and moved them around the floor with confidence and smooth authority. She moved her left hand from his shoulder to

War Record

the back of his neck. On opposite sides of the floor, this maneuver was analyzed closely. His boys exchanged knowing glances while her girls, though envious, wondered if she hadn't been a little too quick.

They liked each other's smell. They liked each other's moves. They especially liked what each of their sets of friends must be thinking about the match. For the two of them, at least, it had been a very successful evening. As they walked home separately, they could each almost imagine the credits rolling.

This was Leo's social environment when he first noticed that there were women in the world as well as girls. It was a shock to him, as it is to most boys, that the half of the population he had found so easy to ignore was suddenly almost the sole focus of his attention. The attraction was powerful, but so was the risk of failure. He hated looking stupid. Nobody likes the thought of rejection. Leo's natural approach to all problems was one of caution, so he studied this one too before taking any action.

At first, he thought of romance in the same way he thought of any other form of competition. There were rules, bounds that could not be exceeded. Within the matrix of the rules, there were techniques that might be more successful or less. Before he really got to know any women, he viewed his relationship with them as a contest to beat the other young men around him to a prize. For success in that type of arena, one needed an advantage, and the more overwhelming the advantage, the better. The primal urge that drove this chase would not forego anything that might bring success. Fairness was not even a consideration.

He smiled when it came to him, a broad self-satisfied smile that bared all his teeth. Before he got started with women, he needed a car.

Even for adults, automobiles were the exception rather than the rule in those days, especially in the city where so many tra-

Mark Zaccaria

ditional methods of transportation existed. This made for both advantages and disadvantages when Leo decided he would get one. For the first thing, he had to learn to drive. Then there was the capital investment necessary to get such a possession. Keeping it in the city would be a minor problem if these first two could be solved. Whatever had to be done for him to get a car would take a huge amount of time and energy. Could he afford those resources at the expense of his work and study?

On the plus side of the ledger, there were some powerful incentives. He would certainly stand out in any crowd if he had a working automobile, practically no matter what kind of shape it was in. A car was personal, portable space. It gave its owner control over his schedule and a little bit of privacy that was quite unusual for those growing up in crowded apartments and public urban facilities. Everyone understood this instantly. The reason there were not more cars in the neighborhoods had less to do with indifference than it did with fear and inertia. Mostly for Leo, it was a matter of always being on the first team. If having an automobile was part of playing in the big leagues, then he would get one, maybe two.

The more he thought about it, learning how to drive wasn't all that big an obstacle. Since driving was such a benchmark of masculinity, there was lots of information on it in all the popular literature. Leo started out knowing where the throttle and brake were and what the clutch and the gearbox brought to the process. Although he had seldom ridden in a car, he saw them every day. This meant that the rules of the road were more or less self-evident. It also gave him a rough eye for how fast was too fast and how slow was too slow, at least in city driving. For Leo, most projects of this sort began at the library, so he read up on the steps and coordination needed for maneuvering an automobile, and then he was ready for some hands-on exercise. How difficult could it be?

War Record

He was fifteen that summer. In the fall, he would turn sixteen and be able to get a chauffeur's license. It was time to get started. To begin his instruction, Leo put on a pair of dark slacks with a good crease, a white shirt, and a dark bow tie. He carefully brushed his black hair back into submission. Then he headed for the trolley.

From the cross street just up the hill from his house, he rode to Maverick Square and the ferry dock. East Boston is an island, and to leave it, one must cross water either by boat, bridge, or later by tunnel. There was no problem. The motorman gave him a transfer ticket, and he rode to the Dock Square terminal in Boston proper. The ferry landed almost at the foot of the looming twenty-two-story Custom House Tower, then the highest building in New England. At the pier was the Dock Square Station and another car for the short ride to Park Street.

The Boston subway system featured four lines, which crossed each other at four main downtown stations. Of the four main transfer stations that formed the corners of the system's central circuit, Park Street was the biggest and best. It went down two full stories beneath the Boston Common. Its granite-and-filigree entrance at the corner of Park and Tremont streets was surrounded by vendors, park benches, plenty of pigeons, and the lawns of the city's best-known promenade. Leo emerged from the station aboard the powered escalator with its interlocking wooden slat treads that disappeared beneath the sidewalk as he made the final grade. People of all ages were walking together on the grass, sitting watching each other, or minding the little children who played underfoot. In the background, there was a newsboy's chant, as distinctive and individual from its cadence even if you couldn't make out the words as those of a priest, a railroad conductor, or a drill sergeant.

"Paepah, paepah. Get ya paepah hee-ya. *Roosevelt* Bucks Congress, *War* Talk in Europe, *Sox* and Braves aah Winnahs. *Read* all about it."

Mark Zaccaria

Leo stood under a bright blue, late June sky complete with white, puffy clouds. It was a beautiful and tranquil moment in the city. He was just up the street from the Parker House Hotel.

The Parker House was a grand, full-service hostelry that prided itself on having all the amenities. Its main door faced the park diagonally, and around the corner, another entrance was just across from City Hall. James Michael Curley himself was a frequent guest of the main dining room. He was a guest rather than a patron. The maître d' was easily smart enough never to render a bill for something so trivial as a dinner served to one who brought so much business in with him and who might shift that patronage if his wishes were not properly satisfied. The carpets in the main concourse were plush. The marble of the foyer and the main salon was gleaming. The staff held their liveried shoulders square and took pride in rendering only the best and most proper service. It was quite an operation.

Leo approached the doorman, standing back a bit and waiting for a moment when there were no customers. As with most busy hotels, the doorman at the Parker House was a minor potentate. John Jay Washington had held the post for only four or five years, but he had apprenticed under his predecessor for two decades. Now that he had the job, it was time to collect some back pay. Mr. Washington was quick to offer any customer a bow and a tip of his ornate cap. He received tips from them with a smooth motion that bordered on legerdemain. During the day, it was nickels and dimes from the brokers and Boston Brahmans. In the evening, there were dollars from the dandies and the elegant diners.

Through it all, the real money came from those who owed their fealty to him. Bell boys, messengers, delivery men, and cabbies alike contributed to Jack Washington's pocket if they wanted to be allowed to ply their trades by his doorway. Occasionally, a cop on the beat would take some back, but in general, Mr. Washington held a tight rein on all the details of his small patch of bustling street enterprise. There was never a bit of trouble at

War Record

the door, and all of the customers were made to feel that they were the center of attention whenever they arrived or departed. He was an expert doorman and was rewarded handsomely for his attention to detail. He was also the only Negro on the hotel's liveried staff.

Jack himself thought that he had the best situation of any black man in the city since the days when Frederick Douglass had been a lecturer at Harvard and the Boston Athenaeum. His income would easily make it possible for his children to go to college, maybe even Harvard. Just the same, he wondered if all that education would let them be able to earn as much as he did.

"Pardon me, sir," Leo said politely when there was a break in the routine.

"Yes, lad?" Mr. Washington inquired with a cocked eyebrow. "How may I help you?"

"I would like to apply for a job."

"A job, is it?" the doorman replied in a businesslike tone.

The boy looked washed and well mannered, so Jack was already beginning to compute what might be in this for him.

"What sort of job do you think you can perform for this fine establishment, son?"

"I would like to work parking cars, sir," Leo answered evenly.

The Parker House had a small lot for automobiles directly behind it, parallel to Tremont Street. The lot took the space where a carriage house had once stood. Those days, more and more of the hotel's dinner patrons arrived by automobile, and even some of its overnight guests were now motoring into the city. The lot saw almost constant activity and, in fact, was nearing its capacity. Before long, customers' cars would have to be parked in the Motor Mart or one of the other indoor garages that were being built in the area of Winter and Summer Streets just a few blocks away.

The doorman couldn't dream of fetching automobiles himself. He barely left his post to use the toilet. None of the bell boys who assisted him knew how to drive. Though they were called boys, they were all long-term employees of the hotel and were all of an age when driving was a very rare skill. Mr. Washington had been prevailing on the cabbies who lined up their cars to be ready for a departing patron. Asking for favors of this sort was not always easy, and it cut into his personal income since reciprocity was in order.

"You know how to drive well enough to handle fine automobiles?" he asked.

"Oh yes, sir." Leo answered smartly. "I come from East Boston."

Washington was unsure at first how coming from East Boston guaranteed skill as a chauffeur. Having never been there himself, he guessed that it must be very rural, making a car a necessity. Driving was a young man's avocation, though, and Jack suffered from the assumption that he, himself, was so important that no mere lad would ever lie to him. This began to sound more and more like a good idea and, where his self-interest was involved, he was used to making quick decisions.

"Okay, laddie," he said without further thought. "I'll see that the hotel pays you ten cents an hour if you will see that you promptly pay it all back to me for getting you this job. All gratuities you receive from customers are yours, up to ten dollars worth per week. Don't laugh. You could easily make that much if you're quick and polite. Tips over and above ten dollars per week will be split fifty-fifty by you and me. Do we have a deal?"

"Yes, sir!" Leo smiled broadly. "And thank you very much."

After leaving his name, Leo trotted off to the lot to survey his new domain. There were several cars parked there: a Buick, a Cadillac, two LaSalle sedans, and a Packard Dual Cowl Phaeton.

Might as well start at the top, he thought, stepping up on the running board of the Packard.

In the mid-thirties, most American cars still used only an ordinary toggle switch of some sort to turn on the ignition. This was especially true of the larger, more expensive models. Key-operated ignition switches and door locks were future enhancements. In the cars of that day, where even a hard top was still the exception rather than the rule, the main anti-theft protection was provided by strong social standards. Thus it was child's play for Leo to get the Packard started. All he had to do was set the manual throttle for a high idle, open the fuel valve so gasoline could go to the carburetor, pull the knob out to close the choke, retard the spark to help the engine catch while cold, and turn it over.

The electric starter for automobiles has been called the single most important technological advance in the liberation of women in the twentieth century. It allowed them, after all, to routinely use cars without having to develop the upper body strength needed to start them by hand. As true as this might be, the electric starter also provided a similar service to Leo. In his mid-teens, he was barely five foot, six inches tall and 135 pounds in weight. He was naturally wiry of build and had the stunning reflexes of youth. He could hit a baseball over a 350-foot center field fence any day of the week, but that had more to do with hand speed than with brute force. If he'd had to turn over the Packard's V-8 engine by hand, he would have needed help.

Without much trouble, though, he had it running. After a minute or two of considering his options, he opened the choke and advanced the spark, releasing the manual throttle when he had the big engine purring like a kitten. Oil pressure came up obediently, the ammeter showed that the batteries were charging, and manifold pressure hovered at twenty-two inches of mercury. It was too soon to worry about water temperature. The next thing to do was try moving it.

He adjusted his seat and let out the clutch, holding its pedal to the floor. Then he went over all the gearbox positions, using the pattern cut into the shift knob. Unlike most other cars, the Packard had four forward speeds. This meant that the floor-mounted gear-change lever traveled the four positions of the *H*-shaped pattern plus one extra outboard slot for the very high road gear. Leo made a dry run only with first and reverse, all he thought he'd need in the parking lot. As the car had been nosed into a wall, he began by backing it straight out. He stalled it once or twice, but pretty soon, he learned to listen to the engine and feel its vibrations in his seat to determine when the clutch was catching.

He pulled straight back a couple car lengths, let out the clutch, and stopped gently with the foot brake. Going forward was even easier; he could see where he was pointed. While trying to be delicate on the way back in, he took a bit too much time before touching his brake. The Packard was barely moving, but the front bumper flattened out just a little on the wall. This was not too big a problem. The Packard's bumpers were actually chrome-plated leaf springs. When Leo disengaged the transmission and released the foot brake, the bumper straightened right back out, pushing the three-thousand-pound car backward.

"Easy, big fellow," he said, touching the brake again.

After two or three more cycles straight back and straight forward without incident, it was time to try turning the car around. The rim of the Packard's steering wheel was a two-part construction of wood that mated over a metal rim that was forged to the metal spokes and hub. The two wooden pieces were riveted together and finished seamlessly with the metal. It reminded Leo of a big, circular knife handle. And big it was. When he first gripped the wheel, he noticed that his hands couldn't reach all the way around the thickness of the wheel. He'd never held a steering wheel before, so he really didn't know, but he had always thought that the metal wheels on the Fords, coated with Bakelite, were much smaller to the grasp. Then, too, the Packard's wheel had big dimples on the backside so that the fingers spread out into deep channels.

When he tried to turn the wheel before backing out, he found out why. In a word, he couldn't do it. He leaned on one side and then the other, but it wouldn't budge. He wondered if there was some sort of a lock on the steering column. Defeated, he returned to the straight-in-and-out exercise. After two more cycles of this, though, he tried turning the wheel again, but while the car was rolling. Eureka.

So it went. In twenty more minutes, he was moving the Packard around the lot with ease. It was time to try one of the LaSalles. In only fifteen minutes, he was an expert at turning it around, which was a good thing because just then, a bell boy arrived to call him up front. There was a car to park.

Leo shut down the LaSalle and was off at a smart pace to the main entrance. There, he saw a big DeSoto sedan with its doors and boot open. The bell staff were removing suitcases and hat-boxes to a shining brass trolley. A middle-aged lady in a stylish hat, a dark suit, and a fox scarf whose spring-loaded mouth bit into its own tail watched the unloading intently. Mr. Washington was also keeping a critical eye on all this. Leo simply stood behind him, cleared his throat, and waited.

In a moment, the doorman snapped to attention and moved to pull open the large, ornate door. Leo hadn't noticed anyone there, but as Mr. Washington pulled it back and touched his cap, a stout middle-aged man in a single-breasted business suit and matching fedora came through without missing a step. The man looked at Washington.

"We're in room twenty-two," he said. "Are you ready to take care of my auto?"

"Yes, sir," the doorman replied emphatically, signaling Leo to the car with his hand. "Room twenty-two for Mr. and Mrs. Miller's baggage, gentlemen," he repeated to the bell boys, who nodded and slid the loaded trolley through the open door.

Mrs. Miller followed the bags into the lobby, causing Mr. Washington to have to wait for her and then step in to hold the inner door. He shot a quick look in Leo's direction, but he was trapped. Mr. Miller walked over to Leo, who was closing up the DeSoto.

"I'll be using the car tonight, young man," he said. "I would appreciate it if you kept it near the front and started it up for me just before seven."

"Certainly, sir," Leo replied in as formal a manner as he could muster. "I'll have it all warmed up. Just mention to the desk that you're ready, and I'll bring it up for you at your pleasure."

"Thank you, my good man," Mr. Miller concluded, smiling and holding out a twenty-five-cent piece. Leo took the coin with his left hand, offering a military-style salute with his right.

"Thank *you*, sir," he replied, thinking that he liked the idea of a salute much better than that of a bow. He got into the driver's side of the idling sedan and tried to decide where first gear might be found.

A DeSoto, he thought. *Very nice.*

The car was parked on Tremont Street, facing north to King's Chapel just across School Street. He used the foot throttle to run the engine up a little higher than idle, just to be sure he heard it. The transmission slid into gear with a silken feel. He remembered to let off the hand brake, and the car moved slowly away from the door, even if bystanders noticed the sound of the high RPMs. At the corner, only two or three car lengths away, he just eased off the gas and held the clutch pedal on the floor. The turn onto School Street would have been perfect if the curb of the sidewalk hadn't stuck so far out into the roadway.

Actually, Leo was too close to the curb all the way. The car had been parked next to it, and he had not pulled out as he left but rather just pulled forward. As he wrestled with the shiny steering wheel, the right rear tire rode up over the curbstone and then dropped off the other side as the DeSoto made its way to the carriage yard. If Mr. Miller or Mr. Washington had been there to see the car bounce on its springs, there would have been some embarrassment. Both of them were inside, though, and the only witness was a waiting cabby who sat in his taxi, just behind the

War Record

DeSoto's starting position. He winced, shook his head solemnly, and then went back to his Racing Form.

Leo was officially a parking attendant.

Throughout July and August, he lived at least one of a schoolboy's dreams. Every day, from late morning until the middle of the evening, he drove some of the finest automobiles made in America, and he got money for his pocket by doing so. Very quickly, the driving part became routine. Even with different controls in different locations on different makes, it was a skill he took to because he thought it important. So before long, it was a matter of what route to take from the carriage lot to the main entrance.

When he drove a car into the lot, it was just around the corner from the main entrance and only two hundred feet down the curb from the side door on School Street. By common usage, though, traffic on School Street was one way. The signs would come later, but the custom was that you had to turn away from the hotel as you pulled out of the lot. Going around the block presented several options, and Leo scouted them all. There was School to the left on Winter to State Street and back to Tremont with another left, but that put the car heading opposite to the entrance. From Tremont, before the hotel, you could take a right onto Beacon, go up a steep grade, and come around to Park Street right in front of the State House. That doubled back to Tremont, where you could make the turn north and pull right up to the canopied main entrance. Or from the lot, you could take School to a right on Winter and then to another right on Tremont Place or all the way to Essex Street. Either way, you then had to circumnavigate the Boston Common to get back to Park Street so the car would face the door.

A block before Tremont Place, there was another right turn off Winter. This was Bromfield Street, and it was technically the shortest route to the main entrance of the Parker House. From the corner of Bromfield and Tremont, it was necessary to make a turn just slightly against traffic. It was done all the time by the cabbies, but Leo reserved it for emergencies. One did not want to pare the opportunity to drive all the way back to the bone, after all.

There could be no best way. There was a shortest, but if it had just been used, wouldn't a change in scenery be in order? There was a school of beauty on Boylston Street as you came off Essex to go around the Common. Sure, that was the long way, but at 3:00 p.m., the girls all came out onto the sidewalk and made their way across the street to Boylston Station. It was an opportunity for chivalry from the front seat of a fine car that was not to be missed. Charles Street, along the back side of the Common, divided it from the Boston Public Garden. It was a much more formal topiary where people stuck to the benches and brick walks, but it was a favorite of the nannies minding their young charges. In other words, each trip to the hotel's main entrance was a brief safari through a different part of the city's downtown residential area.

Traffic on the roadways was never a great problem. Automobiles were so few in number in that part of town that they seldom conflicted with one another. As evening fell, there were a number of horse-drawn landaus and cabriolets that transported those who had a taste for nostalgia. The horses were acclimated to city life, though, and they seldom were startled by a passing car, even if it was a Lincoln Zephyr.

Traffic under the canopy of the main entrance to the Parker House, however, became increasingly complex. Tipping was a new skill for many of the hotel's patrons. Tipping itself wasn't new, but in America, the upper economic class was growing, despite the much-publicized hard times. New people had to adopt the process every day with little more than the movies as a model for this new behavior. They were novices at tipping who

War Record

were still excited just by the fact they were called upon to do it. For Jack Washington and those beneath him in the hierarchy of his little fiefdom, it was a feeding frenzy that caused their appetites to grow faster than the potential satisfaction from this important source of income. In other words, there was no honor among thieves. The pages and bell boys and cabbies all delicately jostled with the doorman to be in position for these handouts, which were increasingly taken for granted. Decorum had to be maintained so the activity of the staff under the hotel's big top was more like competitive choreography. Each server would do what he could, subtly of course, to be the one front and center when the patron's dime emerged.

For Leo, this was just one more new game that he would play to win. He quickly picked up the rhythm of how his part of the arrival or departure transactions usually took place. As he had by accident on the first day, he tried to split the couples. The man would always be in charge of the automobile. If Leo could get him on the outboard side of the car, by the driver's door, that would leave the woman standing alone, a situation no doorman could allow. Taking his instructions on the care of the vehicle with a serious demeanor was always good for at least a nickel, especially if Mr. Washington were not there to exert *noblesse oblige*. Departures were a little trickier if the gentleman held the door for his own lady. If not, the doorman did and Leo had the chance to make some thoughtful technical recommendation as he held the driver's door.

Perhaps his best opportunities came from the liveried chauffeurs who arrived at the Parker House in the real limousines. When a Dusenburg or an Auburn Saloon rolled up, Mr. Washington was totally attentive to the lady or gentleman riding in the back. When he opened the rear passenger door of a long car, he gave his very best performance. He stood at attention. He extended the sincere greetings of the entire staff. He inquired discretely as to which of the hotel's many services he could see to for the patron. In the process, he ignored the chauffeur, who got directions to the lot from one of the bell boys at length.

When one of these glistening barges eased in to his carriage yard, Leo knew that he almost certainly had a big tip practically in his pocket. He could talk to the driver like a normal human, directing him to any supplies or services the automobile might need. He would show him to the hotel's staff entrance and through to the kitchen. There, it only took one word to insure that the driver got all the lunch he wanted. One more word to the sommelier's assistant would normally be good for a bottle of bonded Scotch whiskey or champagne to replenish the car's bar, if it even had one. The hotel was happy to do all this and more in hopes that the favor would be recalled when it was time for his employer to visit again. The chauffeur had all his needs tended to and no one to thank for the consideration but Leo. It almost always meant folding money.

For Leo, all this was a lark. For Jack Washington, however, it was his living. He always got Leo's pay envelope back with both a signature on it and the money still in it. He always wondered, though, just how much of the boy's tips were really coming back. Leo always gave him something extra every payday, but that just meant that he always made the ten-dollar minimum. How much more did he get? Was Jack really getting his share? The doorman had never considered having a parking attendant before Leo presented himself and asked for the job. Now it was time to get someone he trusted for the position, someone who owed him and needed the work.

Thursday was payday. On the last Thursday in August, the doorman had everything in place.

"This will be your last pay envelope, lad. I'm sorry, but there's no more work for you here," he told Leo calmly.

"What do you mean?" Leo asked, truly not getting it the first time.

War Record

"You've done a good job, son," Washington said. "There have been no complaints with your treatment of the automobiles. It's just time for the hotel to have someone there with more maturity. I hope you understand."

Leo understood. The anger welled up in him, flushing his face even through its naturally ruddy color. He thought about the situation for a moment and decided to control himself.

"Sure, Mr. Washington," he said slowly. "I understand completely. Please keep me in mind if you need extra help."

The words were right, but there was fire in his eyes, and he held the doorman's gaze as if with an iron grip. It made a little shudder go through Jack Washington. This allowed him to confirm the wisdom of his decision. Suddenly, he didn't want a boy like that around his customers.

That time, the pay envelope came back signed but empty. As he walked back to the Park Street Station, Leo thought that it was almost time for school anyway. Even so, he made a mental note to go back to the Parker House for coffee sometime relatively soon, just so Mr. Washington would have to hold the door for him. Perhaps he'd even get a five-cent tip.

Now that he had the basics of driving down, it was time for Leo to get a car of his own. After the last few weeks, it didn't seem too farfetched either. In fact, the country's appetite for automobiles had grown so quickly that there were huge numbers of new models rolling off the Detroit assembly lines. All the visionaries or long-distance travelers who wanted a car bought these up. Still, the bulk of the population, especially in the cities, was not involved in the market. What this meant was that new models commanded full price, but the growing numbers of used cars went begging since there were few drivers willing to buy them. A new 1936 Ford V-8 Coupe might cost you close to $800, but Leo got his 1928 Model A Roadster for just $15. That was little more than one week's take at the Parker House, and the vehicle even ran.

There was a leak in the radiator, but the proprietor of the Chelsea junkyard where Leo found the machine had thrown in another, used of course, as part of the deal. For an extra fifteen cents, he bought a gallon of gasoline from the junk man, just to be sure he could make it the two or three miles back to Eastie. The spare radiator sat erect in the open rear jump seat as Leo drove his new chariot home. A hose extending from the top fitting projected out into space and bounced as they traveled the cobbled streets. It was the Grand Marshall of a one-car parade, waving to the admiring crowds. With the top folded back and the sun on his face, Leo was every inch the proud chauffeur and parade organizer. He rolled at a slow pace over the Chelsea Bridge, past Alex Bang's boatyard and the old clipper ship piers. When he turned up the Lexington Street hill, he began to be recognized. Citizens of the neighborhood acknowledged the achievement of one of their own by grinning and waving. The backs of their hands displayed with fingers up, they rotated the hand at its wrist, wiggling more than really waving. It was a sign of respect. Possessions meant something, and driving was a rare talent.

The alley to the right of his father's building widened out just a bit as it got to the street. Actually, his father's garden was five or six feet wider than the house. This was a little unusual, but it made for a perfect off-street parking spot and sidewalk mechanic's work area. Leo backed the Model A in. He put up the top and removed the replacement radiator to close the jump seat. Then it was time to carefully survey his prize.

Though he put a careful eye on the car, it was the wrong moment for him to be critical. The finish was dull, but there was little or no rust. All it needed was a good spit shine. The sand-colored top was creased but not too badly stained. It must have had its top down most of the time. The leather upholstery was faded in the front from wear, but there were no cuts, just some

War Record

wrinkles that were permanent. The jump seat had some grease on it, but the leather looked good. It must have served as a storage bin rather than a passenger compartment. The chrome on the bumpers was scuffed and pitted. They had been called on to do their job more than once. So, too, the radiator cowl was freckled with rust spots in a red haze that was more pronounced at the top than the bottom, probably a combination of the ocean air and habit of letting it run hot. Leo made a mental note to keep the water level up. Maybe the cooling system needed a flush.

He was about to open one side of the bonnet when the physical force of a staccato yell stopped him in his tracks. The pressure came direct to his ear from the diaphragm of a young man trotting up the street.

"*Hey! Guidareio! Che Cosa*, huh?"

It was Vincent Spinelli, a schoolmate and friend. He was breathless from coming over on the dead run as soon as he had heard. "What are you doing with that, *pizan?*"

"It's mine." Leo said, his broad grin putting the lie to the nonchalance in his voice.

"Whaddaya mean?" Vinnie asked, eyes glued to the machine as he circled it. "Does it run?"

"Sure it runs," Leo rejoined. "How do you think I got it here?"

"You drove it?" came the skeptical response. "Since when do you know how to drive?"

"So I learned." Leo shrugged, taking the path of extreme modesty since he felt sure that the attention would remain at a fever pitch. "C'mon," he continued. "I have to look at the engine."

The hood of the Model A consisted of two gatefold, metal panels running front to back on either side of the engine. Leo locked one of the louvered doors up into its open position and peered inside. Silent with the gravity of the situation, Vinnie looked in too. He nodded slowly and adopted a serious expression that he felt was appropriate to the moment.

Had this custom begun with looking into the mouths of horses? Did ancient fishermen inspect the rib work of each other's boats this way? Whatever the origins of the practice, it didn't take long in the twentieth century for men, and finally women, to be compelled to look at an automobile's engine whenever it was exposed in a social setting. Is it possible to bring a new car to a family picnic without lifting the hood so that a small committee can observe studiously?

The Model A's engine was an in-line four-cylinder with an iron block. It had lifters coming up from the bottom-mounted cam shaft and a single-barrel downdraft carburetor sitting on top. Leo's was missing the squat air filter can that should have perched on top of the carb. He didn't think that too great a problem for the time being. The fan was mounted directly to the crankshaft, and a single belt drove off of it to turn the generator. The distributor looked like a spider whose feet spanned the engine block but whose legs were a little shaggy.

"The plugs look good," Vinnie said.

It was important to make a serious comment on the technology at a moment like this. Leo knew that the spark plugs were on the other side of the block and that they were buried in their sockets to begin with. He took the comment as a compliment though.

"The wires could be better," he thought out loud. "I'll need to re-tape them."

By that time, a few more of his friends had begun to drift in, and the sidewalk inspection took on the aspect of a block party. The Model A attracted a lot of attention. Before going into the front door of his family's house, Guido Lessardo saw the commotion and came up to find out what the news was.

"Hey, Gui!" said Leo. "*Come va?*"

"Hey, Lee," he said, returning the salute. "How many marbles did you have to trade for that?"

War Record

Johnny DiNaldo came by. "Hey, *wal-yo!* Is this an ornament?" he asked. "Or maybe a shrine? It's bad enough to put a Blessed Virgin in a bathtub. If you put one in this junk car, the priests will come and get you." He got his laugh.

"Keep talking," Leo advised. "I'm waiting to hear what you say the first time you need a ride."

"You're right! I'd love one," Johnny shot back. "How about tonight?"

"Okay," Leo nodded. "I know you're a virgin, but you will have to work on the blessed part before we can go."

The presence of the car was such an exciting turn of events that before too long, the boys were posing for invisible cameras from its running boards. They were engaged in mock fisticuffs to decide who would get to ride inside and who would be consigned to the jump seat. Each was vying for the attention of the group so that he could tell some story of automotive fantasy, swearing, of course, that it was the absolute truth had from some knowledgeable but unnamed associate. They were all so wrapped up in their little outburst of joy that no one noticed the arrival of Gianfredo Martello.

Martello was a couple years older. He had become acquainted with Leo's family after being attracted to, and then rejected by, Leo's sister Edith. He wasn't tall really, but he looked that way because he was very trim and always wore very tight-fitting clothes, tight-fitting and black, to be precise. His black pumps had pointed toes and were polished to a mirror shine. His trousers might have had pockets, but it was clear to anyone taking notice that he wasn't even carrying change. His short-sleeved black silk shirt had mother-of-pearl buttons down to square-cut tails that he wore outside his trousers, more like a jacket. His square jaw and flattened nose were set off by intense dark eyes,

Mark Zaccaria

and his black, curly hair was cut short and brushed back into a stylish but carefully controlled bob.

He had done a little boxing and still trained now and then. It was widely thought that he worked for one of the businesses that were just as black as his outfit, though no one would say such a thing to him. He knew what was said about him, however, and he made no effort to set the record straight. In fact, it pleased him that when Leo's friends finally noticed him, they fell silent and began looking nervously at their feet.

"Hey, Lee-och," he said gregariously, arms out with palms up to point to the car. "What's this?"

He sauntered over to Leo and gave him a soft slap on the cheek and then pinched it, using the grip to make his head shake once or twice. It was a carefully calculated liberty meant to be just short of what would cause Leo to fight but still plenty to demonstrate to his friends just who was the boss.

"Is this yours?" he asked.

Leo brushed the hand away gently and met Martello's gaze. "Hey, Fredo," he said with a smile. "How come we never see you anymore?"

They all knew that he objected to being called Fredo, and they all knew why he no longer made many visits to the Zaccaria household. When Leo's comments were allowed to pass, the boys scored the salutation portion of this contest as a draw.

Martello nodded, smiling. He walked slowly around the Model A, running his fingertips over the finish, the top, and the single chrome taillight. "Someone said you drove this up here."

Was it a question or a statement? Leo didn't respond.

"So, what are you going to do with it, fix it up and sell it?"

"I'll fix it up," he answered, "but then I'll use it."

Fredo's eyes sparkled at this, and he strolled back over to Leo, holding his stare. "Maybe you could give me a ride sometime," he said. "There are lots of times I could use a man with a car.

War Record

Naturally, I would try to return the favor somehow. What do you say?"

"I'm pretty busy with school these days." It was the best Leo could come up with short of an outright refusal. He looked away as Fredo's eyebrows furrowed into a scowl, although the eyes themselves never even flickered.

"What am I hearing?" he asked. "Would you deny a simple favor like this to a *fratello* like me?" He managed to sound astonished.

The boys worried that he had Leo in a box.

"C'mon, Fredo," Leo said, changing tack. "I'm just a kid, and this old Model A is a heap. I expect a guy like you knows people with fancy cars. No?"

"Please don't call me Fredo," Martello said quietly.

The boys stopped breathing.

With nowhere else to go in this contest, Leo started to get a little angry. He smiled a big, fake smile that managed to show all of his teeth. Both he and his adversary were bound by each other's stare.

"Okay. Fine. What should I call you then?" he demanded, leaning into it just a little too much. "Gian? What's that? John? How about Johnny?"

The boys knew that there was about to be a fight. Silently, they prepared to bury their friend.

This was the scene at the side of Antonio Zaccaria's house when he walked down from the streetcar, returning home from work. He came over to see what was attracting so many to his property. As soon as he joined the crowd, he felt the electricity and could imagine what was going on.

"Gianfredo, are you here for Edith?" he asked. "She's not home now."

His intervention broke the bond of tension between the adversaries. As soon as he thought about it, Martello was just as happy that a way out of the confrontation had been found.

Mark Zaccaria

"Ah. Mr. Zaccaria, how are you?" he inquired cheerily as he turned away from the man's son. "Actually, I just heard about the new car, and I came by to offer my congratulations."

For whatever else he and his associates were or thought they were, they maintained a strict hierarchy of respect. Within that system, Antonio Zaccaria was due some deference. He was a property owner. He had shown them no disrespect. They had no current dealings with him. Martello used this as his opportunity to bow out. He had made his point and could deal with the son later. He made a sort of formal genuflect to Antonio and started off calmly toward the streetcar tracks.

They all watched him walk away. It was Leo's father who gave the sign that the man was officially out of earshot.

"*Basta!*" he said quietly. Then he turned back to his son. "Leo," he asked, "is that yours?"

It was as if the other had never happened. His tone of voice gave nothing away about his thoughts on the car, but this was an enormous asset to be owned by a boy.

"Yes, Pop," came the reply, perhaps a little too bravely.

Antonio walked around the machine, taking it in at his own pace.

"The carburate shouldn't be open like that," he said finally. "I show you how to put a coffee can on it."

There was a silent but collective sigh of relief from the boys.

"I can get another cover from the junkyard, Pop," Leo said happily.

"Save you money," his father advised. "Most of 'em are empty anyway. Just use a can to keep out the sticks and leaves." With this, he pursed his lower lip and nodded at the car in approval.

"You know about cars, Mr. Z?" asked Guido.

"Right after Leo was born, we went to live on a farm in New York," he answered. "I hadda drive a Model T. Same engine. This one got a better gears. Leo, you know who knows about cars?" he continued. "You Uncle Freddie. Talk a to him, hey?" He nodded again and then went inside, smiling.

By the time his senior year of high school got under way, Leo had the car all cleaned up and was looking forward to getting his chauffeur's license. He thought he might even register the car so he could take it on the road outside the city.

The local police precinct was able to provide all the paperwork, including a book of questions to study for the written test. He could get a simple driving license by presenting himself at the Commonwealth's Registry of Motor Vehicles. It was located in an impressive new building at 100 Nashua Street, on the banks of the Charles River, in Boston. To get the chauffeur's license, on the other hand, he had to be nominated by an approved driving school and schedule a road test with a registry officer.

On top of that, the chauffeur's license cost five dollars for a four-year term, but it allowed him to take money for the use of his car, and it also permitted him to drive any registered vehicle. In short, it was what the big boys had. So it was time to find a driving school.

The police at the local station suggested Fitzgerald's Driving School, in South Boston. It was no surprise to Leo that the desk sergeant was also named Fitzgerald. Well, it was as common a name in the Irish neighborhoods as Rossi was in Eastie, and since the days when John Fitzgerald was mayor, it was used more proudly.

Leo made a telephone call from the corner store to be sure of an appointment before taking the trip across the harbor. He was rewarded by a pleasant conversation with a honey-voiced young woman who set a time for him, gave him directions, and said that *she* would be happy to help him out. He always loved the way the Irish girls spoke. They almost sang when they talked. He wondered what she thought she could help him with. Was he overlooking the obvious, or did he just not believe that that was what she meant?

It was late afternoon on a warm September day when he took the car ferry to Dock Square and then drove across the Fort Point Channel Bridge into Southie. The main streets in this section of the city were lettered. There were blocks of three-deckers, just like at home. There were also large areas of factories and warehouses, all of which were near the rail yards and seaport that met each other on the south side of the harbor. South Boston was a booming industrial area because raw materials could be had by rail or sea from anywhere and the finished goods could be shipped out just as easily.

From Northern Avenue, he rolled down D Street to a low, brick building with a parking lot that was surrounded by five-story brick and stone warehouses that all came right to the edges of their lots. The streets were paved with cobblestones that had been rounded over by one hundred years of wear from the iron tires of heavy wagons, some of which still plied the streets, delivering drayage and taking goods away. A small sign by the entrance announced Fitzgerald's Driving School and Livery Service.

Leo entered through a storm door set and found himself in a reception area separated from the main office by a low banister with a swinging gate. The office itself was an open area with space for several desks. There were two glass-doored private offices at the back of the small room. Sitting at one of the desks out front was a young woman. At second glance, he noticed that she was a lovely young Irish woman.

She had dark red hair, curly and long but held up with pins. Her skin was milky white, which set off her freckles and her bright blue eyes. She wore a dark brown, long-sleeved dress with big cloth buttons up the center of the front to a V neck. It was a conservative and businesslike costume, but it also showed off her ample figure to full effect. He took a moment to look her over again, and their eyes met as she was giving him the same treatment. Her gaze was unwavering. Leo thought instantly of Rosalind Russell in *Craig's Wife*. The young woman smiled broadly.

"You'll be Mr. Zaccaria then, won't you," she said with a twinkle in her eye. It was the honey voice from the telephone call.

"Why, I'll be anyone you please, my dear," he returned. "And you are?"

"Colleen Fitzgerald at your service." She smiled. "Now either you've come here for driving instruction or to take me to dinner. I'll happily consider either request, but you will have to pick which one it's to be."

Leo wrinkled his face into a stagy mask of tragedy, clutching his breast. "Ah, Colleen! Why must life always impose such crushing limits on what's possible for us to achieve?" he asked theatrically. Resuming his normal posture and voice without missing a beat, he added, "I suppose it has to be the driving. I'll be back later to inquire about the other, however."

"I daresay you will," she allowed with a chuckle.

Before she could continue, one of the two office doors swung open abruptly, banging against its stop. Out stepped a man in his middle years, walking a little unevenly and observing the two of them through eyes straining a bit to focus. He was tall, perhaps even a full six feet in height. He wore a three-piece tweed business suit, a white shirt, and a necktie. Together, this outfit seemed to be conspiring to hold him against his wishes. The waistcoat buttons strained to clutch his abdomen while the shirt's collar kept a stranglehold on his neck. He seemed resigned to the fact that resistance was futile, but he didn't have to like the situation any. His skin was pale white, but his cheeks and thin nose were bright red. Closely cut brown hair was plastered back against his head.

"Is this our new student, Colleen?" he asked in a strong tenor voice that filled the room.

"Not yet, father," she answered, "but quite possibly in a few moments." Turning back to Leo, she said. "Mr. Zaccaria, may I present Mr. Brendan Fitzgerald, the proprietor of this establishment."

Her father stiffened formally at the introduction and nodded his acknowledgment to the young man.

"How do you do, sir," Leo said, eyeing him.

"Quite well. Thank you, young man," Brendan Fitzgerald began. "Let me tell you about our school. I see you have met my lovely daughter. She is a capable driving instructor, and either she or I will administer both your classroom and on-the-road instruction. I trust that you will be able to maintain a professional attitude toward her?" he asked somewhat aside.

Colleen flushed but didn't respond, so Mr. Fitzgerald continued.

"We will be able to give you all the informative instruction and practical training you need to become a capable chauffeur. Our rates are one dollar per hour for classroom instruction and one dollar fifty cents per hour for on-the-road practice, using the school's vehicle. All fees are payable in advance, of course. We will begin by evaluating you and determining how much instruction will be necessary in your case. Is that an acceptable arrangement, sir?" he asked in conclusion.

Leo thought about this for only a moment, sorry that he had not gotten in the first word. "Actually, sir, I already know how to drive well enough to pass the test. In fact, I drove over here today in my own Model A. What I need is the school's endorsement on my application so that I can arrange a road test with the registry. How much will that be?" he asked, thinking it a logical question.

It was not the response that Brendan Fitzgerald was expecting. In fact, it seemed to take him a moment to digest this new information and to decide how to respond. While he was thinking, Colleen turned and ducked down a bit to get a look past Leo and out the front window. Satisfied that there was a car there, she got up from her desk and stepped around to the balustrade.

She was almost as tall as Leo, and when she came into full view, he could see that she was also almost as young as he was.

War Record

What a delightful combination, he thought.

"Father," she said, "I suggest that since Mr. Zaccaria is already acquainted with the operation of a vehicle, you need only take a short ride to verify that fact. Perhaps one half an hour? Then you could attest to his ability formally. A fair administrative fee for affixing the school's seal to his application might be two dollars, don't you think?" she asked. "After that business transaction is completed, I believe Mr. Zaccaria and I have one other matter of social interest to discuss. Does this sound like an appropriate course of action?" she concluded, holding Leo's eye.

This was all happening just a little too fast for Mr. Fitzgerald's taste. His daughter had given him a clear opening, though, and he took it as gracefully as was possible under the circumstances.

"Why, yes, my dear," he said in his formal and deliberate tone. "That sounds very good. Do you agree, sir?"

"Done," said Leo, extending his hand across the rail to Colleen for the formal handshake.

It was too much to pay for a signature on a form, but there looked to be more to the deal than just that.

Colleen was pleased. Between work and school, it wasn't often that she got the chance to meet any young men from outside her immediate neighborhood. *With a little mustache,* she thought, *he could be Ronald Colman in* Under Two Flags. *How exciting.*

As they shook on it, Leo could see that there was much more to this deal than just the chauffeur's license. *Having a car really is magic with the ladies,* he thought.

The Tunnel

Leo snapped into adrenaline-induced concentration. He was wide awake in an instant but disoriented. His animal half leapt to the fore and he was poised to defend. But there was nothing there.

Then he noticed his crotch was hot. He looked and saw that he was crouched in the tunnel, still guarding the only burning lamp in the works. He had been asleep during an air raid. According to procedure—*Achtung!*—he had disconnected all the large globe lamps…except the one he'd hunkered down with hidden under his greatcoat for heat, and to win a small victory over his captors.

While he slept and while he floated back to Boston and happier days the ground shook under him as British bombs pounded the neighborhood. Leo was long past fearing the bombs. What was the point of the tunnel if there was danger from the bombs? Strangely he had been comfortable as long as the concussions came in regular sequence. It was the abrupt stop that had jolted him upright.

In the silence that followed the raid Leo's hearing was suddenly at highest alert. Were they coming? He heard nothing. Carefully he extracted the large globe and its wiring from under his heavy coat and rose up to hang it back on the overhead hooks. Then he took the other bulbs he'd removed when the raid started and replaced them in their fixtures. In America light bulbs screwed into their sockets. But here in Germany they had saber clips that locked in with a quarter turn. *That was how Christmas Tree Lights were designed at home,* Leo thought. But here the big bulbs, at higher voltage than was ever allowed into American homes, were connected by the same method. After suffering at the hands of his captors for so long and with his future still greatly in doubt, it pleased him to feel superior to the Germans on this small matter.

Back to work.

If he was the first one back at the drill he knew he could expect some slack from the guards when it came to taking worn drill bits off to Vulcan's Forge. So when he never even saw the guards he was pleased with himself for having conditioned them to believe his lies in advance of the time his life might depend on what they would do.

Although the animal in him would never admit it publicly, he was secretly happy that he'd won one, even if it was a little one.

Later on he took the two worn drill bits he'd managed to sabotage and headed out of the tunnel and off to the forge where they could be refinished. As he approached a guard, now lounging near the entrance with his rifle leaning against the rock, Leo held up the two four-foot rods to indicate his errant. The guard showed no reaction and Leo simply continued.

He left the tunnel he'd been working and followed the narrow-gauge tracks leading from it. Where the small tracks merged with a cross tied line he turned left to make his way across all the tunnels, en route to the forge. The tunnel entrances were perhaps 150 feet apart. Before Leo had even made the next opening he came upon one of the small carts that were used to remove the shattered shale after a blast. It was just sitting there awaiting its next call. In its hopper there was a long, stout steel rod that resembled a crow bar. These were used to edge the little rail cars left or right if need be at a switch point.

There was no one else around. It was dark and quiet under a blanket of stars following the nightly transit of the RAF's

Bomber Command. The cross tracks perched on the outside edge of the flat overlooking the river. When he reached the car Leo stopped and looked around to be certain he was not being watched. Beyond the low gurgle of the slowly moving water there was nothing but silence.

Without really planning it out or thinking about a plan Leo put down his two long drill bits and labored to pull the crow bar out of the hopper of the little rail car. Then from inside the rails he extended the bar across both tracks and used it as a lever to tilt the car over on its side. The exertion was almost too much, but he wanted it badly enough that he summoned the energy and once the high-sided car tipped past the point of no return it did a slow roll onto its side. In fact, the energy it had when it landed caused it to slide away from the track until a good portion of its upper structure was hanging over the escarpment. The boxy little rail car seemed to have a mind of its own. It teetered at the edge of the ten-foot drop, as if thinking about whether or not to go for a swim. Then it finally tipped past the horizontal and slid down the steep incline into the River Elster. The water was shallow and the car did not sink out of sight, but unless you were looking over the edge you simply wouldn't have seen it.

The effort to topple the car left Leo breathless. He exhausted great plumes of vapor as he fought to slow his pounding heart. It wouldn't have been such an ultimate exertion but for the fact he was only a starved remnant of the specimen he'd been the day he was captured. The silence seemed to confirm that he had done the deed undetected. So he picked up his two drill bits and shuffled off to Vulcan's Forge.

At the forge the swarthy old blacksmith who maintained the tools gave Leo a look of stark suspicion as he received the two worn bits. How could this American wear out two drill bits per day?

"Arbeit macht frei," Leo said with a shrug.

War Record

The wisecrack brought fire to old Vulcan's eyes, but he dismissed the American with a head nod and began taking it out on the tools instead. As Leo settled in for another nap he could hear the blacksmith hammering the red hot rods of steel with excessive zeal. It was warm in the forge area so Leo silently allowed all the time that was necessary to repair the bits.

He shrugged once and fell sound asleep.

A Night at the Opera

It might have taken Leo longer than some to flesh out his master plan for the conquest of women. When he was ready to put it into action, however, it was impressive in its strategic forethought and elaborate in its detail. If women had been a sports team or an opposing army, they wouldn't have stood a chance.

Logistics alone put him way above the average. He had a car. He had taken the time to do the work on his automobile, which made it both reliable and agreeable to ride in. The engine was in tune, sporting a better distributor and brand-new spark plugs. The wheel bearings had been repacked, and the chassis and steering box were freshly lubed. The interior was clean as a whistle, as was the jump seat. All the chrome had been cleaned and brightly polished, which made the scratches and dots of rust virtually invisible. Having a car of any kind was a remarkable thing, but this one also sent a message of pride.

Target intelligence was an area that had required a little extra effort. Before concentrating on women, Leo had been only an occasional moviegoer. At that, he had always leaned more toward stories of epic adventure than to those of social sophistication or drawing room comedy. Now he forswore the days of wooden ships and iron men for the likes of Noel Coward and Carole Lombard. It was all to make sure that he knew the latest lines

War Record

and had heard the most popular music. He worked conscientiously on his sense of style.

Tactics were straightforward. Like most energetic young field commanders, Leo favored the frontal assault. The social scene had evolved to a point where there were clearly defined times and places for young men and women to meet. It was simply a matter of gathering his troops and getting started.

Leo had always enjoyed a reasonably wide circle of friends in school. With the advent of an automobile, however, young men from his class and all around the neighborhood vied to be his buddy. When it was time to organize a Friday night outing, he had no trouble filling the car with friends. Guido Lessardo sat up front. Bob Cole and Johnny DiNaldo shared the jump seat. The objective was the Oceanview Ballroom in Revere.

Going to a dance was always the great way to get started on the social scene, then as now. Once you got past the small dances held in churches, schools, and community houses, the next step was to go to a real music hall. The Oceanview was only one of a number of large commercial ballrooms that sprang up in the improving economic times of the late thirties. Most of them featured hardwood dance floors that were easily the size of two or three basketball courts. Columns supporting a roof of that size were always necessary but were also always kept to the perimeter of the floor, leaving a broad walkway behind. The trusses between them looked like archways in the wooden structures and usually defined the standing room where people mingled while not dancing. There was always a bandstand because there was always live music.

The house orchestras for ballrooms like the Oceanview were both a potential springboard for the careers of young musicians and an honorable last stop in the careers of older ones. The band leader and a corps of seasoned professionals formed the backbone of the group. These were skilled technicians who had put in their time on the road and prized the chance to have a real home near a steady gig. They constantly auditioned for junior players, though, to get a continuous infusion of energy and the latest in style, not to mention some good-looking youngsters to sit in the front chairs. These bands also always had at least one or two vocalists to let them do covers of popular hits. There were girl singers and guy singers as well as duets, trios, and quartets of every combination. The house band at a commercial ballroom tended to be the first place for a young singer to get noticed also.

The major hotels attracted nationally known touring bands such as those led by Duke Ellington, Woody Herman, or the Dorseys. Whenever one of these came to town, someone from the band would call someone they knew in one or more of the house bands and ask if there was anyone they should listen to. In some cases, a publicist or secretary would be sent out on a Friday or Saturday night to listen to the music at several of the local ballrooms and report back on emerging talents. The fact that such a scout might be in the audience on any given night energized the young players as well as enticing them to work for short money. On occasion, a ballroom might actually book a big-name touring band. If that happened, the young house musicians got the chance to sit in with the big timers while their older colleagues got a rare night off.

It all made for an extra level of voltage in the performances similar to those seen in the minor leagues of baseball where everyone is trying to shine so they can get called up. It was also the reason that the bandstands were large and sometimes terraced so that anyone on the floor could see the players as well as hear the music.

Add to this the sexual energy of a large group of young men and women all gathered together in search of one another and you begin to understand why dancing at a ballroom was the place to be on a Friday or Saturday night.

The Oceanview Ballroom was a particular example of the breed. The city of Revere lies just north of the entrance to the

Boston Harbor. Its land rises from salt marshes and sand bars to meet the Atlantic Ocean at a shallow, crescent-shaped bay. Revere Beach is a four- or five-mile stretch of sandy shoreline that was home to amusement parks, old-fashioned resort hotels, a variety of eateries and bars, and the Oceanview. Revere Beach Boulevard lay on either side of the trolley tracks, so one way or the other, there was easy access to both the beach and the businesses.

The ride to Revere from Eastie took only twenty minutes, but for Leo and his friends, it was a thrill all of its own. They took the route they wanted at the time they wanted to, with no delays to switch streetcars. The personal autonomy imparted to the little band of friends by their motor car was new to them and very exciting. People and street scenes passed before them, and they could slow down to observe more closely or even stop to converse briefly before resuming their trip. When they did have a word with people on the street or the stoops of a neighborhood, they did so from an elevated platform. The Model A was a throne upon which all four of them sat. When they spoke to those they passed or if they were only observed in transit, it was a little event in the day of the people of that block. To the boys, each such encounter was worthy of a short newspaper story whose headline read, "Local Youths Make Good."

As they rolled down Revere Beach Boulevard, the ocean was on their right, a wrinkled and inky plain stretching off to the horizon. From it came a sea breeze that smelled like salt and life. On their left were the buildings that fronted the water. At the far end, there were three-deckers looking just like those in Eastie except for the widow's walks that adorned many of the roofs. Closer to the social center of the beach, the buildings were all commercial. Since they were there to attract customers who were at play, they sported a wild variety of architectures. There was the Spanish castle, a towering wooden frame hotel that featured spires and onion-topped minarets. It was some Yankee's interpretation of a Moorish fortress. There were carousels whose walls could be removed in summer to show the merry-go-round with its carved steeds and gilded chariots. A restaurant shaped like a giant frankfurter on a roll left no doubt as to its main menu item. Kelley's roast beef sandwiches were dispensed from the counter windows of a shack, which was straddled by the huge effigy of a cow. There were bathhouses that strived for the look of elegance. There were stands where saltwater taffy could be viewed being endlessly folded in onto itself and pulled by counter-rotating steel arms.

The entrance to one amusement park was via the open mouth of a smiling clown whose flat wooden face stood three stories high from its chin rest on the sidewalk. Another park offered midway games right on the sidewalk. Behind its wall of low stalls, the wooden structure of the roller coaster known as the Tornado could be seen. It could also be felt since the sidewalk rumbled underfoot when one of the coaster's cars hit the bottom of its steep slope and made a tight left turn up and away.

Standing alone near the end of the beach was the Oceanview Ballroom. It was a wooden building that looked low from a distance because it was so wide. There were large, paned windows in the front that allowed the namesake vista to be enjoyed. The clapboard exterior was painted gray with white trim to simulate the colors of the weathered shakes of nearby cottages. Over the center of the dance floor, the roof was raised in a short cone shape that allowed for a necklace of small windows and made an outside peak for a pennant that fluttered in the on-shore breeze. At the entrance, there was a box office where patrons purchased their tickets to get in for thirty-five cents apiece.

The boulevard was at least wide enough for two cars to travel abreast plus a row of parked cars in each direction. As they drifted past the Oceanview, Leo moved to the left and then traversed the streetcar tracks at the next crossing. He made a smooth U-turn and came back past the ballroom to find a parking spot. There

War Record

were plenty of places on the street because most people took the trolley. When they eased in, it was almost too bad that such a great ride had ended. That thought was short lived though. As the engine went silent, the sounds of the light surf and the muffled music of the big band reminded everyone what was to happen next.

Entering the main ballroom to get a good look at the party, this little band of eighteen-year-olds from East Boston felt like the masters of all they surveyed. They had arrived by car, Leo had the immense sum of five dollars in his pocket, and they came from two towns over, so they had the exotic quality of strangers. Suddenly, their jackets draped just a little bit better on their frames, they each stood a little taller, and their eyes were just a touch more irresistible. All this happened not a moment too soon because each of the two thousand other people in the room felt exactly the same way about themselves.

Above the dance floor was a rotating sphere covered with tiny, flat mirrors. Key lights shined on it from three corners of the room. The effect was to diffuse light in a pattern of stars revolving around the floor and over the band and dancers. The bandstand was more brightly lit, and since it was the summer season, all twenty-three members of the band were dressed in white evening jackets and black tuxedo trousers. It made for a bright spot at the head of the floor that reflected even more light.

Behind all this, the music was a palpable presence. The acoustics of the wooden building were great, especially when it was full of people. Those conditioned by the scratchy sound of the radio or of records were bound to be shocked by the strength and purity of the live sound. There were complex arrangements of instruments, all of which could be discerned if you listened. If you didn't listen, there was an environment created by the music that engulfed you. The dancers glided easily to the 3/4 waltz time or worked athletically to the driving 6/8 time of a jitterbug. Those standing in groups around the floor, behind the ring of roof supports, would also respond differently to the different tempos.

The music wasn't so loud that conversation was impossible. It was clear and pure, though, in a striking manner. This made it a part of everything that went on in the room.

As they took in the scene, they each smiled in anticipation. Leo made a subtle gathering motion with his arms, calling for a huddle, and the others leaned in.

"Keep an eye on the clock," he said. "We all meet right here at midnight. Understood?"

There were nods and winks all around. Lee and Gui sauntered off in different directions. Bob and Johnny stood together for a moment, watching the crowd. Something made Johnny think that he knew which way they should look. He gave Bob a touch with his elbow and jerked his head in the chosen direction. They were off.

They walked together slowly, appraising and being appraised. A group of young men who were regulars noticed that Johnny and Bob were new. This was cause for whispered consultation with serious looks. A range of ages was gathered on the floor, so just as many of the regulars who were a little older took no notice at all.

The opposite happened with the women. When they noticed new blood, there was a smile to accompany their whispers. Just how big a smile and what it really meant were the questions dogging the pair of young men.

Before long, the two boys spotted two girls standing together. They seemed otherwise unattached, and the band had just finished a spirited tune with a Latin rhythm, so something slower was probably up next. Making the decision for both of them, Bob turned in the direction of the two, and Johnny followed smoothly.

"Good evening, ladies," Bob said easily. "I didn't know they let movie stars out on the town this far from Hollywood."

It was to start as a test of wit.

"Is that what they call a line?" asked the taller of the two, a brunette. She fluttered her eyelashes theatrically. "Oh, how sweet."

Her hair was shoulder length and wavy, parted just to the left of center and held back with clips. Her lipstick and eyebrows showed great attention to detail, but her smile was fresh and genuine. She was flattered by the attention.

Her girlfriend was blonde with dark eyes. Her hair showed a tighter wave and was just a little shorter with bangs á la Claudette Colbert. A smile lit up her whole face.

"Hi, boys," she said, veering away from repartee. "You're new around here, huh?"

"Why, as a matter of fact, we are," Johnny chimed in. "I'm Johnny, and this is my buddy, Bob. We're from Eastie, and it was reported in the *East Boston Times* that you two would be here tonight, so, naturally, we had to see for ourselves."

"Well I'm pleased to meet you both," Blondie continued with a little laugh. "You two are such kidders! I'm Jennette, and this is my friend, Mary."

"East Boston?" Mary asked. "You boys are a long way from home, aren't you?"

"Oh, not really," Bob offered casually. "Everyone's heard of the Oceanview. We just thought we'd drive over and join the fun."

The word *drive* was not missed by anybody. Bob was almost too satisfied with himself, but he didn't waste time before moving on.

"Mary, my dear, I have this strange medical condition," he continued. "Right now, I feel a foxtrot coming on, and I might be powerless to stop it. Can I ask you to help me work through the crisis? The feeling will pass when the music stops."

She had actually started to believe him when he mentioned a medical condition. Then, when she realized what he was really getting at, she burst out laughing. His timing was perfect, however. Before she could speak, the band struck up "Begin the

Beguine." He took her hand and led her, still giggling, onto the floor.

As they box-stepped off into the throng, Jennette said, "Gee! They look like Vera Zorina and George Murphy. They're real good dancers."

"Well, let's us give it a try and see who we look like," Johnny said, holding out his hand to signify the offer.

Jennette smiled and blushed. She put her own hand in his to accept. The building itself swayed with the music and the movement. The stars swirled. The dancers did showy steps with practiced assurance. Gable? Lombard? Robert Taylor? Priscilla Lane? Lyle Talbot? Norma Shearer? Someone else? At some point, everyone closed their eyes and imagined. It was the moment that all this had come together to create, the reason for going out on a Friday evening.

On the way home, after midnight, the boys stopped for coffee at an all-night diner in Chelsea. The sidewalks were empty at that hour, and the streets belonged to the Model A. At the counter of the old railroad car, the coffee was strong and hot as the evening's victories were recounted and relived.

"This Oceanview Ballroom is quite the place," Guido allowed, nodding his approval.

"Let me tell you about these two girls Bob and I met." Johnny began a detailed and rapturous description that might have been about two Grecian goddesses from Mount Olympus rather than two stenographers from the General Electric factory in Lynn.

While this was in progress, Bob Cole picked up a copy of the Saturday edition of the *Boston Traveler*, which had just hit the street. An article with photographs about riots in Europe had pushed the lead sports story off of the front page. Absentmindedly, he interrupted the discussion of his own conquest.

War Record

"Geez! I couldn't even spell Czechoslovakia without a crib sheet. How come it's more important than the Red Sox?" he asked.

"It isn't," Guido said flatly. He turned his attention back to Johnny's story, which had continued unabated.

"What's going on?" Leo asked Bob.

"I don't know," he replied, rereading the text. "Germans who have lived in Czechoslovakia for years are suddenly claiming that the government there is persecuting them. They're asking Germany proper to help 'em out."

"Oh?" Leo asked with a wry grin. "Like they helped out the Austrians last March?"

"What Austrians?" Guido asked, wondering what could be more important than the girls at the Oceanview Ballroom.

"Last winter, the German army marched into Austria and made it a part of Germany," Leo said. "Some said the Austrians asked them to come in, sort of like petitioning for statehood. Others say they just stole the country without firing a shot. Now it looks like Czechoslovakia is next." Leo shrugged to show that he was noncommittal, but it did make him wonder.

"According to this," Bob continued, "the French are unhappy 'cause they have a treaty to help out the Czechs. So do the Reds. That'd be team, wouldn't it?" With no audience of his own, even Johnny was listening now. "Great Britain says they'll stay out of it though."

"Stay out of what?" Johnny asked. "Are they going to fight over the legal drinking age in Czechoslovakia? That's crazy! I'll tell you what's important," he went on emphatically. "Doing this all over again next Friday, that's important! Are we on again?"

"We'll see," said Leo with a smile. "I might have to stay home with my mother, you know." He instinctively warded off the blow he received from the front page photograph of a column of Nazi troops.

Looking back the next day, Leo was satisfied with the outcome of his plan for meeting women. He had talked and danced with several girls his own age at the Oceanview. He had enjoyed their touch and smell. He'd been accepted as a suitable partner and could probably expect that to continue. Throughout it all, though, he had a feeling of competition about the process that separated him somehow from the very ones he was trying to get close to. He was learning plenty about women, but he was approaching it all as a competition rather than a romance.

Contrary to what the movies seemed to say, there was more to life than just women. Leo graduated from East Boston High School in 1936. At the time, he was only sixteen years old, so he decided to work for a while before going further with his schooling. He found a series of jobs and approached each with energy and thoughtfulness. He drove for the dairy where his father was employed. He kept stock and ran messages for a greeting card company. He kept several different kinds of shops at different times. Most often, he had several different jobs at one time, using his weekly schedule as a wall that was built up out of blocks of time of different sizes and shapes on different days.

So when he did want to go on with his studies, he looked for a school that would accommodate his need for a flexible schedule. A traditional ivy-covered campus with a rigid academic calendar wouldn't allow him to use the pay-as-you-go plan. Boston has always been a center of education with new institutions and new plans and methods evolving all the time. He had no trouble finding just what he needed.

By the turn of the century, the Massachusetts Institute for Technology had outgrown its buildings off Clarendon Street. By the mid-thirties, it had completed its move to a rural tract in nearby Cambridge. The new campus stretched along the banks of the Great Basin created by the Charles River when the marshy Back Bay was closed off from the harbor with a lock and dam.

War Record

Down Huntington Avenue, back in Boston, this provided an opportunity for growth to Northeastern University. A newer and less well known school than MIT, Northeastern, had to cater more to its students. It offered a full program of evening classes with semester schedules in progress throughout the year. Better yet, their courses were a good deal less expensive. The school began a period of growth as it served students unable to afford full-time learning and a few who were simply askance at traveling all the way to Cambridge just to learn engineering.

So it was that Leo found himself in a second-floor lecture hall above a row of shops on Huntington, near the corner of Gainsboro Street. He sat in a wooden seat with a folding armrest for note-taking. His chair was almost at the center of a steep, fan-shaped bank of rows that curved around and looked down onto a marble-topped lab table. It sported gas jets and a sink with running water. The table was backed by chalkboards in hardwood frames that shifted up and down like giant window sashes. It was the classroom of Professor Heintz Gerber, Chemiedoktor of the Universität von Heidleberg and basic lecturer in wet chemistry at Northeastern.

Leo would never have chosen a seat in the center like this one. He would have gone toward the ends of the row to have easy access to the aisle. He might have taken the very last row so that he could observe not only the professor but also all the student interactions that took place before him. It was not to be though. When he entered the hall, a graduate assistant took his name and directed him to the seat, which had been pre-assigned. Attendance would be taken, it was explained, by matching occupied seats with a master chart.

The room was relatively full. It was small enough so that everyone could see the table and the boards well enough, but there were still as many as 150 students waiting for their instructor to begin the first class meeting. The place on Leo's left was empty.

Mark Zaccaria

Sitting on his right was a young man about his own age. In fact, there were only two or three women in the whole group.

"Hi. I'm Joe Stossel," he said. "You full time?"

"Leo Zaccaria. No. I have to juggle this with work. In fact, I'm just starting out tonight."

"Hey, me too," Joe said. "I've been in school here for three months, but I do have to work to keep up. You live at home?"

"Yeah," Leo answered. "I grew up in Eastie. How 'bout you?"

"Quincy. Hey, look. Here he comes."

Professor Gerber was a man in his mid-fifties. His white hair was much thicker at the sides than it was on top but a bit unkempt overall. His posture was a little stooped and his clothes a bit baggy. He wore a goatee and mustache that still showed a trace of black, but in general, he was the picture of an old man as he shuffled onto his stage, depositing an armload of books and papers onto the lab table.

"Gut morning, chentlemen," he began in a strong, clear voice. Looking up at his new charges for the first time, he scanned the steep slope of seats. "Ah! Und ladies too. Forgive me."

As he looked over the crowd, his eyebrows furrowed in scrutiny and the great power of his eyes became apparent to everyone they fell upon. In no more than a moment, he had seen all that he needed to see. He nodded his approval, cleared his throat, and began.

"Ve come now to your first taste of *applied* chemistry. Both here and in your pure theory courses, you vill hear much about what chemical structure is thought to be. Zum of this theory can be proven und zum cannot today. As chemists, we vill all be involved at some level in doing the laboratory work to either prove or disprove these hypotheses. In the meantime, howefer, both the art und the science of chemistry must be used in daily commerce. The things that can be proven must be used profitably in business chust as they are used in research as the foundation upon which new discoveries are made. It is my hope that these lectures vill be your first introduction to the *practical* uses of the theories you have learned in the abstract.

"I vill discuss with you a range of tools which the chemist has at his disposal. I vill try to show you how these tools can be used to make certain positive analytical determinations. I hope I vill be some small example to you of how you must use your Got-given gifts of deductive reasoning to take several pieces of information which can be proven und use them to eliminate possibilities until you have revealed a new piece of information. Haf you read the stories of the English conzulting detective, Sherlock Holmes? Those of you who are successful vill become chust like this fictional character. You will not solve puzzles of crime, howefer; you will solve puzzles of how the world is constructed and how it works. Much more important, if I may say. Remember, please, that the Englishman who wrote the Sherlock Holmes stories was a chemist. Now I make an example for you of what I mean."

The professor had been standing in front of his lab table with his hands clasped behind his back. As he spoke, he had continued to scan the audience and take in what he saw with a riveting gaze. Now he walked behind the table and opened a cupboard underneath. He brought out a wooden rack and placed it on the table. It held a number of small, brown glass bottles.

"These are reagents. They are chemicals which haff well-known properties und which you vill all have a chance to learn about. Mit diese known substances you vil begin to observe und record certain properties of unknown substances."

At this, he removed one of the bottles. He also took a potato out of the pocket of his cardigan sweater. With a knife taken from a drawer in the rear of the table, he cut the potato into two halves.

"In this bottle, ve haff Lugol's iodine, a liquid made from the crystalline form of the well-known element."

He took the stopper from the bottle. It had a dropper through it so he could dispense a small amount onto the white internal surface of the potato.

"Here ve see that the light brown liquid turns the white flesh of the potato a very dark indigo blue. The potato contains, ah… *Kartoffel Stärke*…ja, starch. The Lugol's is well known to always turn the starch to dark blue." He held the blackened face of the cut potato up for the class to observe. "Does everybody see?"

At this, he removed a swatch of white cloth from the drawer and held it up.

"Here is a rag from an old dress shirt," the professor continued.

He applied a drop or two of the reagent to the cloth, turning it a lighter shade of blue but bright blue just the same. The reaction was almost instantaneous. When it was complete, he held the cloth up for viewing.

"What do we observe here?" he asked.

Everyone knew that he did not expect an answer from the class.

"Here is more blue. Therefore, we must have starch in this cloth chust as it is found in the potato. Notice, howefer, that this color is lighter in shade, meaning that there is not so much starch here as in die *Kartoffel*…the *potato*. Sorry. There remain questions of how much less und how to quantify the difference, but that is the object of this lecture series, to learn these things which can have practical use and to start to use the strongest reagent of them all: your brains."

Herr Doktor Gerber was a maddening combination of intuitive teacher and self-absorbed talker. Sometimes he would speak to the souls of his students, showing them the way to increase their abilities in both the art and science of their chosen field. At other times, he would talk to himself or, worse yet, the blackboard, making it difficult to determine if what he said was important or merely just reverie. Later, as formulae became an increasingly critical part of the work, his most annoying habit was seen. He would make his way from left to right across a chalkboard, writing a formula with his right hand but then erasing it with his left as he went on. One had to see through his head and copy the factors as they were written down to have any hope of viewing the equation in its entirety, and then only from one's own notes.

These little problems, plus the complexity of the subject matter, contributed to a fairly high level of attrition in the class. As the weeks went on, Joe and Leo found themselves meeting in an increasingly sparse group. They sat together because they had to if they wanted their attendance recorded. Gradually, they became friends and one of a number of little islands of humanity in a growing sea of empty chairs.

They both stayed with it though. As they got used to dealing with Dr. Gerber's eccentricities, they also began to follow his logic on the subject of the practical application of chemistry. His suggestion that there were real, profitable things to be done with it provided an incentive for learning all the theory that was required at the beginning of such a course of study. It quickly became difficult to explain the attraction to those not involved with the science. To them, chemistry was some ivory tower of hypothesis and conjecture that was intimidating because of the inference of excessive intelligence required. Leo, Joe, and most of the other students in the class knew that this wasn't really the case. The idea of membership in an exclusive group was implied, however, and as it elevated their class somewhat in the eyes of the beholders, they became less strident in their protests of equality. Like it or not, those who stuck it out were becoming chemists.

Within a year, Leo had found equilibrium with his studies, his social life, and his work. He was employed by the Rust Craft Greeting Card Company of Boston. They had offices, warehouse space, and a printing factory in a building near the downtown shopping district. The company had a number of advantages for him. They were satisfied with the flexible, part-time schedule he

Mark Zaccaria

needed to keep. They liked the aggressive unconventional thinking he brought to problems of getting the supplies they needed and making deliveries on time, despite obstacles of availability, traffic, or weather. They employed a number of young women as secretaries or commercial artists. This, of course, gave him a higher level of interest in routine office work. Perhaps best of all, Rust Craft had a company baseball team that played in the Boston Park League.

Throughout the summer, the teams would play in the early evening on weeknights and in the afternoons on Saturdays and Sundays. There were city parks with ball fields all around town. The most prestigious, though, were the two located on the back side of the Boston Common. There, the teams would find the greatest number of casual spectators, not to mention the greatest cross section. When Rust Craft played the High Hat Club that summer, Leo was in for much more than just a baseball game.

The High Hat was a nightclub renowned for its jazz band. It was located at the corner of Massachusetts Avenue and Columbus Avenue, only two or three blocks from Symphony Hall and Northeastern University.

Columbus Ave had been built up with brick and stone three-story housing some fifty years before. The apartment buildings along the avenue were sturdier than the wood-frame models found elsewhere in the city. They were the product of a boom that had accompanied the filling in of the Back Bay and the development of a great deal of new property. In the teens and twenties, the street had seen a transition from a Yankee middle-class to an Irish middle-class population. In the early thirties, the transition had continued with the black middle class moving in.

Shops and small businesses along the street were owned by people who lived in the apartments above them or at least nearby. They served the needs of the people of the neighborhood for bread, books, laundry, or the like. A number of larger businesses catered to a clientele from across the city. The High Hat Club was located in the second-floor auditorium of a building with round towers, cone-shaped pinnacles, and a main roof of slate. On the street, there was an awning that stretched across the sidewalk to the curb. Here, taxis and hired cars dropped off the mostly white celebrants who came to hear the music and dance while rubbing elbows with a stylish and elegant crowd.

Chick Webb's band was playing an extended engagement at the High Hat that summer. He was the attraction for the real connoisseurs of jazz, and they were the attraction for the camp followers who only knew that the place was stylish. Chick was serious about his music to the point of brooding on it. He demanded that sort of intensity from his musicians, driving them to accept nothing less than excellence and then to push through it to yet a higher level of development. That sort of force cannot be applied without an occasional blow-up. When they came, Chick always remained calm, almost languid.

"Express it in your music," he would tell a player who had leaped from his stand after one too many criticisms. Wide eyes and bulging neck veins would then be stared down by almost sleepy eyes that made no physical threat but which would accept no less than what was necessary. More than once, the drummer and bandleader would smile just a little as he heard the tortured and stratospheric solo that might follow the resolution of one of these conflicts. It could be Teddy McRae's sax, Bobby Stark's trumpet, or Nat Story's trombone. It might have been anybody else in the band. At one time or another, Chick pushed each of them over the edge. The result, however, was ensemble music played in freefall, and in retrospect, they all knew it and liked it that way.

Despite his best efforts, though, it could not always be about the music. His players were young men who were performing at a peak in their professional lives. They had to blow off some steam by performing at a peak when it came to recreation. So the High Hat's baseball team was made up mostly of musicians.

There were one or two bartenders, bouncers, or cooks, but everyone knew it was the band's team.

The Boston Parks Department went about the job of overseeing the summer league with bureaucratic efficiency. They took all factors into consideration and made up the schedules accordingly. Most of the ball fields were located in neighborhoods that were simply known for being Yankee, or Irish, or Polish, or Italian, or black. Without having any sort of written procedure on the subject, the Park's Department schedulers just assumed that white teams would be more welcomed in black neighborhoods than vice versa.

Thus, when the High Hat met the team from the nearby Aolean Skinner Organ Company, they played on a field between Columbus Avenue and Huntington Avenue. The field was just west of Northeastern University. In fact, it was very nearly the same location that the Red Sox had used prior to the construction of their palatial new stadium, Fenway Park. Both teams played that game somewhat in awe of the fact that this was the ground that had seen the first World Series.

Rust Craft was a downtown team, however, and the city's center was considered no one's neighborhood. Thus, for their game with the High Hat, the fields right on the Common were picked. Not knowing this, both teams felt a sense of increased importance going into their contest. How would you feel if your next tennis match were scheduled on Centre Court at Wimbledon?

It was a Saturday afternoon in the summer of 1938. The sky was bright blue with the occasional counterpoint of a little, puffy cloud. The onshore breeze from the harbor made the presence of the ocean known. Team members filtered in one at a time for the 11:00 p.m. start. Many of the Rust Craft players had worked until noon. The High Hat's band had worked until 2:00 a.m. and would do so again that night. They were just waking up and coming downtown for a breakfast of baseball.

War Record

As the players turned up, they would drop their jackets on one bench or the other and walk stiffly out onto the field to warm up. Balls and gloves materialized as they always do. Someone was the first to overcome modesty and take a few swings. Before long, there were two or three third basemen, a pair of shortstops, and half a dozen outfielders picking up ground balls, calling for flys, or just standing at ease and trading quips while the action took place somewhere else on the field.

As the warm-up continued, it became about much more than just limbering muscles. At first, the two teams circled each other, each wondering what the other was thinking. Then, as both sides had the chance to demonstrate a great diving catch or a perfect off-balance throw, there began to be some mutual admiration. Later, a grounder was hit to third and the catcher called for the double play. It went 5-4-3, black, white, black; and everybody cheered. The ice was broken. This was to be a day only about baseball, and the teams were evenly matched.

A game like this develops energy slowly. As it does, though, its gravitational pull increases. Long before the city umpires showed up to officiate, the stands were filling up with picnickers, young families, and other denizens of the Boston Common there to spend an hour or two watching a contest.

Throughout the pre-game practice, Leo shared the shortstop position with Sandy Williams, one of the High Hat's trombone players. He offered a running commentary on both his team-mates and Leo's—who was just here to show off, who should be home minding the children, who had a dangerous stick, who could steal, who needed two bats if he hoped to make contact. It was all revealed with a grin and a staccato rat-tat-tat to the shoulder from a slender right hand. At the crack of the bat, though, he moved fluidly toward the ball, and when it was Leo's play, second base was always covered.

Everyone was struck by the growing sense of fun that was building in anticipation of this game. There was no trophy. This game was for the joy of it.

"Awl right!" said Sandy. "Here comes the man!"

Chick Webb was walking across the Common to watch his players play. He looked frail and painfully thin. He wore a double-breasted suit and two-toned dress shoes. He had a matching fedora with the brim snapped down. His silk shirt was worn without a necktie and with the collar open. His most riveting feature was his dark glasses. To be sure, it was a bright and sunny afternoon. Still, sunglasses were a rarity, and they attracted attention, perhaps making more out of a stern expression than might have really been intended. He looked good, but there just didn't seem to be enough of him there to produce his legendary energy on the drums.

With him was a young woman struggling to match even his slow pace since her high-heeled shoes were not well suited to the soft, grassy soil. She wore a rayon dress with a full skirt, and her hair was bundled up in the net that fanned out from her small hat. She was a little full of figure, but it was her wide, dark eyes that drew the most attention.

The High Hat players started converging slowly on their leader. Sandy tapped Leo on the arm with his glove and signaled him to come along. One or two of his Rust Craft teammates gravitated in as well when they recognized the new arrivals.

"Hey, Chick," said a High Hat outfielder. "We're ready, man."

"Yeah, but they're ready too," said another. "This'll be a game, you know."

A few of the others agreed with gleaming eyes and broad smiles.

"Well, that's good," Chick said slowly and without really looking at anyone. "You don't want it to be a gimmie, do ya? You win this game, you want it to mean something."

There was a short period of general boasting and kidding that covered all aspects of the game and all its players. As this sub-

War Record

sided, the teams started to move to the benches. Williams took Leo by the sleeve and conducted him over to the bandleader.

"Chick, man, this is Leo. He's the other shortie in this game, and I'm afraid we just got to hurt him somehow." He said it quite conversationally.

Chick Webb smiled coyly and extended his hand to Leo. It was cool and dry, but it put no energy of its own into the handshake.

"I see," he said to his cohort. "Should we use a knife or a gun, you think?"

"I'm serious, man," Sandy continued, enjoying this setup to the fullest. "We don't hurt him now, when the game starts, he's going to hurt us, and that's the truth. I've seen him play."

By this point, the trombone player couldn't contain himself, and even the bandleader was snickering.

"What do you know about playing ball anyway, Slideman?" Chick asked. "I think we can let this one live."

Just then, another of his players tugged at him from his right and he turned away.

"Awl right, but you better keep an eye on him," Sandy said, regaining his composure. "Hey, Leo. Say hello to our singer," he went on, turning to the young woman. "This is Ella. She's got a new record coming out."

Ella smiled and extended a gloved hand. Leo took it, and they shook gently. Her eyes were fixed on his, and she was apparently surprised that he returned her gaze. As she retrieved her hand, her eyes widened slightly, a fact not lost on her new acquaintance.

"I'm pleased to meet you," Leo said, talking directly to her. "A record? Congratulations. What's the title? I'll go buy a copy."

"Actually, I just recorded a few tracks in New York last week," Ella said. "There's some post-production work, and the disks won't hit the market for a week or two more."

"Well, I'll just have to drop by and hear your performance some evening." He shrugged.

Mark Zaccaria

"I'd like that," Ella concluded with a smile. "But I do have a couple of records still in print from two and three years back."

"That's great," said Leo, "but I'd still like to hear you in person."

"Be careful now, shortie," Sandy Williams chimed in. "This is Chick Webb's girl. It's an important ballgame, I'll admit, but not important enough for her to be the prize. You hear?"

Ella looked down. For his trouble, the High Hat shortstop got his bicep swatted with a fielder's mitt. Leo smirked and trotted over to his own bench. The umps had appeared, and it was just about time to play ball.

The exuberance and downright joy that the High Hat musicians brought to the game was infectious. Their infield chatter was nonstop and bordered on the poetic. They were also their own best audience, doubling over with laughter or stiffening with mock outrage depending on which end of the joke was pointed their way. The High Hat pitcher worked from the stretch, and as soon as his motion started, all his teammates were suddenly focused only on the play. At the crack of the bat, the whole team moved as one to eliminate the threat or at least minimize the damage. This team gave no gifts.

Individual heroics were recounted to the opposition between plays as the chatter burst once again from its bonds. Boasts and threats about catching anything or firing a bullet from third to first might follow a successful put out. But just as easily, there might be murmurs of admiration if an opponent drove the ball so hard or so fast that no one could have gotten it.

Throughout it all, there was a concentration on the game that forced everything else on Earth from the consciousness of the participants. It was a great afternoon of baseball. The couples and families who collected in the bleachers got double their money's worth.

War Record

In the bottom of the second inning, Sandy came up with the bases empty and hit a long drive to the left field corner. The ball took a carom bounce off the fence, causing the Rust Craft left fielder to overplay it. That was all the base runner needed to turn a stand-up triple into an inside-the-park home run. He beat the throw to the plate handily and then broke into a wide grin and a pulsating dance that carried him all the way back to the dugout.

He was still in motion when the side was retired, still beaming and still dancing around his teammates. It was as if his happiness was just too much for him. He leaped from the dugout and moved out to his shortstop's position by a series of cartwheels ending with a back handspring. It was an acrobatic performance that easily surpassed his demonstration of expert base running. It was also an exhibition that seemed completely unhindered by gravity, by convention, or even by the fielder's mitt he was wearing.

Leo was dumbfounded at the display. He just loitered at short and waited for his counterpart to land there so he could shake the man's hand. Then, while he trotted off to his own dugout, the thought went through Leo's mind that he'd better pull to right this inning.

As the 1930s drew to a close, there was no widespread lack of stimulation among ordinary Americans. There was no impending sense of loss that might have made people value their encounters more. It's true, though, that there was a greater likelihood then that an event in someone's life would become a really peak experience. It might start out as a bush league baseball game or a visit to the Oceanview, but frequently, these common occurrences would assume gigantic proportions in the memories of those who lived them out. It was the payoff that, for most people, made the tedium of existence worth the daily grind. In an age not yet overloaded with items of property, these vivid recollections of a sweet, if mundane, victory were the individual status symbols of people whose actual possessions were remarkably similar.

So it was that night when Leo parked on Mass Avenue and walked back half a block and across Columbus to the entrance of the High Hat Club. By then, he was driving a '36 Ford V-8 coupe. It had a hard top, which made it warm and dry inside. It had a radio that could be played when the engine was running. It had the high gloss and attention to housekeeping that marked all of his cars. Before walking under the awning to the club's entrance, Leo instinctively stopped and looked back at his car admiringly. It was a constellation of lights reflected from neon signs, passing traffic, and the moon. Its image was defined more by where the shine ended than by any visible details of the body. Of course, since it was his buggy, it also served to help define him. Leo smiled at that thought.

Turning to the large, raised-panel door, he adjusted his bowtie and nodded his thanks to the doorman as he walked in. Climbing the broad staircase to the upper entrance, he could hear the hubbub of the throbbing club, and a transformation started to take place that would have made any sorcerer envious. Leo's second-hand tuxedo seemed to hang better on him in the dimming light. His boiled-front shirt stood stiffer the higher he climbed. His white jacket began to give off an iridescent glow, making his face seem older and his features more chiseled. He felt all this, and it made him stand taller and react more smoothly. By the time he reached the top stair, one eyebrow had raised almost imperceptibly and he was ready to go in.

At the upper foyer, he nodded to the maître d' and gestured to the bar, indicating that he was alone and would not need a table. The smartly dressed black man nodded just slightly and extended his arm toward the bar in a sweeping motion, ushering and admitting Leo with that single move.

The main part of the club was dimly lit with a hint of red from the rose-colored chimneys that held a small candle on each table.

War Record

The shape of the room was difficult to make out, but the eye was quickly drawn to the right from the entrance. Past tables and a glistening dance floor was a brightly lit bandstand. There were several levels to it that looked like giant coins or poker chips that had been dropped in a random stack. Each of the bright, white circular platforms held the white chairs and white music stands for ten or twelve musicians. Leo noticed that the bandleader's drum kit occupied the highest ground on the bandstand and proclaimed Chick Webb's name in dark, fluid script on the yellow skin of the large bass.

Leo moved the other way. The bar was off to the left of the entrance. Its facade was bright white in color with a glossy black surface. In the same motif, the stools were white stanchions bolted to the floor. They featured circular cushions in round metal frames that spun on their stands. The frames were painted white, and the cushions were of glossy black leather. Although there was a step up to the bar area, the entire floor, including the dance floor, was done in black linoleum tile that had been waxed and polished to a mirror sheen.

As he slid onto a bar stool, he began to survey the tables and to see who was there. There was a buzz of conversation and a haze of cigarette smoke throughout the room. Waiters moved smoothly through the maze of tables and customers. The round, white tops of the small tables looked like lily pads floating on the surface of an inky pond. Glasses tinkled, and the seated couples oozed sophistication for each other's benefit. By mutual consent of everyone inside the High Hat Club, the boundary between fantasy and reality had been blurred for the evening.

In barely the time it took to notice all this, a barman moved smoothly to face Leo across the glinting black ribbon. He was tall and trim. His smooth, black face was a display of sunken cheeks and clear eyes framed by wavy and perfectly coifed hair. He wore a black brocade vest over his boiled-front shirt, the winged collar held by a white bowtie.

Mark Zaccaria

"Good evening, sir," he said. "What'll it be?"

"Good evening," Leo replied, thinking over what would be best.

Straight spirits would move things along much too fast. A cocktail was an idea, but there was no one yet to impress with the associated ceremony, so the extra cost wasn't worth it.

"I think I'll start with a lager beer. Thanks."

It was the sign of a man keeping his wits together, waiting for something that would happen later.

"Very good," said the barman, instantly producing a tall, cone-shaped glass almost from thin air. He held it for a moment in the horizontal position, mouth facing away. Then he flipped it backward in the air, catching it expertly so that the mouth faced him for an inspection. Satisfied, he flipped it back to its original position and thrust it downward into a bin of crushed ice that Leo hadn't noticed until that moment. The force of it unnerved him just a little. It seemed almost enough to break the glass, but it didn't.

"I'd recommend a snack with that," the barman continued with mock solemnity. "My choice would be the clams casino, but we have some excellent cheeses, or you could just start with a few pretzel sticks."

"A difficult choice," Leo allowed. "I'll try the clams and the pretzels, if you will."

"A difficult choice expertly made," the barman said, writing what looked like a single curved line on a small slip of paper he produced from a vest pocket.

He extracted the chilled pilsner glass from its ice and moved fluidly down the bar to a tap. In a moment, the frosted glass was standing on a coaster in front of Leo, flanked by a shot glass that held a dozen tall, thin pretzel sticks fanning out into a cone of just that same angle.

"The clams will be right up," he said. "I trust you'd like me to run a tab."

War Record

"Yes. Thanks," Leo said with a smile. "That would be perfect."

Just before the barman moved away, he made a tiny head nod across the room. Leo didn't have to wait long to find out what sort of signal it was.

"Hi, stranger."

The voice came from behind, and he swiveled around to find the cigarette girl smiling at him. She was a beautifully proportioned black woman of maybe five feet four inches in height. Tall as that was for the day, it didn't stop there. She wore a black silk top hat and a form-fitting black cutaway jacket that was open to reveal a black choker bowtie and a white silk vest and briefs. Shear silk hose created a sheen on her dark legs, and her black, patent leather pumps had two-inch heels. From her heels to her hat, she was the picture of a formally dressed Amazon.

Holding a tray of cigars, cigarettes, and notions that was suspended from her neck by black ribbons, she asked. "Need any smokes?"

Leo could have responded right away, but he preferred taking a little time to appreciate the work of art that stood before him. She understood the process and didn't rush it. Her large, almond-shaped eyes and full, almost pouting lips slowly turned up together as she completed the picture with a smile.

"Chesterfields please," he answered at length. He really didn't need any cigarettes, but then, few of her customers did.

"This is your first visit to the club, isn't it?" she asked as she extracted the pack from her neat rows of different brands.

"Yes," he said, placing a dollar bill on top of the goods in her tray.

"I'm Josephine. Pleased to meet you. What made you decide to come see us tonight?"

"Leo," he said. "I played a ballgame today with your team, and I got to meet a few of the guys in the band."

"I see," she said, broadening her smile. "So you whooped 'em and came on in to gloat a bit, huh? That's good. They need a little of that."

"No, no. Not at all," he protested quickly. "The game was actually a tie, but I was introduced to Ella, and I promised I'd come to hear her sing."

"Baseball is never a tie," Josephine scolded theatrically. "So we just met and you're lyin' to me already. I just don't know." Then she smiled again. "If you're a friend of Ella's, though, I.guess it's all right this time." The cigarette girl winked at him and turned to walk away.

Her walk was the final brush stroke of a minor masterpiece, and Leo savored every bit of it.

The musicians began to filter onto the bandstand. They wore black tuxedo trousers and white, double-breasted dinner jackets with heavily padded shoulders. Each was made taller and straighter by his formal costume. They carried themselves regally and looked a far cry from what they had been on the diamond that afternoon. One by one, they started organizing sheet music and getting their instruments ready.

One of the club's customers left his table and walked up to the bar, next to Leo. He was tall and thin with shiny black hair brushed straight back to better highlight those freckles. His dinner jacket bloused off of his square shoulders, making it seem that his torso had no mass at all. He motioned to the barman with an unlit cigarette.

Without a word, the barman produced a small box of safety matches. He slid it open and removed one match while never breaking eye contact. With a flourish, he struck it and then kept it back until the chemical flare was finished. Cupping the flickering brand, he held it out until the customer's smoke was lit. Then, with one motion, he snapped out the flame and held up the closed box, offering it with long, outstretched fingers.

War Record

"Thanks," said the customer, taking the small present. It was more legerdemain than magic, but the barman disappeared as smoothly as he had appeared. Turning, the smoker commented, "That man doesn't tend this bar; he's its headliner."

"He's certainly been giving an award-winning performance tonight," Leo said, nodding his agreement.

"I'm Rick Levine," he said, extending his hand, "from Brookline."

"Leo Zaccaria from Eastie."

They shook, and Rick's face registered just a bit of unease as he tried to decide how he would pronounce that last name.

"Look, Leo," he went on. "I'm here tonight with my girl and her sister. We're celebrating the sister's birthday. You seem to be alone. Would you mind terribly stopping by our table for an introduction once the music gets going? I'm sure Anna would love to have a dance."

"Well thanks for the offer, Rick." He was hesitant. "I don't want to impose, of course…"

Rick was trying to read Leo's mind. Of the two choices he thought there were, he began with the one most favorable to his own cause.

"She's all right," he interrupted. "Just twenty tonight and not bad to look at. Her family is from Austria thirty years ago, but she was born here. She doesn't have to get up for church in the morning. I hope that won't be a problem."

Leo's scowl made it clear that it would not.

"Well then, just watch me as I go back to the table and you can decide for yourself. Drop over in a bit and we'll act like old chums. What do you say?" Levine kept up the pressure like a door-to-door salesman.

"Okay, Rick," he replied with a smile. "You tell them you met an old friend. I've got a snack coming. As soon as I take care of that, I'll be over, and thanks."

"Don't mention it!" he said happily as he headed back to the table.

Mark Zaccaria

Leo followed him with a critical eye. Would this be one dance or two? While he was straining to analyze Anna's curly, shoulder-length red hair from his perch at the bar, a hand caressed his shoulder. He was approached from behind.

"Hello again, Mr. Shortstop. Welcome to the High Hat."

It was Ella Fitzgerald. She was ready to go on stage, dressed in a white silk evening dress. It was sleeveless with a deep V neckline and had a full, floor-length skirt. She wore white kid gloves that extended up past her elbows. Her hair was down now, a shiny black mirror image of Anna's from across the room.

"Well, hello," he said, standing and recovering quickly. "This is an unexpected pleasure, but I didn't realize it was your wedding day."

She looked quizzical for just a beat and then laughed with her head thrown back. "Honey, you wait 'til you see a veil and some flowers before you worry about me gettin' married."

Chick Webb had walked out onto the upper tier of the bandstand to polite applause from the tables nearest the front. His tux was all black, and it made him stand out against the high-contrast background. A floor mike stood next to his drum kit, but he ignored it at first. After barely nodding to the audience, he started a three-count time beat for his now-assembled group. It acted as their downbeat and the players began as one. The tune was "Stardust," and the band was known to sometimes take twenty minutes to do the tune every which way there was. They chose a medium swing tempo, but the percussion was building throughout. The maracas, claves, and Chick's drums drove the rendition. Each of the other instruments on the bandstand would get a little piece of the number before the audience was warmed up and it was time to start the real show.

Back at the bar, Ella heard the opening number begin, and she turned to Leo. "I'll have to go in a few minutes," she said. "Josephine told me you were here. I just wanted to say hello and mention that I enjoyed the ballgame."

War Record

"I see I'm being watched," Leo observed. "You ladies apparently stick together."

"Now, Josephine and I are the only two colored girls in this joint," she replied with a conspiratorial look. "You know we watch out for one another." At this, she stopped abruptly and wrinkled her nose. "What is that delicious smell?" Ella demanded.

"Me?" he offered.

"Not on your best day, honey," she said with a smile. "What I smell is food."

The clams had arrived. A little plate with four upturned clamshells had materialized while they were talking. Inside each was the hot mixture of clam, bacon, and garlic that had attracted her attention.

"Clams casino," Leo offered. "Please help yourself, but can you eat just before you sing?"

"You watch me," she said. "I'll just try one, for the taste."

"Well then, let me help. You'd just get your gloves all messy." He took the tiny fork that had come with the plate and held one of the shells while he scooped out its contents. He fed her the morsel, which she took delicately, closing her eyes in delight at the sensation.

"Thank you. That was marvelous," she said when she was finished. "But how dare you introduce me to yet another temptation in a world already so full of them!"

"I'm sorry, dear lady." He smiled. "It's just the devil in me."

"Well, don't you ever change," she added, patting her lips with his napkin. "Look here. After the second show, most of the band goes around the corner to a little place downstairs to jam and relax a bit. Some of the customers come along, so why don't you? They're still talking about that ballgame, you know."

He agreed instantly. She smiled and nodded, but then she had to go. As the opening tune ended, Chick Webb started to make his formal introductions now that he had everyone's attention. His drum set was like the throne at the peak of a musical court chamber.

"Thanks, folks," he said as the applause died down. "Welcome to the High Hat Club, Boston's center for swing and its best joint for jazz." He spoke slowly in a sonorous voice that gave him an air of absolute confidence. "I'm Chick Webb, and this is my band."

At this, applause rose in front of him, as did a small cacophony of drum rolls, trumpet flourishes, and guitar chords.

"We'll be playing 'til midnight tonight for your dancing and listening pleasure," he went on when the commotion faded out. "We'll have some of your favorite popular tunes as well as a few of our own compositions and a style all our own that we hope will get you jumpin'. On top of that, you're in for a special treat tonight 'cause we will be featuring the vocal stylings of Decca Records star Miss Ella Fitzgerald."

His voice didn't rise to an announcer's peak when he said her name. Rather, his voice went lower, giving it an air of importance. Perhaps only a few more than half the audience knew the name, but they all took their cue and applauded loudly.

"C'mon up here, Ella," Chick intoned with his hand extended to stage left.

Ella walked out into the ball of light that engulfed the top level of the bandstand. Her gait was familiar, but her arms were held out theatrically on either side. She faced the audience as she moved. Joining hands with the bandleader across his snare, Ella gave the crowd a curtsy from that tethered position. Her white gown radiated more brightly than either the white stage or the white jackets the musicians wore. She did a slow pirouette across and in front of Chick Webb. The little spin made her flowing skirt fill out, and the light reflected from the gown illuminated his face briefly as she flashed by. His large, dark eyes could be seen for just that instant.

When she came to a stop stage right, her hands were free, and she held them out and down to highlight the band below. They

War Record

launched immediately into a rousing version of "One O'Clock Jump." Ella's face twisted in glee as soon as she heard the driving sounds. She began moving gently with the tune and snapping her fingers to the beat as she slowly made her exit on the opposite side. Chick Webb faced his drums and was absorbed completely in the act of playing the other instrument at which he was a virtuoso: the band.

He led it from his seat at the drums. There had to be signals of some sort mixed into his percussion line. However he did it, he was in undisputed charge of a sparkling and well-drilled corps of first-class musicians.

The music engulfed the room. There was no denying it from any corner of the High Hat. It was not demandingly loud, nor did it coerce the crowd with brute force. It was almost ecstatically pure though. For an audience accustomed to poor reproduction technologies, live performances were the definition of what music should be. The perfection of the individual tones and the acoustics of a good room were always a shock. That surprise was followed this night by the recognition of the beauty of the arrangements and the expert musicianship. The performance could not be ignored because it so magnetically attracted everyone within its reach. Nobody chatted about politics or baseball while Chick Webb's band was performing.

Chick used the music to energize his audience and then hold it at that level. Then he let them down gently with a slower piece. Once he felt that everyone was with him, he offered a long, interpretive variation on the old vaudeville tune "Clap Hands! Here Comes Charley!" Brass, woodwind, and drums each got four-bar solos in the high-energy rendition. Sandy Wiliams's trombone gave the best of the horn riffs, a surprising fact when you considered the extremely fast tempo and the effort needed to keep up with it while pushing a slide. Chick Webb was lost in the music. His frantic drum work was the canvas upon which the song's picture of Harlem and its crowded Savoy Theater was painted. Though he might have looked frail and brittle, when he got cookin', there was no question that Chick was the man who had once drummed Gene Krupa into submission. When it ended, the audience was on its feet. Next came a smooth version of Jimmie Lunceford's hit "Organ Grinder Swing." The audience was catching up to the infectious rhythms. They were on their feet already, so the dance floor started to fill up.

When Ella came back out, she fronted a cover of the Benny Goodman hit "It's Been So Long." She sang from a floor mike at the bottom and to the left side of the bandstand. Although the whole band was still visible, all eyes were on her. Her vocal tones were so pure it was frightening. Her simple, direct style and her eye contact with everyone in the room made folks forget that Helen Ward had ever sung the tune.

With these kinds of vibrations in the air, how could Leo remain seated? He left the bar and traced his way to Rick Levine's table. All that mattered was whether or not Anna could dance.

It would have been unfair right then to force anyone in the High Hat to remember that there was an entire city just down the stairs and out the door. By common consent, the club had become the whole world for those visiting or working in it, at least for that brief moment in time. The band played siren songs, and Ella sang them. Nobody left the room. Nobody noticed the temperature or the tab. Nobody's ears throbbed, but everybody was fully involved in the music. A spell had been cast. The entire throng was in a trance together. Short as that trance would be, its strength was unmatched.

How could you put a price on such a magic moment? Nobody would ever complain about the fact that the evening had cost a week's pay. On the other hand, everyone in the audience would remember their night at the High Hat at least until the day they died, maybe longer.

War Record

Like Cinderella, the customers were surprised and saddened when the clock struck twelve. How could it have come so fast? The Brahmans of Boston were not to be denied, however. An establishment with a liquor license could not be allowed to remain open now that it was officially Sunday. Chick Webb and his band took their bows to roaring and stomping rounds of applause. After the patrons slowly filtered out and the lights were brought up, the magic spell was well and truly broken. The room was littered and disheveled. It looked and smelled as if a small battle had been fought there.

Out on the street, the sky overhead was as black as the High Hat's dance floor and shined as brightly with the splash of stars across it. The world was turned upside down again, and for an instant, Leo was dangling by his feet, looking down at that shiny, black floor in the heavens. The air smelled sweet and clean. As he strolled toward his car, he noticed several members of the band walking in the same direction. They were carrying their instruments, and he was reminded of his after-hours invitation. The room was only a few doors down from where he was parked, and finding it was as easy as falling in step with the sidemen.

It was too late and too dark to really tell what kind of a place it was. It might have been a private social club. The room was large, and a buffet table at one end served as the bar. An iced tub beside it held beers in bottles. The decor was a curious mix of institutional and private. There were tall, round-top tables with foot rails and stools, clearly nightclub equipment. There were also sofas and divans flanked by low coffee tables and plush cushions, a sampling of drawing room furniture from the surrounding neighborhood.

The front door opened to three granite steps up to the sidewalk. There was no anteroom or entryway. If there was a rear exit, it couldn't be made out. The only light came from a handful of candles spread out here and there on tables. Small groups started gathering around each of them. Before long, a muted trumpet could be heard riffing slowly to impossibly high notes. It was like liquid flowing uphill but heard from far away. In the club, John Trueheart had been playing a guitar with a microphone strapped right to it. Here, he had an old-fashioned six-string, and he began strumming chords behind the trumpet's running gold. The twenty or twenty-five people who drifted in didn't begin to fill up the space.

Leo noticed that he and two other couples were the only whites in the room. That seemed only fair since the ratio had gone quite the other way at the High Hat. Still, he could see that the two girls were a little nervous that their dates had brought them here.

As he got used to the dim light, Leo could make out Chick Webb slumped on a sofa, watching one of his players heat something over the candle flame. Dim as it was, he was wearing his sunglasses again. Around the room, four or five heads craned to observe the operation at Chick's low table. Both of the white boys were paying close attention.

Fine, thought Leo. *Let them have the dope, and I'll mind their women for them.* He extracted a beer from its icy burial mound.

Two trumpets played a languid game of tag for a while. Chick had a pair of drumsticks, which he used to keep time on the low table. Before long, he looked like he was barely moving, but the sticks were a blur. The rapid tapping sounded like a kid's bicycle does when he's fixed a playing card with a clothespin so it flutters against the spokes. A clarinet tried to match the tempo.

On the makeshift laboratory table, it looked as though chemists were bending over an alcohol lamp or a Bunsen burner. Leo wondered if the notes in their lab books were detailed as to concentrations, components, titration, and timing. He smirked to himself and settled onto a stool that gave him a clear view of the two white girls. Which one did he want? They weren't sitting together, but he still wondered if there was a chance to get them both to come along? He knew that that was a fantasy, but he still amused himself with it for a while. In fact, he had no place private to go to with even one of them, so his plan became very general once he got her out the door. He'd improvise.

The soft hubbub of conversation and disjointed musical notes made a distracting buzz that separated his daydreams from the room itself. That's why he was so startled when the one word cut right through to his thoughts. He wasn't startled so much. He didn't jump. Still, the single spoken word was full and resonant in his ear. It brought him back and riveted his attention in a heartbeat.

"Leo."

Where had that come from? The tone was pure and deep. It was a sweet voice, a woman's voice. He turned just a bit, and there was Ella, leaning to his ear so that she could be heard.

"I'm hungry, Leo. Do you know any place where a girl can get a bite this time of night?" She was wearing street clothes now, a summer dress with a full skirt that buttoned down the front,

"Sure," he said without missing a beat. "I've got a car right outside. Let's take a ride."

"A car?" she asked, not really believing it. "Honey, if you got a car, then you got a dinner partner. Let's go." She crooked her arm through his elbow partly to simulate a formal promenade pose and partly to yank him up off the stool.

"Should we let Chick know we're leaving?" he asked, not wanting any trouble.

"I don't see how we could get it through to him right now," she answered with a touch of disappointment in her voice. "Anyway, it ain't gettin' any earlier. Are we going or not?"

Standing now, Leo extended his elbow with a small bow. She took it with a little curtsy, and they walked through the door almost unnoticed. Their departure was caught independently by both of the white girls. Each had a look of mild horror on her face as the door closed behind Leo and Ella. It wasn't the pairing that bothered them. The last lifeboat had just sailed away.

"Nice jalopy," Ella said as they walked up to the Ford. "Is it really yours?"

"Of course," Leo replied.

He let just a touch of mock indignance infiltrate his voice. All of a sudden, though, the car looked longer and lower. He held the door for her, and she slid in comfortably.

"I thought we'd have to walk to some diner," she said, pleased that it would actually be much easier.

"Assuming I've got enough gasoline," he joked, "you won't even have to walk back. What's your pleasure? Did you like the clams? There's plenty more seafood down at the waterfront."

"The clams were great," she said as they pulled away from the curb. "But should we be going to just any other part of the city? Together like this, I mean."

"You let me worry about that," Leo answered.

Because the major establishments closed down at midnight, so did the streetcar system half an hour later. Since most people took the trolley, when it shut down, they stayed put. That was one of the great liberating factors of owning a car. So what if it was late? In a city of more than one hundred thousand souls, there were only a handful abroad in the wee hours. Whether because they were forced to work at that time or because they had their own cars, the people you did meet late at night were not the ones who created social conscience or made up the ruling class that passed on issues of propriety.

"There aren't any real eateries open now," he continued. "So we'll never know if they'd have let us in. But there's still plenty to eat at this hour. If you do want fish, the boiler house down on the fish pier uses its steam to keep a kettle of chowder going virtually always. All the workers and some of the fishermen eat there. It's not really a restaurant. It doesn't have a name or anything, but we could buy a couple bowls of excellent chowder that would be hard to finish off."

War Record

"Well, that does sound good," she said, still thinking on it. "I might have a taste for something sweet though. Are there any bakeries open?"

From Mass Ave, they turned right onto Huntington and headed toward Copley Square. The road came into the square at an angle, and on the pointed lot that was created stood a pointed building. It was the headquarters of S.S. Pierce & Company, and it featured a little grocery at street level that never closed. Pierce supplied the best restaurants and a class of individual patrons who preferred to have their groceries delivered. Thus, they needed to be available at all hours if they got a call.

Eating in a car was unthinkable, however, and there was no place to sit down inside the store. They angled right, onto Boylston Street, and headed farther downtown.

"There are several places for extremely fresh bread at this hour," Leo offered.

"It's funny," Ella replied. "I get so hungry I can't see straight, and then, after two bites, I'm fine again. So maybe just a little pastry or something sweet."

"Ah, *zeppelas*!" he said triumphantly.

"Ah, what?" she asked.

"I come from East Boston," he explained. "It's an Italian section. There's a little *pasticceria*, a pastry shop that makes breakfast for the workers at the shipyards. The place is run by Mrs. Delrusso, and she makes the best *zeppelas* in town. That's a Southern Italian specialty, deep-fried pastry flavored with honey and maybe some powdered sugar. It'll be perfect. Trust me."

They drove through Dock Square. Since it was Sunday morning, there was little or no activity at the vegetable market that occupied the old colonial warehouse Josiah Quincy had built. Back then, ships could breast up right along side of the structure and load or unload. By 1938, however, the shoreline had long since crept back toward the channel. The Quincy Market was high and dry, lucky to have even the produce business. It was a shame, he thought, but nothing much more would probably ever become of it.

Just by the edge of the North End, they entered the new Sumner Tunnel, which spanned the harbor channel from below, connecting Eastie directly to the city. The tunnel was tiled in bright white with electric lamps every few feet, and since it was enclosed, the engine sounds seemed suddenly louder. The light was so bright it was shocking after the darkness and quiet of the ride through the sleeping town. Ella looked over and saw quite clearly who she was with. She wondered if she should have gotten herself into this position or not.

"When we get to this place, Leo, is Mrs. Delrusso going to shoot me, you, or both of us 'cause we're together like this?" she asked.

Leo smiled. "Unless you say something bad about the *zeppelas*,"—he chuckled—"you'll be okay. Listen. About a third of all the folks in Eastie come from Naples. My own mother does, and so do both Mr. and Mrs. Delrusso. Naples is a seaport and a trading city, just like Boston. In fact, Mr. Delrusso, who'll be there too, was a merchant seaman in the old country before coming here years ago. So he's certainly been to Africa many times. Traditionally, ships from Naples sail south across the Mediterranean to ports like Tunis and Tripoli. Sailors from those ports call at Naples all the time. Naples is actually closer to Tunis than it is to Genoa. Okay. They won't think for a minute that we're out together for purposes of romance. And we're not, are we? I think you'll find that they know more about being polite to strangers than a lot of folks you might have met."

She thought about that, hoping it was true. They came out of the tunnel and back into the darkness. The toll was five cents. Five minutes later, they were parked in Maverick Square and walking into the pastry shop.

It was a simple storefront nestled between a newsstand on the corner and a barbershop in the middle of the block. The front

War Record

window had a rod across it just above waist height. From the rod hung a drapery that cut off the bottom of the window for no particular reason. The folds of cloth were the same red-and-white checkerboard design as the place mats at the counter inside. In an arc across the top of the window was a hand-painted sign proclaiming "Pasticceria Delrusso."

They sat on stools at one end of the lunch counter. The counter itself was broken in the middle by a glass front display case that held shortbread cookies, marzipan forms, and cannoli tubes. Behind it stood a large cast iron gas stove and all the other oversized kitchen fixtures needed to turn out sweets in commercial quantities.

It was still a little early for the shipyard workers to be coming in. Mr. Delrusso sat at the other end of the counter, sipping a coffee and observing the world. Mrs. Delrusso was working the dough and tending the deep fryer and the ovens. They were both in their early sixties, and both measured about five feet in any direction you chose.

"Hey, Lee-och." She recognized him as he came in. "Long night, huh?" She saw the now-wrinkled and open evening shirt and the dangling necktie.

"Hello, Mrs. D.," Leo said. "Hello, Mr. D."

A nod came from down the counter.

"Do you have any fresh *zeppelas*, Mrs. D.? And maybe some coffee?"

"Whaddaya think we make here?" she scolded. "We better have fresh. Is that all you gonna get for the lady?" she asked, wiping her hands on a dish towel and walking over to them.

"We'll start there, Mrs. D," Leo said. "This is Ella. She's singing with a band in town, and I've been telling her about your pasticcini."

Mrs. Delrusso extended her hand.

"Pleased to meet you," she said with a smile as they shook. "Ella? Ella? Ella Fitz, the Tisket Tasket girl?" she asked, pointing her finger, her eyes wide.

"That's me," Ella said. "I'm glad you liked the song."

"*Mamma mia!*" Mrs. Delrusso exclaimed. "Hey, Geno, the Tisket Tasket girl. We gotta big star in the place!"

From his perch at the far end, Geno nodded with a smile. It was as if recording artists visited his coffee shop all the time.

"Like the song? Sure I like the song. I hear it alla time on the radio. I gotta special treat for you," she said breathlessly as she hurried back to the stove.

Leo was unprepared for Ella's notoriety so far off the beaten path. He had to be careful not to let on that he'd never heard of her until they were introduced. He wondered what a "Tisket Tasket girl" was and made a mental note to ask later.

The *zeppelas* came with strong, black coffee. They were fluffier and yet chewier than a doughnut but had the same color skin. They were about the size of a small apple but were shaped like the big globules that they were. A spoonful of dough was simply dropped into the hot olive oil and left to sizzle until it was done. After it was blotted, it was put into a paper bag with some powdered sugar and shaken to give it a coating.

"You can call it what you want," Ella said when she tasted one, "but this is fried dough, and it's almost as good as my mama used to make." She finished it with her eyes closed.

"This is better," said Mrs. Delrusso, arriving with a new delicacy on a plate. "*Rum baba!*" she said solemnly as she served it to Ella.

It was a soft, round sponge cake about the size of a muffin, and it was saturated with a mixture of rum and sugar water. In this case, Mrs. D. had leaned on the rum just a bit in honor of her special guest.

"This is good," Ella agreed. "The way it warms my throat, though, I think you'd better take half, Leo."

War Record

He did. Then he stepped in on her behalf with Mrs. Delrusso to try and shut off the flow of new and different treats before they were both killed with kindness. As the first of the shipyard workers started to filter in, Mrs. D. proudly introduced her resident celebrity to each one. Some of them looked quizzical. Most smiled and nodded whether they recognized Ella or not.

It was clearly time to go.

Leo started the good-byes. There were loud protests that they hadn't eaten enough. These were followed by whispered advice from Mrs. D. to Ella warning her that "this one" runs around. Forewarned is forearmed. A paper sack of *zeppelas* was provided for sustenance on the long ride home. Leo was commanded to say hello to his parents for the Delrussos. As they left the store, the sky was beginning to brighten.

Even on Sundays, the car ferry operated between Jeffries Point, in East Boston, and Pier 3 on Commercial Avenue, in South Boston. From Maverick Square, it was just a few blocks to the Eastie terminal. Their timing was relatively good. A ferry was just docking as they arrived, and there was little traffic going back.

"This is the coolest and quietest time on a summer day," Leo said. "I always like to relish it a little because when I get home, the flat will be hot and crowded, and they'll wake me up too soon just to remind me that fun shouldn't get in the way of work."

They had cranked down the Ford's windows, and the scree of circling gulls accompanied the musty ocean smell. Ella seemed lost in thought as she gazed out across the channel to the low cityscape that was slowly emerging from the predawn gray.

"Enjoy what you got, honey," she said after a moment. "At least you got family to be with."

This surprised him, and he turned to her profile as she looked away. "I thought the band was pretty much like family and that you and Chick Webb were a number. You don't sound too happy about your situation."

Mark Zaccaria

"The band?" she asked. "The band? They want me to do for them like I'm their mama, so long as I don't scold 'em over anything. They don't think to do for me though. Sure, they want me to be their family, but they don't really want to be mine."

"Okay. I guess that leaves Chick," he said, still trying to make her situation fit what the *Saturday Evening Post* tried to project.

"Oh, Chick likes me well enough, and we protect each other from the outside world in a funny kind a way." She looked over toward him as she spoke, and her eyes held his as she continued. "But he loves his music and he's obsessed with his dope. I can't compete with either of them. Now, to be fair, he started with the dope to try an ease the pain, but it wasn't long before the dope owned him."

"What pain is that great?" Leo asked.

She looked at him with a motherly look. "Chick got something real wrong with his back," she explained. "You ever notice he stands almost like a little hunchback? He says it's TB, but he doesn't cough or anything. Whatever it is it hurts him so bad he needs dope just to keep from cryin' sometimes. So I'm just a woman. I don't think that's enough to take him away from his music, his pain, his dope, and all that. To tell the truth, I'm not sure I want to. When you win the contest, you got to accept the prize, if you know what I'm sayin'."

This brought a smile to her face, and he did know what she was saying. A deckhand waved them aboard, and Leo pulled the Ford up a ramp and into the front position at the gate on the other end. He shut down the engine and stepped out of the car. They were nearly alone onboard, so there was plenty of room for the two of them to watch the South Boston shoreline come up to greet them.

"If you can't get romantic with Chick," Leo asked, "why don't you just find someone else? You'd be quite a prize for any guy."

For a minute, she just stood and felt the constant even vibrations of the deck and railing as the diesel ferry made its way

War Record

across the inner harbor. The motion made a little artificial breeze, and the water made everything seem comfortably cool.

"You're sweet, Leo," she said, "but you don't understand. I don't want to be anyone's prize right now. If I were to settle down and have children today, then all the things I got goin' for me in entertainment would be gone tomorrow. Then all the women out there like me wouldn't have me as an example of what could be if they wanted it bad enough. Does that make any sense? I have to be a lot more careful about what I do with myself than you have to, both 'cause of my sex and my color. If I and folks like me don't act carefully, then things are never goin' to change."

He was trying to understand. "Well, if that's what you want, why not just take over the band or start one of your own?"

Ella smiled. "Now you're gettin' warmer," she said. "There's no way I could take over the band with Chick still around, and I'd have to sell a whole lot more records with a much better contract than I got now before I could afford to bankroll a new one."

Her eyes looked tired now. They were resigned more than fatigued. "Chick loves his music, and he needs his dope." She was almost matter of fact. "One day, he'll play so hard his head will explode or else he'll do so much dope that his heart will. That's a fact. Man like him will never change, and he won't survive it either." She smiled, and the sparkle returned to her eyes. "And that'll be my chance," she said. "Someday, Chick just won't wake up an' I'll play Wendy to all those Lost Boys of his. An' that's okay. Everyone will get what they want when that happens."

Two tugboats were breasted up together at the head of the pier, pointing crosswise at the ferry as it landed. From the low automobile deck, Ella and Leo were dwarfed by the high prows festooned with giant bulbs of cut hawser. It was as if huge theatrical wigs had been stored on their bows. The ships had tall wood strake wheelhouses that were painted red. They rode separately on the chop from the gliding ferry and seemed to be nodding slowly to the new arrival.

Mark Zaccaria

As the Ford rolled over the cobblestones on Atlantic Ave, its vibrations were coarser than those of the ferry, but they were still a reminder. They turned up Essex Street and skirted Chinatown as they made for the Common and Huntington back to Mass Ave at Columbus.

When they stopped at the High Hat Club, she leaned over and kissed his cheek. He didn't lean away, but he was too self-conscious to try to press for more.

She certainly smells like any other girl, he thought. *Very nice.*

"Thanks for the ride and for the shoulder to cry on, Leo." She got out of the car on her own and came around to his window. "I've seen more of the city tonight than in all the times I've been here before. I liked that, being with the real people and taking a moonlight cruise," she said, patting his forearm as he rested it on the window rail.

"Well, it's been a treat for me too," he said, "a real night to remember. Maybe I can get back here again some Saturday night."

"You do that," she said. "We can go out after for some fried dough."

He smiled at her and put the car in gear. They each felt the sincerity of the other's promise. Somehow, though, they each also knew that it would never happen. She waved sweetly as he pulled away.

Like most young men, Leo started out thinking of getting to know women in much the same terms as he thought about a game of Capture the Flag. Energy has its merits, of course, when it comes to romance, but there are limits to how far that alone will take you. As he grew, he learned that the objects of his quests were not just trophies but people and that knowing them was of more value than just having them.

You're in the Navy Now

You could look at the summer of 1939 as the final curtain call for an optimistic and naive society that was about to be transformed. The character of the world was being rewritten, and the new players that would emerge from the chaos and change would look and act much differently than any of their predecessors.

To most in Boston that summer, the continent of Europe was very far away, both in distance and in importance. That feeling was even more pronounced the farther west one traveled in the United States. Direct memories of Europe were frequently decades old and confined to family stories of the place of someone's birth. There was no concern with international relations on the continent, much less geopolitics. It was thought that rich people traveled to Europe to do the grand tour, some sort of combination vacation and rite of passage for the elite. The actual number of these visits was generally thought to be quite small, and there were no strong business ties that were recognized by the American masses.

In short, it was hard for most people in the States to understand why anything that happened in Europe even mattered. When that painful recognition was thrust upon an unsuspecting nation, it happened in degrees, and the shock built up gradually.

On September first, before the summer was really even over, the German blitzkrieg struck a Poland desperately trying to avoid the clutches of its enemies as well as those of its allies. Two days later, both France and Great Britain declared war on Germany, and even the World Series was squeezed off the front pages of the Boston papers.

Try as they might, Bostonians couldn't ignore the growing conflagration across the Atlantic any more than the rest of the nation could. By the twenty-eighth of October, the first German warplane was downed on British soil. Enemies though they had been in the early days of the Republic, there was a bond of far more than just language between the Yanks and the Brits. Monarchies abounded throughout both Europe and the rest of the world, but it was the British royal family who got all the ink in America. British tea was a staple of the local breakfast tables just as British poetry was the backbone of drawing room bookshelves. American children were terrified by the prospect that the ghosts and goblins menacing their English cousins that Halloween were very real indeed.

Little guarantees of stability in life were being stripped away one at a time. No one such change was unduly threatening. After a while though, it became noticeable that things had been altered in a big way, and for good.

Before the summer even started, Chick Webb was dead at the age of thirty. Ella took over leadership of the band, moving it to Hollywood and moving herself toward the big time.

The fight for air superiority being waged over the United Kingdom was christened The Battle of Britain. The name alone was a stroke of marketing genius that made American public support of Churchill a virtual certainty.

Overly detailed and easy-to-ignore newspaper stories were superseded by first-person radio reports recorded right where the war was happening. Long, unpronounceable place names and essays on diplomacy were replaced by stark descriptions of bombs falling on neighborhoods just like yours. It took effort to read all the way to the end of a story in the papers. Sitting before the radio in dull shock at what all this meant, people practically had no choice but to listen to every bit of it. When they heard about the little band of heroes climbing their Hurricanes and Spitfires up to meet the incoming challenge, Americans felt redeemed, and that moved them.

At the Oceanview Ballroom on Revere Beach, the dance band played Friday and Saturday evenings, as usual. If anything, the crowds grew larger and more eager.

Since their invasion of Manchuria in 1931, the US had been complaining about Japanese aggression in the Pacific but doing nothing about it. The 1940 US decision to stop selling steel and scrap iron to the resource-hungry empire sealed the fate of the Dutch East Indies, an alternate source for such strategic materials. The continuing display of weak American resolve in the

War Record

Pacific would ultimately have even more ominous effects closer to home.

American attitudes on the spreading conflict were not molded much by the government's official position of neutrality. Public comment on the policy was intermittent, tepid, and not very compelling. Popular opinion was, however, at the mercy of Hollywood and such anti-Nazi films as *The Mortal Storm*, *Escape*, and *The Great Dictator*. After all, any force that could so threaten Robert Taylor and Norma Shearer had to be evil, and any person who deserved the ridicule of Charlie Chaplin certainly deserved no respect from the population at large.

At Northeastern University, as across academia, there was studious concern on the part of the faculty even if there was intent apathy on the part of the students. When a notice was placed on the chemistry department's bulletin board that Civil Service examinations were being offered for staff chemist positions in the federal government, Leo viewed it as just another job opportunity. That it was actually part of a gradual mobilization of American productive capacity was way beyond his recognition.

After more than two years in the university's program, he had become a capable laboratory technician, and he was still an eager student of theory. His first attempt to find work in his chosen field had been a disappointment. He'd applied for a job at the New England Candy Company in Cambridge. He expected that the NECCO position would only involve a limited area of organic chemistry, namely that involving sugars and starches. Even so, Leo was attracted to the post since he knew that almost eight hundred young women worked in the factory's production areas. Although he was ready, willing, and able, someone else was chosen.

Oh well. The government probably dealt with more interesting science. The notice indicated that he would need to fill out an application, submit references, and await an interview for any opening that came up based on his position as determined by the test's score. It seemed he should get started with the task of satisfying the bureaucracy just in case there was a job possibility at some point. All the forms had been left with the department's secretary.

That afternoon, he managed to schedule an office meeting with Dr. Gerber. After taking three of his lecture courses and one of his labs, Leo was known to the professor for more than just having stayed with chemistry beyond his freshman year.

"Gut day, Mr. Tzacharia," the old scientist greeted him. "Haff we a problem today?"

"No, sir," Leo began. "I would like to apply for a job in chemistry, and I hoped you would be kind enough to write me a letter of recommendation."

The professor beamed at the request. "Naturally, I cannot say what isn't zo, but I would be pleased to offer a positive evaluation of your present abilities. What sort of job is it you zeek?"

"The title is staff chemist," Leo noted. "I would be a civilian employee of the US government. Depending on openings that come up, the job might be with the army, the navy, or maybe the agriculture department. There's even a form to fill out, which should be simpler than having to write a letter from scratch."

As he described the position, he noticed that Dr. Gerber's expression became serious. The professor took the government form and looked at it.

"Listen here, Mr. Tzacharia," he said after a moment. "You want this job und I want you to haff it. But what I think is best is that I speak to my colleague, Dr. Jenkins, und we get him to make out this recommendation form."

The teacher carefully watched his student's reaction to this suggestion and noted the lack of comprehension in the young man's face.

"As things are going right now," Gerber explained, "I don't think you want to submit a recommendation from someone who sounds German for a job in the US government. That is especially true if the military is involved."

"But I thought you were Swiss?" Leo asked.

"I am," he answered, "and never more so than now. In fact, I believe I will haff to be even *more* Swiss in the very near future. I did graduate from the Universität Heidelberg, howeffer, and that may be German enough to complicate your application for this job."

"Aren't some of the best chemists supposed to come from Heidelberg University?" he asked, still protesting, still failing to understand.

"Ja. Of course many in Heidelberg are very pleased to think this," Gerber went on. "Sure, every doktor from Heidelberg must first create a new and neffer-before-discovered compound before receiving his degree. Don't underestimate yourself and the training you get here though. When you work hard, you are every bit as gut a chemist as anyone on Earth. So is Dr. Jenkins. He learned here, from me. Alzo, don't underestimate the importance of an English name and an American degree to the US government right now." Heintz Gerber was adamant. He had built a case for his hypothesis that was unassailable. He now waited for the inevitable assent that was due his position.

"I guess you really think that this war in Europe is going to draw us in."

Leo was beginning to get it.

"Ja, Mr. Tzacharia, I do," the professor said sadly. "I haff seen it all before, und this time, the world is an even smaller place. It will all happen faster and bring even more pain. A piece of advice. Take this job and perform your wartime service in the laboratory, not on the battlefield. This will be better for you."

Three weeks after filing the paperwork, Leo received a letter from the US government. It came in a regular business-sized envelope, but one which was manila yellow in color. The return address was preprinted on it, as was the franking notice that enabled it to be delivered without a stamp. The only intelligible thing that could be made of the return address was that it was in Washington, DC. His name and address were typed on the face of the envelope. All these features added up to create considerable concern in Maria Zaccaria. Her years as a dilettante anarchist had prepared her to be skeptical of any action of government that was directed at an individual by name. When her son returned home, she confronted him with the letter. She shook it at him and flashed a stern look as she demanded satisfaction.

"Leo! What's this?"

The maternal protective reflex is a wonder. Through it, fear turns almost instantly to anger, which then acts as the voltage a mother needs to overpower almost any foe in the animal kingdom. When that threat is not at hand, however, and especially when it is *the government*, a force neither fish nor fowl, that anger still has to be directed somewhere. So it was that Leo came home routinely after class and found himself indicted by an inquisitor of his own flesh and blood.

"I don't know, Mama. What is what?"

Bewilderment was not an acceptable response to her question.

"What is what!" she repeated, her anger now fully targeted on him. "What is this letter! What a you doing with the government, hah?"

"Well, let me read it and maybe I'll be able to tell you."

Leo chuckled just a little when he finally recognized what was going on. He saw that she was just looking out for him. She wondered briefly how he could smile at a time like this but could not argue with the logic of reading the letter. To her credit, it was still sealed. There was no way to tell, though, just how many times it had been turned over in front of a bare light bulb before she surrendered it to him. As he opened it, she stood at his shoulder. Rights of privacy extended only so far, after all. She handed it to him unopened, but she still meant to know its contents at the same time he did.

War Record

The letter was from the Civil Service Administration. It was an invitation to take the government service exam and a specialty test in chemical technology. The tests were to be administered one week from Saturday at the main post office building in Boston. A stamped card was enclosed. It was the credential Leo would need to be admitted to the test session.

"There, you see," he said cheerily, offering his mother the letter for a closer look.

His pause made her eyes flair. He was on thin ice, and this was no time to joke with her. Finally, he let himself off the hook.

"I'm going to take a test to see if I can get a job as a chemist with the US government, Mom. This is the notice of the test date and a ticket to get in."

"Oh," she said, brightening to the idea. "How come you gotta take a test? Don't they know you good enough?"

Leo smiled again and gave his Mother's cheek a playful pinch. "They got rules, Mom. Everybody's got to take the test."

As he walked through the kitchen to the room he shared with his brother, she watched him. Slowly, her body sounded the hormonal all-clear, but she was still not completely satisfied at the thought of close dealings with the government.

The main post office branch in Boston was located off Federal Street on a block appropriately named Post Office Square. It was a ten-story bastion of office windows and marble fascia with the words "US Post Office" carved in large letters on the lintel of the main entrance. It housed the only class A post office in the city. That is, at least one window was open for business at any hour of any day except Christmas and New Year's. Along with a major league ball team and a choice of daily newspapers, having a class A post office was one of the things that allowed a town to think of itself as a city rather than just another burg.

In addition to the postal operation, the building housed the administrative outposts of all other federal government departments not otherwise represented in Boston. In a large second-floor hall that was equipped with classroom chairs with arm rests, twenty-five or so young chemists gathered to take the tests.

"Hey, Leo! You didn't tell me you were taking this exam." It was Joe Stossel from school.

"Joe! I see you're always on the lookout for an easy buck."

They shook hands.

"Sure," Joe said. "I don't mind feeding at the federal pork barrel, but I understood that you had far higher aspirations." His tongue was placed firmly in cheek.

"Ah!" said Leo, recognizing the joke. "You heard about that opportunity I looked into at NECCO. It is a shame they didn't come to their senses and hire me. Do you know that the man they did take was almost *fifty* years old!" Leo managed a painfully high level of indignation and briefly considered crocodile tears. "What a waste of concentrated womanhood," he concluded with theatrical dejection.

"So, do you have any inside dope on something that's available through this one?" Joe asked seriously.

"No, no. Not at all," Leo answered. "This is just to be allowed into the personnel offices at the Natick Army Labs or other places like that."

"Yeah," said Joe. "I'm just taking this one on a lark too. I guess we really won't know what could come of it until we see our standings after we get the results."

They chatted about school for a few minutes, and then the test proctor arrived. The proctor was a middle-aged clerk who administered one government test or another on every Saturday morning. Appointment examinations for the military academy, language tests for the diplomatic service, and application testing for would-be postal workers made up the bulk of it. He gave whatever test was scheduled though.

War Record

He opened a box that contained the examinations and first removed a sheet-sized card that had instructions printed on it in block letters. These he read to the testees in a perfect monotone. The answer to each question would be marked in pencil. If a correction was made, the first answer should be erased completely. When finished, one could turn in the test materials at the front of the room and quietly wait outside until everyone was done. Once the test began, there would be no talking or other excess noise of any kind. Were there any questions?

Then he handed out test booklets and answer sheets. The civil service exam was first. Its question books were well worn. The answer sheets were paper about half the size of a standard sheet. They were printed with a matrix of a hundred numbered boxes, each of which had the letters A, B, C, D, and E in parentheses.

The clerk sat dully until the first test was turned in. As the testee left the room, the clerk took out a key to the test. It was a standard answer sheet that had been glued to a stiff cardboard backing. The correct answer to each question had been removed with a paper punch. When he lined up the key with the answer sheet, he just had to look for any hole that had a white spot in it. These he marked through with a red grease pencil, showing the error and noting the correct response in one stroke. He went methodically through each answer sheet as it came in, placing his red dots here or there as necessary.

When Leo stepped out of the exam room, Joe Stossel was already standing in the lounge area, smoking. They talked about the test for a moment. One or two of the other testees listened in. Then something caught Joe's eye through the glass window in the door to the exam room. The clerk was holding up his key to get a better look at it before the light. He checked the answer sheet, and then he checked the key. He put them back together again and looked very carefully at the set. Ignoring his own prohibition against noise, he tapped the end of his grease pencil on the desk and stared at the answer sheet with a perplexed look.

Mark Zaccaria

Four weeks after the examination, Maria Zaccaria was given an even greater test of her own calm. This time, the government sent a large manila envelope that looked as if it was crammed to overflowing. *What an enormous amount of information it must contain*, she thought.

When Leo arrived to open the package, he found that it was fifty copies of the same letter.

```
Mr. Leo V. Zaccaria
63-A Lexington Street
East Boston, Mass
```

Dear Mr. Zaccaria,

This is to notify you of your success-ful completion of U.S.C.S.A. Test PV4-4A, Sub-ce.; the US Civil Service examina-tion with specialty testing in Chemical Technology, of 9 SEP 39.

Your test scores place you number 11 out of 2,359 tested nationwide on this date.

This score places you in the *immediately hirable* category. This letter will serve as certification of that fact. Please attach one copy of this letter to all applica-tions entered at the personnel offices of any federal installation currently seek-ing workers with this specialty.

Please note that in certain instances, to be determined locally, more than one copy of this letter may be required.

You are further advised that these results may be superseded by requirements imposed by either the Department of the Army or the Department of the Navy on

active duty military personnel. In such
cases, please check the standing orders of
your commanding officer for clarification.

If you have any questions, or if you
require more copies of this letter, please
contact the undersigned.

Sincerely,

Dep. Civ. Serv. Eval. Administrator

P.O. Box 113, MS2457
Washington, 3 DC

The letters were fastened with a heavy-gauge staple at the upper
left corner. They had been printed using a diagraph-type fiber
stencil and dark, black ink. As Leo looked farther down into the
stack, he noticed that the reproduction quality deteriorated to
the point that it was almost an act of faith to use the last few for
informational purposes.

That's all there was.

Over the next two weeks, he trekked dutifully through the application process at the US Army Natick Labs, the Watertown
Arsenal, The US Naval Hospital in Chelsea, the Boston Naval
Shipyard in Charlestown, the US Fish and Wildlife Laboratory
at Squantum Point, and the Post Office Department lab at the
South Boston Annex. Personnel clerks at each of these locations
promptly gave him the forms he needed and received them back
without reaction.

At the Watertown Arsenal, he was asked to wait while a telephone call was made. The clerk returned and asked if he could
report to the chemical laboratory for an introductory meeting
with the chief chemist. Naturally, Leo agreed and was given directions to the building deep inside the heavy industrial complex.

As he walked from the visitor's parking lot, he could hear the squeals and screams of furnaces melting metal and foundries pouring it. As he passed the massive open doors of one shop, he saw that a roof crane held a massive block of metal suspended by a chain made from what must have been links the size of suitcases. The huge block dangled just above the floor, and workers strolled calmly around it, going about routine tasks in utter disregard of the amazing feat on display before them. They must have seen such things every day.

As he passed a second shop whose doors were also open, Leo saw what seemed to be a ship's mast held horizontally on a giant lathe. It was turning slowly, and as he looked closer, he saw that it was actually a gun barrel, probably being machined or rifled.

What sort of artillery uses cannon that big? he thought. *It must be a naval gun,* he concluded, *for how could anything that size be maneuvered over land?*

As he reached the chem lab, it crossed his mind that no one had stopped him to ask who he was. He wondered whether or not this kind of military production should be guarded a bit more closely.

The lab was housed in a converted machine shop. The building had a granite foundation and brick walls. Large areas of the walls were taken up by windows composed of iron lattices that held two-foot square panes of dimpled glass that had been made with a chicken wire core to prevent shattering. The windows admitted light but completely obstructed vision. The roof of the building was corrugated metal. Leo entered a door at the street level and climbed one flight of stairs to a landing with a small reception window. It had a hole through it to permit speaking, but there was no one there to let him in.

No matter. The lab door was unlocked, so he just walked in. He entered a large, long room from about the middle of its long wall. There were three ranks of lab tables standing at the ready along the room's long dimension. Each had gas piping, and maybe

War Record

one in three had a sink for water. On the far wall from the door was one of those translucent windows that took up about half the area. The bright light from the window was blinding and made the rest of the room seem dark. On either side of the window space, there were wooden shelves that held hundreds of boxes and bottles of various chemicals and lab supplies. At the right end of the room, as he entered, Leo saw a large sink and counter area covered by a hood. This was to ventilate fumes, of course.

The only thing the lab seemed to be missing was activity. There were three people in evidence, sitting at different parts of the huge lab. One had some glassware assembled but seemed to be ignoring it. One was reading the paper. The third was making notes in a lab book from a series of perhaps a dozen brown glass jars with cork stoppers. Each had a paper label on it, and he seemed to study each one and then write something in his book. Leo walked over to him.

"Hi," he said, getting the technician's attention. "Where can I find the chief chemist?"

"He's in his office," the man replied without hesitation, pointing to a door in the left end wall of the lab. "Right down there. Just go on in." The man went back to his study of the jars.

Leo knocked before entering and was a little embarrassed to find that he had entered an ante room with some file cabinets and a secretary at a desk. She was a woman in her mid-thirties, dressed properly but without too much attention to beauty.

"Is this the chief chemist's office?" Leo asked.

The woman smiled and said, "Oh, you must be the gentleman sent up from personnel. Please go right in. Mr. Smythe is expecting you." She extended her arm, gesturing to the inner door.

Leo knocked again and then entered. The office was at the end of the building, so it, too, featured a large, milk-colored window on its back wall. This one didn't face the sun, so it wasn't as bright. There was a credenza in front of it with piles of books and papers. Floor-to-ceiling bookshelves flanked the office on opposite walls. They were filled with all types of reference books. In front of the credenza was a large oak desk. In an oversized leather swivel chair, Osgood Smythe sat, facing Leo across his blotter.

"Come in, my boy. Come in," he said, putting down some papers. He motioned to one of the two captain's chairs that faced his desk from the corners. "Sit down, please. Let's talk for a minute. What did you say your name was?"

Smythe was a man of about sixty. His white hair was a halo around his red head and face. He had a bushy but well-trimmed mustache that acted as the foundation for his small, bulb-shaped nose. It, in turn, held up a pair of rimless glasses over which the chief chemist observed Leo. He wore a white dress shirt and a brown bowtie under a white lab coat. On a coat rack by the door, there was a brown suit jacket hanging on a wooden hanger. No doubt there was a morning and evening ceremony of swapping coats.

Smythe was animated and interesting, though. He was eager to hear about Leo's training and to tell about the sorts of support activities that the lab provided for the production shops at the arsenal. Since before the Civil War, this government factory had been in the business of building big guns and the ammunition they fired. Smythe told Leo about projects the lab took on to improve lubricants for the cutting oil used in the various machining processes. He mentioned metallurgy in passing and explained that the lab did strength tests on proposed new formulae. He spoke at length about the protective coatings they devised to prevent corrosion on the steel barrels, both inside and out. Finally, he mentioned that there were no openings at the moment and that he didn't really know when he would be authorized to increase his staff.

Leo was a little confused. "Thank you for the explanations, sir," he said. "I do appreciate the opportunity to hear some details about how a real lab works. May I ask, though, why you agreed to see me if there were no openings just now?"

"Frankly, my boy," the older man said, looking right at him, "I wanted to see the man who scored so high in the GS exam."

War Record

"So high?" Leo asked.

"Yes, indeed," Smythe continued. "I've never had the chance to interview anyone who has done so well. I wanted to see if you really were that much better than the rest or whether it was just luck."

"I see." Leo nodded, smiling. "So which is it?"

Mr. Smythe laughed. "Too early to tell," he said, "but you seem to know the basics pretty well. Do me this favor. Drop by and see me every so often. I'd like to keep in touch because sooner or later, something will come up."

The meeting lasted a few more minutes. Leo was shown an old photograph of a railroad flat car carrying a huge cannon whose breach diameter was extremely large compared to its muzzle and whose length overall made it extended a foot or so over each end of the car. Before it stood an array of twenty or thirty men, tiny formal attendants to the big gun. There was pride in the work done at the Watertown Arsenal. There had been for a long time.

That night at class, he asked Joe Stossel how his test had come out. Joe seemed a little uncomfortable at the question.

"Actually, Leo," Joe said. "I got number two twenty-seven. That was in the top ten percent of the whole country. It's like getting a ninety on a nationwide test, and the letter said that I would receive *strong consideration* for any open posts." He was clearly happy with the results. He even seemed a little humble about it as he continued. "I didn't want to say anything until I heard how you had done."

There was a pause.

"How did you do?"

Leo's eyebrows went up. He was in a bit of a spot. "Actually, Joe," he started awkwardly, "I did even a little bit better than that." He met Joe's eyes. "I guess Doc Gerber was right. The chemistry we learn here is just as good as anybody else's." He was relieved when he saw Joe smile and soften.

"I guess it is," he said, happy to be able to talk about it.

Mark Zaccaria

In November of 1939, Soviet troops invaded Finland as the Germans had Poland two months earlier. The Finns waged a furious defense for over three months but were ultimately defeated by sheer numbers. This put the Baltic states of Estonia, Latvia, and Lithuania in the jaws of a Russian vise.

In Western Europe, the war had gone from blitzkrieg to sitzkrieg, as all sides took a breather for the winter. There were occasional border skirmishes or artillery barrages but no major campaigns. The French were on record as giving credit to their Maginot Line, a massive defense network that, in one form or another, ran the entire length of the Franco-German frontier. The British felt secure in the protection afforded by their large navy. Newspaper and magazine articles began to come out of the European democracies, which predicted that there would be no large-scale war. The German press offered no such punditry. Ignoring this, countries outside Germany used the lull as an excuse to further delay, putting their economies on a wartime footing.

In Boston, Herr Doktor Gerber was made very uneasy by what he considered to be the calm before the storm. He took to using at least a part of each of his classes as an opportunity to exhort his students to worry over the condition of European politics. He repeatedly made the point that this European conflict would engulf the entire world in war, just as the last one had.

In April of 1940, the quiet was shattered. Germany swept into Denmark and Norway. Virtually defenseless, the former was overrun in a single day. Although the latter's government fled with its army to the central regions of the country, it required only two days for the Germans to take over all major Norwegian seaports. This included Oslo, of course, whose capture was a deathblow to Norwegian pride. Before the month was out, Norway's King Haakon VII escaped to London with his cabinet to establish a government in exile.

War Record

Just a month later, on May 10, 1940, Germany invaded the low countries of the Netherlands, Belgium, and Luxembourg. That same day, Winston Churchill succeeded Neville Chamberlain as Britain's prime minister.

Near the end of March of that year, the city of Boston had enjoyed an early taste of spring. The ground was still frozen, but on sunny afternoons, the warmth and promise of what was just ahead made everyone want to be out of doors. Leo used the excuse that he had to make a drive over to Watertown to check about a possible job opening. When he arrived at the arsenal, he could see the increase in activity. He could smell the foundries and hear the forges ringing blows down on elastic steel. On top of that, he couldn't find a parking place. Being resourceful and realizing there were no traffic cops on a federal reservation, he pulled up onto a small traffic island.

At the lab, he saw the same three technicians. This time, however, there were glassware arrays standing on a number of the lab tables, and the chemists were moving between test setups and carrying two or three lab books each. When he got to the chief's outer office, the secretary was busy at her typewriter. She seemed to be fighting with it, forcing her fingers into a series of its tender spots and smiling at the noises of mechanical pain it made in response. Leo walked up to her desk, and when she still didn't notice him, he cleared his throat.

"Oh, I'm sorry," she said, pausing in her labors. "Everything has to be done in duplicate these days, and it takes a combination of brute force and concentration to get a decent carbon. I hope you haven't been waiting long."

"Oh no," he said pleasantly. "I just got here, and I was enthralled to see an artist at work."

"Sure." She smiled. "Does Mr. Smythe expect you?"

"Actually, no," Leo confessed. "I just had a spare afternoon, and I thought I'd drop in. He did ask me to do so from time to time."

"Why, you're lucky you got such a nice day for it," she said knowingly. "He has only a half hour or so until he's due at a meeting, but if you make it brief, you should be okay. Go ahead in."

He knocked and then entered. Mr. Smythe was sitting at his desk. He looked up, almost startled, from a report he was reading. He was quizzical for just a moment, and then a smile of recognition came over his ruddy face.

"Oh, come in, please, Mr...uh..."

"Zaccaria," Leo offered.

"Yes, yes. Forgive me please, Mr. Zaccaria," Smythe went on without hesitation. "I'm actually very pleased to see you."

"I can see that you've gotten busy over the winter."

"Yes. The arsenal's orders have increased. I'm sure you'll notice all the extra activity. As it happens, Mr. Zaccaria," he continued. "I was just thinking about you yesterday. Are you still in search of a laboratory position?"

"Yes, of course," he answered quickly. "That's why I came by today. Do you have an opening I can apply for?"

"Well, no actually. I was talking to a colleague at the navy yard, however, and he is in need of a young man to do some very particular work on the various carbonates that precipitate from seawater. Are you familiar with the phenomenon?"

"Why, yes. Certainly," Leo answered without taking a beat. He made a mental note to read up on it as soon as he got to a library.

"Good, good," he said with growing excitement. "I trust that working in Charlestown would be no great burden to you?"

"Why no, sir. In fact, Charlestown is considerably closer to my home than Watertown is."

"Ah. Excellent," Smythe said, rummaging through his government telephone directory. He traced down to the number he

War Record

wanted, and then, as he reached for the phone, something else came to him. He looked up at Leo sternly, suddenly sober.

"I'm about to call the chief chemist of the Boston Naval Shipyard and suggest that he interview you. He and I are colleagues, and we help each other out in many ways, so I wouldn't want to steer him wrong. Aside from being an MIT graduate and the author of numerous articles and studies on ocean chemistry, Fred Hemmings happens to be a Negro. Will that pose any difficulty for you, Mr. Zaccaria, to work for a black man, I mean?"

"Of course not," Leo replied with almost a trace of irritation in his voice. "And, in point of fact, it wouldn't be the first time."

"Oh really?" Smythe beamed, knowing there must be a story behind that answer. "Well, fine then. Let me make the call."

Barely one hour later, Leo pulled up to the main gate of the Boston Naval Shipyard, which also served as headquarters for the First Naval District. There was a granite guardhouse with a stop sign for vehicles just in front of a granite archway that stood with its spear-topped iron grate gates open. Unlike Watertown, here there was a marine guard in dress blues who challenged every car or wagon. Leo pulled up as instructed.

"Good morning, sir," the guard said, leaning down to observe him through the Ford's window. "State your business, please."

"Uh…I have an appointment," was the best he could do at first. "With the chief of the chemical laboratory, Mr. Hemmings," he added after a short pause.

"Very good, sir," the marine replied, returning to attention. "Proceed straight ahead, please. The roadway before you is A Street. Look for Building 11, on your right, six blocks down. Please observe the posted speed limits and watch carefully for construction vehicles. Park only in designated areas." At this, the guard waved him in with a stiff, ceremonial right forearm that ended the move in a perfect salute.

What a soldier, Leo thought, as he pulled into the yard feeling very rumpled.

While the Watertown Arsenal felt like any heavy industrial factory complex, the Boston Naval Shipyard was different from any other manufacturing facility Leo had ever seen. Everything about the place spoke of tradition and age.

For one thing, everything was nautical. There are no human pursuits based on traditions any deeper than those having to do with the sea. For another, the navy yard was a real military installation. The base flagpole stood directly in front of the admiral's quarters. That house was a large, antique colonial with a widow's walk not because of any sense of style but because that was what was thought of as fitting over a century before when it had been built for the purpose it still served. The flagpole was flanked by two twenty-four-pound naval cannon because they had been standard equipment when they were first requisitioned as salute guns. Every morning and evening, weather permitting, there was a formal ceremony to show or strike colors. When the band played the national anthem, people in the yard stopped their cars, got out, and stood with hat in hand.

To be sure, a good deal of heavy industry took place there. They built ships. They also re-fit and repaired ships from throughout the fleet. There were construction shops in the yard where every shipbuilder's specialty was practiced with distinction. Engineers worked on plans and modifications for the largest as well as the most minute of ship's details. Boilermakers installed and repaired the power plants that drove modern fighting ships. Riggers lifted heavy equipment on and off the vessels under repair. Painters used the newest techniques of sandblasting to clean hull plates to bright metal and then airless spray painting to coat them with protection against the harshest elements on Earth, those at sea.

Even though all this was in progress around the clock, the base had the clean, crisp look of an orderly military installation. The shop buildings were built almost completely of New Hampshire granite, and all sported slate roofs. While this made additions and modifications difficult, it gave the yard an air of timeless stature. Pier One, directly abreast of the main gate, was too short and too far up the channel to have the draft needed for modern ships. Its granite pier house had long since been converted into an officer's mess and commissary. In the 1920s, the admiral who commanded the First Naval District wanted to have an appropriate place to display his flag. So he had an old wooden warship that was still at the yard moved over to Pier One, and he asked that it be spruced up. Thus, the *USS Constitution* had been rescued from the sea worms to stand as a tangible monument to the nautical traditions that could be felt everywhere in the shipyard.

As Leo drove through the main gate that first time, he noticed the dark blue flag bordered in gold fringe and bearing two white stars. It flew just below the national ensign atop Old Ironsides's mizzenmast. He wondered briefly what it meant.

Building 11 was a long, narrow, two-story building that ran parallel to A Street. Its granite block construction seemed powerful if only because of the mass involved. The blocks themselves had been worked by stonecutters more than one hundred years before, and each had a smooth, finished band of precise dimension bounding the rough stone of its bulk. The blocks were four feet long and perhaps a foot and a half in height. They mated perfectly to those on all sides. Lead plates between them were masked by the grout work in the seams. Leo entered through an arch at the center of the long wall fronting the street. The archway had clearly been sized for the narrow wagons of a different age. There was a wooden staircase leading up to the laboratory space, but beside it, thick hemp rope hung from shiv blocks and tackle leading to a trap door above. Large objects came in and out routinely. All in all, Building 11, like all of its counterparts in the yard, had been built with an attention to aesthetics that gave it a strange sense of industrial grace. All this further fed the feeling that the shipyard was a place of stature.

At the top of the stairs, he came to a glass receptionist's window. A young woman sat behind it, palpating a typewriter with great determination. When he tapped on the glass, she stopped with some apparent relief. She took a standing wooden block away from the inside of the window's voice hole and leaned toward the opening just a little as she spoke.

"Good afternoon, sir. May I help you?" she asked.

"How do you do?" he replied. "I'm Leo Zaccaria. I believe I have an appointment with Mr. Hemmings."

He was ushered into a laboratory space that looked remarkably like that of the arsenal. This time, they moved to the right from the center entrance. The tables and gas jets were the same. At first, he thought that the room wasn't quite as long. As it turned out, the space had been broken up with partitions paneled in dark tongue-in-groove pine. At these partitions were the sinks and hoods and electrical outlets. The windows were smaller, inset into granite archways in the outer walls. They were of clear glass, though, and hung with venetian blinds through which there was a view of the harbor behind. As he followed the receptionist through two successive spaces that were laid out about the same, Leo noticed not only manpower but activity. There were lab setups everywhere. Some seemed to be sophisticated collections of glassware apparently intended for delicate or involved wet chemistry. Others seemed as simple as large beakers of water just left to evaporate. In one corner, a massive serpentine forged steel beam rose from a platform of gears and wheels. Hung from it by two thick bolts was a piece of deck plate approximately the size of a sheet of paper. The plate was bolted to a part of the platform at its bottom. As they passed, a technician was winding a screw wheel even tighter to test how much strength was needed to pull the plate apart.

There was a lot going on at the chemical laboratory of the Boston Naval Shipyard.

The receptionist walked him into a narrow anteroom near the end of the building. A secretary was seated there at her desk, and Leo's escort spoke briefly to her.

War Record

"Jean, this is Mr. Zaccaria, to see Mr. Hemmings." After making the statement, the young receptionist gave the secretary a formal, constricted smile lasting about one heartbeat. It was some sort of signal that reaffirmed the hierarchy between them.

The secretary smiled at her new visitor and stood. She was not terribly old but already matronly in both her dress and demeanor. "How do you do, Mr. Zacceria?" she asked pleasantly. "My name is Jean. Mr. Hemmings told me to expect you. Let's go right in." She conducted him to a raised-panel door on the rear wall. It was a lighter color wood and bore the gold lettering "Frederick Hemmings, Chief Chemist."

Once again, the inner sanctum was at the end of the building. On its back wall was a window framed by a double arch in the granite. It gave the room back light as well as a fine view of the end of Building 9 just across the alley. To the left and right of the window were bookshelves. On the left-hand wall, however, was a lab counter with gas jets and a sink. Above it were glass-fronted cabinets holding a variety of items from chemicals in bottles to glassware to what seemed to be large pieces of corroded metal. The lab counter was in inspection order. The large wooden desk, at which Fred Hemmings sat, was strewn with letters, notes, and stacks of files.

He, too, was a man in his sixties. His curly hair was white and, although it covered most of his head, was closely cropped. His white mustache was the foundation block for a small but bulbous nose. He, too, wore rimless glasses and tilted his head down just enough so that he could look at Leo over them. His complexion was roughly the color of coffee with cream. Although his color was more ruddy than red, he bore a remarkable resemblance to Osgood Smythe. Certainly the white dress shirt, bowtie, and lab coat were the result of an identical sense of style. He stood as his guest was ushered in.

"You must be Mr. Zaccaria," he declared in a friendly tone. "Please do come in. Have a seat."

Mark Zaccaria

They shook hands, and he gestured Leo to a bow-back arm-chair that faced the desk.

"I understand you're seeking employment as a staff chemist," he said when they were situated.

"Yes, sir," Leo began. "I've taken the necessary government service tests, and in fact, I've already filed an application with the shipyard personnel office."

"Ah, then you've met Mr. Holloway?" he asked. "Our head of personnel."

"No, sir, I haven't," Leo answered. "When I visited the office, I was given the forms to fill out and told there were no openings at that time. I just left the paperwork with the clerks there. I believe they put it all on file."

"Well, no matter. Let's talk chemistry first."

Hemmings asked how Leo had come to take up chemistry. He wasn't told about the involvement of Miss Emily Derby, but he did hear that it had been a goal since before high school. Leo spoke of his interest in understanding how materials merged and coexisted. He talked about his belief that in chemistry, there was the opportunity to witness some startling advances over the next two or three decades.

The discussion moved on to Leo's training, and he was pleased to learn that Mr. Hemmings knew of Dr. Gerber. As they talked about texts and methods, Hemmings put his guest at ease by comparing them to the ways he had been taught and what had been known in the early 1880s. He'd attended MIT when it was located off Copley Square, on Clarendon Street, in Boston. He made the point that both his school and his chosen field had come a long way since his graduation in 1884.

The chief then changed the subject. He started talking about his project by first taking about the chemistry of seawater. He went on about its solvent abilities and the vast mineral resources it carries with it. He noted the presence of metallic ions in fairly heavy concentrations. Thinking about this point, he seemed to be taken back for a moment.

"Do you know what my first job was after leaving MIT?" he asked. "Of course not," he answered quickly. "I was hired by a wealthy industrialist from Maine to develop and perfect a process for extracting gold from seawater. What do you think of that?"

"Is that possible at any kind of scale?" Leo asked.

"Well, scale is exactly the issue, young man. Since all the metals in seawater are ions in an electrolyte, I was able to plate them out quite easily by electrolysis. Then the problem was separating them and getting enough gold to make the effort worthwhile." He smiled to himself to think back on the project. "I spent two years at Bar Harbor, a beautiful but desolate place, building a full-scale separator. There are approximately one to two grams of gold per every one hundred liters of seawater. Someday, when you wish to overload your cerebellum, we'll try to compute just how many of those hundred-liter units there are per cubic mile of seawater and then how many thousands of cubic miles there are in the world's oceans." Mr. Hemmings chuckled at the thought. "It was the very size of all those numbers that kept my patron interested for as long as he was. To make a long story short," he concluded, "the process worked quite well, but our best estimates of the cost per ounce of fine gold was above two hundred dollars. So since we know the treasury is going to regulate the market price of gold at only thirty-five dolalrs, there's no sense in pursuing it."

From the romantic challenge of turning brine into gold, the talk turned to the problem at hand for the navy department. Mr. Hemmings explained that there had been a recent directive to dramatically extend the amount of time a fighting ship could remain at sea in a battle ready condition. While there were many parts of the problem, the Boston lab had been tasked with that of improving boiler water treatment.

"Any boiler is just a big tea kettle," the chief said. "When you boil off the water to make steam for the engines, you leave behind all those minerals we've been discussing. That means a good deal of calcium, magnesium, and, of course, sodium carbonates concentrated on the watersides of the cooker. When these things fall out, they settle and cut down on heat transfer efficiency by insulating the steel surfaces. Sometimes they can completely clog the pipes."

"The sodium carbonate should be pretty soluble in the incoming water, shouldn't it?" Leo asked.

"Right you are, and there's really only a trace of magnesium carbonate. It's the calcium salts that really gum up the works."

Mr. Hemmings outlined his plan to create a training school to teach ship's firemen to chemically treat their feed water to minimize the problems. At the start, it would take a chemist to make up the course and then to teach it to the men.

He went on to mention such other areas of chem lab interest as cathodic protection for ship hulls, the non-destructive testing of weld joints in steel, and monitoring the formulations of the navy special fuel oil that most ships burned. Each of these was something Leo was at least able to discuss intelligently, although as the interview went on, he felt he had less and less of a grasp of all the job entailed.

"Okay, Leo," Mr. Hemmings said finally, "do me a favor, will you? Take a run over to the personnel office right now and see Mr. Holloway. Just mention that I asked you to see him. Can you do that?"

"Sure," he said without a second thought.

"Good," Hemmings concluded. "It's getting late, and you have one more stop to make this afternoon. Let's plan to talk again next Monday." Without anything more detailed than that arranged, the chief stood up and escorted his young guest out of the office. "Jean," he said to his secretary, "will you take Mr. Zaccaria's telephone number and then show him out? Thank you."

War Record

The personnel office could be reached from outside the main gate. As he drove back out A Street, Leo thought about the intricacies of the chemistry and the position of responsibility he would have if he got this job. He felt the aura of the navy yard all over again as he saw the Constitution riding at her moorings on the incoming tide.

When I talk to this guy again on Monday, he thought, *I'm going to have to really push to get this slot.*

When he walked into personnel, he asked for Holloway by name.

"Come right in, young fellow," said a jovial man in shirtsleeves as he emerged from a back office. He scratched absentmindedly at his bald head as he stood by to let Leo go in first. "I have some papers for you to sign."

Holloway presented him with a form letter offering employment and a paymaster's form. "I haven't had time to have the titles and so forth typed in," he said when they were seated. "We'll just do it in pencil so you can have the carbon copy. The starting pay in your grade is twenty-two fifty per week. I think that's pretty good. I hope you do."

To say the least, Leo was confused.

Fred Hemmings had telephoned personnel as soon as he finished the interview. They did talk again that Monday. It was when Leo reported to work.

Battle Stations

Fred Hemmings was every inch the scientist, so without giving it a second thought, he took a simple, scientific approach to training his new staff chemist. He took the time to show Leo around the laboratory and to explain each of the projects that were underway. Lab books for each were reviewed, and the chemists or lab assistants who were managing them gave Leo a quick summary of the progress.

At the relatively tender age of twenty, Leo was a bit surprised to find that several of the people working in the lab were assistants who worked under the direction of one of the chemists, such as himself. They were civilian workers who had bid for the positions from just about any other shop in the yard. It was inside work in the winter, after all, and Building 11 was a far shorter walk from the streetcar stop at the main gate than the graving docks or ship-fitting piers at the far end of A Street.

Fred's orientation included issuing a number of project assignments to Leo. These were for relatively routine tests or inspections, all of which were replications of previous, well-documented analysis. It also included some of his own insights into the boiler water problems and a discussion of the design and operation of the boilers Leo would be working with.

Destroyers had evolved over the last hundred years of naval operations to be the smallest but the most maneuverable of ocean-going warships. They were initially intended to dart in under the guns of bigger capital ships, as the battleship and heavy cruiser crews still liked to refer to their boats. The Destroyer's job had first been to deliver an offensive blow against its bulky targets in the form of torpedoes. That was a bit like taking a bishop off the chess board with a pawn, and if an outright trade was necessary, the Destroyer's side made out better in the transaction cost wise.

During the Great War of 1914-1918, a critical defensive role had developed for these agile hunting cats of the sea. Submarines had nearly succeeded in blocking all supplies to the island nation of the United Kingdom in the early part of that conflict. At first, freighters traveled alone in hopes of avoiding detection and were easy prey for even the rudimentary subs of that time. Once convoys were formed to protect merchant ships in huge groups, it was natural that Destroyers should roam their perimeters as the first and most potent line of defense for the whole mile-long phalanx.

By the end of the Great War, naval visionaries had also begun to see the potential role of the airplane in operations against their capital ships. This suggested an anti-aircraft responsibility that lay ahead for Destroyers as well.

Because they were the smallest ships in the fleet, Destroyers were subject to the greatest amount of damage from waves and weather while simply steaming in the open ocean. Because their maneuverability and swiftness were their greatest assets in combat, these little ships of the line were often operated at flank speeds of more than thirty knots. That was something analogous to driving Leo's '36 Ford in excess of one hundred miles per hour on the roads of that day. It could be done, but it was by no means routine or even safe.

Both of these factors made for more wear and tear on a Destroyer's power plant than there would be on those of any other type of fighting ship. The basic design of that power plant, as Fred Hemmings explained it to Leo, made it known as the marine D-type boiler. These steam machines featured a big manifold on the top and bottom. They were parallel pieces of large diameter pipe, actually, that were closed at each end. Between them ran as many tubes as could be efficiently fit. The tubes interconnected the two drums. They were seamless steel pipes perhaps one inch in diameter. In place, they bloomed up from the bottom manifold and cascaded down from the top one to form a tube sheet at both the fore and aft ends of the device.

From the side, you could see that one set of tubes was longer than the other. For that to work, the longer set had to bow out and take a bend to come back whereas the other set was more or less straight. This gave the basic design the look of the letter *D*, for which it was named. Power plants of this type were always constructed in place as the ship was being built.

This whole piping set was encased in a covering of brick and steel, which formed the boiler's firebox. Flames from the high-pressure oil burners would blast across the tubes. The piping array was kept about half full of feed water. When it was generated, steam would rise to the top and pressurize the system while precipitates, minerals, and organic material would fall to the bottom. Thus, the top manifold was called the steam drum while its counterpart on the bottom was known as the mud drum. The general class of boiler was said to be a water tube type because the water was inside the tubes. Smaller vessels using package boilers that were installed ready to go used fire tube boilers, carrying the hot gasses through the center of the kettle and out to the stack.

"Here are some samples I've collected for you," Hemmings said. "These will give you an idea of the problems Destroyer men are up against at sea."

He took a wooden milk crate from behind an empty lab table. The crate seemed heavy as the chemist lifted it. It was sturdy, though, and its smooth, cut-out handles made it manageable. Almost everything in the lab was inscribed "Property of US Government," including the pens and pencils. The lettering burned into the panels of the crate said, "Return to Whiting Milk

Company." It was comforting to Leo to see that at least some of the shortcomings of the real world had found their way into the yard. It made him more confident that he could measure up.

The crate contained a collection of pieces of boiler tubing that had been cut with a hack saw to lengths a little under a foot each. Fred picked one up and looked through it like a spyglass.

"Take a look at this one," he said, handing it over. "You can see that the scale is beginning to build up."

Leo took the piece and looked inside it. A bright orange scale was caked to the inner surfaces. He was able to pick out a plate of it the size of a half-dollar coin. Putting the tube down, he inspected the piece of scale. It was brittle and broke with an audible click along a jagged line when he bent it.

"It's tempting to just call this rust," the young man said, thinking out loud. "And it probably does get its color from iron oxide, but the color masks another substance, a carbonate you say?"

"Almost certainly," Hemmings replied. "Think about the insulating qualities of this kind of build-up on the inner walls of the tubes and what that does to efficiency." He was rummaging around in the crate for a second tag piece. His face brightened as he brought out the one he was looking for. He was animated as he spoke, he but he looked and gestured only at the sample, not at his new colleague.

"Here's a good example of the very worst that can happen."

He handed it across. This piece of tube was at least twice as heavy as the other. The inch or inch and one quarter inside diameter was filled with a yellowish solid such that the opening at the center of the tube was about the size of a pencil.

Leo first took a coin from his pocket and tried to chip off some of the material. The coin was useless, so he took out a small pocketknife. Even with this, it was difficult to break away any of the eggnog-colored mass. Its crystalline structure was visible though when it was scraped with the knife.

"You can imagine how much extra oil it would take to put enough heat through this little darlin' to get any steam," Fred went on. "And even if you did, there isn't enough room left for water to give you more than a bucketful of steam anyway. But that's not the worst part. Boilers fire an atomized combination of oil and air under pressure. The flame can get over eighteen hundred degrees Fahrenheit as it comes out of the nozzles. Steel has a melting point a bit higher than that, depending on the alloy, but those temperatures can still make it cherry red and subject to distortion. Why do you think the whole boiler doesn't melt the very first time they fire it up?"

Leo was at a loss. He hadn't put that set of facts together for consideration at the same time before. Why didn't it melt?

"I'll tell you," the chief chemist said as soon as he saw the question in the novice's eyes. "It's because of the water inside the tubes. Before you can melt the steel, you have to heat all the steam up to that temperature or at least drive it all off. Naturally, the operators are cagey enough to keep feeding in new water, so they cool down the tubes and use the fire's heat to make steam rather than to melt tubes. When this kind of insulation builds up, however, the tube develops a hot spot. Look closely and you can see that the outside of that piece has begun to drool just a bit."

Sure enough, there were slight ripples in the outside skin of the sample tube.

"Before long," Fred concluded, "this tube would have gotten hot enough to melt right through, and then you'd have a leak in the system as well as a kettle that wasn't using all its design surface area to make steam."

"The heat on this one must have been tremendous," Leo observed, picking again at the deposit. "That must be why the deposit has so much cohesive strength."

"The heat didn't help any, but this is calcium carbonate, and it's naturally the most difficult of boiler water residues to do anything about."

War Record

They spent a little time discussing the composition of the feed water used at sea. Steam-powered evaporators that boiled ocean water and condensed the vapors produced it. The resulting fresh water was used both for drinking and firing the boilers.

Then they talked about the different methods of chemical intervention they could use to keep the carbonates from setting on the insides of the tubes. They had to pick one that would work at least reasonably well but which wouldn't use exotic or unstable chemicals and which could be administered by the seamen who manned the boiler plants.

Since he was allowed to do a great deal of the work, Leo did just that. He took the lead in making estimates of the time it would take and the costs for special materials and equipment. He was pleased to see Fred Hemmings nod studiously when his first choice was explained. The plan was to suspend the carbonates so they would not fall out of the water. It involved adding a combination of chemical salts to the feed water to approximately 1 percent by weight of the total. But neither the volume of chemicals that would have to be carried at sea, nor the method of introducing it would pose any but the most minor problems.

"There will have to be fairly careful monitoring to be sure that the levels of these salts are constant," Leo said. "We might have to have some sort of training program at first to test the crews' ability to comply with the regimen."

Fred agreed. "We'll also have to monitor the operation of a couple actual boilers to verify that our treatment program really, really does some good," he added, making a point that Leo hadn't thought about up to that point.

By the end of his first week at the lab, Leo had sketched out a workable plan for the process. His boss looked the proposal over and said that it was time for his new chemist to go aboard ship and start to figure out how his plan would work in a real boiler room.

"I'll make arrangements for you to go aboard one of the Destroyers we have in overhaul at the moment," the older chemist said to the report he was reading. "You'd better get a look at where this work is really going to be performed and who is really going to do it for you."

Leo had his project.

When the whistle blew that afternoon, several of Leo's colleagues from the lab invited him to "stop off for a few" before heading home. He thanked them but declined the offer; he had a date that night and hoped they would understand. They winked at each other and said that there would be another Friday night, perhaps even next week.

I'll have to go with them at least once or twice, Leo thought. *It looks like it's expected if I'm going to play on this team.* For the time being, he had offered the one excuse that would be considered acceptable for not joining them. Even that one wouldn't work forever though.

———————————

Her name was Ellen, and she came from Belmont, a tiny community of gentry farmers northwest of Cambridge. The town lay along the newly rebuilt and resurfaced Route 2. They had met at a dance held at the Commander Hotel just outside of Harvard Square. She'd been there in search of college men. That was fine; Leo was a college man, and he had a car.

In fact, she had a car. She also had a horse. It was boarded in the barn out behind the family home.

"Oh, it's just another house in Belmont," she'd told him

When he saw it he made the silent comment to himself that it wouldn't have been "just another house" in Eastie.

She had been two years to Simmons College in the city. Now she was "looking for something acceptable." Did that mean work?

War Record

It really didn't matter what that meant. She was blonde and beautiful. She was sure of herself, and when she spoke to you, her blue eyes bored in on yours like searchlights. She was adventurous without being foolhardy. She was energetic, so she was accomplished. Her father was well enough to-do that one of his hobbies was indulging his only daughter. Ellen was used to being permitted to act on her impulses.

On top of all that, she filled out a sweater like Lana Turner in *Johnny Eager* and had a set of legs that reminded him of Marlene Dietrich in *Manpower*.

If she was "looking for something acceptable," Leo hoped he was it.

That night, they drove even farther out to the Concord Inn. It was a celebration of his new position. They had dinner and then danced to a six-piece band. He was animated as he explained his new job. He sounded authoritative as he interpreted the design of steam boilers on fighting ships. He'd studied all the diagrams, after all. About the time he was describing colloid chemistry and how it might help with the process of improved water treatment, Leo noticed a smirk on Ellen's face. She was listening and she was watching him closely, but she was bemused.

"Ah. I take it my explanation has gotten a bit overboard?" he asked.

She reached across the table took his hand, her arms outstretched. "I love to see you so interested," she said. "It sounds important, and you sound excited about being involved. What could be better at the start of a new job? Daddy was in the navy," she went on. "Why don't you come around tomorrow afternoon? We can exercise Montie, and you and Daddy can swap sea stories. What do you say?"

What would anyone say?

As they danced, they showed each other off to the crowd. They joked about "Don Winslow of the Navy," a serial from Universal that preceded action pictures. Leo began to realize it would always be impossible to really explain his work and what went on inside him when he did it, even to a girl like Ellen.

Over coffee the next morning in his mother's kitchen, Leo talked about his new job with his father. Antonio Zaccaria had gone in early to help with a special order. Since it was Saturday and he only worked a half day, he was home by 11:00 a.m. and could sit with his oldest son. Over the years at the dairy, he had taken a simple skill that everyone from the ranch life of his youth possessed and turned it into a master craft. He was a cheese maker. As a boy, he'd made cheese in a pottery bowl. Now he supervised five helpers as they made a thousand pounds at a time in porcelain-lined steel vats. Pumps, piping, valves, and especially steam were matters he dealt with every day.

As Leo spoke, he became animated again regarding both the chemistry and the functional steps he was trying to devise to treat boiler water at sea. His father sensed how serious he was about it all. The discussion of chemistry might as well have been conducted in Greek as English for all he really understood of it. When it came the steps the boiler men would have to take to do what his son asked, however, he followed intently.

"These guys got a plenty to do," he advised. "You need a be sure you don't ask for somethin' at's too hard or a too deligade."

His version of the word *delicate* was pronounced with feeling and three equally stressed syllables: "del-ah-gahd."

"Sure, Pop," Leo answered respectfully but without really understanding. "The crews in the boiler rooms of these ships drill all the time, and they do everything according to some military procedure. All I want is to have them make up a mixture in water and add it their feed once every hour."

"Okay, kiddo. Okay," the father replied, not wanting to dull his son's enthusiasm. "Do me a favor though, hah? Go look at a what they do before you tell 'em what they oughtta do. Okay?"

War Record

"Sure, Pop." Leo was a little surprised by the suggestion. Of course he was going to visit a ship before finishing the project.

His Father nodded. He knew his son would go to a boiler room. He hoped that when he did, he would see what was there.

Maria Zaccaria moved quietly around the periphery of the kitchen. She was cleaning up after breakfast and beginning to get ready for dinner. She was pleased that her husband and her son were entertaining themselves with man talk around her table. It was good that the kitchen was still the center of the family.

Shortly after noon, Leo was ready to leave again for Belmont. Ellen had said there would be a picnic, so he didn't have too much with his family. He dressed up just a little to try to fit in. He wore a collared shirt, open at the neck, and a blue suit coat as a blazer. On the drive out Route 2, he felt like an aristocrat.

When he arrived, Ellen's father answered the door. He, too, wore a blue blazer. His had brass buttons, though, and some sort of badge embroidered on the breast pocket. In his open collar, there was an English cravat bunched up at his throat.

Even so, Leo thought, *for a kid from Eastie, my shot landed pretty close to the mark.*

"Ah. You must be Leo," he said, offering his hand and a hardy welcome.

Ellen's father was thin, and his face was weather-beaten. His graying hair was swept back and parted jauntily, but it was his erect posture that most communicated his warmth, his energy, and his authority.

"I'm Jack Hurley."

"How do you do, sir? It's a pleasure to meet you."

They shook firmly.

"Ellen is out back, putting Montie through his paces," he said, showing the young man in. "Let's go out and join them."

The house was of wood frame with cedar shingles painted gray surrounding bright white window and lintel trim. It was a big house, though, and even with this standard construction combination, it didn't look ordinary at all. The front door was a massive raised-panel oak portal hung on bulky brass hinges. Over the doorway was a fan-shaped transom with clear window-panes that were roughly triangular, their apexes coming together at the middle of the bottom. In the door's main center timber, between the two upper panels, there was a carving of a pineapple. The door was a caramel color perhaps from age but more likely from numerous liberal doses of varnish.

The foyer was easily larger than Leo's parent's sitting room. It ended at the foot of a broad center stairwell that split at the first landing so that the climb to the mezzanine could be finished in either direction. Overhead, there was a huge electrified chandelier. Leo thought of the front entrance of the main branch of the Boston Public Library, except in brown wood rather than white marble.

To the left and right of the front part of the foyer were a formal dining room and a parlor. If you moved around the foot of the staircase to the right, there was the door to Mr. Hurley's study. They went around to the left and past a door to the kitchen. They went past a back stairway and out through a dark, paneled hallway to a rear door. Leo must have been craning his neck to take it all in.

"Do you like the house?" Jack asked conversationally. "Stanford White designed it. My grandfather originally had it built as a wedding present for my parents. I've never really lived anywhere else."

Nice dowry tradition in this family, Leo thought.

Outside the rear of the house, they crunched across a gravel yard where Ellen's car and two others were parked. At the rear of this parking area stood a tall old barn. It was large but much more the work building than was the house. The barn was gray, too, but

War Record

the color was natural to the weathered broad pine planks standing vertically as its outer skin. Trim boards were painted white. There were wide double doors that swung open. Today, they were latched back, revealing a broad oak floor down the center of the building and another door, open, at the far end.

"These days, we mostly use the barn for cars," Jack went on as they mounted the short ramp up to the open front doors. "Ellen is intent on keeping me a gentleman farmer, however, so we have to maintain a place for Montie in the back and keep some hay and grain for him in the loft."

Once inside, the planked floor and the empty expanse of the closed-in space amplified their footsteps. The barn was dark, and there were just enough farm and feed smells in it to make a pleasing counterpoint to what passed for normal in a society edging away from the land. The two men walked purposefully, and they sounded like a squad of troops as they marched in step.

The barn had clearly been originally built for draft animals. By now, the carriage spaces had all been cleared out for automobiles, and most of the horse stalls had fallen to use for equipment storage. At the far end, there were two closed and probably heated stalls that faced each other across the center aisle.

As they walked out the open rear door of the barn, Leo noticed that it was a more traditional wooden slider hung on cast iron wheels and a track of iron band. Once they were back in the sunshine, there was the muffled sound of hoof beats on the early autumn breeze. Ellen was cantering her chestnut stallion around a paddock that was bounded by a white post and rail fence.

"Ah. There she is now," Jack said.

The small note of admiration in his voice was natural for a father. Even so, he'd understated the obvious. There she was indeed.

She wore brown leather riding boots over tan jodhpurs. Her cashmere turtleneck sweater was almost the same dark Earth tone as the horse's body. Montie's muscles rippled and his breath heaved as he floated around the perimeter of the fence. Her tight trousers and loose, flowing sweater gave a pleasing suggestion of her taut form. The appearance of floating came as much as anything from the union of horse and rider. Ellen moved up and down with her mount in what looked like complete harmony. The only indication that they were changing vertical direction came from their hair. She did without her black riding helmet, so her golden hair flowed back in the breeze and bounced with the horse's gait. At the same time, Montie's mane and tail trailed back from his forward motion and jounced in parallel with his rider's tresses.

As she rode, Ellen leaned forward, holding her wrists together above the saddle's pommel in perfect English form. When she came around and passed the approaching gentlemen, though, she smiled at them and waved with one hand. All in all, it was an image that deserved a sonnet, and Leo was sorry he couldn't freeze it in time by commemorating it in verse.

The two men leaned on the top of the paddock fence, and each rested one foot on the bottom rail. They spoke congenially but without looking at each other. There was only one thing to watch just then.

"Ellen tells me you've entered government service," the elder began. His tone of voice gave the term *government service* a sound of importance that Leo hadn't thought it deserved until that moment.

"Yes, sir," he answered. "I've just started at the Boston Naval Shipyard as a staff chemist."

"Sounds commendable," Jack replied. "What sorts of projects will you be working on for the navy?"

"There are lots of routine tests and evaluations, of course, but my main project will be to develop a workable method for treating boiler feed water on Destroyers."

War Record

"Really?" the older man asked with interest. "As Ellen might have mentioned, I sailed on a four-piper myself during the last war."

There was a pause as Leo thought about two things. He hadn't heard the term *four-piper*, but he was stopped more by Jack's tone of voice. He said "the last war" not as if it were the final one but rather as if it were just the most recent. That brought Dr. Gerber to mind.

Perhaps only one beat late, Leo replied, "A four-piper?"

The older man smiled. He understood the question and set about answering it at once.

"Back then," he said, leaning on the age issue just a bit heavily, "the standard design for a naval Destroyer featured a smokestack for each of the four boilers. This gave the ships a distinctive silhouette with the four thin stacks, or pipes, jutting up above the superstructure. Today, as I understand it, the boiler exhausts are paired, so the average tin can has only two stacks. Since both of these are larger in diameter, it makes the ship's proportions look more like those of a Cruiser, only smaller. I'm not sure which ship is more insulted by that," the old Destroyer man concluded. "But there you have it. From a distance, the enemy has to look twice to be sure which type of vessel is steaming in on it. Also," he continued, "the term *tin can* refers to a Destroyer because of its small size and relative lack of armor. The ships have thin skins like tin cans. By the way, do you have any ideas on why the navy is suddenly interested in feed water for Destroyers?"

"I only know what I've been told by my boss, sir," Leo answered.

His eyes were still riveted on Ellen and Montie. Even though he paused each time the two of them thundered by, he was warming quickly to her father, and his mind was fully involved with the conversation.

"There's been a directive from the navy building to take steps to increase the average time a Destroyer can stay at sea and stay battle ready. Yards all over the country have been given specific tasks to help with this. Mare Island in California has the job of making improvements in hull painting so it can be done less often and attract less sea growth for the duration. I believe Baltimore's engineers are looking at hull structure and equipment mounts trying to improve durability under stress. There are several other projects. Boston got the one for feed water, and I was hired to do most of the basic work."

Ellen's father nodded. He, too, was looking at the poetry in motion of horse and rider. Like Leo, though, his mind was elsewhere. He understood everything the young man had described, but unlike him, he knew what it all meant. He was grave for a moment or two but then put it out of his mind. He stood up straight and pushed back a bit from the fence.

"Young man," he said, "may I offer for inspection the sixteen-cylinder engine of my new Lincoln over here."

Leo joined his host as they walked back through the barn to the 1939 Lincoln Zephyr parked next to Ellen's Packard. The car was a little larger than Leo's Ford, and its proportions were different because of a slightly elongated hood. This one had a soft top, however, and since it was down, the car appeared to be very long and very low.

As her father opened one side of the engine bonnet, Ellen could be heard slowing her mount to a walk to begin cooling the big horse down.

Jack and Leo were intent on their inspection of the machinery by the time she climbed down and began to loosen Montie's tack. The car, after all, had a straight block engine with a single giant distributor cap sprouting wires all along its nearly five-foot length. It did feature two oversized carburetors spaced out along an intake manifold that looked a picket fence. Jack explained some of the engine's intricacies with obvious pride as ambling hoof beats resonated on the oak floor inside the barn.

"The carbs look so big because each has two barrels. It's like having four carburetors overall," he pointed out.

War Record

Inside the barn, Ellen was stowing her gear and wiping Montie down after his workout.

"That's the reason that, big as she is, she can really get up and go when you step on it. You can see that the manifolds each have *sixteen* branches," he continued. "It's a wonder that any fuel gets to the far ends."

The two men in blue blazers were bent over the elongated engine as Ellen walked up between them. She stretched her arms wide, putting one hand on the outside shoulder of each, perhaps not knowing or caring at first which was which.

"Now I'm jealous," she said with mock seriousness. "Imagine being forsaken for a greasy valve cover!" Her father smiled and stood up from his inspection only very slowly.

"My dear girl," he said, just as theatrically stern. "It seemed the only way to get you to pay any attention to us. And by the way," he demanded, "where do you see grease on this exemplary piece of machinery?"

Jack closed up the bonnet, and the three of them moved to the rear of the car. Ellen chatted with them both and was pleased to see they were getting on well. Her father opened the boot of the fashionably hunchbacked Lincoln. Inside it, there was a small leather carrying case strapped in a standing position beside the wheel well. He unstowed and opened it to reveal a bottle of scotch whiskey, a soda siphon, and a nested stack of sterling silver tumblers.

"Care for a bracer?" he asked.

"Just ever so small a splash for me, Daddy," Ellen said. "What I need right now is the water, not the whiskey." Her father poured her barely enough scotch to tint the soda.

"And what about you, lad?" he asked Leo, not waiting for an answer before making them each a drink. "We'll have to take it English style I'm afraid. It's tough to store ice in the car this time of year."

Did that mean he managed it in winter?

Ordinarily, Leo stayed away from scotch. Perhaps medicine had to taste bad to be good, but surely not cocktails. This moment was anything but ordinary, however.

Was it the silver tumbler or the freshly siphoned soda that made this drink taste so good? Maybe it was the expertly balanced mixture, surely a skill born of practice. More likely, it was the rarefied atmosphere of an opulent home, a civilized discussion, and a gorgeous young woman on horseback. Were any of his friends from East Boston spending this Saturday afternoon in a similar fashion? Leo was in his very own movie.

Whatever it was, this scotch and soda had a pleasing flavor of bog peat and wood smoke straight from the misty Highlands. Its Earth taste fulminated as the husky liquid bubbled on his tongue. Before long, it began to warm him from the inside out. He stood there at the long car, dwarfed by the house and barn, ringed by tall oak trees just starting to go orange and red in the yellow sunshine. He felt that the drink was the perfect mark of punctuation for such a moment.

On Monday morning, when he got to work, Leo was immediately asked a leading question about how the weekend had been. What could he tell them? He couldn't possibly explain anything about his time with Ellen or his feelings for her and still remain a gentleman. How could he express the towering heights of self-satisfaction he felt at having been able to move smoothly through her world? Already, he was too much the scientist to realize that they didn't actually want a play-by-play rebroadcast. His colleagues only wanted him to make any general statement that would validate the opinions they already held.

"It was great!" he said, taken back to it for a moment by his thoughts. "Just great. What else can I say?" At first, he was a little embarrassed that he was simply unable to elaborate.

War Record

"You don't have to say a thing," Arnie Cohen told him with a knowing smile.

Arnie was a chemist who had been at the lab for eight or ten years. He shared a leering grin with the three or four other lab people gathered around for the fun. They all winked and nodded at one another.

They wanted to live vicariously through their new single-combat champion of bachelorhood, so they did. Each one scripted Leo's weekend differently in his own mind, depending on the author's own feelings. They all imagined that their fantasies were much better than anything that could have actually happened. Only Leo knew differently.

When Fred Hemmings came in, he spent ten or fifteen minutes in his office and then asked Leo to step in.

"I hope you had a restful weekend, young man," he began. "I've just arranged for you to start some real work. As soon as you get the chance, I'd like you to go down to Dry Dock Two and go aboard the *USS Monaghan* for a tour of her machinery spaces. You can't miss it. The number three fifty-four is painted prominently at its bow. Have you ever been on a military ship before?"

Leo shook his head. "I'm sure I can manage it," he said.

Fred explained that all he had to do was go up the main gangway and speak to the boatswain's mate, who would be standing guard. "Tell him you have an appointment with Lieutenant Commander Dobbins, the executive officer. I've spoken to him, and he will introduce you to his engineering staff. By the way, military have to salute the ship's flag, salute the guard, and then ask for permission to board. In the yard, civilians aren't held to that protocol, but it wouldn't hurt to just look in the direction of the flag for a moment and then nod to the sailor on guard and ask rather than tell him that you want to see the XO."

"Oh. No problem at all," Leo said. "But, uh…where will the flag be on this ship?"

"Good question," Fred answered with a smile. "You probably know that the rear end of any ship is called the stern. The very end of the main outside deck is known as the fantail, and in the middle of it, there should be a short flagstaff with the national ensign and a small commission pennant on display. Sometimes while a ship is in repair, the staff is taken down. Just do a little genuflect toward the blunt end of the boat and you'll look like you know what you're doing."

Leo smiled at the joke but understood what he had to do to get along.

His boss got serious as he continued. "Mr. Dobbins has agreed to let you inspect his boiler rooms. He will provide you with an escort who can explain everything to you and help you get your bearings prior to developing your training plan and the technical orders for how to treat boiler water. Today, you're just there to observe and learn." Fred lifted one eyebrow and looked directly at his young charge.

Leo nodded his understanding.

"Good," Hemmings concluded. "Just one last thing. As a navy employee, you are authorized to use the base clothing store. It's over on C Street in Building 37. If you decide to spend some time below decks on the *Monaghan*, you can find the right work clothes there at the right price."

Fred explained that the *Monaghan* was sitting alone in Dry Dock Two, so it would be no trouble to find. Across the pier from it was Dry Dock One. This was the yard's shipbuilding basin. It was a good deal wider, although not any longer than number two. Even so, it usually held several small ships at a time. Within the hour, Leo was off to find his Destroyer.

The orderly stature of the administrative areas of the Boston Naval Shipyard broke down somewhat when it came to the real working areas. Dry Dock Two was a graving dock. That is to say

War Record

that it was built right into the floor of the harbor like a giant sunken bathtub. When the water was pumped out of the closed dock, it created a hollow below sea level that was more than large enough to take a Destroyer.

At the ocean end, dock two had a movable cofferdam, or gate, to close it off from the bay. This large barricade was a small boat in its own right. It would be filled with water and sunk into its socket in order to close off the dry dock for pumping. When the dock was empty, the intricate pattern of its granite block construction could be seen on its long, flat floor, but not for long.

The dock was pumped only so that the great, wood-topped concrete blocks that formed the ship's cradle could be rearranged for the next occupant. The dock crews wasted no time in bringing up a crane to change the pattern as soon the water was gone. Each ship had a docking plan that specified the exact locations of hard points in the hull that could stand the strain of keeping the ship upright when it was high and dry. The blocks were moved to precise positions on a grid of the dock floor. Then the wood butchers came in to add or subtract timbers on the blocks and then chop out the resulting wooden pads so that each one closely matched the curve of the underwater body at its point of contact.

When this was done, the dock was flooded again and the cofferdam pumped and floated out of the way. Then the ship was brought up by tugs. Lines from many points along both sides of its weather deck were passed to corresponding capstans on the gunwales of the dock. That's when the real fun began. The dockmaster was always a savvy old shipbuilder with ice water in his veins. He would stand on a platform at the fore end of the dock and direct the slow movement of the ship into position directly over the blocks.

For docking, a ship would raise a special staff directly vertical from its bow. The dockmaster used this to sight the vessel onto the centerline of the now-submerged block pattern. From his perch at the head of the dock, he would signal his crew to use the slow, controllable capstans to draw the ship forward and to adjust it left or right until it was perfectly positioned over the blocks. There were no telephones connecting all the crewmembers to allow the dockmaster to coordinate them. The signals he used ranged from flags to throwaway arm motions to head nods sometimes punctuated with expertly spit tobacco juice. All the while, the ship's master stood on his bridge, wondering if this was the day that some civilian was going to cost him his career.

In fact, there was a good deal more Kentucky windage involved in dry docking a ship than anyone would ever have admitted publicly. The whole process was as much art as science, but people took responsibility for what they were expected to do, and nobody, all the way up to the navy building in Washington, concerned themselves with the ramifications of failure. Rather, they simply scheduled their operations based on the assumption of success.

After the whole ship was in the dock, the cofferdam was towed back into place and the dock's rear door was closed. When the water was pumped out and the ship had settled onto its temporary stand, the shipbuilders started to make connection after connection between the boat and the pier. First came a gangway that would remain at whatever angle it first held since the ship was no longer subject to tidal swells and falls. Shore power, water, and sewerage were attached. After that, there was an endless array of hoses, lines, wires, pipes, and conduits. Each of these carried something either onto or off of the boat to support one or more of the work items being attended to by the yard.

When the repairs began in earnest, the general noise level suddenly came way up. Needle guns driven by compressed air were used to scale off rusty spots in the ship's paint. Arc welders crackled with flickering light that seemed painfully bright even at noon on a sunny day. Rivet guns sounded like jackhammers. Although they were smaller, they drove against the steel skin of the ship, which acted like a sounding board. Engines roared to drive generators and compressors. The deafening hiss of sand-

War Record

blasting would indicate that some surface was being cleaned down to bright metal. Above all these sounds of industry came the intermittent cackle of the ship's loudspeaker as orders and information were passed to the crew. Such orders came only after the signature whistle of the boatswain's pipes became an amplified shriek throughout the ship.

"Now! Second watch fall in at quarters for muster and inspection!"

When Leo rounded the pier house and saw the *Monaghan* for the first time, what he beheld was a fish out of water. With all the cranes and lines and bridges to her, the ship looked like Gulliver held down on the beach by the thousand trusses of the Lilliputians. Not really knowing what to expect, he accepted what he saw as the way things ought to have been.

The day was gray, and so was the ship. The dark water of the inner harbor was placid beyond the dock, but there was the feeling that the *Monaghan* couldn't tell that since it was headed in to the dock and had its stern to the sea. Leo took a walk down the pier before going aboard. He wanted to take all this in and maybe even to understand it. The closer he got to the vessel, the more difficult it was to decipher what was going on. Before he'd made it down the dock quite as far as the fantail, though, help arrived.

"What'cha need, buddy?"

The question came from a beefy middle-aged man in a rumpled suit coat, necktie, and a steel hard hat. He had a cigar butt in his teeth, and his pale cheeks made a striking background for a network of tiny red blood vessels.

"I'm the dock super. Can I help you with somethin'?"

No doubt it was Leo's white shirt and necktie that made the superintendent take the diplomatic route with this intruder.

"Ah. Yes, please." Leo fumbled a little for his words. "My name is Zaccaria. I'm new at the chem lab, and I'm supposed to meet the *Monaghan*'s XO."

"Sullivan," he barked. "Call me Sully or I won't know who you're talkin' about. Pleased to meet'cha." Sully spoke in short bursts, directly to the point. "The gangway's back there. You do have some shipyard experience, don't you?"

Leo didn't like the inference of this last question, especially since it looked like he had to plead guilty. "Well, I did spend some time at Alex Bang's yard." He gestured across the channel. "What I was really hired for was my chemistry though." He was trying to divert his new adversary.

"Cap'n Bang's a good hand," Sully said with an approving grunt. "I take it you don' know anything about ships."

They were nose to nose, and Leo blinked. "I suppose there's always more to learn," he said with a smile.

Without so much as a second breath, Sully smiled too.

"Follow me, kid," he said over one shoulder as he started to walk farther aft on the stone pier between the two docks. "Let me show you a couple things."

Leo followed him. They went down a long, wooden staircase into the bottom of the dock. Once down there, it was curiously silent. The hull of the ship bowed upward and curved away from them, blotting out most of the sky. It seemed smooth and cleanly designed. It also seemed immense. Sitting on its series of docking blocks, the hull's curve made it look like the great weight of the vessel had forced the whole structure to distort and bulge as it sat there.

"See that?" Sully demanded. "Fresh paint on her underside. See where the blocks hold her up? No new paint there. Every ship has at least two docking plans. Where she sits on the blocks only gets paint every other time."

They were walking back toward the after part of the ship. Above them, the two propeller shafts exited the hull and ran along under the fantail. Halfway from the exit point to the giant brass screws, each shaft ran through a bearing that was held by a

War Record

wide brace to the upper part of the hull. Between the shafts and running beyond them was the rudder.

"See those arms? They're called struts. See the part of the hull above the shafts? That's called the counter. Now let's go forward."

Three quarters of the way to the bow, the block pattern seemed to be interrupted. There was a space of perhaps ten or fifteen yards with no blocks at all. The reason was that the ship's hull had a protrusion hanging below it at this point. It looked like a little gray boat hanging down from the bottom of the big one. Sully stooped to duck walk under the bottom of the hull. Leo had a real question about the wisdom of this, but he knew he had to follow. They were stooped under the center of the ship's hull. The *Monaghan* loomed above them, tens of thousands of tons of metal and machinery held three or four feet off the granite bottom of the dock, and they were the meat in the sandwich. It was cool and damp and almost silent beneath the ship. The whole sensation was eerie. He had the strong feeling that he ought not to stay there because the *Monaghan* could settle down on top of him at any moment.

"Here's the keel," Sully barked. "This is a sonar dome." He patted the sharp rear end of the teardrop-shaped housing that hung down from the keel. "It sends out signals to locate subs. But it's almost like a secret weapon, okay? We try not to talk a lot about things like this." As he craned to get a better look at the seam between the hull and the dome, Leo learned why Sully wore a steel hat. When they scuttled back out from under the smooth hull, Leo felt its weight being lifted off his shoulders.

Once they were standing again between the ship and the dock's wall, Sully reached over without asking and inspected Leo's scalp. It was bruised but not bleeding.

"You should get a hard hat," he said matter of factly. "At least wear a cap with some rags in it, will ya?"

They walked all the way to the bow of the ship. Its knifelike point where port and starboard met widened out below the waterline to form a bud or bulb where it met the keel. Just back from this bulb, there was a small oval hole cut in the hull plate. Wires and hoses ran up into the hull through the hole, and light could be seen inside. Sully walked past the opening and stood right at the bow, looking aft. From there, you could see the smooth sweep of the hull and observe the complex curves as it bowed out to a pendulous bulge amidships. Since the hull widened out to fifty or sixty feet of beam at its waist, everything above the dock floor was blocked from view. It was quiet, and they seemed to have the place to themselves.

"This is beautiful," Sully said, almost with emotion. "Take a look. I always come down here when a ship docks. Cans are my favorite."

Leo stepped into position and saw what he meant. People live in a world where the term utilitarian design usually means a box. A ship's hull is designed for the world of fishes, though, where it costs far too much to push a box along. So the shape of the hull was a work of simple function, but just like a shaker chair, it was also a work of art. The finished hull itself became an industrial sculpture. It was unusual, so it was beautiful. Beyond that, Sully felt a sense of ownership since he'd helped build it; if not this one, then others like it.

Leo appreciated being taken into the gruff superintendent's confidence like this. He had a question about the hole in the hull just aft, however.

"Why is the hull cut open like that so far below the water line?" he asked.

Sully shifted gears without even batting an eye.

"Lots of things go in and out through the hull," he said as if nothing had happened. "Weld is stronger than steel. When the cut-out's replaced, it's like it never happened." He walked back to inspect the opening. "The inside of the bow is called the peak. This cut goes into the peak tank," he explained. "The peak takes more stress than any other part. So it's got more structure in it. Take a look," Sully commanded.

Leo stuck his head through the hole very carefully. Inside, there were bars and beams and plates with circular cut-outs in an almost-chaotic profusion. The effect was as if a load of steel parts had been dumped into the wide top of the peak and, being of different sizes and lengths, they had each jammed into random positions and locations all the way down.

"Things are crowded in the peak," Sully allowed. "So it's usually a fuel tank. Especially on small ships like cans."

"Why is this one open?" Leo asked, taking it all in.

"The cleaners were in there, swabbin' it out. Looks like they're settin' up to paint."

Leo didn't believe it. "Men actually went all the way in there?" he asked. "I could never do that."

"O' course they go in," Sully shot back, irritated at being challenged by a college boy who knew nothing about ships. "How else could you get it clean? Never say never, kid. Since nobody likes doin' this job, it pays more than most. You stick with this trade long enough, you'll do a peak tank or two. C'mon. Let's go topside."

As they climbed back up the wide wooden stairs, the noise level began to mount. From the top of the dock, all you could see was a jumble of angular and pointed shapes. The *Monaghan's* superstructure looked like a hodgepodge of boxes, turrets, and towers. It was studded with ladders and cables, and a handful of radio antennas sprouted from its mast and stacks. It all seemed to extend too far up into the air to be stable at sea. For as smooth and clean as the underwater body was, the ship's topside was a frenzy of hard-edged shapes that made a confused counterpoint to the hull's simplicity. But then the topside of a ship lives in a different world than the hull does.

Mark Zaccaria

Sully kept a brisk pace along the dockside to the ship's after gangway. He motioned Leo ahead as they took it up to the main deck. Leo instinctively held on to the smooth rope handrails, moving his arms along them in opposite stride to his legs. The gangway was pitched up just a bit. At the top of the ramp, he stopped just long enough to look aft and then turned and nodded to the sailor standing guard. The man held a clipboard and was wearing a sidearm in a covered leather holster. He stood on the walkway by a small desk that was rigged to the outboard rail just across from an entryway to the gray structure of the upper decks.

"May I...uh...see the exec?" Leo said, confused about whether to be courteous, conversational, or commanding.

Sully was right behind him.

"This man's here to see the XO," the super announced. "He aboard?"

"Yes, sir," the seaman answered. "Check the wardroom. First deck, forward."

"Thanks, Bos'un," Sully said. "Follow me and watch your step, kid." He hunched just slightly and climbed through an oval-shaped door in the steel wall of the superstructure.

The ship had a main fore and aft passageway with ladders leading up or down on either side at regular intervals. They entered at the main mess area and then went forward through the chief's quarters and all the way up to officer's country and the ward room. By then, Leo was completely lost. He hadn't really watched where he was going. Rather, he'd paid particular attention to the problems of stepping over hoses and watertight thresholds on the deck and ducking under the cables and ropes that festooned the overhead. All the while, the aroma of dust, diesel, paint, and new rubber replaced the salty smell of the sea air outside. Everywhere you looked, there were people at work on something or other.

The door to the ward room looked like a real door made out of polished metal. There was a small brass plaque on it that identified it. Sully knocked twice and was greeted with an abrupt reply.

"Come!"

He opened the door and revealed a rather small room roughly in a *T* shape with a metal table occupying the long leg. There were several naval officers sitting on the built-in bench that surrounded the table. They were working on various pieces of paperwork either alone or with one of the two yard workers who were there carrying blueprints. Sully walked in with Leo in trail.

"Mr. Dobbins," Sully said directly to one of the officers, "this guy's from the chem lab. Says he has an appointment with you."

The lieutenant commander put down his clipboard and rose from his seat at the forward end of the table. "Thanks, Sully," he said. "I've been expecting him." He extended a hand to Leo and they shook.

"Leo Zaccaria."

"How do you do, Mr. Zaccaria?" Dobbins asked, getting the pronunciation right the first time. "I understand you're working on water treatment procedures for our boilers."

"Yes, sir," Leo answered. "I know enough about the chemistry to understand what will work in the laboratory. Now I'd like to learn a little bit about where this chemistry will really have to be done so I can figure out what will be practical as well as effective."

As he spoke, an older officer at the rear of the table began to take notice. When Leo finished, the other officer spoke.

"Is this the gentleman working on boiler reliability, Bart?" he asked.

"Yes, sir," Dobbins replied. "Mr. Zaccaria, this is Captain Baker, the *Monaghan*'s skipper."

Leo nodded in the captain's direction.

"Mr. Zaccaria," the skipper continued, "this is an important project for us. If there's anything we can do to help it along, just say the word." He looked at the XO. "I assume Smitty is aware that this gentleman is coming aboard?"

"Yes, sir," Mr. Dobbins answered. "Was just about to call him."

The captain nodded once and went back to the report he had been reading. The XO spoke to a steward who was manning a coffee pot at the rear of the room, beside the door. Leo didn't see a telephone, and Dobbins was returning to his seat. Leo wondered what the next step was, but he didn't wonder too long. The speaker system hissed to life, and the static reproduction of the boatswain's whistle made Leo jump.

"Now. Mr. Smith to the wardroom. Engineering officer to the ward room."

In ten minutes' time, Leo was following the engineering officer below to the forward fire room. Smith was a lanky Midwesterner, five or six years out of the naval academy. He seemed too tall for the cramped spaces of the Destroyer's lower decks, but he seemed to slouch naturally and glide over or around all obstacles as they made their way through the machinery spaces.

Finally, he looked over his shoulder and said, "Here it is."

They were facing an oval hatchway. It was closed, and two of the upper latches were dogged down. Smith threw the levers up and pulled the watertight hatch open. Leo closed the hatch behind him and followed his guide down a steep ladder perhaps twenty or twenty-five feet to what passed for the floor of the boiler room.

That floor was actually a series of steel grates. They were made of parallel and perpendicular bands stood on their sides to create little box shapes perhaps one inch square each. These were cut to fit into frames made of inverted *T* bar. Beneath the honeycombed deck plates, the piping and curved hull of the bilges could be seen. The deck plates were narrow, though, because everywhere you moved, there was piping and machinery. The overhead was low, and Leo felt the need to stoop just a little even though he probably wasn't too tall for the walkways.

War Record

Mr. Smith's lanky form seemed to make *S* shapes in both directions as he slithered around the levers, gauges, and valve stems that crowded the eye levels of the space. The steady noise was intense in the boiler room, just as it was in the rest of the ship. There was banging and scraping going on at all quarters. Suddenly, though, a screeching noise escalated to a really painful volume and pitch in an instant and then stopped just as abruptly. Instinctively, Leo hunched farther and looked to his right. The engineering officer didn't seem fazed at all by it, however. He simply swung around the edge of a silver-painted structure near the floor by holding a black vertical pipe to help him pivot. He held the pipe and used it for support as he squatted down to peer into a floor-level opening in the casing.

The metal grating screech flared again just as loudly and quickly as before. The noise seemed to be coming from the oval steel opening. Mr. Smith hefted a ball peen hammer that was lying on the deck grate and banged three times on the opening. Hoses leading into the man way started to rustle a little, and then a sailor's rust-stained face poked out of the hole. The man in the boiler was wearing a traditional American sailor's cap, but it had been navy blue before its exposure to the rust. He winked his eyes to clear them. Then, seeing the officer, he nodded once and began extracting himself from the bowels of the machine.

By the time he stood and brushed himself off, Leo had been backed into some of the adjoining structure, just to make enough space. Mr. Smith held on to the overhead with one hand so he could suspend his upper body outboard of the deck grate. He used the other hand to wave Leo forward. From his position amongst the gauges and valves, Smith made the introductions.

"Chief Pickford," he said, pointing to Leo, "this is Mr. Zackah-reye-ah from the yard's chem lab. He's here to look into our options for feed water treatment at sea."

The sailor was older than Leo, a little shorter, and even more wiry. He had pale blue eyes and reddish hair, although it was cropped too close to tell easily. His pale skin and freckles made red a good guess for hair color though. He made the start of a move to shake but then showed his palm, ruddy with rust and dirt. He made a little high sign instead.

"Chief James Ravenell Pickford, at your service, suh," he said with an almost liquid Southern drawl.

"Can you take a break from the tubes, Chief?" Mr. Smith asked.

"Yessir," the sailor replied. "I just done the last of 'em on this powah plant."

"Good," Smith said. "I'd like you to brief the chemist here on our boilers and their water supply. He'll have some questions. Please be of any assistance." Turning to Leo, the engineering officer said, "You're in good hands. Let me know if you need any further help."

With that, Mr. Smith lurched off around the machinery and on to his next duty. His movements through the forest of metal objects in the cramped boiler room reminded Leo of a horseman swinging left and right in the saddle to avoid low tree branches. Smith kept his waist and legs directly over the deck grates as he walked away. His upper body moved constantly to and fro, however, to clear the various hanging or protruding obstacles that crowded the fire room while it was under repair.

"He's too tall to have this job," Chief Pickford observed laconically, "but he's too good not to have it." Turning to Leo, he said. "Ah appreciate you gettin' me out of the mud drum fo' a while, suh. How may ah help you?"

"Maybe first you can tell me what that screeching noise was," Leo said.

Smith's footsteps could be heard clanging upward and away on the steel ladder.

"Oh, that was just a compressed air gizmo I put together to clean scale out of the tubes. It's a little air motor on the end of a hose with some cable pieces on its shaft. When you turn the air on, the little cables spin like a propeller and drag the whole thing

War Record

up through the tube to the steam drum." Pickford paused and then smiled. "'Course, you can only use it when we're cold iron."

"Naturally," Leo replied.

Even he understood what the chief had meant. In doing so, he passed his first test.

"It certainly makes enough noise."

"Yessir, it does," the chief allowed. "I usually chew on a little tissue paper and then put it into my ears before I start. That helps with the noise. If we start to fire our five-inch seventy-five gun, you'd better do the same thing."

Leo nodded at the obvious wisdom of this advice.

"I'm here to learn a bit about your boilers, Chief," Leo said, getting down to business. "My assignment is to make it take longer for those tubes to scale up and cut into your efficiency."

"Ah'm all for that," the chief answered, "but there seem to be some few things which are guarantees in this life, and ah believe that scale in the water tubes is one of 'em. May ah ask how you propose to accomplish your assignment, Mister...uh?"

"Zaccaria," he said. "I don't think I'll be able to eliminate the deposits altogether. I do hope to treat the feed water with some chemicals that will suspend the particles of scale before they attach to the tube walls and keep them floating until they can be drained out."

"That all sounds fine, Mr. Zack," the chief allowed. "For the time bein' though, let's just pretend that ah'm from Missouri, if that's all right with you?"

"Fair enough. For right now, though, I'm completely lost. Can you tell me a little about your machinery and how it's laid out?"

"Sure thing." The chief smiled thoughtfully. "Let's talk about propulsion on a fightin' ship. This here's the number one fire room. That's the foremost of the two boiler rooms aboard. Each fire room has two boilers. See here how they face each other?" Chief Pickford pointed through the forest of piping and temporary hoses.

Sure enough, just across the grated walkway, almost hidden among the lines, there was a second man way just like the one he had crawled from moments earlier.

"That's the mud drum of number two," the chief announced.

Leo was beginning to see the looming shape of the steel-encrusted fire box as it rose from the bilges and came to a head at the exhaust stack perhaps fifteen feet above.

"Right behind this fire room, there's an engine room. The steam made here turns the turbines and reduction gears in there. Next space aft is the number two fire room, with two more boilers jes' like these. Then there's number two engine room, and by then, we're almost out of ship. Just the shaft alleys after that and the scuppers and stuffing boxes where the shafts finally get wet. Simple, huh?"

"If you say so, Chief." Leo actually thought he was beginning to understand the layout. "Does each engine room turn only one of the two shafts?"

"Why, give that man a cupie doll!" the chief mugged. "Ladies and gentlemen, we have a winner. Step right up. That's exactly how it works, Mr. Zack. Forward engine room turns the starboard shaft. That's the long one. Aft engine room turns the port. That's the short one. Now you'all can teach the class."

Pickford did his job amicably, and before too long, the clutter of piping, stanchions, and valves began to resolve itself in Leo's mind into a unified system. The chief explained how evaporators make pure fresh water by distilling brine from the ocean. He made the point that navy practice measured the increased salinity of the make-up water in the evaporators so that it could be discharged and replaced before it became so brackish that it caked the heat transfer surfaces.

Leo seized on this idea to explain exactly what he meant to do in the boilers.

"That'd be called blow down, Mr. Zack," the chief explained. "We do that now when our boiler water gets too foul. The problem is it costs us too much in lost heat, so we're real careful about how often we empty out these tea kettles."

"Oh, I hope you can actually exhaust the water *less* often if my process works," Leo advised. "I hope the chemical treatment will act partly to keep carbonate particles floating and partly to keep them lubricated so they flow better. If I'm right, your occasional blow downs should do more to eliminate contamination than they do now."

––––––––––––––––––––

Leo was careful not to take too much of the chief's time on any one day. He divided his own time up between the lab and the Monaghan. On the ship, he learned about where there were fittings that could be used as injection points for the orange soup he concocted in the lab. From his desk, he did the research that told him which chemicals were already available from naval stores for use nationwide. From Chief Pickford, he saw where sufficient quantities of these chemicals could be stored on board, near enough at hand to the fire rooms to be useful.

As a few weeks went by, Leo began to appreciate Pickford more and more. The sailor was only interested in keeping his machinery working well, so he was sincerely helpful to anyone with the same goal. More than that, the chief knew his job and his vessel so well that he was always able to expedite modifications. If a little welding was needed here or a new fitting spun in there, the chief could either do it himself or trade a favor with one of his shipmates to make it happen in jig time.

In the lab, Leo ran test after test on the residues from evaporated water, both with and without his treatment. He was convinced by volumetric and by scale analysis tests that his plan was a sound one. Most pleasing of all was the fact that Fred Hemmings agreed.

Leo wrote up a procedure for mixing and injecting the water treatment chemicals. He tested it out for himself by crouching next to the feed water inlet line and installing a bottle of the mixture on a hanger so that it would drip slowly through a rubber tube. While the ship was still on the blocks and the boilers were open and cold, he couldn't actually try the process. He did ask for Chief Pickford's opinion though.

"Glass jugs like that don't last too long at sea, Mistah Zack," he said after simply casting a glance at Leo's rig. "When we get to bobbin' around like a cork, that glass'll smash first thing. Then I wonder how air is goin' to get in as the chemicals run out. Is there a vent? Have you ever tried to drink beer from a steel can when only one hole's been punched in it?"

Canned beer was a relatively recent development that had been made specifically at the request of the US Navy. The officers in charge of such things were realists on the subject of making beer available to their sailors, but they also knew why having glass containers aboard ship was against the unwritten rules of the sea.

Leo hadn't actually seen a can of beer until he'd started working at the shipyard. He had come across the odd, pointed tool that was now more common on the rear end of a bottle opener. He'd heard what it was for and had imagined a can of peas with beer in it.

"Ah think what you need here is a submarine bottle," the chief continued studiously. "Ordinarily, they are as hard to find as a chicken's lips, but for this project, I might just be able to swing it for you."

The diesel electric submarines being turned out by the Electric Boat Company down in Groton, Connecticut, were growing bigger and better with each design class. They were still small vessels, though, and were subject to even more battering than Destroyers. While the generations of hulls and power plants came along at slow intervals during peacetime, there was considerable attention being paid to the items that could be retrofitted to the existing fleet. One of the recent small advances was a screw-top bottle made entirely out of polyethylene. These one- and two-quart containers were almost a military secret. The plastic material was scarce because it was still produced in virtually laboratory conditions. Since its properties were not well understood, the submarine bottles had been constructed of very thick, molded walls of the stuff.

They were shatterproof and pliable, though, and within a week, Chief Pickford had two cases of them under lock and key. He drilled two small holes in the screw-tops. One was for a surgical rubber tube that ran down to the feed water fitting. The other sprouted a shorter tube that was tied back up to the bottom of the bottle once it was inverted to let the treatment chemicals flow out. That made a vent. As long as a restriction in the outflow tube kept the rate of drainage down to a drip, it didn't matter that the vent was wide open.

"That was actually a pretty good idea you had there, Mr. Zack," the chief observed when it was all in place. "It only needed a little fixin' up, an' now I believe it'll work jest fine."

Leo took that as a compliment.

In April of 1941, the Monaghan was floated out of the dry dock and brought along pier side for the finishing touches in its overhaul. Hull painting and tank cleaning were complete, and she rode easily at her moorings on the gentle swells of the inner harbor. Oil was taken aboard along with potable water. Stores of all kinds began to make their way up the gangplank and down from the yard cranes. The pipes and hoses only stretched to the ship from one side now. The Monaghan was beginning to look seaward.

Dock trials were scheduled for the boilers, so Leo stayed away for a few days until all the ship's high-pressure systems could be recertified. When he did come back aboard, it was with a certain sense of anticipation. It would be the first real test of his water treatment program.

When he climbed down the long ladder to the deck plates over the boiler bilge, Leo was struck by the heat and the strong smell of oil. The number one boiler was running. It made a constant roar that almost became loud silence after you listened to it for a minute or two. It was actually comfortable working in the space until you had to say something to someone. Then you realized how loud you had to speak just to hear yourself over the din. Chief Pickford spotted him and came over. He bent to talk directly in Leo's ear, and he spoke so loudly that it hurt, but he could still barely be made out above the roar.

"Welcome to a real fire room, Mr. Z," he shouted. "Take a look at how your water treatment rig is working out."

Leo saw that a rope mesh harness had been made to hang above the inlet fitting, which was down at deck level. The harness was like a holster, and a new bottle could be dropped in at any time. Swinging next to it was a small clipboard with a hole drilled in its bottom so a lanyard could secure it to the mesh. It didn't even take a conscious thought on the chief's part to insure that the clipboard would not become a piece of flying debris, but it took Leo a moment to work it out. Even then, he understood about shipboard motion at sea only in the abstract because Pickford had made so many points of preparing for it.

The clipboard was to keep a log of how much water treatment was put into the feed and when. Each fire room already kept a complex log-on system efficiency like every other major boiler installation either stationary or afloat. After operating for a while, the actual efficiency of the treated boilers could be compared with historical information from the last time an overhaul had been performed. Leo assumed that the inevitable drop in efficiency would take longer this time because of the benefit of the treatment. He also assumed that someday, the long, boring task of writing up a spreadsheet showing those values would fall to him. He loved to put on lab goggles and do some wet chemistry, but he didn't relish the thought of wearing a green eyeshade

War Record

and sleeve garters. Yet somebody had to do the accounting. He was still missing one important point.

"Ah'll be doin' that part of it, Mr. Zack," Chief Pickford shouted conversationally. "It's too important a matter for me not to know right away. If it works, I'll see to it that the watch is faithfully maintained. If it doesn't, I'll jest throw the rig overboard and have one less thing to worry over. And, anyways, suh, we'll be ten thousand miles from here before we get your numbers. Unless you're comin' with us, it'll have to be me."

When he emerged from the fire room Leo was reminded that there was an entire ship around him. While below, he had only seen and heard the boilers and piping. His mental picture of where he was and what was happening had been restricted to that little world of ship's engineering.

On Friday evening, he took Ellen to dinner. Leo was unaware of how animated and descriptive he became when he started talking about his project. He was always surprised when she made a comment that showed how much she knew about it. He really thought he stayed away from it as a subject for conversation because it was so remote from anything she would know or be interested in.

She actually enjoyed listening to his effusive explanations of the minutiae of marine power plants. Coming from anyone else, the subject would have been boring to the point of tears. It was clearly important to him, though, so it was also important to her.

"That mesh holder for the bottle sounds like Montie's bridle," she observed over salad. "If it works out, I know several good tack shops where you could have something made up in leather with brass hardware."

Leo smiled, but he saw her point.

"The hanging bag was made up on board from knotted lanyard line," he told her. "It's a traditional approach to dealing with

Mark Zaccaria

ship's motion, and you'd have to see it to see what a good solution it is. You're right, though, dear lady," he continued. "If this becomes a permanent part of shipboard life, there will have to be a permanent fixture." He couldn't help but smile. "It might be made by a defense contractor rather than a tack shop, however."

As he reached across the table for her hand, he deserved both the smack on the wrist and the smile in return that he received.

"I like the sound of this Chief Pickford," Ellen said as desert arrived. "I wonder if he'd like to join us sometime? He sounds like someone my cousin, Betsy, might like."

"Your cousin who?" Leo asked.

"Haven't I ever mentioned Betsy?" she asked, really wondering. "She's older than me and was always my helper and heroine when we were kids. In those days, she showed me all about underwear and snuck me cigarettes and did other important things like that during family get-togethers." Ellen thought about it for only a moment and then jumped back to the conversation, almost with a start. "She's only a few years older than me." It was a point that must have required emphasis. "Ever since she graduated from Simmons, she's been teaching there, planning improbable literary projects and staying single, much to the dismay of her mother."

"Ah," Leo said. "The old salt and the old maid."

Ellen's eyes flashed at that. "She's not an old maid at all," she shot back. "In fact, you're not allowed to look at her any more than social courtesy requires. The reason I think they'd get along is that he seems to be an expert at something, and Betsy constantly complains that she can't find any men of substance in this modern world. Besides," Ellen concluded slyly, "the longer she stays single, the longer the heat stays off of me. Unless you have any other suggestions, that is?"

Leo was lightning-quick to shift the focus of the conversation.

"There is a slight barrier between Chief Pickford and me because of our positions," he allowed, nodding studiously. "But

War Record

it's not as if I were an officer or anything like that. Sure I could bring him along sometime."

Back in the lab on Monday morning, Leo began the day by checking his scale build-up experiment. After hanging up his hat and coat, he went directly to a lab table. It was just like the one Dr. Gerber used in his amphitheater lecture hall.

On it, Leo had two similar bell jars. Each was half full of water that was boiling, as both apparatuses were on stands over gas flames. Sitting in the boiling water and rising above it inside the jars were short tag pieces of boiler tube. Each bell jar was supplied from off the flame by a reservoir bottle that was stoppered. As the water boiled off and exposed the glass and surgical tubing conduit between the jar and the bottle, vapors would be able to go into the sealed reservoir. This let more water into the jar but also sealed off the tunnel between the two.

In one jar set, there was plain tap water. In the other, the orange stain of the treatment chemicals was a dead giveaway as to what was in progress. Both kettles had been boiling away for weeks, and a small residue of mineral deposit could be seen in the area of the water line on each test piece of tube.

Leo refilled the reservoirs and made some notes in his lab book as Arnie Cohen strolled by and inspected the setup.

"Have you tried running electrical current through the water?" he asked.

"Why, no," said Leo, looking up. "I hadn't even thought to. What do you think that would do?"

"I'm not sure really," Arnie replied truthfully. "I've been working on some hull corrosion problems, though, and we know that a slight current is formed between the salty seawater and the steel. That current accelerates corrosion. It's a process a little like electroplating. That's why zinc cathodes are bolted to the outer hulls of steel ships. They give galvanic protection to the under-water body.

"It might not do anything," he said with a shrug, "but it's one more thing to try, and, hey, it couldn't hurt."

Leo nodded and thanked the older man for the suggestion. He made a note of it in his lab book but also wrote that the problem with boiler tubes was the build-up of minerals on the inside, not the reduction of metal due to corrosion.

In the recent past, electricity had been only partly understood, so it had been popular in the names of both research and quackery to use it for a wide range of things. All sorts of devices had been constructed to use both low and high-voltage current for tasks as diverse as curing illness, inducing sleep, treating petroleum, and repelling insects. Every time a seemingly outlandish use for this invisible energy was proposed, it was followed by some equally improbable discovery that was actually true. In this way, the development of electromagnets, x-ray photography, and even the radio made it easier for people to believe in the electro-harmonizer for a healthy brain, the coil energizer for automotive fuel lines, and the electro transporter that was developed by Dr. Zarkov and used to such good effect by Flash Gordon.

Still, if the mineral particles could be made to take a charge, then they might be attracted to an anode or cathode of the opposite charge. Leo was just about to start looking for some large dry cell batteries when Fred Hemmings emerged from his office and came into the lab.

"Leo, may I speak to you for a moment?" he asked.

"Yes, sir," he replied.

In just a few months of working around naval personnel, he had picked up the cadence of the standard military form of address and had adopted it as useful in talking with everyone.

The two men walked back to Fred's office, where he motioned Leo to a chair. They talked about the water treatment project, and

Leo added detail to the written reports he had been filing for the chief chemist. Finally, Fred Hemmings got around to the point.

"I've had a call from the *Monaghan*'s executive officer," he said.

"Mr. Dobbins?" Leo asked, wondering if there was something wrong.

"Yes," said Hemmings absentmindedly. He was searching through the papers on his desk. When he found the one he was looking for, he read it briefly and then looked up. "Lieutenant Commander Dobbins tells me that his engineering officer is giving him good reports about your work below decks. He also informs me that with dock trials and steering tests complete, they are going to take the ship out for sea trials in ten days' time. You'll be expected to be aboard to monitor the operational ease and effectiveness of the new procedures you've instituted."

One by one, the ten thousand Lilliputian lines that had bound the Monaghan to the beach were taken away. By the time Leo went aboard her to ride along on sea trials, there were only four or five hawsers left. As he came aboard, he felt a steady vibration in the deck. It made his feet tingle at first. With shore power and water disconnected, the ship was running its boilers and evaporators. A plume of white vapor issued from each of the two stacks and looked to be contributing to the wispy puffs of cloud that dotted the blue sky.

First, he reported to the ward room to be signed into the ship's log. Mr. Dobbins welcomed him and made arrangements to show him to his quarters.

"Mr. Sullivan has had to stay ashore at the last minute," the exec explained in a businesslike tone. "That makes you the ranking civilian aboard, Mr. Zaccaria." Once again, he got the name exactly right. "The skipper has asked if you would care to take your meals here in the ward room."

"Thank you, sir," Leo responded smoothly. "It's an honor I haven't earned yet but which I'll gladly accept."

"Good. And you'll share a stateroom with Ensign Davies, if that's all right," he said.

Once again, Leo was well aware that it wasn't really a question with two possible answers. A steward showed him to his quarters.

It was a small, oddly shaped room. The door looked like a steel version of a regular wooden door rather than an oval water-tight hatch. It opened from one side of the base of a triangular set of walls. To the left, as you entered, there was some cylindrical structure occupying space from the deck to the overhead at the apex of two bulkheads. Perhaps it was a service trunk or a conduit for piping. Extending from it for six or seven feet were two bunk beds bolted to the wall one over the other. Two narrow lockers filled the third side of the room, and just to the right of the door, there was a steel hand basin with a single faucet and mirror above.

A young man dressed in khakis was sitting on the bottom bunk. He looked up as Leo was shown in.

"Hi! I'm Jim Davies," he said, extending his hand. "I guess you must be the fellow from the chem lab."

"Leo Zaccaria. Pleased to meet you."

They shook firmly.

"I guess I'm on top?"

"If you don't mind," Davies replied. "Mr. Smith says you're doing some sort of scientific work in the machinery spaces? It's not weapons related, is it?"

"No. Nothing like that," Leo replied. "Boiler water treatment. I'm trying to find a way to extend tube life while the ship is underway."

"Oh. Good," Davies said, visibly relieved. "I'm supposed to be a deck officer with some weapons responsibility, and I wanted to be sure I hadn't missed anything. Have you ever been to sea on a can before?" he asked.

War Record

"I've never been to sea on anything before," Leo answered.

He looked over the cramped cabin, feeling a little bit confined. The air was fresh, pouring in from a six-inch tube that ran halfway down the crotch between the conduit and the bunk wall. There was no window or porthole though.

"This must be an interior cabin," he concluded out loud.

"It's not quite the *Queen Mary*," Davies observed. "You'll get used to it though. Stow your gear," the ensign suggested. "Let's go up on deck and watch the show."

They stepped back into the sunshine on the port side of the weather deck. Port is left on shipboard, but it's also the side most often tied off to a pier. Thus, it's where you go to get to the seaport, the shore. A thousand years ago, there had been good reason for this. The steerboard, or rudder, was then always an external device, lashed to the right-hand gunwale, which would be fouled if the boat was positioned to put it between the hull and the beach. Gradually, that whole side of the boat became named for the rudder, starboard. Modern ships could be breasted up to deep-water piers in either direction and sometimes were if need be. Still, it was tradition to have the gangway on the port side.

Leo had been to the movies enough to know that cowboys always mounted their horses from the left. It seemed to him the same sort of thing.

"Our weapons are all locked," Davies said. "Let's go forward."

They walked toward the bow of the vessel, where there was considerably more space to move around. This was because there were two gun turrets mounted there and the big muzzles had to have room to train through as large an arc as possible.

"This big set of tubes forward is our main battery," Davies explained. "It's a twin five-inch, seventy-five mount, and back up there is a single three-inch, fifty. That's our secondary."

The large forward turret had an oval watertight door in the rear and two long tubes protruding from the front. It sat on the main deck. Behind it, on a structural platform extending maybe

Mark Zaccaria

five feet up from the deck, there stood a smaller gun housing with a single barrel.

"Naval guns are described by their bore size and the ratio of the length to that bore," the young weapons officer went on. "So the barrels of the five-inch guns are seventy-five times their projectile diameter, or three hundred and seventy-five inches, a little more than thirty-one feet. It's a standard size for small guns in the navy."

The gun tubes lay out at a horizontal pitch. Part way down their length, they were supported and secured in place by a steel bar hinged at the deck with a stirrup on top. Their muzzles were plugged with bright red wooden stoppers that sported polished brass stars in the center.

From the forward area of the deck, Leo and Ensign Davies could hear the regulated commotion from the bridge as the ship's master and the officers of the watch eased her away from the pier and headed down the channel. There were orders shouted through megaphones for the remaining lines to be slipped. There were orders relayed through the deck watch and telegraphed to the boiler rooms below. There were commands both shouted and signaled to the yard tug, which stood by to guide the *Monaghan* out into the channel and down the outer harbor to the open ocean.

At first, Leo noticed that the gap between the ship and the pier widened at an almost imperceptible rate. Then he noticed that the voices and machinery noises coming from the yard were less distinct. Before long, the ship just seemed to be gliding slowly down the harbor. He saw the warehouses and the old clipper ship piers of East Boston on his left and the Coast Guard boats at Sullivan's shipyard in the north end on his right. By the time he thought to check for it, he had to look over his shoulder to the left to pick out Captain Bang's yard. From the harbor side, it looked like a random pile of small hulls stacked ashore with two or three working boats tied up alongside. He couldn't make out any figures moving around in the yard, but he assumed the old salt was there somewhere and that he had taken note of the movement of the sleek, gray fighting ship as it slid down the harbor.

"You must be off watch right now," Leo commented to his companion.

"Yes and no," Davies replied, watching the shore parade by. "I've been asked to show you around and make sure you get oriented to departure and seagoing operations."

"In that case, let's go aft for a look."

From the fantail, they could hear the staccato flutter of the ship's pennant. They could also feel the quiet boiling rumble of the water at the stern as the propellers made slow turns out of sight in the brine.

Looking back, they watched the navy yard receding. Now on their left as they moved backward was the army base in South Boston. Across the harbor to their right were mud flats stretching pungently from Jefferson Point to Winthrop. Because that shore of the harbor channel was so soft and shoal, it was unusable for shipping. A part of the flats was used as an airfield. There was a hangar there these days, and a signal tower. The whole thing had been named after a Boston airman killed in France in 1918. Even so, Logan Airport and the cloth-covered bi-planes that buzzed around it like bees were considered an oddity, something to be done in space like this that had no commercial purpose.

On the left, Castle Island came into view. Its massive Civil War battlements had been built on top of those of the Revolutionary Era. Just off the tip of South Boston, it was the perfect location for shore batteries to defend the harbor, although no artillery pieces could be seen on the bastions.

Boston's outer harbor is littered with islands. Some had military structures on them that had fallen to disrepair and others still held working garrisons. Boston Light, a massive hundred-foot-high lighthouse, stood on one and marked the harbor's position. When the *Monaghan* rounded Boston Light, it swung north.

Mark Zaccaria

Long Island, Greater and Lesser Brewster's Islands, Spectacle Island; Leo had heard their names all his life but really didn't know from sea level which one was which.

As the Destroyer cleared the harbor islands, the yard tug that had accompanied it was just a bobbing dot receding in the distance. It headed back to its inner harbor berth as the *Monaghan*, now fully in its element, churned up foam at the transom as it gained cruising speed and began to turn east toward open water. Looking aft from the fantail, Leo imagined that he could see the crescent sweep of Revere Beach just north along the shore from Boston. He fixed a point along it where he decided the Oceanview Ballroom must be. It was odd to envision his old stomping grounds in such expansive terms, taking it all in essentially in a single broad view.

There was a feeling of constant acceleration as the ship cruised eastward. The deck plates vibrated evenly underfoot from the complex conversion of oil into forward motion. The ship itself rocked gently from left to right, or rather port to starboard, as it made way. This gave Leo the feeling that the *Monaghan* was constantly leaning forward as a runner does, straining to break the tape at the finish line of a race. The whole vessel resonated with the barely contained energy of its propulsion machinery. Even Leo would know the moment the engine room answered the captain's call for a change in power.

The ship at sea bore no resemblance to the passive mass Leo had crouched beneath when it was in dry dock. In fact, at that spot just then there was a constant battle of forces in progress as the steel hull resisted the fluid abrasion of the sea rushing by. The shallow alluvial sands of the coastal sea floor passed beneath the *Monaghan's* keel and then began to drop away into the canyon depths of the open ocean.

As the ship gathered speed, it created its own fresh breeze. Its bow churned up spray that came back along the superstructure in tiny droplets. Even in the bright sun, these two facts combined to

War Record

make it increasingly cold and uncomfortable. The shoreline was receding quickly now. Ensign Davies tapped his charge on the upper arm with the back of his hand. It was a silent signal, and without a word, Leo followed him below.

Now that they were under way, Leo assumed that he could check in with Chief Pickford without getting underfoot. He made his way down the familiar passages and ladders. Something was different though. On the one hand, even the cramped quarters of the Destroyer's innards seemed roomier now that all the excess gear, hoses, and shipyard tools were removed. On the other, as he walked, he seemed to be putting a steadying hand on one bulkhead and then, in a few more steps, on the other. As he descended the ladders, Leo noticed that there was more stress on one hand and then on the other. Below decks, there was no visual reference for the ship's motion, but it was an unseen hand that urged the sailors first left and then right or forward and then aft.

All of the sailors compensated for the gentle motion without thinking about it, and so did Leo. He became more deliberate in holding the rails and planting his feet. When he stood still, he began to adopt a relaxed posture that included holding on to whatever pipe or conduit was just overhead. Like the rest of the crew, Leo would not resist the tendency of his body to bow outward at the middle to and fro from the hard points of his foothold and handhold as he stood in conversation.

Something else was different. As he slid down the last long ladder into the forward fire room, he was lowering himself into a roaring oven. It wasn't just too hot; it was way too loud. In that first moment, Leo realized that his khaki trousers and long-sleeved shirt were far more than was needed with the fire room living up to its name this way.

Chief Pickford stood by his engineering station, crouched to peer through the sight glass and decide for himself about the size and color of the flame in number two. He steadied himself in that stance by holding on to a valve wheel. It was draped with a rag for insulation, and he turned it slightly to adjust the flame. He wore bell-bottomed fatigue trousers and an undershirt whose thin straps looked brown rather than white. He was glistening with sweat, and what there was of his ribbed cotton shirt was slicked to his thin body. On his head, he wore what was left of a white sailor's cap, squared now from having its sides rolled down so tightly and yellowed almost to brown where grimy hands had done the rolling.

Leo walked up to him and tapped his shoulder to get the chief's attention. He rose with a broad smile and bent to the chemist's ear in order to be heard over the din of machinery.

"Welcome to the gates of hell, Mr. Z." He grinned. "I heard you came aboard for the shakedown. Ah'm happy to see that you were able to make your escape from officer's country."

Life on shipboard always seems to reduce itself to practice quickly. By early the next morning, Leo had acclimated to the vibrations of the decks, the gentle motion of the vessel underway, and even to the staccato and rather hydraulic snoring that marked Ensign Davies's sleep. The ship was quiet just before dawn, and like most of the rest of the crew, Leo slept soundly and at peace.

It was quiet in the *Monaghan*'s bridge. Dim red lights illuminated the surroundings enough so that the three sailors standing the last watch could make their way around the space without stumbling. Outside, the late summer sky was just turning gray with the promise of a clear sunrise. The calm sea that lay before the destroyer glistened just enough to allow the deck watch to make out its surface and distinguish the horizon. The helmsman had an easy job of holding the ship on a course of 075, magnetic. As they glided along on a heading just north of due east, the officer of the deck was looking to starboard and awaiting the emergence

War Record

of the sun. The ship's clock showed 0558 and 30 seconds sweep when the Bo'sun's mate stepped up to the OD and spoke.

"Request permission to pipe reveille, sir."

The officer glanced back briefly at the large clock mounted on the rear bulkhead. "Permission granted," he said, thinking about coffee.

As Leo sprawled out in the upper bunk of the small stateroom, he had become accustomed to all the background sounds of the moving ship. There was actually a fair amount of noise, but it was all constant, so it all faded from one's attention. When the room's intercom speaker crackled to life, however, this was something different, and he opened one eye to focus a question on it even before its message began. The time was 0559, straight up.

First, there was the shrill, three-toned attention signal of the Bo'sun's whistle. The mate actually blew his pipe into the microphone where its piercing tones were amplified and left no one wondering if they were actually hearing NBC.

"Reveille! Reveille! All hands heave out and trice up!" It only had to be said once.

Lights came on in the crew's bunk spaces and the officers' staterooms alike. There was softly padding foot traffic throughout the ship as the plumbing in the heads came gushing to life. The few new recruits were eager. Their excitement at their first morning at sea was obvious. Old salts watching from the petty officers' quarters smiled with feelings of both irony and approval. Stewards in all three mess areas set about making coffee, but somehow, the chiefs always got theirs first.

The captain arose, dressed, and climbed the ladder from his stateroom directly to the bridge. There, he turned a practiced eye to the weather, scanned the horizon to be sure it was clear, and asked the OD for an informal report. A steward presented him with a mug of coffee as he was glancing at the ship's log before retreating to his quarters again to prepare for breakfast.

By 0630, the lines were beginning to form in the crew's mess and the cooks were starting to dispense heaping mounds of scrambled eggs, sausage, dry toast, and oatmeal. Tonight, there would be roast beef for dinner, so tomorrow morning, the new recruits would get their first taste of creamed chipped beef, on a shingle of course.

The Bo'sun's whistle rent the air again. "Attention in the ship. The smoking lamp is lighted."

After a cramped and abbreviated morning toilette, Leo followed Ensign Davies to the ward room for breakfast. Once again, he was surprised at how small the ward room actually was and that even though he took up an extra place, it was not at all crowded. They sat around the narrow table that occupied the tail of the T in the small space. Coffee was poured from steel pots that clipped into sockets on the coffee makers right there. Stewards arrived with plates of eggs, sausage, and pancakes. They seemed to take it personally if you didn't accept more of everything.

Leo's place was at the part of the table that opened out onto the rest of the room and the door. Davies sat across from him. He wondered why the far end of the table was reserved for the ship's master and the highest-ranking officers; it was the most inaccessible, after all, once everyone was seated. The question didn't distract him from applying syrup to a stack of pancakes. From the other end of the small table, Mr. Dobbins, the executive officer, spoke up.

"Mr. Zaccaria, it seems that our sea air agrees with you. Your appetite appears unaffected by a night at close quarters with Ensign Davies."

Things like snoring quickly became common knowledge on a small ship. Davies looked a little sheepish but actually pleased with the attention. He could have gotten a reputation for any number of things more embarrassing than snoring. He took it in good fun. After all, what choice did he have?

War Record

"Yes, sir," Leo replied with a smile. "I'm well-rested and ready to get to work."

"Excellent," the XO continued. "And just what will your work consist of on this short trip?"

"Mostly, I'll be observing the operation of the water treatment system I've devised for the boilers, sir. Chief Pickford has created a rig that seems to be quite workable for introducing the necessary chemicals into the feed water. I'll be watching to see how easy or difficult it is to actually do it under sea conditions," he explained. "We don't want to ask the fire room watch to do a task that is too difficult or gets in the way of some other function. After a couple months, I'll also be reviewing the ship's efficiency figures to try to estimate how much good all this has done."

"Very well, Mr. Zaccaria," Dobbins answered. "Our sea trials will consist of a series of high-stress maneuvers followed by ordinary steaming while we evaluate the ship's performance. I daresay you'll have the opportunity to observe your treatment system under extreme operating conditions." The captain raised an eyebrow at this last statement. He cast a critical eye on the young chemist and then back at his executive officer.

The intercom speaker came to life with a brief static hiss that served just as well as the Bo'sun's call for getting the crew's attention.

"Now. All hands fall in at quarters for muster and inspection." The time was 0745.

Leo descended the long ladder into the fire room by using his hands as brakes on the smooth tubing of the handrail. His feet were poised to take over if something went wrong. They just stood by, though, while he regulated his rate by tightening or relaxing his grasp in fine degrees. As he slid down, the noise and the heat assaulted him on two fronts. Suddenly, his ears hurt, and if he breathed deeply through his nose, his nostrils burned. Chief

Pickford's comment about the gates of hell went back through his mind.

But there was the chief, tending his equipment, seemingly unfazed by the cacophony around him. It was unnerving to Leo, but Pickford acted as if he was right at home. They quickly began to communicate by hand signals. The chief got the chemist's attention with a touch and then handed him a clipboard. Leo saw that it was a log of the times and amounts of the introduction of the treatment chemicals into the feed water of the number two boiler. The figures were symmetrical. Every four hours, the submarine bottle was refilled, and it was coming up on time for it to be replaced again.

When Leo noticed this, he looked up, and Chief Pickford read him like a book. With a pointed finger, he directed Leo's attention to the bottle and hose hanging from their harness just above the feed pump. As he checked it for fill level, Leo became aware that it was swinging gently from side to side. With all the heat, vibration, and noise in the windowless space, he had forgotten that the ship was rocking as it made way.

As Leo tried to grab the bottle to replace it, he was suddenly keenly aware that he had to hold on to something in order to put a grasp on his target. It seemed that half the pipes overhead were too close together to provide a good hand hold, and the rest were too hot. There were levers, chains, and valve wheels all around. Each of them were controls, though. If he grabbed one to steady himself, he'd change something. As he stood trying to decide how even to approach the water treatment rig, his mentor stood by with a knowing look, just watching the wheels turn in his charge's head.

Finally, Leo grabbed a rag that was tucked behind an electrical conduit. He used it as insulation for what he hoped was the least hot of the accessible handholds, and he let himself down to secure the bottle. How to unscrew the stopper? How to remove the empty bottle with one hand? How to steady it for the transfer of the reddish brown liquid from the five-gallon ready can that was lashed to a rib along the hull? All in all, it took Leo more than fifteen minutes to refill the bottle and get it all set up.

Hand signals were fine for simple exchanges. For complex thoughts, one still had to bend to his shipmate's ear and yell, at least here in the fire room.

"This takes too long," Leo strained. He remembered that his original plan called for each of the four boilers to get this attention at the same time. "We'll have to stagger the refill times," he concluded.

"Ah already have, Mr. Z," Pickford shouted back with a smile. "Watch this."

With that, the chief made his way over to the number one boiler. There, he began to replace the feed bottle for that system. Pickford used his hat for insulation, but he held on in almost the same place Leo had. The chief took an alligator clip from his pocket, though, and used it as a clamp on the surgical hose leading from the bottle to the black iron nipple off the check valve into the feed water line. Then he just peeled the hose back and removed it. When he pulled the bottle from its harness, the chief dropped it down far enough so he could unscrew the cap with the bottle upright. He put the flexible metal spout from the ready can into the soft neck of the submarine bottle and then tipped them over together. He didn't lose a drop. He reversed the process and was done in under five minutes.

"They' ahs no tellin' what else might pop down here when you have to do one of these drills," he shouted again at close range. "So ah scheduled 'em for one boiler each hour. That way you always have some time in case somethin' more important comes up."

Leo could only nod his agreement. He had new respect for what the chief could do in a crowded machinery space. He also knew that his water treatment would do some good if it was only introduced every so often. Anything that made it easier to use would make it more effective.

He was relieved to realize that the operational part of his plan was workable at sea. With that off his mind, he could remember again that the room was heaving gently and that it was noisy and way too hot.

Leo had almost convinced himself that he had acclimated to his strange new surroundings when all hell really broke loose. So far, the intercom speakers in every space had always come to life with a Bos'un's whistle. This time, there was a klaxton that sounded like an aoogah horn on a kid's jalopy, except it was loud and harsh, even in the fire room.

"General quarters! General quarters! All hands man your battle stations!"

The needle of the ship's telegraph swung back and forth, clanging the bell at both ends of its arc before coming to rest at flank speed. Chief Pickford leapt to the cast iron stand with its brass scale-and-ebony handle. He jammed the handle to the stops in both directions, again clanging the telegraph bells before stopping it directly over the needle at the highest forward setting. From there, he raced to fuel valves and stack, air, and flue settings as the noise level suddenly soared to unbelievable levels.

The klaxton sounded again. The voice that followed was lower than before, more stern and very serious.

"General quarters! General quarters! All hands man your battle stations! Attention, all hands! This is not a drill!"

Leo was immobilized. He had no idea what was going on, and his attention was drawn by several different danger signals almost at the same time. Chief Pickford was excited beyond anything Leo had seen so far in the taciturn snipe. There was something in the air, a smell perhaps that told him that the Destroyer man's actions were being driven by more than just a sense of duty.

War Record

Overhead, there was a shuddering clang. The watertight hatch in the deck above had been closed abruptly. There was no mistaking that. Through the din, Leo could even hear the metal-on-metal screech as it was dogged down to make its seal. At the same time, the ship's vibrations began to catch up in intensity with the new, higher noise level. The *Monaghan* was answering her master's call for top speed and battle readiness.

Instinctively, Leo backed away from the main passageway between boilers, as much as that was possible. He found handholds on one of the ship's ribs and on a turnbuckle that kept stress on a structural member. He wondered how long this could go on and how long he would have to wait for whatever was going to happen next.

As Chief Pickford brought both of his boilers in the forward fire room up to full power, he reviewed the gauges once more and then moved over to the small engineering station. There, he picked up an oversized telephone handset and took it with him as he stuck his head into a three-sided wooden box that was padded with a bunk mattress. The box had been incongruous among the pipes and conduits before. Obviously, it had been rigged to give the chief some small hope of talking on the phone at times like these. In a moment, he emerged, put the phone down, and opened a nearby tool locker, coming up with a roll of toilet paper.

He quickly made his way to Leo. Even shouting into one's ear would be useless now. Pickford unwrapped several turns of the toilet paper and handed them over. Then he took some for himself, crammed it in his mouth and began to chew. He gestured to Leo to do the same. Before it got too soft, he took out the wad, divided it, and put some in each of his ears. Again, he insisted with a look and a motion that his charge do the same. Leo didn't stop to think; he just followed orders.

Even with all that was going on, a new sound commanded attention. It was as if someone was using a small hammer on a tightly stretched steel cable. It made a pinging sound at a high

Mark Zaccaria

pitch, and it seemed to reverberate. Every few seconds, there was another ping.

Pickford went back to his duty station, but not before sternly pointing to Leo's handholds. "Stay put, Mr. Z. We ah in fo' a bit of action."

Leo's hand and wrist felt it first. He was grasping the *T*-shaped top of one of the ribs so closely spaced along the tin can's hull. What he felt was something at first like the shock that runs up your arm when you hit a baseball with a cracked bat. It was of a lower frequency, though, and much more powerful. As soon as this first feeling registered, he was overwhelmed by the second. The entire fire room shook once as if it had been kicked sideways in the water. It was past the point where anything more could be heard, but Leo's entire body shuddered so violently that his vision blurred and he felt as if he'd been dazed by a solid right to the button. For just a moment, his only ken was of his two hands and their tight grip on something solid. This was all that kept him upright.

When he came to, he thought for a split second how unusual it was that the lights stayed on. Then he snapped to full attention as it occurred to him to look for a wall of water rushing into the space, but there was none. The search was frantic but brief. Nothing seemed too different after the shock subsided. At least until his hand and wrist told him it was happening again.

It's both right and wrong to say that he was ready for the second reverberation. It wasn't such a surprise, and it didn't blur his vision. It was nothing a person could get prepared for, however. The hull jumped again in the water, and he thought it a wonder that nothing in the fire room came loose. Once he realized he wasn't going to die that second, he started to get angry.

There was the rumble and the jarring jump, and it happened again.

Something inside Leo started building fury. He wanted to fight, but there was no one to punch. He wanted to do some-

War Record

thing, but even Chief Pickford was really just looking on as he monitored his two tightly wound boilers.

Kawhomp! The shocks were coming at even intervals. There was only a second or two in between.

He felt trapped. He had no target for his anger and no choice but to stay where he was. In his mind, he knew that the ship was doing some heavy maneuvering and that they were somewhere off the Maine Coast. What he didn't understand was the announcement that this was not a drill. There was a force inside him that was almost apart from his normal self. This animus was bound by his conscious self but was raging against that bondage.

Kawhomp!

Suddenly, he was straining at his handholds. The ship must have been leaning over into a steep turn. Running sounds shifted. Leo didn't understand that at least one of the ship's propellers had cavitated in the turn and that with the sudden loss of resistance, it had gurgled and oversped. The boilers and machinery kept up their steady din. He had no idea what was happening.

Kawhomp!

His anger might have turned to panic if he had truly thought himself helpless. Something in the fury made him keep searching for a target though. He never got to the point of giving up.

In all this other confusion, he missed the jangle of the ship's telegraph. He only noticed that something was different when the next expected shock finally failed to materialize. There was Pickford frantically pulling and turning his controls to slow down the production of power. Behind them, the big shafts started turning more slowly, and all at once, it was as if the whole ship fell silent. Then the ship's aft lifted as it was pushed briefly by the wake it had been trailing at the higher speed. It wasn't at all quiet, of course; things had just dropped back to their normal roar, and after the last few minutes, it seemed quiet.

Mark Zaccaria

Once he stabilized his machinery and checked his gauges, the chief turned to Leo with a huge grin on his face. He made his way over and punched the chemist gently on his upper arm.

"Hey, bubba," he mouthed, "you stood that all right."

"What was it?" Leo spoke without hearing himself or knowing if he was being heard.

"Depth charges," Pickford answered. "Anti-submarine weapons. They're two hundred and fifty pounds of TNT in a weighted can with a timed fuse, so they go off under water at whatever depth you want."

"I don't want them going off at all." Leo couldn't shout or get angry with the chief, but as he spoke, his eyes were on fire and riveted to the only other person in the space.

"Well, it could have been worse," Pickford said, still grinning. "You could have been in the sub."

"What sub?"

"I don't know, but that was the captain talking when they announced that this was not a drill."

"Now. Secure from general quarters. Secure from general quarters."

Just after things got back to normal, Leo's chest had been heaving as he gasped for breath. Then there was a period of euphoria. Everything felt great. The fire room felt cool and serene. He felt free again when he heard the hatch above being reopened. Even the chief was almost dancing around his machinery and making notations in his engineering logs with a bounce in his step.

They had survived. Now there was even a target for Leo's fading rage. The thunderous reverberations hadn't been aimed at him, after all. It was the sub. He grinned a fierce grin when he thought that, baring his teeth.

Pickford pointed out that it was time to refill one of the water treatment bottles. The whole project had disappeared from Leo's mind. That alone was something to be learned from the time at sea.

Back in his stateroom, he was drained. He was drenched with sweat, and he just sat on his bunk. His back was bowed forward so that his head didn't touch the overhead. He clasped his hands and leaned on his forearms just so he could sit without using any muscles. His mind was blank.

Eight bells sounded over the ship's intercom. It was four in the afternoon.

Ensign Davies returned to stretch out on his bunk and reflect. After settling in, he spoke. "Some fireworks, hey?"

Leo didn't respond.

"I didn't even know we had live weapons aboard until after we were underway," he went on. "There's some five-inch and three-inch ammo as well." He was chattering now, relieving his own stress. "That's not what the book says for first trials. They're hurrying us up for something."

"Was there really a sub?" Leo asked.

"I don't know. We were vectored to the area by the coast guard, and that new sonar gadget certainly got some exercise. They're the ones who gave the command for weapons release. We only dropped one pattern of charges, so we didn't try too hard if there was something down there. I don't know.

"If there was and it was one of ours, we played pretty rough with it," he went on. "We stood by for an hour, looking for wreckage and survivors, but there wasn't anything. If there was a sub, I imagine it got the message that the welcome mat was not out."

"I sure got that message," Leo said.

The Monaghan steamed into the harbor at Bath, Maine, just after sunrise. There had been a slight chop to the water's surface offshore. Once they rounded the headlands of Pond Island and moved briskly up the two-mile channel between islands,

Mark Zaccaria

however, the early morning sea became like glass. There was an even deeper feeling of serenity about the ship as it glided past Southport on the port side and Boothbay Harbor on starboard. Leo stood at the rail on the forward weather deck, taking it all in.

Fishing trawlers were already making their way seaward. Their crews just stared back impassively as the larger warship slid by. After making eye contact with one deck hand fifty yards off, Leo waved his hand to the man almost automatically. It was an impulse. He didn't know where that had come from, but he was rewarded with a subtle nod from the Mainer as a return salute.

Further up the channel, Leo watched as a single old man stood in a dory with shipped oars and pulled a rope aboard. The man had a gray beard and was wearing a brown oil skin sou'wester hat with matching bib overalls and a wool sweater. There was a pipe clenched in his teeth, and he was oblivious to the passing destroyer as he bent to the task of slowly hauling up something heavy. Leo was almost beyond the tableau when he saw a wooden cage perhaps half the size of the dory break water. The lobster-man pulled the trap out entirely and rested it across his gunwales while he opened the door on top and removed his writhing catch.

Life was normal here. The day was starting off as tens of thousands of days before it had. The noise and heat and profusion of conflicting sensations of time and place that was the fire room existed only on some other world. The lobsterman was in complete control of whatever he did next. In the fire room, Leo had been a small part of a large organism. He had been at the mercy of the actions of the group. Worse yet, he hadn't even been able to see what was going on because his vantage point didn't allow it. Life on a fighting ship was not for him. He wanted to be more in charge, even if that meant doing smaller things.

He didn't realize that he was already just a small part of a large organism, and precisely because of his remote vantage point, he couldn't see where his society, his country was heading.

War Record

The little town of Bath clung to small hills that rose steeply out of the estuary harbor. By the time it flowed all the way to Bath, the Kennebec River had split its waters around three or four islands and had mixed them thoroughly with the salty sea. Bath Iron Works was a cluster of black buildings with slate roofs that stood guard over a series of piers, dry docks, and shipways leading to the deep channel. For as much of a reputation as the iron works had for world-class craftsmanship, it seemed small when you saw it huddled into its few acres of coastal plain. It was framed by the dark hills and white clapboard houses that rose behind it. This made it seem all the smaller and more compact.

Leo could have left the ship at Bath and taken the train back to Boston. Enough of his work on the water treatment system was done. That was out of the question though. He had become part of the ship's company, if only for this one voyage, and he had to see it through. Still, his days at sea were numbered, especially if it came to a fight.

Mark Zaccaria

Pushed to the Edge

Suddenly there was fear and fighting. Leo came to as he was being manhandled by a pair of the old guards. His rage was immediate and the two could barely hold him as he wrestled with them instinctively. He became conscious and tried to look around. He was being roused from his nap at the forge and the two guards who had his arms were accompanied by two more who looked on with boredom and resignation at first.

One of the two extra guards slowly cycled the bolt on his rifle. Then with no particular sense of urgency he brought it to his shoulder and pointed the muzzle at Leo's nose, from about an inch away. It was time to stop fighting.

Leo went limp, but kept his eyes on the small dark circle from which his death could come at any second.

Over the months of his captivity Leo had developed a rudimentary level of skill in the German language. It was a survival requirement. None of the guards spoke English, and they all had guns. Now, though, the fourth guard began to speak but before long it all started coming too fast and too complex for Leo to keep up. In fact the guard gradually began screaming at Leo. The more the old fellow ranted on the more red in the face he became and the more passionate and angry he became. You didn't have to have any vocabulary to understand that Leo was getting the tongue lashing of his life. The guard's body language alone made that clear.

"Hieraus mit die! *Schnell!*" he concluded as the two guards began dragging their prisoner out of the area. At least the old Mauser rifle got re-slung on the shoulder of the guard who'd been aiming it at Leo. They dragged him back in the direction of his assigned tunnel.

The problem became clear to him as they dragged him up to the spot where the push car for hauling stone debris had gone over the edge. *How did they figure it was me?* he thought. *What a bonehead move this will turn out to have been. It's going to cost me, for certain.*

The escort detail became a work party as a handful of prisoners were brought out from the tunnels, along with some stout rope and an assortment of shiv blocks to boost the mechanical advantage. They would need to rig a block and tackle set up if they hoped to have the emaciated prisoners pull the car up the embankment by hand.

As the guards were laying out the lines one of the faceless ghost soldiers edged nervously up to Leo and spoke under his breath.

"Was it you that tossed that cart over?"

"Yeah," Leo grunted.

"Nice," the skeletal prisoner answered, nodding his approval. "Too bad you were the only one outside the tunnel tonight. They had the goods on you as soon as they checked the count. I hope you live to brag about this."

Damned German efficiency, Leo thought. *They document everything. What a bonehead.* He wondered about what would happen to him and he got angrier and angrier with himself. After all he'd done to ensure his survival he goes and trips himself up for no good reason. *What will happen now?*

He didn't have long to wonder about it. As soon as the lines were laid out and the tackle belayed to a stone foundation the head guard came over to Leo with the running end of the rope in hand. He gave the rope to his prisoner and pointed him over the edge.

"Binden sie das Seil am Wagon, Herr Schweinhund," he said roughly, smiling victoriously after he'd issued his order.

Leo just looked at the guard. The temperature was above freezing, but not by much. It was early April and it was the middle of the night. He'd never be able to get into the water and then have the strength to get back up. He was angry at himself but now he got angry at the guard. They locked eyes and the whole transaction took too long for the guard's liking.

He unholstered his Walther P-7 pistol and brought it to the vertical position as the staring contest continued. "Macht Schnell, Bitte," he said quietly, but with a sneer.

If Leo got into the water he ran a high risk of dying. It might be hypothermia. It might be a fever some days later. He might be swept away by even the slow moving current of the Elster since he'd never be able to swim at this temperature. On the other hand, if he didn't get into the water he'd be guaranteed a sudden death, and then one of the other guys would have to go in.

"Klein Moment, Bitte," Leo growled at the guard. "Meine Kleidung ist zu schwer." He began to unbutton his greatcoat. He removed his field jacket and blouse. He took off his undershirt and then his trousers. He left his boots and his skivvies on. The last time he'd checked on his feet they were purple and his socks had virtually liquefied. Just then he didn't even want to find out what their condition was by now.

He took the rope and pulled it taut to the edge of the bank. Tossing the running end down onto the upended cart he walked backwards down the escarpment. He was shivering. He was furious. But by now this was his only possible way out.

When he got to the water there was a revelation waiting for him. It was *cold*. He'd known it had to be cold but there was a tremendous gap between reason and reality. He'd hoped it would be only as cold as the Boston Harbor when he'd been a kid, dared to jump in. He thought it could not have been as cold as the Pacific Ocean off St. Louis Obispo when he'd volunteered to take a line out to a truck that had been stranded by the tide. That was cold. But this? It was liquid ice. He couldn't describe it, even to himself. The numbness this water created in him made him even more numb, mentally. Still, he had to go on.

As he got in around knee deep and started to fish in the inky fluid for the axle of the cart his body started to shut down. He could barely move his arms and legs. When he reached in to pass the rope through the coupling eye at one end of the cart his chest got wet and his breathing just stopped.

It was a moment that easily could have killed him. To survive there had to be some unique factor that pulled him through.

And there was. Anger.

At that moment Leo Zaccaria felt fury welling up in his entire being. Something inside him was not going to let this stupid circumstance be the end for him. He'd carefully planned and executed his way through too many dangers to let one random, boneheaded act spell curtains for him. His limp arms twitched and then passed the rope through the eye. He stood up in the waist-deep stream to throw a series of half hitch knots into the bite of rope he'd made and then shouted with a fearfully powerful animal voice.

"Pull!"

As the rope tightened and the prisoners bent to their task God must have been watching because the little rail cart somehow righted itself and began rolling on its wheels. Leo's back was against the wagon and he held on to the rope, walking clumsily with his salvage prize but actually using the power of his fellow prisoners to move him back up to the top of the bank.

Meanwhile, high above this little drama four flights of British Lancaster bombers were heading inbound for a live weapons run on the industrial sites of Berga. The flight's lead navigator had been unable to pinpoint their primary target that night so when

Mark Zaccaria

fuel became a consideration he'd asked the flight's commander to divert to their secondary target. It proved to be the night that Bomber Command saved Leo Zaccaria's life by staging a second, unexpected attack.

As the cart was brought back to a crosswise position over the narrow-gauge tracks the first concussion shook the ground. Leo was oblivious. He could think only of his greatcoat and the warmth, protection, and survival it meant. He was fumbling with it and planning to take the rest of the pile of his clothes with him when the guards and the other prisoners made a break for the tunnels. They all went to nearest opening, which was one tunnel up from Leo's. He didn't make a calculation to separate himself. His intellectual functions were not operating at that level right then. He simply headed back to where he'd started.

He shuffled into the tunnel but then kept going, even as the lights were being doused. A force within him drove him like a homing pigeon to the very spot where his rock drill still lay. There he used his last ounce of energy to take down the large illuminating globe, turn it on, and stuff it under the coat to begin returning heat to his frozen limbs and core. The guards would never be able to pick him out by looks. All the skeleton prisoners looked alike. If he could get his clothes on after the raid he'd be anonymous again.

He would survive.

For now he basked in the purloined heat and fell instantly asleep.

Sea Changes

In early April of 1941, Germany mounted simultaneous invasions of both Yugoslavia and Greece. Military planners in Washington were more than just concerned over the seemingly effortless expansion of German authority. Objective estimates of the effectiveness of the Yugoslavian and Greek armies were almost nonexistent, so it was assumed that the Germans were routinely overcoming stiff opposition. Surely, soldiers fighting in and for their homeland gave it their all.

War Record

Contributing to this perception was the sad plight of His Majesty's forces in the region. Although the Royal Navy had evacuated British troops in Greece safely, they had lost all their heavy equipment once more, just as they had at Dunkirk. When the Germans advanced again, this time on Crete, they short-circuited whatever power the Royal Navy had at sea by launching an airborne attack. The British Admiralty had given no thought to how they might counter waves of paratroopers descending directly to the battlefield. When the Germans did it, they left the British ships of the line as mere observers.

In June of that year, word came of the Third Reich's invasion of the Soviet Union. In remarkably quick succession, there was news of German victories at Riga, Gorodno, Brest-Litovosk, and Minsk.

American policy became preoccupied with the growing war in Europe and the Middle East. Lend/lease had been successfully sold to the country as an economic action bringing jobs to US shipyards. Now that American freighters were increasingly forming the backbones of the convoys in the North Atlantic that were Great Britain's sole source of supply, it seemed proper that the military should protect US business interests in international waters. The air and sea patrols protecting the convoys on the western half of the route became mostly American. Hadn't the United Fruit Company received the same treatment just fifty years before?

In the small, inner circles of American government, there was no doubt that the United States was adopting a posture of support for the United Kingdom. Rhetoric about the defense of freedom notwithstanding, the reason was to put as strong a buffer as possible between Washington and Berlin.

For the man in the street in Boston or New York, it was still a little difficult to see all of what was happening. Photographs seldom accompanied newspaper stories of the war, and their copy only covered the essentials of action that had occurred in

Mark Zaccaria

places few had ever heard of. A small corps of radio journalists was gaining increasing influence over American public opinion. Their first-person reports from the front lines were gripping and immediate to the audience at home. That was because they put things in human terms. It was all simplified greatly and disconnected from the underlying geopolitical causes of the conflicts. They sure did sell corn flakes, though.

Average Americans knew that there was a conflict in progress between good and evil. They assumed that they were on the side of good. They also maintained the attitude that it was all happening very far away and would never have any real impact in their own front yards. A few of the working men and women whose tastes ran to discussions of politics after Sunday dinner might even be heard to pronounce that this European War was a good thing for America because "it got our factories going again."

Nobody in America seriously factored Japan into their estimates of what the future might bring. Vague talk of the "yellow peril" was mostly heard only in California. Even there, it was thought to refer to all of Asia and to be as much of a social menace as a military one. Those who had helped to mediate the end of the Russo-Japanese War were both out of office and out of fashion in Washington. The few voices there were that sought to remind the American government of Japanese pride, Japanese honor, and even the concept of Bushido were buried deep within the Department of State. There, they were barely audible and went wholly unnoticed on the national stage.

So when Leo went in to work that summer, he was once again stepping from one world into another. In Eastie, people bustled into the shops and elbowed their way onto the streetcars in a daily ritual of just living that carried them along week to week, month to month. What was so wrong with that? they thought. There was food on the table, there was wine in the jug, the family

War Record

was together, and people were happy. Life was good! In Belmont, there were examples of mild concern over places vaguely known because friends or acquaintances had once visited them. Even that concern was disconnected from the day-to-day routines of those expressing it though.

When he passed through the gates of the Boston Naval Shipyard, however, Leo stepped into a little world that was gearing up for war, perhaps without really understanding that was what was going on. As a group, the yard was working itself hard in order to cope with needs that existed over the horizon. The pace of activities was gathering speed, and things in the well-ordered military facility were beginning to get crowded. Stores piled up to overflow the areas designated for them, and materials were left temporarily in sections usually reserved for other types of items. Even a year before, that would have been unheard of.

Ship fitters and shop engineers were getting plenty of overtime. Schedulers were having to get creative with their planning for the jobs being forecast to them by the navy building in Washington. No longer could last year's schedules simply be copied and used again this year. Now, when traditions or even regulations were bent a little bit, there wasn't a peep out of management. Everybody was starting to think only of the goal, of getting the job done. Their focus was completely on the yard. With such concentration, they couldn't possibly notice that the same thing was happening at every other production facility in the nation.

As he pulled through the main gate in mid-July, he noticed that the *USS Monaghan* had been moved to the pier opposite the *USS Constitution*. Leo smiled and nodded as the marine guard waved him through with a typically crisp motion.

That was strange, he thought, looking back to his right.

The admiral liked to have the old sailing ship stand alone at its berth of honor, not to mention that it was always said that the water in the area of Pier One was too shallow for modern warships at low tide. They must have done some dredging because they wouldn't let the *Monaghan* settle into the silt on her sonar dome twice a day.

Leo's work at the chem lab became more frenzied as well. He was teaching classes now in boiler water treatment for the engineering staffs of every vessel that put in to the yard. The number of lab books on his table had grown also. It seemed that there were more and more little experiments that the navy wanted done. Some of them made sense, and some didn't. A telegram would arrive from Washington instructing Fred Hemmings to test the effects of this chemical or that seawater condition on some grade of steel, brass, or bronze. Results were to be reported by order number.

Contacts with the labs at other navy yards had once been rare events. Now Fred's counterparts in New York, Philadelphia, or Baltimore would actually telephone from time to time when they needed to trade supplies or ask for preliminary results. More than once, Leo had actually taken crates to South Station in his own car to get them to a train that would ship them to one of these other yards by the next morning.

What product or material could be so scarce or so important, he thought, *that you would ever require an overnight delivery?*

On his return from sea trials, Ellen had asked Leo for all the details of his adventure. He hadn't been briefed not to talk about the depth charges. Strangely, though, none of the ship's officers had discussed the matter in the ward room during meals. From that, Leo took the cue that it was not a matter for comment. He told Ellen about maneuvering at sea. He described the physical difficulties of performing a delicate task like feed water treatment while riding a roller coaster. He marveled at Chief Pickford's mastery of his cramped machinery space and especially at his love of performing the role of boiler engineer under unbelievably difficult circumstances. Leo even mentioned the Yankee lobster man and the incredible beauty of the stillness at early morning as the *Monaghan* glided up the Kennebec estuary into Bath.

He didn't mention the depth charges, though, and his questions about what their target might have been remained unspoken. Somehow, he thought it was his duty to stay mum on that one.

She took it all in, happy to be the one he could talk to about the things that defined him so. She asked again about getting Chief Pickford together with her cousin, Betsy. Right after the short voyage, Leo was still hesitant, based mostly on concerns of class. He felt that he was in over his head, not with Ellen but with her family. For as much as he admired the petty officer's technical skills, Leo still felt that he was even further down the social ladder. He didn't want to risk being unmasked as a commoner by attending a royal function with a companion whose behavior he couldn't predict. So it hadn't happened that fall.

By the spring of 1941, however, Leo's contacts with the chief had become fewer and farther between. The young chemist was dealing with the initial briefings of Pickford's counterparts on all the other fighting ships that that were beginning to clog the yard. At the same time, the *Monaghan* was tending to those final touches that would bring her to that peak of mechanical readiness only achieved in the peacetime navy as a ship steamed back out to sea from a major overhaul. Logs of her boiler functions still made their way to the lab, though, and in the *Monaghan,* Leo had his clearest picture of the results that now could be expected from his process.

As she lay at pier side, the ship was pointed down the harbor and out toward the open ocean. The smoke now sometimes climbing gently from her two stacks gave testimony that the vessel was under its own steam more and more regularly. It was the ebb of the tide that made the *Monaghan* drift forward, gently straining the hawsers to hold her fast. Even so, when Leo saw her like that, he couldn't help feeling she was both looking and leaning seaward, itching to be back in her real element.

Off her starboard bow and across the mouth of the Charles were the remains of Sullivan's shipyard. The frigate *Constitution* had been built there, and now the property hosted an increasing coast guard presence. Off *Monaghan's* port bow was a thousand yards of the main channel of Boston's inner harbor. At the far side of the channel was Captain Bang's yard and East Boston. Just across the Chelsea Creek from Bang's, young Jim Monroe was now running his family's boatyard and marine railway. The creek was spanned by an antique drawbridge, further closing in the channel. *Monaghan* was certainly protected, but she was also cloistered. An ocean-going vessel needs to have nothing on the horizon but horizon in order to be truly free, and it was almost time.

Now in the middle of summer, Leo was just a little surprised to see the chief himself report to the chem lab with the latest set of figures. They greeted one another with a handshake, and Pickford got a brief tour of the lab. The hardwood floors creaked a little underfoot as they stepped around crates and fiber drums of test materials. All of the marble-topped lab tables had at least two different tests set up. Nowadays, lab books stayed with their experiments rather than with a single chemist in charge as everyone took a turn at recording data on whichever test they were attending that day. Most of the exposed granite block walls were covered in diazo print charts of past results or future expectations. The chemical laboratory of the Boston Naval Shipyard was bustling with activity.

"Plenty of room for you here," he observed. "Nice and quiet too."

"And just a five-cent trolley ride to Fenway Park anytime you want to catch a ballgame," Leo added, trying to give as good as he got. "What really brings you here, Chief?"

"Well," he said slowly, "we just got our steaming orders, and I thought I'd come over and rub it in a little." A broad smile broke on his thin face, making it light up. "We cast off in two weeks bound for Pearl."

"Pearl?" Leo asked. "Is that a place?"

"Pearl Harbor, Hawaii," Pickford replied wryly. "It's only the best home port assignment a single sailor could have. By Thanksgiving Day, when it's really starting to turn cold in these parts, I'll be in Honolulu, eatin' pineapples and chasin' hula girls!"

"That's great, Chief," Leo said, picking up on the man's excitement. "It couldn't happen to a nicer crew."

"Yeah," Pickford went on. He was looking down just a little now, but his grin was unabated. "We bunker at Newport the day after we leave here. Then it's a speed run to Mayport, Florida. There, we form up with two other vessels for a trip through the canal and on to San Francisco. We'll get a week or so on the Barbary Coast, and then it's off to an outpost in the sun far away from the problems of the world." Pickford looked up at his colleague, and the sparkle in his eye put the lie to his "aw shucks" grin.

"Y'all are just strapped to the beach." He went on, "Boy, don't you just wish you was me!"

"I guess I do," Leo mused.

The thought of an exotic port of call like Hawaii was exciting indeed. He envisioned narrow, white sand beaches bordered by blue water on one side and palm jungles on the other. Naturally, the fantasy included dusky native women wearing only grass skirts and exotic flowers in their silken black hair. Would there be a tall, cone-shaped volcano at the center of the island lazily emitting smoke into the cloudless sky?

Then he thought about the six weeks, more or less, standing watch in a cramped fire room that frequently did its own rendition of the hula dance. Leo remembered why he could never be a snipe.

Chief Pickford saw the wheels turning in his friend's head and was pleased to imagine it as envy.

"Ah'll telegraph you mah next report from Panama City," he replied in an off-handed way designed to milk the moment for everything it was worth. "Maybe ah can also send you some numbers from San Fran, but Pearl is probably just too far away."

"And, of course, you'll be kept quite busy on the beach," Leo said, finishing the thought and letting the sailor bask in the moment. "This calls for a celebration, Chief. Can I invite you out for a night on the town in the company of my girl and perhaps her cousin?"

Betsy Fletcher was a woman in her late twenties who had exactly the life she wanted because she had subtly worked the system to her own advantage. Bred to keep up with the intellect and the wit of those around her, she had been spoiled for ever voluntarily taking a backseat to anyone. There was the problem of society's expectations, however. So finding refuge from a predictable marriage and an even more predictable set of social duties had taken a little creativity.

Growing up, Betsy knew she would never be permitted to simply run away to the circus. To tell the truth, with her accumulated tastes and values, she wouldn't really have wanted to. Still, there were only a limited number of acceptable alternatives to becoming a young matron and treading the well-worn path. She simply chose the one best suited to her and followed it.

As a student at Simmons College for Women in Boston, she had been spared the need to put up with young men or to posture before them, except in social settings where the terms of the competition were more favorable. With that distraction eliminated in the classroom, she had been able to concentrate on the stimuli of the subject matter. Rising to the bait offered by her professors, she'd contended with them on points of philosophy until her academic skills had become finely honed. She came to regard the college as a gymnasium of the mind and herself as the intellectual equivalent of the German gymnasts of the middle of the last century. They had developed their bodies to unheard-of levels on political and philosophical grounds. Then they had been sought after around the world as athletes, trainers, and especially as bodyguards. Alan Pinkerton had used German gymnasts to form the core of Abraham Lincoln's presidential guard. Now Betsy Fletcher aimed to achieve that same level of excellence without the need to have all those unsightly, bulging muscles in evidence.

College gave her an acceptable excuse for four years, but what then? Why, teaching of course. Betsy happily returned to her alma mater and simply changed sides of the academic table to continue the mental weightlifting. She loved teaching because the topics of inquiry meant something to her. She was good at it because she never let any of her students hide in her classroom. Everyone was engaged in the intellectual deliberation, and everyone was critiqued without being judged. With that kind of attention to be had, it wasn't long before students were on waiting lists to get into one of her classes.

Betsy also put the lie to the traditional idea of the egghead. Coming from a successful family as she did, Betsy was supported in reasonable style by a trust fund first set up by her great-grand-parents. Neither she nor the rest of her family was rich like the Rockefellers. The interest from her part of the family trust made a nice supplement to the minimal salary offered by Simmons, however, and frankly, her expenses weren't all that great. She still lived in her parents' home. Since a car was thought to be a liability in the city, she took the streetcar to work. On the weekend, if Betsy Fletcher needed an automobile, she could simply borrow Daddy's. Clothing was important to her. As a younger member of the college's faculty, she felt the need to dress well in order to clearly display which side of the line she now stood upon. Even so, two or three conservative daytime suits and a small range of appropriate blouses completed her professional wardrobe quite

Mark Zaccaria

nicely. It was, after all, an age when clothing was cut from heavy cloth and stitched to last for a lifetime. Her closet, like those of most in her social circle, contained several items that had been handed down by a mother, aunt, or grandmother. These hand-me-downs weren't a matter of charity. They were items that were still both acceptable to a traditional sense of fashion and serviceable for routine wear in conservative settings.

So Betsy was in a position to devote herself to style for style's sake just a little in her personal life. One way or the other, she always turned up at social events in a good-looking party dress that flattered her hourglass figure. She had always taken the time to learn the latest dance or to see the latest picture. In the off time her academic calendar afforded her, she was known to travel to New York City with her mother to shop on Fifth Avenue and perhaps take in a show. She might just as easily be found in slacks and a pullover, helping her cousin Ellen swamp out Montie's stall. Everything about life interested Betsy Fletcher, and she was far from ready to close off any of her options. That made her circumspect on the subject of romance even though she was always on the lookout for an acceptable escort.

When Leo called and suggested that the four of them make a night of it, Ellen didn't even think to consult with her older cousin; she just accepted for her on the spot.

When he pulled up to the Monaghan's gangway that summer Saturday afternoon, Leo was surprised to see that the sailor stepping down, ramrod straight in his crisp, white uniform, was actually Chief Pickford. His hair was freshly cut, and he was freshly shaved and scrubbed. The average civilian would not have thought it possible to starch even a cotton uniform quite that much, nor to make it that white. His black low-quarter shoes were polished to a mirror finish. If he'd looked down at them while he was walking, he would have seen huge, distended legs trailing off below to tiny swinging arms and a pinpoint of a head looking back up at him. He wasn't looking down though.

"You're lookin' pretty sharp, Chief," Leo said as the sailor slid into the Ford's passenger seat. "These girls don't stand a chance."

"Ah sure hope not, Mr. Z," Pickford replied. "After as much gettin' ready as ah did tonight, ah surely hope not."

Leo thought there was a strangely businesslike quality to his voice.

"Now, where can we get some flowers?"

On the way across the causeway from Charlestown to Boston proper, Leo made the mistake of suggesting that flowers were a bit obvious and perhaps even trite. This got him a detailed lecture on how to treat a lady. Pickford claimed no special abilities with the fairer sex, but he was a sailor, after all, and that meant that he had a certain standard to maintain. Women, he pointed out, *want* to see their men make all the obvious gestures. Perhaps flowers and candy were a predictable opening gambit, but they always worked. Since it was too warm for candy, the chief reasoned, it ought to be a bigger bunch of flowers.

As they came alongside North Station, Leo stayed straight and headed down past India Street to the Haymarket. There, his mentor cast a critical eye on all manner of cut flowers sold from stalls and wagons in that oldest of farmer's markets. Finally, Pickford decided on a mixture of crocuses and chrysanthemums. The white-and-yellow bouquet looked airy and cool, just right for a summer's evening. Taking the hint, Leo picked daffodils and carnations, also in yellow and white. Then it was off along the Charles River, down Massachusetts Avenue through Central Square, Harvard Square, and past the Cambridge Common. They took Alewife Brook Parkway to Route 2 and were on their way to Belmont.

At the massive oak front door to Ellen's home, the chief rang the bell and then stood at a modified parade rest position with the flowers held at low port. The man knew about drill and ceremonies, and he'd stood this watch often enough before to be confident that he had it right this time as well. Leo noticed Pickford's calm self-assurance just in time to feel a little awkward himself and just in time to see the door open.

It was Ellen, gorgeous in a light-colored rayon sundress and then suddenly made radiant by the smile and the excitement that overcame her when she saw the flowers and the tableau of the young gentlemen come to call. She swung the door wide, taking Leo's crooked arm and conducting them both into the foyer. She kissed his cheek, thus simply and quickly informing the chief about who was who and what was what.

"Welcome, boys. Come on in," she said. "You must be Chief Pickford. I've heard so much about you. It's a pleasure to finally make your acquaintance."

She offered her hand, and he took her fingers, gently bending them a little toward her palm. He didn't shake it so much as hold it up almost at eye level for what was more like a salute. It was a gesture that in another age would have preceded a formal kiss on the back of her hand.

"Ma'am, the pleasure is all mine," he replied with a suddenly smoother and more mellifluous Southern drawl. "Ah now know why our chemist heah is in such good sprits every Monday mornin'. Mah compliments." The effect was perfect and well practiced, no doubt.

Ellen looked down, and a warm flush came to her milky cheeks. Score one for the navy.

"Why, Mr. Pickford, you ah quite the flatter-ah," she answered, looking up and demonstrating how the New England twang can also be used to good social effect. "I do so like that in a man."

The chief smiled, hoping that Leo was taking note.

"Now, please let me introduce my cousin," Ellen continued, nodding at the parlor archway to the right of the door.

Betsy emerged on cue. She wore a cotton sundress in a pastel print. Its full skirt accentuated both her hips and slim waist

War Record

while its scooped neck brought the sailor's heart into his throat. She was almost as tall as he and looked the picture of a cover girl as compared to his wiry, muscular workingman's frame. On first impression, each was quite pleased with the other.

"Mr. Pickford," she demurred, offering her hand.

"Miz Betsy," he replied, taking it, "ah am overcome."

Overcome? Leo wondered briefly what he meant by *overcome*. In the next moment, though, he recognized that Betsy and the chief were performing a *pas d' deux* at least as complex as the foxtrot.

At his comment, she lowered her eyes. He shook her hand delicately, lowering it when he was done rather than just letting it go. He presented the flowers, and she brightened as if she was just then noticing them. She accepted them in both hands, took a long sniff to enjoy their smell, and then turned to show them to Ellen before turning back to her caller.

"Why, thank you, Mr. Pickford. You shouldn't have," she said.

But by now, even Leo knew that he most certainly should have.

Their greeting was a tableau played out as precisely as any scripted scene in the movies. Even the set was perfect. The rich, polished wood surroundings and the high ceiling of the Stanford White foyer with its formal staircase as a backdrop made the whole picture one of knowing elegance. Each was playing a role that he or she cherished, perhaps mostly because it was not the one played every day. All was justly proud of the fact that they got their own lines and blocking just right. Moreover, each was visibly pleased that the other was doing such a good job of it as well. To a couple raised during the age of the silver screen, this was exactly how the perfect blind date should begin.

"Miz Betsy," the chief replied in his most courtly manner, "ah'd be pleased if you would call me Ravenell. It's my middle name, but it's how my closest friends address me."

Leo hadn't known that.

"Why, Ravenell," she replied, "here and we've only just met. I'd be flattered to call you by your given name, especially since it's as important a name as it is in Southern history."

The chief's polite smile became a grin from ear to ear. He was pleased that she knew already what a proud name it was and, therefore, why he liked to use it. Score one for the well-read college girl.

Ellen intervened to move things along. "Let's get these lovely flowers into some water, Betsy. Would you gentlemen mind saying hello to Daddy while we search out a vase or two?"

The question was rhetorical. She was already moving toward the library door with the whole party in tow.

"Daddy," she asked at the door, "would you entertain our guests for a moment while we put these flowers in water?"

Her father put down his glasses. He got up from the typewritten papers he had been reading and came around from behind his desk to greet the young men. "Come in, gentlemen. Come in," he said warmly.

"Leo, it's good to see you again," he said, offering his hand. "Chief," he continued, "I'm Jack Hurley. Welcome. I hope you're finding our port to your satisfaction."

They exchanged a decidedly more masculine handshake.

"Yes, sir," Pickford replied smartly. He spoke as if he was addressing the captain of his ship. "Our overhaul is just about complete. The craftsmanship has been first class at the navy yard, and the hospitality has been great all around the town, although never more so than right now."

"Well thank you, Chief. It's our pleasure. Do I understand that you're soon to shove off for more sunny and exotic climes?" he asked.

"Yessir," Pickford answered, beaming broadly at the recognition. "We're bound for Pearl in less than two weeks. After a couple stops, we should be there by Thanksgiving. Do I under-

War Record

stand that you used to sail on a four-piper, sir?" the young sailor went on.

"That's right, Chief," Jack said proudly. "I did some convoy duty in the last war."

There it was again, the last war as opposed to the next one.

"It must have been tough," the chief offered. "Those boats were smaller and even less comfortable than ours are today."

"I suppose so," Jack agreed, enjoying the role of old salt. "But we didn't think so at the time. All we knew was that our four-stacked oil burners were a site better than the baby dreadnoughts the Spancos had to sail before us. It must be the same for every generation at sea," he mused. "Twenty-five years from now, there will probably be dancing girls and full orchestras on all the battleships and the Destroyer men will feel slighted because they can only have a four-piece combo."

Chief Pickford ceremoniously scratched the back of his neck as he slowly shook his head at the very thought of such a thing.

It was remarkable to Leo that the two men should so instantly forge a relationship based on the common bond of naval service. Their ages, backgrounds, educations, and futures were far different one from the other. Yet, that single intersection of experience made them like fraternity brothers from different chapter houses. Within a moment of shaking hands, they were relating just like old comrades. Pickford might or might not have known that Ellen's father had been an officer. Leo couldn't recall if he'd mentioned that. Since Jack was the older of the two, he was treated like one, though, just because that was the rule. Both sides knew just how to act, and both sides were pleased to see that the other did too.

In fact, the chief's general acceptance almost made Leo feel a little left out. Ellen and especially Betsy seemed to know enough about what he did aboard ship to at least speak some of his language. They purred over his uniform, which made him stand just a little taller and straighter, if that was possible.

Everyone in the house but Leo seemed to understand the situation before it had even begun. Betsy and Ellen felt that every girl should spend at least one night on the arm of a sailor. Jack knew that part of the culture of navies all over the world was that while ashore, the men served their ladies. Once they were back at sea, of course, it was time to put such things out of their minds and focus on the ship as an organism that could only function when everyone aboard did their jobs at a peak level. To them, having a sailor as a guest was an opportunity to hear a little about a world they might never experience firsthand, just as it would have been to host a violinist from the Boston Symphony Orchestra.

Leo was learning, however. A social evening like the one that lay before them was actually a conspiracy on the part of all concerned. Each entered an unspoken agreement to play their own part in a grand set piece. The better they all handled their roles, the more memorable the evening would be. He felt a little sheepish that he had been concerned about a mismatch of the social hierarchy. All the rest, including Chief Pickford, knew that this was not about living happily ever after. It was just about having a lovely summer evening out. As he thought about it, Leo could almost imagine Glenn Miller's swing band striking up the perfect background music for the scene *In the Mood*.

Realizing all this, he smiled. He relaxed and got ready for a night of dining, dancing, and romancing such as future generations might only read about in books.

As the Monaghan was pulled away from Pier Two for its final trip down Boston's inner harbor, Leo stood by to watch her sail. A small navy band played "Anchors Aweigh" and the ship's company was turned out in dress whites along the rails of the weather deck as a final salute to the yard. Leo didn't even bother to try to look for Chief Pickford. He knew that the chief would be where

War Record

any good snipe should be, below decks, manning his post and tending to his machinery.

As she cleared the yard's pier and bulkhead line and had turned fully down the channel, there was a sudden increase in the white smoke pluming up from her two stacks. Leo noticed it, but it didn't mean anything to him until he heard a couple navy men next to him exclaim.

"Uh Oh!" the one said to the other with a conspiratorial grin. "Here it comes."

Just then, the dark blue water at the *Monaghan*'s stern transom bubbled and boiled as it churned white with a sudden cavitation of the twin screws. The ship went visibly tail down and fairly leapt forward as a curved and foaming wave formed along its raising bow. Leo thought of it as a smile on the ship's face as it came out of the starting blocks on a sprint back to sea. Then the sound broke across the small crowd on Pier Two. It was a sudden rush of growling machinery and burbling water as the ship expressed raw power and lurched ahead.

There were signs posted on buoys in the channel limiting vessels to five knots speed and no wake. These now bobbed wildly back and forth. They were the pendulums of some great inverted clocks as a wake suitable for a Hawaiian surf rider trailed along both sides of the harbor channel. At Sullivan's shipyard, the little coast guard launches juggled up and down at their moorings like the pistons of some open engine. At Alex Bang's boatyard, the clutter of small craft and nautical debris chattered and plashed as the water's edge churned in the passing wake. The old captain looked up from his whittling and cast a critical eye down the channel and an approving grin on the farewell being paid to the port by these navy boys. Down at his pier, though, his son, Val, cursed quietly as he struggled to keep a hemp fender between two small lighters that might gore one another if they jostled metal to metal.

Mark Zaccaria

All the way down the harbor, boatmen, wharf rats, and land-lubbers of every stripe stopped what they were doing and looked up at the flashy departure of the sleek Destroyer. Comments of envy, of wonder, of surprise, and of grumpy disgust followed the *USS Monaghan* as she departed Boston. Of course, the harbor-master's launch also followed it out toward the harbor islands. It had no chance of catching the warship and administering punishment to the ship's master for his showy exit. If the truth were to be told, it probably had no real desire to do so either, but certain appearances had to be kept up.

So the city and the navy both winked at the *Monaghan*'s performance and were secretly proud of it, even though it reminded them that they were strapped to the beach. Leo followed the ship from his post on the pier for as long as he could. He watched it plowing up water and dragging a horizontal plume of white smoke as it heeled into the port turn that took it around Jeffery's Point and out of his sight for the last time.

The next day, there were reports in the newspapers that President Roosevelt had ordered all Japanese assets in United States' banks to be frozen. Those who read beyond the headlines learned that this action had been taken in response to the fact that Japanese Imperial military forces had moved into Indochina. The freeze was accompanied by a warning from the government of the United States of America against any further Japanese advances into Southeast Asia.

A few in America who considered themselves close observers of foreign policy wondered at what role France had played in this action. On the one hand, France owned Indochina and stood to lose the most from any Japanese takeover of its rich resources of rubber, rice, and relaxed colonial living. On the other hand, Nazi Germany, as it was now being called, had occupied France for over a year. Was the US dealing secretly with the Free French in

Morocco? Had the Vichy government made a request that had prompted this action? If so, did that mean a subtle shift toward US support of Hitler?

All these questions focused on the European angles to the story. The average American was still not hearing about Japanese plans to take over either the British Colonies of Malaya and Burma or the Dutch holdings of Java, Sumatra, and Borneo. No public comments were being made about the fact that the resource poor island nation of Japan now had six million men-at-arms and the third largest navy in the world. Third though that navy might have been, it was first in the Pacific.

It might have been that no analysts were thinking about the fact that to hold these potential conquests, Japan would have to reach beyond them to New Guinea, the Celebs, the Solomons, and, of course, the Philippines. If they were, they were not raising any public alarm about the certainty of a major naval conflict in the Pacific when all this began to occur. Of course, there were no first-person radio reports from places like Singapore or Batavia, so matters in the Pacific remained outside of the ken of most Americans.

In essence, the country was vaguely aware of the need to protect itself from another European War. The people of the United States had numerous links to Europe and thought of the people there as their equals or even their betters. Japan was largely ignored, however, mostly on grounds of racial and cultural prejudice. They looked different from most Americans. They spoke a language that might have come from another planet, not just another country. Worst of all, they seemed to work together as a single horde, focusing the entire power of their nation on one project at a time. To a fractious polyglot nation like the United States that barely controlled its teeming and contentious masses with an equally cacophonous government, this last idea was frightening because it was beyond comprehension by American standards.

Mark Zaccaria

A few historians might have pointed out that it had been only fifty years between Admiral Perry's arrival in Tokyo with a single wooden warship and the Russo-Japanese War. In that time, Japan had changed itself from an isolated medieval kingdom of feudal warlords and court intrigues to a modern international power that had crushed what was thought of as one of the largest war machines in Europe. Some might have remarked on the amazing adaptability of a culture that could transition from plutocracy to technocracy so quickly. Others might have noted the galling humiliation of being forced to allow Perry's men ashore simply because they lacked a single cannon and the silent vows never to allow a travesty of that sort again. A few who had attended the conference in Portsmouth, New Hampshire, that had ended the Russo-Japanese War might have reminded one and all that it had taken threats of annihilation by both the US and Great Britain to get the Japanese to the table in the first place. They had simply seen no need to sue for peace with an enemy they felt they could destroy.

All of these ideas might have been put before the American people, but they were not. As a result, most citizens of the United States, psychologically at least, stood facing Europe, thereby ignoring the trouble brewing in Asia.

One thing was certain, however: the Great Depression seemed to be over in more and more places around the country. Perhaps it was the fact that manufacturing was building back up in order to support the growing needs of the combatants abroad. Maybe ordinary people had just adapted to an economy, which had made the painful transition from being mostly agrarian to being mostly cash based. It could have been that all the debts had been retired and all the bankruptcies absorbed, or it might have been that folks were just plain tired of thinking in gloomy and pessimistic Depression terms. Whatever the reasons, in the fall of 1941,

War Record

more and more Americans thought that things were generally getting better.

In a strange way, the Depression had united Americans more than any other event in over 150 years as a republic. In one way or another, it was the one national event in which everyone participated. As a result, it caused the average man in the street to think, *We're all in this together.*

Although the melting pot had always contained distinct ethnic communities that refused to dilute very much in the mix, there were more things that gave the country a common bond than just hard economic times. Radio and the movies had worked together to fabricate a common social experience, even if some only had it vicariously. This common experience led to common standards of behavior, even if these were only in the background behind the regional differences that were still very definite. Of perhaps more importance was the fact that these emerging standards of behavior spanned class lines in addition to geographical boundaries. How and when to doff your hat to a lady became part of this common pattern of social behavior. Farmers who had never seen a taxicab still knew how to hail one on a New York street, how to enter and exit it, and what sort of tip to offer the driver. There was a growing body of common knowledge on how to be an American.

The Thanksgiving holiday was an excellent example of how the social fabric was being woven. Other holidays had different levels of observance and even acceptance in different parts of the country. Thanksgiving dinner was a symbol everyone could accept, however.

Catholics and Protestants differed greatly on such basic matters of Christianity as saints' days and what to make of them. Each regarded the other with suspicion and hostility as a result, and both were very wary of the Orthodox penchant for iconography. So the Good Shepherd's flock didn't congregate very much when it came to holidays. Even the Irish Catholics of South

Boston celebrated St. Patrick's Day in a way far different from their relatives did in Dublin, where the pubs were closed and the churches open to honor that nation's patron. Jewish celebrations of the high holidays were respected by the largely Gentile population, but they, too, served as a reminder of the differences between Americans. Other religions might just as well have been practiced in the catacombs for as much attention as they received nationally. The annual pow-wow of all the tribes of the Plains Indians usually got feature billing in a newsreel, but few outside the reservations recognized it as a holiday, much less a religious celebration.

Non-religious holidays were easier for everyone to understand but sometimes more difficult for them to accept. Although the city fathers were beginning to consider it more seriously, Vicksburg, Mississippi, had yet to resume public celebrations of Independence Day. Folks there still smarted from the federal siege and occupation which had destroyed the town nearly eighty years before, and they were not alone among Southerners in snubbing the Yankee government this way. Washington's birthday was a bit more palatable. He was, after all, a Southerner, but Lincoln's birthday? Please.

Local holidays made for a rich patchwork of folk festivals that existed in a vacuum, unknown to other localities and so not regarded by them as being part of the national heritage. Perhaps folks had heard of Mardi Gras in New Orleans, but few outside the Crescent City itself had actually attended. In Chincoteague, Virginia, the annual Pony Penning Days were essentially an aquatic rodeo and had much in common with the Carson City Round Up in Wyoming. Few in either place had even heard of the event in the other, though, and even if they had it would not have occurred to anyone to link the two in any way. Those on their way to a grunion run in Los Angeles might not know about and would almost certainly never attend a crab boil in Chesapeake Bay or an oyster fry in Charleston, South Carolina.

War Record

So these opportunities for forging bonds across the nation based on common experience went mostly unexploited.

Thanksgiving was another matter, however. Everyone could identify with its origins. For Northerners and Southerners, there was no problem since the events everyone agreed it was based on happened long before Secession. For new arrivals to the land of opportunity, the tale of the pilgrims and their struggles and ultimate triumph made for the quintessential immigrant story. For religious people of every stripe, there was no contest. Having just come through a national time of hardship, the idea of a feast had at least as much resonance with the populace as did the idea of giving thanks. In short, there was something in Thanksgiving for everyone in America.

In East Boston, Mary Zaccaria prepared for an annual round of good-natured battle with her husband. Roast turkey was just not a part of the traditional Italian diet. While Tony was always ready to host a feast, he was also particular about the kinds of things he would allow to be served to his guests. The radio was a powerful adversary for him, though, when it came to the Thanksgiving menu. Everybody had turkey on the last Thursday in November. Mary knew that. She had heard it all over the radio and read about it in the Globe, the Post, the Herald, and the Traveler. Tony knew it too. He saw the papers and listened to the radio. That didn't mean he could just acquiesce though.

"Mmm…" he said thoughtfully as he opened the oven door to inspect what was cooking. "At's a big chicken. I might not have a room for pasta after. Maybe we should invite more people?"

"We got enough," Mary said. She was all business as she moved purposefully around the small kitchen. "An you got no problem 'cause we got no pasta today."

She moved pots, pans, and plates in precise flanking movements within the three-dimensional space. A chess master look-

Mark Zaccaria

ing in would have recognized a final gambit unfolding. Neither Tony nor the bird stood a chance.

"No pasta?" he asked in mock surprise. "Are you sure you from Napoli?"

He sat in the small kitchen, enjoying the moment. There was a jug of wine on the porcelain sheet metal tabletop, and he felt like a king to have a whole day off in the middle of the week like this.

"With turkey, you get potatoes," she said. It was a summary judgment. "You a farmer." She went on with a wry smile. "You must like potatoes." Turnabout was fair play, after all.

Leo and his kid brother still lived in the downstairs flat with their parents. Both of the girls were married. Edith and Frank had taken the apartment on the top floor for a while before they moved to a small double-decker in Winthrop. Now Rose and Paul had the third floor of Tony's house on Lexington Street. By whatever route, they would all make the pilgrimage to Mary's table that day.

At the appointed hour, that kitchen table underwent a metamorphosis. Growing to its full length, it moved into a diagonal position across the kitchen floor, which made maneuvering difficult for the people and opening the oven door impossible. The turkey was already out, though, on display for the diners to admire as they squeezed into their seats.

Tony took careful time with his flint steel hone as he expertly brought a large carving knife up to razor sharpness. He dissected the bird with the sure confidence of a skilled surgeon. As he sliced the breast meat ever so thin, he was more like a barber carefully shaving his patron. He even puckered his lips and forced them to one side as he concentrated on the task. He was applying imaginary body English to the carcass in order to get the difficult slices just right.

"*Va co ci*," he said silently to the bird.

War Record

Placing the cut pieces on a platter, he had the esthetic touch of an artist arranging a still life that could be commemorated in oils, or just consumed for Thanksgiving dinner. His performance was as much a magnum opus as Mary's cooking had been, each made even better by the presence of an audience. The family expected nothing less from their patriarch and matriarch, and nothing less would be delivered.

Soon, the kitchen was awash in the hubbub of clinking cutlery and simultaneous conversations. So much heat and light was concentrated in the small room that the two windows that faced each other at the corner were both opened wide to admit the icy freshness of November in Boston. The cold blast could not be noticed even a foot or two away from the windows. The family, which had once dined together every day, now took the more infrequent opportunity of a gathering to energetically exchange information about all that had gone on that fall. There was talk of babies and of school sports. Expert criticism of the dairy industry was followed by talk of Christmas and who would do what to prepare for that feast. Fashion and the movies held the floor briefly at one end of the table while at the other, there was talk of the relative benefits of brass versus bronze for large marine propellers.

So it was in Belmont at just the same time. Ellen's family convened in the formal dining room, cut off from the profusion of activity in the kitchen. The more refined setting made everyone at table take their responsibility in the unfolding drama all the more seriously. There, too, an unusually large number of family members was assembled, and they all took full advantage of the opportunity to catch up on everyone's comings and goings.

When another large turkey, roast to a turn, was presented at the head of the long mahogany table, Jack stood to perform his ceremonial duties just as Tony had. His carving knife was equally sharp, but he, too, took a public moment to touch it up with a flourish. He made ever so slight a show of furrowing his brow as

Mark Zaccaria

he touched the finished edge with his finger before silently pronouncing it fit with a broad smile.

In fact, the same tableau was being played out in a remarkably large number of the homes, farms, and apartments all across the forty-eight states. America was made as truly united in this ritual feast as it had ever been by anything in peacetime. As the late afternoon flowed serenely across the country from east to west, the whole population showed the aftereffects of a high-protein meal. A ripple of contentment traveled from Atlantic to Pacific. Old people sat back in comfort. Young people began to itch for something to do. Children were bored, wondering when they could doff their best clothes and shoes and get back to the serious business of play.

Tony Zaccaria sat alone in his kitchen in East Boston. The table had shrunk to its ordinary size and retreated to its normal position. The women were all in the front room, locked in an animated conversation and oblivious to anything else on Earth. The young men were outside, taking the air and looking studiously into the open engine compartment of one automobile or another. Tony sat quietly, sipping on homemade grappa and carefully analyzing how well this batch had turned out. He smoked a harsh, rock hard Italian stogie. Its acrid smoke cut into his lungs and made them tingle even as it made his head a little light. The moment was made even more satisfying by his own recognition of the skill with which he handled the choreography of the glass, the cigar, the ashtray, and his peaceful thoughts.

He had eaten well. The family was together and happy. Life was good. When his eyelids dropped involuntarily, he sat up with a start.

That's right, he thought, *the only thing that could make this moment better would be a little nap.*

Always one to take an active role in solving his own problems, Tony put down his stogie and finished his drink. He slouched just slightly in the ladder-backed kitchen chair and folded his arms. His chin settled down onto his chest, and the day got just a little better. He had been at peace. Now he was also at rest.

In Belmont, Jack Hurley sat in a wingback leather chair, facing the fireplace in his study. He watched the dancing flame and savored a perfect scotch and soda. He puffed on a briar pipe mostly for something to do, and he, too, was at peace. His wife appeared briefly at the library door. She observed him for a moment as he felt the warmth of the fire on his closed eyelids. Taking note of his even but slightly heavy respirations, she smiled and quietly closed the door. Outside in the barn, Ellen and Betsy smoked cigarettes and talked about love.

A little later on, Leo excused himself and drove off toward Route 2. Not long after that, Ellen checked her watch and decided to go inside and get ready.

You're in the Army Now

In the United States, the calm and peace of Thanksgiving Day 1941 was something of a mirage. In order to feel it, Americans had to ignore the gathering storm of war, and they did. Some had to work pretty hard to disregard all the danger signals. They overlooked them successfully, however, choosing to believe instead that the oceans and their own lack of understanding protected them from the confusing contest of forces underway in the world. They clung to the notion that because everything felt good on Thursday, November 27, things would always feel that way.

On the East Coast of America, it was late Sunday afternoon, nine days later, when the first reports of the attack on Pearl Harbor shattered the illusion of well-being. They seemed to come out of nowhere. People were beginning to concentrate on Christmas shopping and their preparations for the winter that was settling in. Sunday afternoons were traditionally very quiet times in those days, long and languid. Shops were closed, very few people worked, and sports events were few and far between. That late in the day, most church services were long since over. The great majority of people were relaxing in their sitting rooms.

They read and chatted while the ubiquitous radio played calmly in the background. It was too early for any of the important serials or adventure dramas to be on the air, so music was the almost universal background to the family still lifes being played out in the parlors of America.

"Your attention please, ladies and gentlemen! Urgent news has just reached us from the US possession of Hawaii in the Pacific! Please stand by!" That strident lead was followed not by a headline, not by a commercial message, and not by a return to the music. It was followed instead by that most unusual and unnerving of radio phenomena: dead air. The music had been interrupted in mid-passage. An announcer unfamiliar to the audience had broken in with a breathless statement that something was up and that it was big. Then there was silence. There was never silence on the radio.

Everywhere in America, people looked up from their reading. They put down pieces of jigsaw puzzles, forgetting about the patterns. Even small children who had been bored and making a nuisance of themselves just for something to do went silent as the droning radio did too. Everyone looked up. They looked at the radio, wondering what was going on and waiting for the next thing to happen.

Meanwhile, in local stations all along the network, the junior staffers who manned Sunday's skeleton shift were being faced with huge decisions that they knew they weren't allowed to make. Frantic network traffic was issuing bulletins from Washington about an air and sea battle in which US warships were being sent to the bottom by the score. The loss of life was said to be enormous. Worst of all, it was reported to be a surprise attack, that absolute antithesis of everything average Americans believed about fair play.

Even the youngest of the radio engineers on duty that day at the smallest of stations in the most rural areas of the country had vivid memories of the Orson Welles broadcast called *War*

War Record

of the Worlds. In 1938, it had sent millions into panic by making them believe that Martians had invaded the United States. Each of these youngsters had gruff older bosses they had to answer to if they made special announcements, and the bulletins coming along the net this afternoon were almost as fantastic as Welles's story about invaders from another planet. In many cases, frantic telephone calls were made to the homes of station managers before these bulletins were read.

The hesitation that marked the initial announcement of the attack made the process seem fearful and disorganized. That was a fairly accurate assessment of what was really going on. So when the information was finally broadcast, it was the way in which it was reported that triggered at least as much concern on the part of listeners as did the details themselves.

"We interrupt this broadcast to inform you of a massive air and sea attack that has been made today on US military forces in the Pacific! Approximately one thirty this afternoon, Washington time, elements of the Imperial Japanese Navy bombarded US Army and Navy installations at Pearl Harbor in the Hawaiian Islands, an American possession in the Pacific Ocean!" Unfamiliar broadcast voices tried valiantly to get out sentences that were far too long to afford them any breath. Local programming was canceled, and the feed was hastily switched to newsrooms in New York and Washington.

Short of the notorious Welles broadcast, nothing like this had ever been covered before by the radio networks. Presidential elections, for example, were scheduled years in advance, and their results took several days to develop. Radio, as the neural network of the nation, had never been tested in time of national tragedy before. No one knew what would happen when this electrical jolt was sent out from broadcast towers all over the country. What did happen was a massive twitch. It was an involuntary nervous response that would have stunned even Galvani because it wrenched the muscles of an entire country.

Across America, eyes went wide. Stomachs knotted up with a sudden sense of vulnerability. Mothers feared for their children even though they were right there at their feet. Fathers, uncles, and older brothers were hastily called in from the yard or the barn. They dropped what they were doing to tractors, bicycles, washtubs, coal bins, or a hundred other pet projects, and they raced in to find out what was wrong. Was it a death in the family? In a strange way, it was, sort of.

An innocence about national affairs and America's place in the world died that day for the great naive majority of the US population.

In East Boston, as everywhere in America that evening, families looked to their leaders for answers to the question of what was going on. Matriarchs and especially patriarchs were uncomfortable because they knew that it fell to them to explain and then direct the next steps that should be taken. How could they though? They knew no more than their sons or daughters did. Everyone listened to the same news about the attack. Those held responsible for leadership, even in family groups, knew instinctively that they were powerless to do anything effective.

On Lexington Street, in Tony Zaccaria's front room, the radio dispensed reports with ever-increasing detail. There were descriptions of the wave after wave of torpedo bombers wreaking havoc on warships moored in their homeport. Enemy fighters and dive-bombers were reported to be soaring with impunity over the army air field. They were said to be strafing American aircraft parked on the ground before any pilots could make their way out to them, much less climb aloft to oppose the onslaught. Tony's youngest son, Tony Jr., was taking it all in and trying to make something out of it.

"What's goin' on, Pop?" he finally asked.

War Record

How could Tony answer that? He knew little about military aircraft and naval warfare. He knew nothing of the politics behind the launch of such an attack. Oh, he was enough of a cynic to understand that governments are run by men who get crazy on power. In Italy, he had seen that the line between bandits and local political bosses was sometimes blurred, depending more on who was "in" and who was "out" than on anything else. How could he scale that idea up to make it apply to an entire nation and beyond to an alliance of nations? Then how could he explain all that in a way in which it would make sense to a thirteen-year-old?

He was frustrated, and he felt helpless. This led quickly to anger, but it was anger that had no place to focus as yet. These conflicting emotions were distilled into a one-word answer to his son.

"*Basta!*" he said gruffly, cutting off any further debate on the subject.

So it was all around the country. The traditional sources of policy and opinion that fed the collective consciousness of America were unable to cope with a problem of this magnitude. Something like this had never even been considered before. People were stunned, and they were at a loss to explain what was going on.

When Leo came in, attention shifted to him. He knew about these things. He worked for the navy. Surely he could tell them something. As he walked through the door, he could feel the fact that all eyes were upon him.

He didn't have any special insight either. He knew that he had to try to keep everyone calm, however, so he did the thing he knew how to do best. He began to analyze the situation methodically.

"This attack is a very serious matter," he explained to his younger brother, as everyone else listened in. "There is no question that it means war with Japan. Next, a naval vessel is a large, expensive, and very complex item. If that many of them have really been lost, it will take a terribly long time to replace them and train new crews. In the meantime, our ability to hold off the Japanese navy will be a real question. This is not good news."

Was he trying to make them feel better? It is possible to be too frank and honest.

"There's another problem," he went on. "The Japanese have a very close working relationship with the Germans. If Hitler takes this opportunity to come at us from the other side, we could be in even bigger trouble than we are today.

"We have a couple of aces in the hole though," he said, realizing that he had to redeem his audience and give them something to look forward to. "We have a population that is far greater than that of Japan and Germany combined. We have at least as many factories as they have, and probably more. We have thousands of miles of ocean between our shores and theirs. They won't be able to bring a real army across that kind of a barrier for quite some time.

"Nothing bad will happen to California or Massachusetts right away," he concluded, "although I'd be pretty worried if I were in Hawaii tonight."

All around America, similar assessments were being made as people began to come to grips with what lay ahead by trying to apply logic to it. The shock of the sneak attack was palpable. You could feel it in every household. What was harder to notice that first night was the bond of resolve that was already starting to harden over the whole nation.

The next morning, when Leo arrived at the Boston Naval Shipyard, there was no question that he was entering another world. There was a line of three cars waiting to enter the main gate. This was the first time he had ever had to stop and wait before being admitted. He was almost insulted at first. An automobile was a ticket to freedom. Drivers didn't expect to have to wait for anything, much less other motorists.

As he inched closer to the gate, Leo saw what was holding things up. He calmed down immediately. There were three marines at the guard post. They wore olive green fatigues, side arms, bloused combat boots, and soft, olive green hats that looked like smaller versions of the billed caps worn by railroad men. The marines also wore very stern expressions and carried carbine rifles slung over their right shoulders.

When Leo's turn came, a grim-looking sergeant bent down to the Ford's window.

"Good morning, sir. May I have your name and department please?" he commanded.

"Ah. Why, Leo Zaccaria from the chem lab," he stammered.

The marine started writing on a clipboard he was holding.

"Would you spell that please, sir?"

He had no list. He was merely taking down the names of everyone who entered. After they went through the spelling, the marine folded the clipboard under his left arm. He looked at Leo with iron eyes.

"Sir, as you might imagine, there will be stringent new security measures instituted at this facility today. Please enter and park as you normally would. Be aware, though, that unless there is some operational reason for you to use a privately owned vehicle in this yard, you will not be permitted to do so probably starting tomorrow. You will be issued a personal pass by your supervisor today. Please keep that pass with you at all times while on post. You will be required to show it both when entering and exiting at any gate. If you are issued an additional pass for your automobile, it will have to be kept plainly visible in the driver's side windshield at all times. Do you understand, sir?"

"Why, yes. Of course," he managed.

With that, the sergeant stood erect and waved the car on with a move that was more like a salute made as extended fingers and a horizontal forearm snapped across his chest. Leo let out his clutch and slowly pulled ahead.

What a soldier, he thought.

At the laboratory, things seemed strangely normal. The typist who sat by the main entrance, acting as receptionist for the office, had puffy red eyes and was barely holding back even more tears. Fred Hemmings's secretary, the only other woman in the lab, was showing grim resolve. As for the rest of the chemists and technicians, though, the level activity hadn't changed from the busy pace that had been developing for some time now.

All the same test setups were there to be inspected, and readings were taken as usual. By all of only eight in the morning, there hadn't been time to establish much in the way of new emergency experiments. There wasn't a lot of talk among the colleagues. Each had a slightly vacant, incredulous expression. When they glanced at each other, the questions were obvious without having to voice them. It was equally obvious that no one had an answer, so there was little or no chatter.

Fred Hemmings was nowhere to be seen. It soon became apparent that a meeting of all department heads had been the yard superintendent's first order of business this Monday morning. In Fred's absence, there was nothing to do but to continue the work that had been left off on Friday. So for most of the morning, everyone kept to the existing laboratory schedule. The difference was the level of effort. Unconsciously, each worker in the lab was putting far more into his or her work this morning than they ordinarily did. It wasn't that people ordinarily took it easy. Far from it. It was that as the enormity of what was happening settled in on people, they knew they had to do something.

The same thing was happening in every other shop around the shipyard, as it was in every office, factory, and farm across the United States. America was already beginning to fight. It was too soon for any leaders to have issued orders or to have sent instructions to people. Individuals were simply realizing that whatever

War Record

their job was, they had to do it better. People were putting more energy into their normal tasks because that was all they could think to do right away. It was nervous energy, but it was about doing something. It was not about becoming frozen. America had been stunned by an attack that everyone took personally. It hadn't happened to military assets in some remote Pacific outpost.

It happened to us, they all thought.

Horrified though they all were, the attack would not prevent Americans from acting. Quite the opposite; it triggered them into a frenzy of defensive responses.

The very first of those in almost every case was to take whatever productive task lay at hand and to perform it with all your might. Thus, when Fred Hemmings returned to his chemical laboratory in the late morning, what he found was a beehive of activity. He saw at once what was going on, and he was pleased.

It's almost too bad, he thought briefly, *that most of the tasks being tended to so energetically are to be superseded.*

On Monday, December 8, 1941, in the United States of America, virtually every existing priority shifted and a new order of things fell into place.

Fred didn't have to formally call the meeting he needed to have with his people. When he walked in, everything gradually stopped and everyone was slowly drawn toward him. He had news, and everyone wanted to know what it was. Fred got as far as the center of the main lab room, at the intersection between four large lab tables. There, his nineteen or twenty staffers surrounded him, and the meeting began more or less on its own.

There really wasn't much to say beyond the obvious. It still took over an hour for the chief chemist to say it all amid the barrage of questions that were often repeated at different times from different quarters. The nation was almost certainly at war. Although the declaration of war would be against Japan, that nation had attacked both Pearl Harbor and the British colonies of Malaya and Hong Kong on December 7, that almost certainly meant an alliance between Britain and the US in the Pacific; but since the United Kingdom was also at war in Europe, it was thought to be only a matter of time until America was fighting there too.

Operationally, the importance of the chemical laboratory was stressed. It was one of the necessary functions in a military shipyard that happened to lie on a Great Circle route between North America and Europe. The yard could expect to see an increase in business as British, Canadian, and other Allied ships began to call for docking and repairs.

Fred mentioned Leo by name. He had a car, and if he agreed to continue using it for the odd official errand, he would be issued a pass for it. Leo's broad smile and the twinkle in his eye at that suggestion constituted his acceptance of the offer. Everyone was issued a stiff paper pass that had been turned out that morning by the yard's reproduction office. They had mimeographed a simple typewritten form onto heavy manila stock. Its title said what it was, a worker's pass to the Boston Naval Shipyard. There was a place for the worker's name to be printed and for his or her department to be listed. Then there was a line for the worker's signature and one for the supervisor's. High security.

Fred finished by explaining that as events unfolded, there would be lots of changes in what was going on in the lab. He instructed everyone not to be offended if their own favorite project was suddenly canceled or if they did not always understand why the navy building wanted this experiment or that done on some impossible schedule.

"As of right now, we are all part of the most enormous war effort the world has ever seen," he stressed. "The important thing is protecting our country and its way of life. Everything else is negotiable. Any questions?"

There were no questions, and no one in the room really thought that anything was negotiable. There hadn't been enough new information presented to have made a decent cut-in news bulletin on the radio. Even so, everyone felt like they had just gotten an important pep talk from the coach, and they all left energized. There was iron determination in the spirit of every member of the laboratory to do whatever he or she had to do to help the group prevail. No one could imagine the hardships that lay ahead, and that was just as well. No matter what they were, this little team was now ready to greet each one with a simple question: How do we lick this one?

It was mid-afternoon before the *Monaghan* came to Leo's mind. For a few minutes, his thoughts were with Chief Pickford and the crew he had known for all those months and sailed with that once.

"Shipmates," he muttered bitterly to himself.

It laid a sudden rush of adrenaline and a pang of sorrow on top of the nagging fear and anger that had been brewing in him overnight. It also slowed down his efforts to recalibrate a wet chemistry test setup he was supposed to be working on. He stowed his concerns and got back to work, but his anger continued to well up inside.

All over the country, emotions rose and fell. In most places, the roller-coaster ride was even more extreme. At Leo's lab, everyone wore the mantle of the US government. They felt closer to the heart of the country's leadership, and they felt like they had a responsibility to provide an example for others whom they increasingly referred to as civilians. In the ordinary offices, as in the mines and construction sites across America, however, spirits went up and down like the elevators people rode back and forth to work.

Fear of an impending invasion was rampant. Was Pearl Harbor just the first action in a coordinated effort that would strike at one hundred different US locations before anyone had time to react? No one stopped to think about the fact that the combined armies of the entire world did not posses enough manpower and material to launch that many simultaneous attacks. Fear is that way.

Rage reared its ugly head rather quickly. Someone or something had to be the cause of this atrocity. It's perhaps a measure of how little was generally known about Japan that morning that the top vote-getters for "target of irrational rage" were Satan, Hitler, Stalin, Social Security, and the Republican Party.

"It's that damned Social Security!" exclaimed those who saw the program as a newly established drain on the national treasury. "It's sapped us of our strength and left us wide open for this sort of kick in the pants!"

Pronouncements on other simple targets of rage were equally illogical. They served as a vent for the pressure that built up in response to fear, though, and they could be heard almost everywhere in the hours following the news of Pearl Harbor.

The one thing everyone wanted desperately was news. Every radio in the country was left on, and every time there was a bulletin, telephone lines would hum as the latest word was relayed and rehashed. By the time President Roosevelt addressed the nation that evening, the cluster of microphones he spoke into were a direct link to the consciousness of the population. One hundred and twenty-five million central nervous systems were fused together as one in a phenomenon of collective will that was still not fully recognized by government leaders, even if executives in Hollywood were quick to spot it.

Grim statistics were announced. Over two thousand naval officers and men were lost as five of the eight American battleships in the Pacific were either sunk or crippled. The army lost over two hundred men and almost as many aircraft at its airfields at Hickam, Wheeler, and Ford's Island. Loss of life was still shocking to a society not yet deadened to such news by a steady diet of carnage in its entertainment and public affairs reporting. Loss of property was also a very big deal to people just at the dawn of the age of consumer products. Even more, loss of pub-

War Record

lic property was an assault on the sanctity they subconsciously invested in government. That really got to the root of the reaction in American society. The nation felt insulted.

When the president announced that war had been declared, there was no political dimension to the statement at all. No one opposed the idea. Everyone would have been completely stunned if America had taken any other course of action. No one really wanted war. It frightened everyone who thought about it. There was no choice, however, and the declaration was a simple formality that was executed quickly and in a businesslike manner.

Three days later, when Germany and Italy declared war on the United States, the country was already over the initial shock. None of the other ninety-nine invasions had taken place yet. Recruiting offices were already clogged with lines of young men responding to a call that had not yet been made. At those offices, the strict quotas that had marked the peacetime army and navy in the thirties were being completely ignored, even before official orders to do so could be passed along. Everyone was getting some paperwork to fill out. A massive list began to be made, as the million-man US military got ready to double in size and then to double again.

Back at the chem lab, Fred Hemmings took Leo aside and made sure he understood one thing.

"I gave you the car pass because you're about the only one here who drives all the time," he said. "I had one to give out, so I did. I don't really see that we will be asking you to drive for the yard. It won't be long before a lot of things change around here, and that quaint little custom will be one of the first to disappear. I just want to be sure you've thought about one other matter. It won't take long before just about every drop of fuel America produces will be sent directly to the army and navy. You'd best not get too used to driving because it will get real difficult before this thing is over."

Leo thought about it and saw the logic behind what his boss was saying. That night, he took two five-gallon jerry cans with

　　　　　Mark Zaccaria

him from the lab's surplus stores. On the way home, he filled up the Ford's tank and got an extra ten gallons for later. When he got back to Eastie, he lugged the two cans into the garden and just left them along the fence at the rear of the little quadrangle. By the time the ground began to thaw in March, things had already changed to the point that he was uncomfortable having the gasoline cans visible like that. He buried them and immediately began to look around for two or three more cans. By then, though, the cans were not the problem; it was the gas.

During the first few months of the war, the news seemed to be all bad. The mood of the country quickly changed in a number of obvious ways. Suddenly, everyone knew a good deal about the geography and recent history of the Philippines, Singapore, Java, Sumatra, and Ceylon for starters. There was also quite a lot of casual talk about the pros and cons of various types of military strategy and heavy weapons, although this was more so among those in midlife and the very young.

Those who were just coming of age were also coming to realize that they were the ones who were going to have to fight this war. Young men and women alike pondered the fact that they would be called upon to volunteer in one way or another. More nagging than that, though, were the all-too-common thoughts that they were being cheated somehow. It crossed many young people's minds that they were being robbed of opportunities that they had been promised.

Leo, like many around him, became an angry young man without really understanding why. He saw Ellen as much as he could. She, in turn, seemed to be clinging to him far more than he would have thought a capable young woman should. Certainly, it was more than he could appreciate in his increasingly inward state of mind.

Although his emotions, his upbringing, and his habits kept him heading back to Belmont, it was getting more difficult to conduct a romance all the time. When the war broke out, the whole

War Record

country went through a number of reflex reactions. Everyone stopped spending money on anything that appeared frivolous. Entertainment budgets were quickly diverted into savings just on general principles. Whether or not that needed to be done in the early months of World War II in America, it certainly was being done. That meant that nightclubs and restaurants scaled way back or shut down completely. Hotels no longer ran dance parties in their ballrooms. Movies were shown to packed houses, but there wasn't as much else for a young couple to do as there had been.

Leo had a job that was sure to be there for the duration. His natural talent at deal making had fallen somewhat into disuse now that he was having steady paydays. Still, he always had $20 more in his pocket than had originally been in his pay envelope. Money should not have been a problem, but once the war broke out, somehow, it was just not right to spend it. With no place to go as nightlife shut down all around them, Leo and Ellen couldn't even take a drive. It was almost unpatriotic to use gasoline for socializing while General MacArthur and his outnumbered garrison of US and Filipino troops were under siege on the Bataan Peninsula.

With the use of the car as a personal private space eliminated, staying at home was all that was left. Ellen's parents were good about leaving them alone. Still, there was always the possibility of being intruded upon to put a damper on romance.

"What's happening to this crazy world?" she finally asked in frustration. "What are we going to do?"

She looked up at him, and it was clear that she wanted him to have concrete answers to questions that were not really about statecraft.

He was frustrated and confused too. Then he was embarrassed because he had similar questions and none of the answers. His embarrassment turned immediately to anger.

Why is it suddenly my job to know everything? Doesn't she under-stand that there is a war on and that it is going badly? "I don't know what to tell you," he said with none of the tenderness he should have said it with. He shrugged and looked away.

It was one more sign to her that the world was falling apart.

In a strange way that nobody thought about, the world was fall-ing apart.

World War I had been a shock to the planet, and nowhere more so than in the United States. The carnage had been enor-mous. Mechanized weapons tore men limb from limb as gener-als followed outdated plans based on chivalrous fantasy, sending wave after wave of foot soldiers into the maw. Clouds of mus-tard gas drifted lazily across the battlefield. They dispensed their death or permanent pulmonary agony on friendly troops as fre-quently as on enemies. Living conditions in the front lines were as mean as any that history had ever seen, allowing diseases of all types to flourish and take as many lives as did the shot and shell.

In World War I, Europe devoured and digested an entire generation of its young men. That wasn't clear to the Europeans until it was almost done. Americans, though, had the example of the War Between the States still fresh and in living memory. Americans understood from the start that everyone was going to die a horrible death in the Great War. They openly wondered what could possibly make such a sacrifice worthwhile.

It was the war to end all wars.

That's how it was sold to America, and that's what people believed. When the veterans who could returned to family life and raised the generation that would fight the Second Great War, they were convinced that it could never be so. The Civil War was terrible. The World War was unimaginable. The next step in such a bloody progression would surely be more than humanity could endure.

War Record

So it must be true, they thought. Wars had ended. The veterans and the women who had waited for them all dearly hoped that it was true. Every parent wants something better for their children than what they had. So American parents in the 1920s accepted the idea that war was over. They had been so scarred by it that they couldn't conceive of subjecting their precious children to such agony. Thus, the promise was born. It was the promise of no more war and a better life ahead.

Whether they had ever been told this outright or not, Leo and his entire generation were taught to believe that war had ended. Their whole social order conspired to make that promise to them. Advances in science and industry confirmed that a better and better quality of life was what the future had in store. Such unabated progress was to be possible exactly because the destruction and chaos of war would be absent.

The many utopian views of the future that were popular in 1930s America all depended on populations of normal men and women who went along with the social dictates that would lead to a well-ordered, perfect life. At some level, virtually all the men and women who would be the ones to populate these Elysian communities accepted the promise in return for a commitment of their own to go along. It was part of what motivated a mass exodus from the American farm as young men looked increasingly to great corporations for their livelihoods. The nation of shop owners and small farmers that had been America in 1880 underwent quite a change in the fifty years that followed. That change was forced by economics and based on the efficiencies of scale. The Great War and its lesson that history had made a sharp turn accelerated it. The change in America was virtually finalized by Leo's generation as they accepted the promise as the basis for their budding careers.

So, out of the shambles of the Great Depression, a new world order would emerge. It was to be a phoenix rising from the ashes of the last great indignity forced upon mankind by the old way.

America has always been a naive and optimistic place where impossible things routinely occur because no one understands or accepts their impossibility. The west had been won. The nation had been forged in war and girded with a sash of cities that were economic powerhouses furiously producing capital by means still only dimly understood. The continent could be crossed by train in a few days with the traveler couched in upholstered luxury, dining and relaxing the entire way. The Empire State Building had been erected and was a wonder of the world. When the French faltered, the Panama Canal had been built and trade all around the world had gotten faster and easier.

Look at all the evidence Leo saw growing up. Is it any wonder that he believed it, along with most Americans of his age? Doesn't it follow that the young men would seek out technical employment with the giant industrial organizations that were to be the engines of prosperity? Isn't it obvious that the young women would prepare themselves to manage the families and rear the next generation of loyal and happy workers? Of course, and this almost universal undercurrent explained much about the behavior of the American generation that was about to go to war. Social mores and taboos could all be traced to it, as could scientific and academic advances and even the economic growth of corporations as their manpower needs became easier and easier to fulfill.

It all worked like a unified plan until the promise was broken.

When America was plunged into war, the society that had devised, nurtured, and proclaimed the promise was shaken at its root. People were dazed. Everything they had learned was proven wrong. Everything they had been told was shown to be a lie. Their parents, the very people they trusted and relied on most, had misled them. American society, that most complex and pervasive construct, the very matrix upon which the promise balanced, had failed them. Leo and everyone he knew felt betrayed.

It's difficult, of course, for the betrayed to act in a civilized and genteel manner.

War Record

Leo met Ellen in town a few times after it became clear that driving to Belmont was out of the question. She took the train in, and he met her after a short streetcar ride.

As a city dweller and a young man with numerous contacts around the neighborhood, Leo was aware of which night clubs were still open. More likely, he would have a line on a private dance party being held someplace. These would be very off-the-cuff affairs. Frequently, they were organized by the three- and four-piece combos, that provided the music. Always there seemed an almost underground air bout the entire event. Maybe there was nothing illegal going on, but it still felt like a return to the speakeasy days. Passwords or signals were exchanged between arriving revelers and taciturn bouncers. The small cover charge was always paid in an almost surreptitious manner, with a young lady looking away demurely as her young man handed a few dollars to a figure standing in the shadows. Those wishing to drink usually brought their own to the small social clubs or fraternal or union halls where these parties took place.

Leo first took Ellen to one of these parties worried that it might be beneath her. He was concerned that she could feel this was slumming it just a little too much. The party was all that was going on, though, so off they went.

Arriving at the dimly lit hall, they immediately had all of their senses assaulted at once. The dancers were whirling around to a waltz number being played maybe half a measure too fast. It was a visual blur in the soft light. The hubbub of the dancers was competing with the three-piece band pretty evenly as they entered at the back of the hall. Their ears had to work to distinguish between the two. The size of the crowd in the packed hall and the athletic nature of the dancing combined to give the party the strong, warm aroma of a handball court mixed with substantial traces of perfume and cigarette smoke. Somehow, it all combined to attract and arrest the attentions of the revelers so fully that they forgot about everything that was going on outside. This was a party, after all, and no one wanted to dwell on what was happening beyond its walls.

When Leo led Ellen into the whorl on the dance floor, he was a little surprised by how tightly she held on and how quickly she seemed to be lost in the frenetic dance. There was no dance space between them, nor did they want there to be. This wasn't a performance for anyone else to see. As he engulfed her, he moved her around and back and forth to the music. She clung to him with eyes closed and a cherub's smile. It added an exciting tactile sensation to the overall mix. Leo thought this a little aggressive on Ellen's part. He wondered at her appetite for him and how it was being displayed in public now a little more strongly than it had been in the past. That was quite all right, you understand; it was just unlike the girl he had known so far. Leo smiled hard, watching through narrowed eyes. The dim light glinted off his teeth, and he scanned the floor as they danced.

Around the room, the dancers were groping and grinding to the music. The crowd was almost unnaturally coupled off. Every guy had a gal, and there didn't seem to be too many partygoers standing alone at the edges of the floor. The crowd was expressing an enormous sexual energy. Leo was surprised to see the women participating as willingly and hungrily as they were. It was quite a change from the more staid, standoffish, and painfully proper approach that would have been almost universal among young women before the war. None of the young men seemed to mind. They were all happily taking advantage of the situation.

When the music stopped, the players had to mop their brows and their instruments. They took a short breather before striking up the next number, and the dancers stood at rest while waiting for more music. Couples all around the floor were standing together with arms around each other's waists. Girls rested their spare hands on the chests of their partners and massaged them gently, enforcing property rights. Guys held their free arms akimbo or thrust the extra hand into a slash pocket, looking around the room and posing for the others.

"Hey, Jimmy!" said a young man standing near Ellen and Leo.

"Gino, hi! What'cha know?" was the response from one half of a nearby couple.

"Not much, Jimmy. It's good to see ya. By the way, say hi to Angie."

"Angie. What a great name. I'm pleased to meet'cha. An' this here is Betty. How do ya do?"

The two couples faced each other and chatted briefly while the band got ready. As the next tune began, a sudden smile came to Gino's face. He had just thought of something.

"Hey, Jimmy, let's switch for this dance. Whaddaya say?"

For a moment, the free arms went out and the two couples became a foursome, only to divide again with the opposite pairing. A samba reenergized the floor, and the dance ground back into motion. Gino and Betty and Jimmy and Angie were like interchangeable parts as the band played on.

The fact was that young women were stunned by the broken promise even more than young men were. They had been playing a waiting game in return for the guarantee of a safe life of being well provided for in the new day that was supposed to be dawning. Now they were more than just betrayed; they were women scorned. War was something women could never understand, much less control. It dominated their world, but they were not part of it. When war broke out, they were unable to accurately predict what was going to happen next: a very disquieting situation for the ladies.

What women saw in the chaotic first days of this new world war was a series of savage attacks on families. They saw mothers unable to defend their children and houses and whole communities destroyed wantonly. Worse yet, there was nothing any woman could do about it. There was no one to go see to demand that these useless hostilities end right now. The governments and armies just would not listen to feminine logic.

So the world *was* coming to an end. There certainly seemed to be no future, at least not the rosy future they had been promised. Without any real understanding of what was going on, there was no real way for women to predict how long it would be before they themselves were engulfed in the flames. With that sort of doom impending, the thought of losing oneself for a few hours at a dance party became very enticing. It gave them a. moment to rest in denial and forget that impossible things were going on just over the horizon. To many, in fact, the broken promise also meant a release from the unwritten contract that bound them to be good girls and to wait. There was no reason now to deny any urges or appetites. Ave Emerator, Nostramus Moriaturi Salutant!

To be sure, not every young woman felt this way as the new war unfolded in those first few months. Enough did, however, to quickly fill the dance halls and honkey tonks of America from sea to shining sea.

At the same time, a general swing occurred in the moods of most young men. They knew all too well who was going to have to shed the blood and suffer the direct violence of this fight. They knew it, and any of them who had any intelligence at all were scared to the bone by the prospect. What they did as a result of that fear was another matter.

Some retreated into what had been the comfortable patterns of pre-war life. They worked the farms harder than they had in the past or spent as much time as they could on shift at the furnace or factory. Many rushed to formalize their romantic affairs, and more than one young bride was whisked to the altar in a flattering rush of emotion and attention. Some of this haste was made in a fatalistic rush to get started with the next generation before these new fathers could be sucked into the vortex of war, probably to be lost forever.

War Record

A less noble response was made by quite a few. They didn't really want to propagate the species, just practice at it a bit. In fact, a large segment of the nation's young men reacted to their fears by thinking only of themselves. They were ready to go. There was no question that if the country needed them, they would serve. Before that time came, though, they felt there were some beers to be drunk and some women to be chased.

This last kind of young man found his kind of girl at dances like the one Leo and Ellen went to that night.

For Ellen, the party was a new experience and an exciting diversion from the steady stream of bad news that was the first few months of the war. Like most women, she'd begun to think quite a bit further ahead than her beau from the moment she made her own internal decision to accept him. Even though it was difficult with the trains and all, she had jumped at the chance to join him for a night on the town. She was comfortable with him and truly liked him, so it was also pleasant to maul him a bit and to be mauled as they worked their way around the floor at the impromptu dance, very pleasant, in fact.

Still, she noticed Leo watching all the mating rituals in progress. He scanned the room with interest, stopping to observe this couple or that. The entire dance floor squirmed and undulated. Wherever a rather more extreme display of affection was taking place, he stopped his sweep of the place to observe for a moment, and his tight grin grew tighter.

She could see what was going on. She saw the changes in all the young men, and so she was quick to spot them starting in him. He was distant in a way he had never been before. Things irritated him these days too. Ellen understood some of what bothered him, but there were other parts of it that baffled her.

Men, she thought. *Why do they have to work so hard at every decision that they overlook the obvious answers so many times?*

They left the party like Siamese twins and just caught a streetcar that would get them to North Station in time for the last train to Belmont. Steam rose from their warm breath as they walked down the deserted platform in the chill dark of the February evening.

"Sleep well," she ordered impishly as they said good night at the door to the last car.

"As well as I can," he replied with a wink, "since I'll be sleeping alone."

This rather direct response gave her a happy twinge. She looked down as the heat rushed to her cheeks. He crooked an index finger under her chin to softly tilt her head back up toward his.

"So long, sweetheart," he said.

She mounted the steps to the car and quickly took a seat by the nearest window. There he was below, waiting to see her situated for the twenty-minute ride home. The railroad car had steaming breath as well. It was real steam, though, and it rose up between them for just a moment as the night air stirred capriciously. From her seat, Ellen pantomimed a kiss blown from her fingertips, through the glass. On the platform, Leo's head spun away from the force of the kiss, striking him on the cheek. He staggered as though Joe Louis had landed a right cross, overplaying it nicely. In the warmth of the car, Ellen giggled at the performance. Holding the side of his face in mock agony, he smiled and then turned to walk away.

When the car lurched and began to move forward, he remained in Ellen's sight for just a moment, receding. His shoulders and his head were down. His hands were thrust into the pockets of his overcoat. From the back, there seemed a hint of sadness about his stride. The joy and exuberance of the theatrical joke had dissipated in an instant, and something was wrong again. As the car passed him by, she knew that he was walking away from her in more ways than one. The train gained speed as it crossed the Charles River on the Prison Point Bridge and made its way through a darkened Cambridge. She cried a little bit, but

War Record

she understood that everything was changing and that most of it was changing for the worse.

As the weeks of worse and worse news wore on, Leo worked hard, but he also began to play hard. House parties and dance parties in clubs and halls were always on his schedule. He called Ellen once or twice after their last night out together. They chatted aimlessly for a few minutes, but each was aware that it was different now. When Leo went out, he went alone, and that was better. He was searching now and wasn't interested in a partnership, just in searching.

At the chem lab, the work was really piling up. Orders from the navy building were streaming in now. Information on the effects of seawater on just about everything was being urgently sought by the naval engineering department. On top of that, every pier in the harbor was suddenly full and all of the berths at the naval shipyard were being used for repairs. Now that America was officially in the fight, British warships could call at American ports, and ships of every flag hauling cargo to that war-torn kingdom could load and sail at will from harbors that just weeks before had to observe strict rules of neutrality.

Boston, although farther South, was actually better situated for crossings to the English ports of Plymouth and Southampton than were the Canadian ports of Montreal, Québec, or even Halifax. Within just a few weeks of December 7, there were freighters of all kinds marshaling at the President's Roads anchorage near Boston's outer harbor. Convoys were being raised weekly as Destroyers of every Allied flag could now shuttle all the way across and all the way back. A road was being paved through the ocean that would ultimately inundate the British Isles with stores, manpower, and the material needed to form a bulwark against the enemy.

Mark Zaccaria

The Boston Naval Shipyard was used to making voyage repairs to American fighting ships. The yard knew the detailed process of following a huge specification of repair while filing paperwork for the extra work items to cover engineering that had been changed at sea and could not have been changed on the ship's drawings in Washington before the work began. Now the men and women of the Yard had to contend with battle damage, on-the-spot choices as to what minimum work had to be done to get a vessel underway again, and the constant pressure that came from time always being of the essence.

Laborers were quickly being promoted to welders or ship fitters. New laborers were being hired as fast as the employment office could process the paperwork. A second and then a third shift were laid on. More and more decisions were being made on the floor of the graving docks rather than waiting for the naval architects to survey the hull and make a detailed drawing. Personal networks were springing up all around the yard. On different shifts, there were different people involved, but at any time in any of the specialty shops, there was someone who knew someone in one of the other departments who would trade something they had for something they wanted. In this way, tools, fittings, scaffolding, hoses, pumps, and even hull plates were quickly allocated to the docks and ships that needed them most. The clerk of the works kept up with the paperwork pretty well. His staff was growing as fast as anyone's. When it came time to getting something done, however, no one allowed the lack of forms or signatures to be an obstacle.

The chem lab was no different from any other shop in the yard. There were readings to be taken at a dozen different times on every ship under repair. Potable water tests, tests for explosive atmospheres in fuel tanks, tests for oxygen levels in ships' food lockers, and tests for wall thickness in hull plates and boiler tubes were just a few of the tasks that kept Leo and the other chemists racing back and forth between the lab and the docks.

War Record

Three or four times daily, the lab assistants had to be sent out behind the building to dip up fresh five-gallon cans of seawater for the many tests. This was a difficult process in winter to begin with. Now, though, every inch of waterline in the yard had a ship or a fueling barge or a floating platform of some kind breasted up to it. This made it tough to find a spot where the cans could be dropped in on a line. There was also the increasing problem of the contamination of the water pier side. Little thought was given to the discharge of fuel slops, kitchen garbage, bilge water, or human waste from any of the hundreds of ships coming or going at the yard.

One day in the commissary, Leo took an empty seat to have his lunch and to wind down for a few minutes. It was at the end of a long table, and he nodded to the young man seated across from the chair he wanted.

"Mind if I sit?" he asked.

"Be my guest," the tall curly haired fellow replied in as fine a New Hampshire twang as Leo had heard in some time.

The man extended his hand as if to offer the chair, and Leo put his metal cafeteria tray down.

"I'd be glad fo'ah the company."

He was dressed in a clean flannel shirt and twill trousers in contrast to the others at the table who were all grimy in the same way and busily huddling over lunch together, discussing the work that made that happen.

"I'm Leo Zaccaria, from the chem lab."

"Butch Lombard, assistant stationary engineer at the pow-ah plant."

The two men shook across their casseroles.

"How's it goin' at your shop?"

"Fancy cars and big cigars!" Leo said without a thought. "We've got nothin' to spend but time and money." He dug into his lunch, starved because he hadn't had anything since breakfast six hours before.

"Ay yuh," Butch answered with even slower and more deliberate attention to his accent. "It's much the same in ow-wah department." His answer was delivered completely deadpan.

Leo's ace service had been returned with a passing shot. He burst out laughing.

"Well said."

They chatted over the abbreviated lunch, and like everyone else in the yard, they talked about work. Actually, they were exchanging information so that each might better know how to use this new contact. Leo's work with feed water treatment in marine boilers was of obvious interest to Butch. There was no reason that the same process shouldn't be established at the stationary plant. Its three boilers were enormous compared to those of a Destroyer, but this made it just that much bigger a job to shut one down for repairs. Anything that would put off that sad day could be worth money to the yard's boiler house.

"Butch, listen," Leo said. "It's no problem for me. I'll send you over a drum of the prepared mixture with my compliments. You try it for a while, and if your efficiencies stay higher longer, you can requisition all you'll ever need from central supply."

"Much obliged," Butch answered. "It sure sounds like it's worth a try. I wish there was something I could do for you in return."

Leo thought about that one for a moment. "Do you have any reliable underground prints for the yard?" he asked.

"Ay yuh," Butch said without twitching a muscle. "Reliable's the only kind we keep around."

He paused just long enough so that Leo felt the needle.

"What'cha lookin' for?" he asked, having made his point.

"Seawater," came the reply. "We need lots of it for our experiments on ocean conditions, and we're having the devil's own time keeping up. I was just wondering if there was a drainage tunnel we could pump from or perhaps a fire fighting main we could tap into for a few gallons."

"Chem lab, huh?" Butch said, gazing off into space as he thought about the yard's piping system. "That's Building Eleven, isn't it?" He knew it was. "There's a feed line to the pow-ah plant's cooling system that runs through the storm drainage tunnel just at the east end of your building. That's a branch from the main seawater intake, and it's on this side of the pumping station out by Pier Six. How much did you say you needed?"

"Initially, I'd like to fill up the largest tank I could find and then just keep a trickle coming in to replenish the supply and keep it fresh," Leo said, thinking out loud.

"And just how big is the biggest tank you could find?" the young engineer asked thoughtfully.

"Oh, seven or eight hundred gallons if I could swing it."

Now it was Butch Lombard's turn to burst out laughing. "Eight hundred gallons isn't even enough for a decent lobster tank," Butch said after quickly recovering his composure. "I thought you were looking for tens of thousands or more. What you want is a bathtub. I'm sure we can work something out."

Three days later, Leo received a phone call at the lab.

"Thanks for the drum of chemicals," Butch said. "And thanks especially for the carbon of that report on the results you got on that tin can. You have to understand that the chief engineer would rather give you one of his daughters than one of his boilers. Guaranteein' the steam output no matter what is the only thing that's important to a stationary engineer. We'll have to do some tests with your juice, but I suspect that once he sees it won't hurt anything, we'll start to use it in all three."

"That's great, Butch," Leo replied, genuinely happy that he was able to help.

"Ay yuh," Butch said, changing the subject. "That's not the reason I called though. I had the chance to finagle the maintenance schedule for our cooling system. Well, change it really. Point is, I'll be supervising the installation of a new isolation valve in our cooling water intake line. The work starts this Thursday night.

To put in the new twelve-inch gate valve, we'll have to shut down and empty that line goin' by your building. If you're of a mind, I could probably have a two-inch black iron pipe boss welded to a convenient spot in that drainage tunnel. Naturally, I'd put a valve on the boss, but after that, you'd be on your own to pipe up to the lab. That'd give you all the seawater you need for your experiment. Interested?"

On the other end of the line, Leo grinned slyly. "Butch, that sounds great! Tell me when the party starts, and I'll be there with bells on."

So at ten o'clock that Thursday evening, Leo lowered himself down through the manhole in the cobblestone street to find Butch Lombard already there, surveying the cast iron seawater line. There was a surprising amount of room in the tunnel. Leo could almost stand up. Light was supplied from a series of portable lamps that the power plant crew had mounted on tripods of small-gauge pipe. The glistening walls of the tunnels went from rusty brown granite to a black void in the course of perhaps fifteen feet in either direction.

One of the lab assistants followed Leo into the hole. He'd come to the lab from the pipe shop, and with him was one of his friends from that apprenticeship program. There was a brief discussion of the engineering details with the power plant crew.

"Since the main is cast iron," Butch explained to Leo, "we couldn't cut a proper fish mouth and insert the pipe boss into the line."

The boss was a simple four-inch piece of steel pipe with female threads at one end. The unthreaded end would be welded to the twelve-inch main.

"It's tricky to cut cast iron with a torch," Butch continued, to the nodded agreement of the two pipe fitters, "so pretty much as soon as we got a hole, we left it to cool. It's jagged and a little undersized, but it'll do what you need it to. Then we ground the butt end of the boss a little to make it fit the curve of the main before welding it on.

"Welding to cast iron creates some problems too," Butch said apologetically. "Where there's two different kinds of metal, you're askin' for corrosion. This joint between the iron and the malleable steel will probably only last eight or ten years before it springs a leak."

"If we're all still here then, we'll come back and fix it," Leo said, trying to let the rangy engineer off the hook.

With that, one of the tripod lamps was turned around to reveal a perpendicular tunnel that ran directly under the chem lab. Several pieces of seamless two-inch black pipe were handed down through the hole. Almost miraculously, it was cut to a length that just allowed it to make the corner. The boss was attached at the four o'clock position on the main so that the new piping could run down the perpendicular tunnel. Where the first run of black pipe hit the floor of the tunnel, the two pipe fitters spun a forty-five-degree elbow into place, and the straight lengths were laid out along the floor of the tunnel all the way to a second manhole, which Butch indicated would lead to the lab entrance.

The two pipe fitters worked fast, cutting and threading the two-inch tubes with hand tools so that the floor of the tunnel would support the weight of the new line and so that the vertical run up into the lab would go just where it was needed. Leo mistook their haste as an eagerness to be done with it before the authorities noticed.

"I guess this has to be a midnight operation for it to be all in place before anyone notices," he observed.

"Not really," Butch said. "It's got more to do with the tide. In another hour or so, our feet will be getting wet. Your boys seem to understand that though. They're doin' good work, and they're doin' it fast."

Well before midnight, they were out of the second manhole and running the pipe along a wall in the carriage entrance to

Building 11 and up through the trap and into the second-story work area. Butch took a moment to look over the straight run from the hole up along the exposed wall and into the lab.

"That probably won't freeze except in the coldest weather," he said to no one in particular. "It'll get heat from the tunnel by conduction. Still, it might be a good idea to insulate this exposed section."

"It's all taken care of, Mr. Lombard," the yard pipe fitter said. "A buddy of mine in the lagger's shop owes me one. There'll be a crew here in the morning."

So there it was. A little before 1:00 a.m., Leo thanked each of his two after-hours plumbers. The ten dollars cash he gave them each ensured that either would be receptive to any future special projects he could come up with. The line had been installed, and a second valve was hanging in the air next to an area of the lab floor that had been cleared to make room for the tank, which would be built the next day.

It was just after 10:00 a.m. when Leo got back to the lab the next morning. When he arrived, he saw that a stack of four thick, green-tinted deck house window panes had been delivered from the yard glazing shop. Meant to shield the bridge of a Destroyer from both sunlight and small arms fire, the panels of glass were almost two inches thick and were actually a sandwich of thick polyethylene between two slices of hardened glass. The panels measured three feet high by nearly six feet wide. The lab's seawater tank was to be transparent so that test pieces could be observed without removing them from the briny bath.

Arnie Cohen was examining the stainless steel channel pieces and rubber gaskets that had been supplied to join the four sides of the tank together. Carriage bolts and cap nuts completed the set. On board ship, these windshields had to be weather tight.

Everyone agreed that their regular fasteners would be strong enough for this job.

"Good afternoon!" he said with a good-natured grin that became a broad smile when Leo replied with a shrug. "Fred's been asking for you."

Sure enough, Leo had barely hung up his coat and opened his first lab book when Fred Hemmings emerged.

"May I speak to you for a moment in my office, son?"

Once they were inside the paneled room, Fred made a little show of checking his pocket watch. Then he looked up at Leo with a fixed stare.

"I suppose I can understand you being late on Monday mornings," he began thoughtfully. "After all, the weekend can be quite an exertion. And I guess Thursday mornings can be explained by the rigors of Wednesday night. What is it you call it now… hump day?"

Leo looked down. He didn't want to be disrespectful, but he had work to do and he wanted to get to it.

"Now you're late on Friday morning," Fred went on. "Are you sure your constitution can stand that much socializing?"

"Look, sir," Leo began, meeting his boss's gaze. "You're right. I have been going out too much. Last night was a different story though."

As he began to explain and describe the new fixture he had organized, Fred Hemmings was disarmed. He shook his head slowly in bemused resignation.

"So I guess I'll have to sign your time card again this week," he offered. "Okay. You lie and I'll swear to it. But do me a favor, will you? Try and keep a reasonable schedule next week."

Leo smiled sheepishly and nodded. As he started to get up, Fred continued.

"One more thing. At this week's department heads meeting, the superintendent read a signal that had been passed on to him from the admiral. The captain of the *USS Monaghan* sent many thanks for the good work that the Boston yard did last year, claimed it helped the ship hold together under fire on December seventh. You worked on that ship, didn't you?"

"They're still afloat?" Leo asked, his heart in his throat.

"Absolutely," Fred replied. "They were on routine patrol, or they got underway in a hurry, or something, but they sank two mini subs outside the harbor entrance. Confirmed. They thought they got three others, but there was no wreckage. Apparently, they returned anti-aircraft fire all day and didn't sustain a single casualty."

Leo's emotions soared. He imagined Pickford in the fire room for ten or twelve hours, seeing to it that the ship answered every bell. He knew the shuddering concussions that had to have gone on almost ceaselessly as the depth charges were dropped. He thought for only a moment about what must have gone through the minds of the sub crews as they listened to the twin props of the *Monaghan* scream by overhead.

He and Fred exchanged ferocious grins. It was the first good news he'd had for too long.

"Fred, I'll try to do better about the work schedule," he said.

His boss nodded, and he took his leave.

Doing better about the work schedule proved to be more difficult than he had first estimated. While he was at the yard, he worked as hard as anyone, and he worked smarter than most. Outside of the workday, though, he was in another world.

He looked around at the city and saw only minor inconveniences for a bustling population. At nights, window shades had to be drawn so that incoming bombers would have no navigation references. In fact, the gold leaf on the dome of the state house had been hastily painted over in a dull gray-brown color so that no moonlight could reflect off of it. It quickly became a custom that everyone followed happily, especially because the bombers never arrived.

Beyond that, there was little more than inconvenience in the daily lives of Bostonians during the early days of the war. Shops stocked all sorts of groceries. Butchers had beef for sale. Bakers had bread. Even the Old Mr. Boston distillery was operating around the clock. On top of all this, with the dramatic increase of activity all along the waterfront, there were jobs for virtually everybody, so the Great Depression ended in Boston in December of 1941. News from the radio was frightening, but what the average citizen saw when he or she went out into the street was comfortable and remarkably normal.

Leo saw all this normalcy, and for reasons he couldn't describe, it made him feel uneasy. There was a conflict between the news photos of smoke billowing up from the hulk of the battleship *Arizona* and the vista of bargaining shoppers and neighborhood contentment he saw in the stalls along Hanover Street in the North End. Increasingly, he sought out the temporary respite from this disparity that he found at nightclubs and dance parties.

Despite its long history of conservative stoicism and outright theocracy, Boston was also well known to sailors around the globe as the port where the anxieties that built up over long weeks at sea could be relieved the quickest. The pragmatic Yankees had long ago realized that they couldn't eradicate excessive behavior, so they settled for containing it. Every seafaring man in the world knew that when he landed in Boston, he had only to find his way to Scullay Square for his carnal needs to be ministered to quickly.

The Old Howard Theater, just off the square, offered a winning mixture of the most hard-hitting burlesque comedy and the most revealing anatomy lessons ever referred to as dance numbers. The many bars and cafés around the square promised all the firsthand contact with the locals that any sailor could want. In the process, the area provided a playground not just for curious college students but also for the more dedicated of metropolitan

Mark Zaccaria

partygoers. This last was true for both male and female celebrants. Despite its "anything goes" atmosphere, there was a strong sense of ethics as they related to ladies among all the denizens of Scollay Square. The line between professionals and amateurs was assiduously maintained. As a result, it wasn't a bad place to take a girl you'd just met at a dance for an after-hours drink and a laugh.

Now not everyone attended smoky backroom dance parties and had a sandwich and a beer in Scollay Square after hours. Increasingly, Leo did though. He knew what it meant for him in terms of fatigue come morning, but he was attracted to the excitement, and suddenly, it was a great time to meet women. The combination proved irresistible more and more frequently.

When he went to work, he fit in with all his coworkers, his job was something that everyone agreed was important to the War Effort, and he was safe from the perils of the front lines. So why did it bother him so much? What was it about this seemingly perfect set up that made him so unhappy? The more he spent his nights on the prowl, the more Fred Hemmings became unhappy too. More and more, Leo would leave word that he had an early meeting in this fire room or that machinery space to run this test or that crew training program. These messages always indicated that he would report to the lab directly after he was done.

In June of 1942, he received a draft notice from the army. Prior to that time, the explosive increase in the number of men in uniform had come solely from volunteers lining up to go fight for America. That alone had kept the army bloating its rolls at more than the rate they could comfortably absorb for the first six months of the war. It was only then that they had become organized enough to go to the draft registration lists that had been compiled over the last couple years.

The draft notice came complete with instructions on how to receive a deferment if you were an essential employee of federal, state, or local government. Forms could be obtained from the employment office or your supervisor. There was no question in Leo's mind that he should start with the employment office. Sadly, when he got the form, it still needed his boss's signature before being returned.

Fred looked down at the form for longer than was necessary as his angry young chemist stood there in front of his desk. Then he looked up slightly, raising one eyebrow to give Leo "the look" for just a beat before sighing and signing the paper. Deferred for six months.

Leo celebrated by going out that night. It was a Wednesday, and the only thing that even resembled a party was a dance being sponsored by the YWCA just off Copley Square. He thought he'd start there and move on once he'd found some company. Arriving, he noticed a couple of disturbing problems. The hall, just off the main floor lobby, was a gymnasium, and although it had been decorated with streamers and balloons, it was brightly lit enough to conduct a basketball game. He was asked for his name when he arrived by a charming-looking older woman at the door. She was sweet and cheerful, but she was certainly also a chaperon. Did they mean to check him out also and keep track of who he left with? Strangely, it was the last of his troubles that night that gave him the most difficulty.

Fully half of the other young men attending this dance were in uniform. There were brand-spanking-new soldiers and sailors sprinkled around the floor. Each stood tall in his new Class A's. Each had one or two friends with him who were still in civilian clothes, and each of these groups had several young women clustered around. It made the serviceman the center of quite an intense little bit of attention and public approval. It made Leo silently angry.

As he looked around the room, his recently practiced eye stopped on a girl standing alone. She was leaning against the back wall of the gym with her arms folded and a frown on her face. She had shoulder-length hair, dark and curly with bangs. Her makeup was just a little more evident than most, and her

Mark Zaccaria

thin frame was accentuated by a tight-fitting, floor-length black rayon evening dress. With brows furrowed, she surveyed the floor. Evidently, nothing she saw was a cause for joy.

"Are we having fun yet?" Leo asked as he leaned up beside her and folded his arms.

"Sure," she said ruefully. "A barrel of laughs. Can't ya tell?"

"It's my first time at one of these," Leo said truthfully. "Is it really going to be that bad?"

"Take a look," she demanded with an outstretched arm and upward palm. "There's enough light to do surgery. The armed guards all over the floor don't bother me, but the matrons guarding the door scare me plenty. This isn't going to be a dance. It's a recruiting poster, for gosh sakes."

"I'm Leo," he said, laughing, "and I like the way you think."

"Trixie," she replied, glancing sideways. "Pleased, I'm sure."

"Okay, Trixie. If it's going to be that bad, let's go someplace else."

She stood up straight and turned to him. Her arms were still folded, but her face brightened.

"I'm here because my mother said she'd kill me if I didn't come. Okay. I came. Now the problem is getting away. Got any ideas?"

"A few," he allowed as the music came up for the first dance. "Follow me."

They began to dance, and Leo held her at an exaggerated distance, taking pains to bring his foxtrot box step to a complete halt at each corner. All the while, he held his nose up and with a theatrically aloof expression on his face.

"How's this?" he asked. "Think we can avoid detection this way?"

She chuckled and got into the part herself.

"The sad thing is, Leo, that no one will notice. We fit right in. Look around."

War Record

It was true. There wasn't a really stylish couple in evidence anywhere on the floor. That probably meant that everyone else was playing it safe too.

He maneuvered them down along the side wall of the gym toward a regular-sized door. When she frowned at him, tiring of the game, Leo gave her a wink, and she played along. Sure enough, the door was clearly marked with stenciled lettering, "Janitor's Closet."

"Got a hairpin I can borrow for a minute, doll?" he asked with a grin as they stopped dancing and he stepped back from her with a little mock bow. Trixie knew something was up even though she didn't know what it was. Still, it was the only game in town, so she was willing to go along. She reached up into the back of her hairdo with both hands, arching to the side just slightly as she hunted for the pin a little longer than she needed to. The pose, combined with the form-fitting, shiny, black dress made a picture that convinced Leo he was on the right track.

"A gentleman always carries a handkerchief," he said with a grin as he removed his from his breast pocket and accepted the wire hairpin she offered. He folded the cotton hankie over the U end of the pin, leaving the two prongs exposed. "Cover me!" he said in his best George Raft impression. "I'm goin' in!"

With that, he opened the door to the closet and, sure enough, there was a single electric outlet. It was contained in a box mounted on the wall just below the fuse panel. He couldn't guess how much of the building this fuse box controlled, but almost certainly, it was for the gym. Leo stuck the prong ends of the hairpin into the two slots of the outlet, and the lights went out on the dance.

He slid out of the closet and closed the door. There were emergency lights by two exits, but they barely cut the gloom compared to how bright it had been. There was suddenly a hub-bub of giggles and gleeful screams, but the band, true to the code of musicians everywhere, kept playing. Leo took Trixie by the hand and drew her in close to him.

"Now, let's dance," he said, meaning business.

She responded with a smile as her left arm slid around his neck up to the elbow. They began to slink along with the music as if they had been partners for years. It was just as well that no one could see the show they put on as he guided them along toward the main door. There was quite a little consternation among the house mothers of the YWCA. This was a situation they weren't ready for. The maintenance man wouldn't be back until morning, and frankly, they didn't know where to start when it came to troubleshooting an electrical problem. It was really rather easy for the two of them to slip right out of the gym, stroll hand in hand through the lobby, and walk out the front door. Naturally, he held the large oak portal for her and waited while she passed before stepping out behind her.

As he thought about it afterward, he began to understand what bothered him so much about the young servicemen he was seeing more and more around town these days. They were in, and he wasn't.

It was just that simple. He felt as much kinship to his country as they did. He was as willing as they were to use all his talents in his country's defense. He was as capable as any of them. Still, they were in, and he wasn't.

He felt guilty because perhaps he was not doing enough. His work was making every fighting ship in the US Navy more battle ready for longer periods of time. It could be described in only slightly inflated terms as a contribution way beyond what the average soldier was able to make, at least in terms of the country's war-making ability. Yet every time one of the guys in the neighborhood came home on leave after making it through Parris Island, Leo was faced with another marine dress uniform and another of the amazing transformations the corps performs so routinely. And who did the girls want to speak to?

Leo was beginning to think that war is hell even when you're not in it.

After analyzing the situation, the corrective action seemed simple. He called his old friend Joe Stossel. Joe worked for Osgood Smythe over at the Watertown Arsenal, and the two stayed in touch both through government channels and at school. The mere suggestion that they get together for a beer instantly set up a meeting.

The bar at the Eliot Hotel on Commonwealth Avenue was a cozy little place. The hotel served a mainly professional clientele, although its location a short walk from Fenway Park also made it a routine stop for the sports crowd. The bar was old oak, and so were the raised panels on the wainscot all around the small taproom. Joe and Leo sat at a tiny round table, looking at two tall pilsner glasses and dining on pretzels. They yakked a bit about the old days at Northeastern. They each brought up the names of classmates whom the other remembered but whom neither had heard from. Each one spent a few minutes bravely describing the intricacies of the work they were doing. Joe had become almost a metallurgist, first testing and then specifying the formulae for the alloys used in big guns.

"Yeah," he said, finishing up his story. "After firing as few as thirty or forty shots, the big naval artillery barrels can have their rifling completely worn off. Retooling the bore is no big deal out at the works in Watertown, but trying to do it at sea, even on a battleship, is out of the question. So I've been working on a task force to come up with a removable sleeve so that spares can be carried and the guns can fire indefinitely."

"Sounds pretty important," Leo said thoughtfully. "You happy?"

"Happy? What do you mean, happy?" Joe's face had a look of incomprehension.

Mark Zaccaria

"I don't know," Leo answered. "Does it ever make you uncomfortable to see everyone else going off to the service while you're staying behind?"

Joe was stopped dead in his tracks. They just looked at each other for a moment before he said anything.

"Yeah."

Leo felt a little better that everything he brought up about being bothered by all the new soldiers was something Joe felt too. They acknowledged that their jobs were important, but they each admitted that someone else could learn to do them. Then they began to negotiate about which of the services they would join.

"I've always thought about the navy," Joe mused, "traveling the world, breathing the fresh sea air, that sort of thing. What do you think?"

"That all sounded pretty good to me too, until the first time I went out to sea on a Destroyer. Take it from an old salt; you don't get to call your own shots when you're on a ship," Leo replied, shaking his head. "Frankly, I'd be interested in artillery. Isn't there a lot of math involved in aiming and correcting for windage and temperature?"

"Not as much as you think," was Joe's reply. "Mostly they use charts that look like log tables. Eggheads and very intelligent young ladies do the real math over at MIT. And I bet you've never been near one of those things when they go off, have you?"

"No," said Leo. "I guess not. Pretty loud, huh?" He thought suddenly about the depth charges.

"Loud isn't the word," Joe said, shaking his head. "I sat through a firing exercise out at Devens, and I thought the cannon did almost as much damage from either end. The ground shook with every shot. I literally bounced off the ground each time, and this was with hundred-and-five-millimeter howitzers. That's a peashooter compared to a twelve- or sixteen-inch stationary piece. Real artillery? No can do, GI."

They sat looking at their beers for a minute.

War Record

"What about the air corps?" Leo asked.

"Sounds great," Joe said. "Probably because I don't know anything about flying. I thought the air corps was pretty elite, tough to get into."

"You never know until you try. By now, we must be making so many planes that they can't be as picky about who gets to fly them. You want to give it a try?"

Sure enough, when Leo looked at the recruiting reports that were found on the bulletin boards at the navy yard's commissary, he found that a special call was going out for cadet aviators. When actually faced with the step, he was apprehensive, so he called Joe back at work.

"You really want to give it a try?" he asked.

"I don't know," Joe answered nervously. "Do you really want to give it a try?"

"I don't know. It wouldn't hurt to fill out the paperwork and then decide. You think?"

"I don't know. I guess so."

The more he thought about it, the more it sounded like a good idea. He got the forms and spoke briefly to a recruiting sergeant in the office that was set up right in the yard. He was told that a special eye test and a written exam for spatial relationships and map reading would have to be passed but that college credits were important in the army air corps. He was also told that there were increasing quotas for pilots. The recruiter emphasized that the need for pilots was based on the growing number of new planes being turned out by factories all over America. Leo didn't dwell on the substantial aircraft losses that were being reported; he thought instead about the increasingly crucial role of air forces in the recent victories at Midway and the Coral Sea.

As he started thinking seriously about the air corps, he began to feel better about himself. In fact, Leo thought it sounded like a good idea right up until the moment he walked into his mother's kitchen and mentioned to her what he was thinking.

Mark Zaccaria

Mary Zaccaria ordinarily stayed out of men's business. She expected them to stay out of women's business in return, of course. She observed the boundaries between these two areas of interest and concern rather naturally. In most cases, she had no interest or concern for the things that attracted men. In fact, many times, she didn't even understand the attraction in the slightest. Men were different. That's all. She'd kept to herself about this World War business. She didn't understand it, and it frightened her. She was happy that her son Leo had a government job where he could stay for the duration. It wasn't war she was afraid of so much as armies.

She'd had a favorite uncle back in the old country, and he had served with the Italian forces in Ethiopia. He was her favorite uncle because he was her mother's favorite brother. Although it was before Mary was born, her mother had been frantic the whole time her brother was away. When he came back, he had blood-curdling stories about the conditions and the atrocities of the action he saw. He was supported by his family's business while he was in Italy, and he was supported by his family's money when they all immigrated to America.

Anytime it looked like real labor was about to be suggested for him, he would tell a story about men being buried up to their necks in an African ant hill and then having honey poured over their hair. With the passage of time, he probably became confused as to whether that had happened to him or just to someone he knew or even just heard about. It didn't matter. The story always served to get Mary's mother, Philomena, exercised to the point where she was convinced that her baby brother shouldn't be forced into such an exhaustive effort as working for a living. To know Philomena was to know that her will could not be opposed.

Mary might even have been slightly amused by her mother's instant irrational fear when it came to her brother, Antonio. Any such amusement was gone forever, though, the moment Leo mentioned joining the army.

War Record

The first words out of her mouth were like mourning cries. She spoke rapidly, with great excitement, and in Italian. As she rose to the challenge of trying to express her emotions, fear became anger and the object of her love became the target of her antagonism. She gestured to Leo menacingly with a long wooden spoon. Before long, she was advancing on him with it held forward, promising a thorough beating if he chose any course but pacifism. She exhorted him against the mental illness that would be suspected if he volunteered, and she cautioned him that humans were not meant to fly. Finally, as Tony Zaccaria came into the house, wondering what sort of emergency was underway, there was a solemn promise of the *Mal Occhio* upon her son and everyone around him if he did such a thing.

Leo was stunned. He never expected a reaction like that. When his father figured out what was going on, he felt sorry for his son, but both men knew that there was no contradicting this strong a position once Mary had taken it. Tony understood his son's need to join in the national effort. He still wondered if flying an airplane could compare with galloping a horse, but he assumed that if he were young, he'd want to try it just like Leo. Too bad it couldn't happen now.

Leo had no choice, and it made him even more angry and sullen. Joe Stossel joined the air corps. In December of 1942, when his first deferment was about to expire, Leo went back to the employment office and then went through another session with Fred Hemmings to reinstate his exemption from service.

The early months of 1943 went by in a blur for Leo. So did the spring. Despite the work he still continued to do in the navy yard, he was not satisfied. He knew what the problem was, and he wasn't doing anything to fix it. The patchwork quilt of dark parties and late dates that was his social life became defined for him by his memories of a string of young ladies whose names he couldn't quite recall.

One night, he breezed into a smoky gathering at a union hall in Southie. As he was surveying the crowd, looking for likely companions, an arm started to wave wildly above the heads of the crowd. Unaware, the other partygoers parted long enough for a young woman to hastily emerge. Her dark, curly hair and fair complexion struck a chord with Leo, but he couldn't put his finger on who she was right away.

"Hey. How ya doing?" she asked breathlessly as she made her way over to him. "Leo, isn't it? I'm Trixie, remember? We met at the Y and then ducked out for a night on the town…"

It took him a beat before his face brightened.

"Ah. Oh! Yes, Trixie," he said, taking a moment to resolve who she was and where she fit in to the last few months. "How's it going with you, beautiful?"

She misread the lack of recognition in his face.

"Oh. I get it, Leo," she said knowingly. "So what's your real name? You can tell me."

What's yours? he thought, even more crestfallen by her assumption. It was clear even to him that he was going nowhere with this behavior, but he didn't know how to change.

His parents watched him withdraw and stay away for days at a time.

Tony Zaccaria shrugged it off. *He's twenty-two years old,* Tony thought. *How much can I tell him about what to do when he's outside my house?*

Mary was sad because her son was sad. She was worried, however, just as every mother was worried during wartime. She worried that she had somehow made Leo sad, but she worried more about what would happen if he got his wish.

By the end of April 1943, the Allied ground forces had repelled an attempted Japanese invasion of New Guinea at Port Moresby. This, along with the earlier Allied naval victories, made things seem hopeful in the Pacific. At the same time, German forces had finally failed in their attempt to capture Stalingrad, having lost more than two hundred thousand men. In that same month, American and British forces met in Tunisia, virtually surrounding the remnants of Rommel's Afrika Korps. The surrender of the elite German desert force seemed only a matter of time.

Everyone was aware that there was plenty of fighting ahead. The feeling was that the tide had turned though. American factories were churning out war materials at unheard-of rates. British and American bombers were making nightly raids deep into Hitler's industrial heartland, destroying the enemy's capability to make the steel and chemicals and finished armaments that would be necessary for the Reich to fight on.

Optimism began to sprout with the crocus flowers that spring, and it made Leo even bleaker. He wouldn't be a part of the fight after all. At the beginning of May, he decided to take a vacation. He didn't plan to go anywhere special, just to play. It would have been better, of course, if he'd mentioned that ahead of time to Fred Hemmings or even to his parents. They would only have objected, though, so he didn't bother.

When his second deferment expired on the first of June, he hadn't been around to file for another, whether or not he even could have at that point. By June 15, his draft notice arrived and his future was settled no matter what anyone thought. The family's reflex response was to throw a party, but at Leo's request, they did not. He left his car in the care of his kid brother, but only after removing the license plates. On the appointed day, he boarded the train at North Station and rode off to Fort Devens to report.

Epilogue

Much more had happened to get Leo Zaccaria to Berga, of course. There was much more to be re-dreamed, to be reexamined and savored as he waited for reality to act on him once again.

What would become of him? Was he simply waiting around for his own execution? Was he to be just another nameless statistic of a world at war? The prospect aroused the anger of the beast he'd become.

"Not if I have anything to say about it," he fairly growled from his crouch next to the window.

It was time for the tired guards to come roust out the exhausted and crippled survivors of the *Kriegs Gefangenehmen Stammlager Berga an der Elster*. The old Germans shouted as best they could. Most of the crushed Americans somehow found strength to get to their feet.

Before long, the sorry-looking contingent was making its painful way toward the tunnels. How many of them would return that night? How many of them would survive captivity and then survive the war?

That day, as he trudged onward, Leo was aware that much more lay ahead.

He couldn't know that nearly Sixty Years were still before him. As day began at the camp his eyes were narrowed to slits, focused only on surviving until tomorrow. But even then he'd dream more dreams of the world he'd lost, if only to find the key that would let him survive Berga.

War Record